ONLY YOU

ONLY YOU

a novel

R. F. EISEN

Editors: Deborah Froese, Megan Mitchum, Jorge David Remy
Cover and Interior Design: Emma Elzinga

Indigo River Publishing
3 West Garden Street, Ste. 718
Pensacola, FL 32502
www.indigoriverpublishing.com

Ordering Information:

Quantity Sales: Special discounts are available on quantity purchases by corporations, associations, and others. For details, contact the publisher at the address above.

Orders by US trade bookstores and wholesalers: Please contact the publisher at the address above.

Printed in the United States of America

Library of Congress Control Number: 2024918874
ISBN: 978-1-964686-15-8 (paperback)   978-1-964686-16-5 (ebook)

First Edition

This book is dedicated to my parents, Robert and Lucille Eisen,
and to their friends, who inspired this story.
They were all members of The Greatest Generation.
And to my wife, Charlene, for her support.

What people commonly call fate is mostly their own stupidity.

– Arthur Schopenhauer

God, grant me the serenity
to accept the things I cannot change,
courage to change the things I can,
and wisdom to know the difference.

– Reinhold Niebuhr

1

NAVY DESTROYER

The towering comber roared toward me, a fusillade of black water unfurling, smashing through the windows, shattering the glass. Futilely, I tried to escape–sloshing through knee-deep water for the door a few feet away. Only a step outside the bridge, the titanic wave swept me over the side. I crash landed on the deck below, slamming into the steel bulwark. A sharp pain shot through my skull. I saw stars. Though dazed, I am pitifully aware that the ocean's murky grip is sucking me into the abyss. The ship lost her battle with the hurricane, spiraling to her new home at the bottom of the sea.

Will I join her? I wonder as I am submerged in black water.

Instinct propels me to the water's surface seeking lifesaving air. Greedily sucking in oxygen, I struggled to regain my faculties. I frantically paddled my arms, desperate to stay afloat. My head was pounding like someone struck me with a sledgehammer. I rolled my tongue around my mouth, trying to determine the source of the pain in my cheek. I lost a tooth, maybe two. *I might have a broken jaw or even a concussion,* I concluded. Tenderly, I felt the back of my head. The saltwater burned in the wound; it was slick with blood.

Ellen's image flashed before me. *Will I see her again?*

A huge swell lifted me to its foaming crest. I choked on seawater as I dropped. My stomach plunged in a free-fall. The sensation reminded me of the Coney Island roller coaster, when the car passes the first peak after its long climb upward.

I was churning in the trough of a monstrous swell, like the one that claimed the ship. I feared its spumy crest would bury me in its curling wake.

We were nowhere near land when the ship foundered. My only chance for survival now was to stay afloat until rescue arrived. *For that*, I reasoned, *I'll need all my strength.* I had been close to death aboard *South Dakota*, but was this my fate? How long could I ride these mountainous swells before I had nothing left? One hour might be too long. I had never been put to such a test, but how could I have been—there were no tests in my naval training for this! What training could possibly prepare me to be aboard a sinking U.S. Navy ship amidst a hurricane?

Pondering the outcome terrified me, but there was no time to dwell on fear. I acted on the reflexes ingrained in my training. With renewed fervor, I vowed I would not swallow that first life-ending drink of salt water or take my last breath before submerging into the watery bottomless pit surrounding me. I searched the swirling sea for something to hold on to; any floating object that would keep my head above water while I figured a solution to my predicament–if there was one to be found. In the minutes before the ship met her fate, I had not grabbed my Kapok life vest: too occupied as EO (second in command) alerting the crew to abandon the ship. I thought I would have time to take care of myself after I had taken care of the others. That was a colossal mistake, one I regretted. It was a foolish decision my training should have prevented. I just hoped it was not a fatal blunder.

The mammoth, undulating swells would not relent. The towering gray walls of ocean were suspended in midair like looming petrified hills. My breathing was labored, and my muscles ached for relief from fighting the waves. I scanned the sea, desperate for a lifeline. I feared I would not last much longer.

Then, finally, through the sleeting rain and brine stinging my eyes, I saw something a few yards away bobbing in the water. Was it a person? Some object that would help me stay afloat? It was too hard to see clearly. I struggled to reach it, expending the last of my energy. It was a life jacket; "USS Warrington" stenciled on the border. The name of my ship. I grabbed it before a wave could steal it from me, holding the vest in a white-knuckled grip as I gathered my ebbing strength before attempting to put it on. I must not lose it. It would mean certain death if I did. I wrestled to strap the jacket over the sodden weight of my uniform that clung to my body like glue. It took a while in the huge swells. Once the vest was firmly bound, I instinctively fell into the eggbeater kick I learned in my naval survival training at Fort Schuyler. Although that action brought immediate relief, my mind wandered to desperate thoughts. How long could I do this? Would it be long enough for rescue to arrive? What if *Hyades* suffered the same fate as *Warrington*? What if no one knew of either ship's demise? If that were the case, there would be no rescue. This vast ocean would be my watery grave.

The sea brought bone-chilling shivers, but the movement of my arms and legs warmed my body temperature to a safe level. I maneuvered into a sitting position as best I could in the swells, keeping my head perpendicular to the surface of the water–hoping to increase my visibility amid the spume, scud, and rain of the huge swells as I searched for other survivors. *I cannot be the only person alive out of a crew of three hundred men,* I determined. *Surely everyone could not have been lost.*

Hoping to find others in the raging sea, I strained to rotate in a wide circle. Anxiously, I rode up one undulating wave to its white foamed crest, then plummeted like the drop on the Parachute Jump at the fair to the trough below before ascending the next swell to its foaming crown.

The turbulent swells made me nauseous. I vomited bile, which retched up my throat from my nearly empty belly. I should have forced myself to eat more solid food as the storm approached. My training had taught me that a person can get just as seasick in the water as they can aboard a ship. The queasiness made me crave my bunk to lie down, but it was already on the way to the ocean's floor. There was no escape.

I am not sure how long I was in the water because my wristwatch, a gift from Ellen–so I'd think of her whenever I looked at the time–was broken. The crystal had shattered against the deck railing when I was propelled overboard. The time did not matter anyway, as I had no appointment to be on time for, but the sentimental value of the watch was overwhelming. I thought of Ellen once more. *Will I see her again?*

With no other option but to ride the combers and focus on searching for others, I prayed for another miracle. For rescue to arrive. I recalled our fruitless efforts to make radio contact with *Hyades* shortly before foundering. Our SOS signals had been unanswered. The weather most likely disrupted the radio frequencies, but that wasn't unusual–nothing we hadn't experienced before, even in good weather and calm seas. Still, were our calls for help heard? I hoped our pleas were received by someone who could save me and that rescue was on the way. That possibility kept me going.

An enormous wave propelled me to its Alpen peak, abruptly dropping me into its deep trough. I was surrounded by a wall of black water. As another towering swell loomed over my head, I reflected on my life. I hoped reliving the memories would pass the time and allay the fear rising from my gut to my chest. I prayed it would be long enough to survive this catastrophe to return home to Ellen and our future, to start our life together. Nothing else mattered. *There must be hope*, I thought to myself. *Afterall, I already survived the worst time of my life when my father died.* I vowed then to change my circumstances, living the words Ralph Waldo Emerson wrote, "The only person you are destined to become is the person you decide to be."

I recalled that fateful event when my father passed.

2

A MAN AT TEN

DAD'S WAKE AND BURIAL, GLENDALE, NEW YORK, JANUARY 1929

It was winter in New York City. While normally a period of freezing temperatures and snow, the weather that year seesawed between bitter cold and spring-like temperatures. Those fluctuating extremes caused my father to develop a hacking cough. His persistent cough, thought to be an outcome of the unusual weather that season, eventually developed into stabbing chest pains, shaking chills, and shortness of breath. No matter how much pampering my mother administered, my father's condition did not improve. He shrugged it off, heading early each morning to those jobs he was lucky to garner. A plumber by trade, he often suffered cuts on his hands that needed mending when he returned home each night. My mother cleaned his sores, fed him hot pea soup, and urged him to bed early to rest to build his strength for the next day. Sometimes, when the thermometer indicated he had a slight temperature, she sat on the edge of their bed and applied a cold washcloth to his forehead. That was followed with a spoonful of cod liver oil she hoped would break the fever that invaded his body.

I recalled the dreary, pitch-black night when our world changed. My father came home from work that day, later than usual. When he entered through the front door, the sleeting rain and howling wind whooshed in behind him and he fell to the floor like a dead weight, his satchel of tools spilling by his feet. His pants and shoes were soaked to the bone.

"Charles!" my mother screamed, racing to his prone body lying in the entry. "What's happened to you?"

Too weak to speak, he feebly uttered, "Help me."

We raised him to his feet and, each taking an arm, led him into the bedroom. There, we removed his rain-soaked clothes and wet shoes and laid him on the bed and covered him with a blanket. Feverish, he grabbed his chest and moaned in pain. My mother snatched the thermometer from the bathroom medicine cabinet and took his temperature while I held a damp washcloth to his forehead. The reading, almost 104 degrees. He burned with fever. My father did not believe in spending money needlessly on medical treatment, but this was an emergency. Surely, he would agree to see the doctor.

He was wreathing in pain and delirious. I mopped the sweat from his brow while my mother pleaded with him to beckon the doctor. He finally ceded, and the doctor arrived early the next morning. After a quick assessment, he arranged to have my father, too weak to protest, admitted to the hospital. By then, though, it was too late. We could see his sickness was too entrenched in his weak body. The diagnosis of viral pneumonia was beyond treatment; there was no medicine to cure him. He would surely die.

He lapsed into a coma that afternoon and, with nothing for us to offer him other than a reassuring hand, we kept vigil at his bedside. The warm sunlight streaming through the window from the mild 45-degree weather outside gave my father's face a serene countenance. That night, when death claimed him, the temperature had plummeted to a frigid 18 degrees. The wind was howling in protest. He was forty-six years old—a young man, in the prime of his life cut short because he would not spend money on medical treatment when food on the table for his family was deemed more important.

His death changed my life.

Our economic circumstances did not allow for a wake at Werst's funeral home so, with financial support from her sister and her husband, my mother arranged for a viewing in the parlor of our house. The undertaker prepared my father's body and placed the plain wooden casket on the same spot my mother said I was born—where one life was given, and now one life taken.

I had never seen a deceased person before and never imagined the first would be my father. I never told him how much I loved him for all that he did for my mom and me. That hurt most of all. I always meant to, but somehow never did. I convinced myself it was because he was never there to tell as he toiled from sunrise to sundown every day except Sunday when he attended Mass and enjoyed an afternoon dinner with family.

The casket sat on a raised platform near the front window. The air was heavy with the scent of the sympathy flowers of chrysanthemums and late roses from relatives, close friends, and neighbors arrayed on each side. The heart-shaped arrangement of red roses from my mother sat atop the casket with a card saying, "Forever in our thoughts. May you rest in peace. Your loving wife and son."

As we were viewing the floral arrangements my mother said to me, "You should spend the day with Howie. His parents suggested it would be a good idea."

Howie was my best friend who lived on the street two doors down.

"No, Mom. I want to be here with you, and Dad."

"Well then," she said in a hushed whisper, "put on the suit you wear when you attend Sunday Mass with your father."

"I will, but Dad is no longer with us."

"I know," she sobbed. "Go. Get dressed. People will be here soon to pay their respects."

I dressed as my mother asked and before visitors arrived, we knelt before the casket and quietly prayed for my father's soul. She grasped his hand and, when I looked up into her face, I saw a stream of tears flowing from her eyes down her cheek. I don't know why I didn't cry. Too stunned by his death, I had to be strong for my mom. She needed me, now more than ever.

A tentative knock at the door woke us from our reverie. My mother glanced out the window and saw several people on the front steps. She took a hankie to wipe her tears.

"John, the mourners have come. Please answer the door and take their coats."

They were dressed in dark wool overcoats and galoshes as the weather was a wintry mix of snow and ice with temperatures hovering around 25 degrees. The people crowded into our small parlor offering their condolences to my mother and patting me on the head as I took their coats and placed them on the bed in her room.

As more and more people came to pay their respects, the overflow spilled into the dining room and then the kitchen. After viewing my father with a prayer, they departed, making space for others to fill the void. I was not surprised by the large throng of people since my mother was a popular person in the neighborhood.

When the sun faded into night, and darkness settled in, Father Coogan, our parish priest, came to the house. He shared with the family his stories of my father and offered a prayer for his salvation. He intoned: "The Lord is my shepherd; I shall not want. He makes me lie down in green pastures; He leads me beside still waters; He restores my soul."

My aunt and uncle arranged for refreshments to be delivered from Dick's Luncheonette. They were placed on the old oak table in our dining room. Following Father Coogan's words, we sat in the parlor reminiscing about my father while we ate. I sat quietly in the corner listening to the conversation. I learned a few stories about him I had never heard before.

The undertaker arrived early the next morning with his hearse to remove the casket and flowers from our parlor and deliver them less than a mile away to All Faith's Cemetery. The sun was hidden that day behind gray clouds. The wind blowing through the naked trees across the snowy ground reflected the somber mood of a burial. Only family and a few close friends braved the frigid temperatures to be there, walking through the blanket of snow that covered the ground, shivering around the gravesite in a silent stupor waiting for Father Coogan to speak. Two lone grackles perched on the bare limb of a nearby oak tree watched the proceedings with their beady eyes. Grave diggers had dug a hole several feet deep in the frozen earth to accept the casket, the dirt from their efforts disturbing the glistening white snow.

Pallbearers removed the casket from the hearse just as a flurry of large snowflakes began to fall. They struggled up the icy slope to the burial plot, setting the casket down next to the hole in the newly fallen snow. The undertaker placed the floral arrays from our parlor, along with the heart of roses, on top of the casket. After a prayer from Father Coogan, the casket was lowered into the hole, and a guttural shriek from the grackles pierced the silence, marking the end of the service. A light dusting of snow now covered the dirt from the dig and erased the footprints of those at the burial.

After the mourners dispersed, walking toward their cars, I stood peering into the hole at the flower-covered casket. The snow changed to light rain. That was the moment the reality of his death hit me. I cried, realizing I would never see my father again. I didn't know it then, but in that moment, I became a man at the tender age of ten. My mother needed me as much as I needed her. I ran to her walking with Father Coogan, the rain turning the snow to slush. I vowed to rise above my meager circumstances. My father shouldn't have died at such a young age. If only he had enough money for medical treatment when he first became ill things might have turned out differently. Maybe he'd still be with us.

There were severe hardships for my mother and me after my father passed. The Great Depression soon invaded our lives, and we struggled to survive with little money left for food. We continued living on Brush Street among our friends paying thirty-two dollars per month rent. My mother earned a small income cleaning houses for people in the neighborhood. Thinking back on it, I'm sure it was a subtle form of charity from those who knew our circumstances. That income, together with welfare payments of twenty dollars per month from the City of New York made possible our survival.

When I reached the age of thirteen, I contributed to household expenses by taking a job after school at Bill's Grocery stocking shelves with inventory. My mother initially refused the money I offered, but I insisted she take it and felt better when she did. Although we were barely living above the poverty level, we had the enduring love of family and friends and that helped us through the really trying times.

To rise above my paltry circumstance, I needed a good education. An education that would lead to a good paying job. A job that would leave money for medical expenses. I kept my nose to the grindstone, graduating from Richmond Hill High School in 1935 with marks that earned me a scholarship to St. John's University School of Commerce. A college degree, and hard work, were the keys to economic freedom, but I knew that in-and-of-itself did not equate to a perfect life. A life worth living, to be complete, needed the love of a woman and a family to share it with. I learned that from my parents, aunt and uncle and cousins. My father, bless his soul, despite his simple circumstances, was richer than most men could dream of being. He had the enduring and nurturing love of my mother until the day he passed.

I had great friends who guided my life's journey, from the time we met in elementary school and into adulthood. They strongly influenced my development into the man I became. Howie Dehls, his affable, easygoing personality, and friendly demeanor always nudged me to loosen up, to be less intense in the pursuit of my goals. "Ridge," he would say, "you don't have to strive for perfection in everything you do. No one is perfect. Live a little. Enjoy today because you don't know what tomorrow may bring. You might not be around to see the other side of six feet under." He was right. Gus, my other best friend, was a great athlete. He excelled in football and held the swimming records at the local YMCA. I strived to match his athletic ability but never reached his level. I played baseball and found satisfaction in managing the team as the captain. Howie's older brother Warren, known as "Chubby," showed us how to talk to the girls. That knowledge became more important as I got older. Other friends who impacted my life were Buddy Svensson, Johnny Faeth, Ernie Stenzel, Paul Kubik, Marty Golden and the two Artie's: Hagenlocher and Gladden.

I appreciated the job at Bill's Grocery and the support Bill gave me and my mom during hard times. Once I started college, he encouraged me to apply for other positions. I successfully landed a full-time job at Bank of Manhattan as a clerk in the credit department at 40 Wall Street. The officers at the bank advised me that a college degree in accounting would serve me well if I wanted to pursue a career in corporate lending at the bank. I took their advice to heart as I surveyed the luxurious surroundings where they worked. Each officer occupied a highly polished mahogany desk and had his own telephone, lamp, and name plate with their title. Their secretary screened calls, made appointments, and took dictation for memos, correspondence, and customer interviews while they entertained important clients of the bank in the executive dining room on the third floor.

Motivated for that career in lending at the bank, I attended St. John's year-round in the evening. I earned my degree in 1939 with honors, accepted into Delta Mu Delta Honor Society. I received a commemorative Gold Key with my name engraved under their motto "Power thru Knowledge."

Although my schedule of school and work was superhuman, I was committed to overcome all obstacles in my path. Little did I know that the same tenacity would save my life sixteen years later.

3

THE HURRICANE RAGED

BATTLING MOUNTAINOUS SWELLS, 13 SEPTEMBER 1944

The driving rain stung like shrapnel, but slapping waves provided temporary relief, washing away the pain until the next comber appeared. Surrounded by frothing white-capped waves in a sea the color of coal, the windswept spume made breathing difficult without swallowing briny water. Teeth chattering despite my aching jaw and dizziness from the bump on the back of my head, the cold water invaded my core. Prolonged exposure could lead to hypothermia and mental confusion, so I flapped my limbs under the constraints of my waterlogged uniform, hoping that would combat the problem. It seemed to work, as the rapid movement brought my body temperature to a safe level.

To ease my anxiety, I thought of the important events in my life that had led me to this dire situation. I prayed that my story wouldn't end here in these bitter waters, but with my return to the loving embrace of Ellen.

★

I was born in 1918 when the war in Europe ended. National pride propelled our country forward. The United States emerged in the following decade, known as the Roaring Twenties, as the most powerful nation in the world. It was a period of unbounded prosperity and opportunity–for everyone, it seemed, except my family.

Although my mother planned to deliver her baby in the hospital, the baby had other plans. Her birth pains came so suddenly that she dropped to the floor in our parlor when her water broke. My father, in a panic, raced down the street to retrieve the doctor, who arrived just in time to deliver a healthy, nine-pound baby boy, the first—and only—child of Anne and Charles Ridgeway, baptized John Thomas Ridgeway by Father Elmer Coogan at St. Nicholas Roman Catholic Church.

Our two-family brick row house at 44 Brush Street in Glendale, New York was illuminated by gaslight until electricity arrived in the neighborhood in 1924. When I was older, I wondered why it took so long for us to get electricity while the bright lights of Manhattan glowed for years across the East River, washing away the stars. The ever-changing horizon of skyscrapers sprouting in the city symbolized prosperity to me. While Glendale, surrounded by farms of German immigrants and cemeteries, just starting to attract people and housing to support its nascent manufacturing, characterized an earlier time. It was as if the past was looking through the window into the future.

Even when our home had electricity, we still hadn't caught up to the twentieth century. The wooden outhouse in the backyard attested to that. Our neighborhood had no sewers for indoor plumbing and the dirt road of Brush Street made it feel like we lived in the last century.

I was a youngster but vividly recalled the clambake on my aunt and uncle's twentieth wedding anniversary, a gala affair in their backyard that brought the family together. Everyone claimed to have a "ring-a-ding" time probably because the beer and whiskey was plentiful despite Prohibition. I remembered walking with my father to Myrtle Avenue to McGrath's Tavern for a growler of beer for the party and then making several more trips with him to refill the empty jug. Even though I was eight at the time, I learned a life lesson about drinking alcohol. Several of the younger adults at the party drank too much hootch, and they suffered the consequences, vomiting the jiggle juice into the bushes on the side of the house where no one could see them. I vowed never to drink like that. It wasn't the way to have a good time. Regretfully, however, I forgot that lesson and many years later, succumbed to my own learning experience with too much to drink.

4

ANOTHER SURVIVOR

A MIRACLE IN THE STORM, 13 SEPTEMBER 1944

Beyond the foaming crest of the last swell, I noticed a dark object bobbing in the water. Is it a broken buoy or a person? The driving rain, slicing the skin on my face like knives, makes vision impossible. I hope it's a person, and not my crazed imagination playing tricks. Acutely aware of the task, I make my way to the blob. I rolled onto my back and, peeking over my shoulder, a wave blurring my vision, I blink away the water to see. I start heading in the direction I need to go, riding up the threatening swell, hoping to reach the blob before it disappears in the swirl of the trough below. When I neared where I thought I needed to be, I turned onto my stomach, the waterlogged uniform making maneuvering difficult, like Houdini twisting and turning as he struggles to escape a straight jacket. It was a person looking up at the emerging swell. Another survivor. I doggy-paddled to him, calling for his attention, but an erupting wave engulfs us. My voice is drowned in a low gurgle by the roar of the turbulent sea. He didn't hear me. He turns away from the curling crest forming above his head. I see his face. Schultz, our assistant gunnery officer, wearing a life jacket. He moves towards me, and, when we reached each other, we unite arms, hoping to gain strength from the other, believing two are stronger than one. Realizing the seeming hopelessness of the situation, I nervously exclaimed, "Don, fancy meeting you here!"

"I'm glad to see you!" he gasped.

"There must be other survivors," I said. "We have to find them."

"Just before the ship foundered, I saw men launching a Carley float, but a wave washed over me and, when I looked back, they were gone."

Looking up, I saw a gigantic swell forming, ready to unfurl. "Watch your back!" I shouted. "Behind you! We'll be buried!"

The curling crest crashes upon us before we can react, driving us down under. We popped to the water's surface seconds later just as the next developing swell sweeps us to its peak. We are careful after that to ride the swells up and down while we drifted along with the Gulf Stream, searching for other survivors.

"How'd you make if off the ship?" I asked, once we settled into a safe rhythm riding up and down the swells.

"I heard the order to Abandon Ship from outside the CR."

"What'd you do?" I asked.

"I saw Greene and several others huddled in the companionway. They were hopping into a Carley float when the ship suddenly turned into a swell, tossing them hard against the bulkhead."

"Did they make it onto the float?"

He nodded. "They relaunched the raft."

"Why didn't you join them?"

"I was about to, but then another wave flipped the float against the side of the ship. They were thrown into the water again."

"Did they get the raft righted?"

"Yes."

"Then they're out here somewhere. We must find them," I uttered in exhaustion.

We drifted in the swirling waves, squinting through the scud and driving rain, searching endlessly for Greene's raft. Then a giant swell carried us to its foaming white crest to reveal a couple dozen men riding a Carley float in the trough below. There was hope. Again, I pondered, were our SOS calls heard? Will we be rescued?

"Let's make it to the raft," Don urged. "It may be overloaded, but we can hold onto the trailing lines."

We paddled towards the raft, screaming for their attention, but a huge wave crashed over us, smothering our cries for help. They hadn't seen us. I gulped a mouthful of water I barely spat out through the pain in my jaw. My arms and legs were dead weights, pulling me down.

Don hollered in my ear, "It's Greene! He sees us! Hang on!" I feel a hand grabbing the back of my vest, pulling me to the raft where the men are waiting to hoist us aboard. The water is turbulent, the raft in danger of flipping over. Greene grabbed Don's vest. Don held me to the side of the float to keep me from drifting away while Sapp struggled to get his hands on my vest. The others on the raft leaned away from the action to keep the float balanced as they pulled us in, depositing us on the webbed grid of wooden slats that made up the floor.

Once we were securely on the raft, Don told Greene, "I sure am glad we found you."

"We almost didn't make it off," Greene said as a wave crashed over us. Everyone held tight to the webbed gridding as the raft rode up into the next swell.

"I know. I was watching when it turned over."

"It flipped, but we righted it. I thought we'd get sucked under with the ship, but we managed to get away."

"Luck was with you."

"Yes, but there were about thirty men on the raft by that point, way too many to keep it stabilized."

Sapp, spitting some water, added, "We were on the right side of the ship when she went under."

LaTronica said, "It was scary, though, because, when the ship sank, the suction took us down with her. I clawed like a madman for the water's surface."

Hart said, "I felt like I was caught in a whirlpool."

"Some of the men got tangled in the net and drowned when that happened," Greene said.

Laying against the side of the raft, I heard their voices, but they faded from my consciousness. Gripped with overwhelming tiredness, my eyes, burning from the salt water, closed. Holding tight to the strap, I recalled my first tangle with a hurricane. That one almost cost me my life, but I survived. I hoped I would survive this one, too.

5

LONG ISLAND EXPRESS

Glendale, New York, 21 September 1938

I was twenty when we were battered by a massive hurricane. I was sitting in the parlor with my mother, listening to the static-filled news on our second-hand Radiola. An emergency weather bulletin interrupted the regular programming to announce a destructive hurricane would assault New York City and Long Island the next day. Intrigued by the news, I told my mother, "I'm going down the street to Myrtle Avenue to assess the situation."

She pulled the curtain aside and peered out the window. "John, it's raining. This must be the beginning. Be careful."

"I will. Don't worry."

I plucked my umbrella from the closet and left the house in a hurry. Walking briskly along Myrtle Avenue, I peered at the sky through the leafy Elm trees in the cemetery across the street, looking for an ominous sign of a hurricane—menacing black clouds, thunder and lighting, strong wind gusts, anything that evidenced danger—but nothing. Everything appeared normal. A soft breeze rustled the leaves in the trees and the rain abated into a light mist. No hint of danger. If the storm were to be as devastating as the weathercaster predicted, there would surely be some indication of impending doom.

People from the neighborhood streamed up the side streets with their open umbrellas, congregating in small groups along Myrtle Avenue, chattering about the forecasted hurricane and the havoc it would wreak. I heard someone say, "lives will be lost." The more they talked, the more they worked themselves into a frenzy. Customers stampeded into Bill's Grocery and Otto Herrmann's Hardware to stock up on food and kerosene lanterns before the shops closed for the evening. Being young, it seemed silly to me to hoard supplies for a storm that would pass through in an hour or so, with a little wind and some rain. *But*, I thought, *what if I'm wrong and everyone else, with their years of wisdom, were right about the danger of the storm?* I hadn't spoken to my mother before I left the house about her experience with hurricanes, so I didn't know her thoughts about the situation. Swept up in the crazed mania of the people on the street, I figured the prudent thing would be to buy some essentials—items Mom and I would consume no matter what. I entered Bill's walking straight to the dairy department, where I grabbed a half-gallon bottle of milk, a dozen eggs, and a package of American cheese, before I scurried to the bakery section for a loaf of Wonder Bread. I snatched a jar of Skippy peanut butter from a shelf and several Hershey's chocolate bars on my way to the cash register. *That should hold us*, I thought, *until after the storm passes.*

I trekked home in a light drizzle, with the umbrella open and the groceries carefully balanced in my other arm so not to break the eggs. I passed a steady stream of people heading to the stores on Myrtle Avenue looking to restock their pantries. The news about the hurricane was spreading. One geezer, in a hurry with his head down bumped into me and I almost dropped my bag. Lucky, I made it home in one piece with no broken eggs or spilled milk.

When I entered the parlor, my mother was sitting where I left her, still listening to the news. She said the weatherman kept to his forecast of a deadly storm, saying it would arrive during the next several hours.

"Mom, the weather doesn't seem so bad," I said, placing the grocery bag on the dining room table. "Only a light sprinkle, so I don't know what to expect. Seems like a lot of hoopla to me. But to be on the safe side, I stopped in Bill's for some food to hold us over just in case. Everyone on the street was doing the same, and I passed more people on the way home heading to the stores. We'll have a good breakfast tomorrow."

"Thanks John," she said as she emptied the contents of the bag. "We should be okay, but I'm not sure I can wait until breakfast for this food. How about you, want a cheese omelet now?"

"Sounds good to me."

My mother had a calm demeanor and wasn't as concerned as everyone else about the potential devastation. "Don't worry," she said while we were eating our omelets. "If the hurricane becomes life threatening, we'll take refuge in the basement until it blows over. We'll be safe there."

We stayed up late that night waiting for the storm to make its appearance. Finally, we drifted into a restless slumber with the window cracked open so we would hear the first signs when it arrived. However, it was as quiet as a mouse all night. When the rain stopped, a calm stillness filled the void.

We awoke early the next morning with the rising sun burning away the soft morning fog. Mom prepared scrambled eggs with toast, and we ate our breakfast listening to the latest weather forecasts.

Finally, just after midday, the weather began to deteriorate. The wind increased in intensity and a steady rain blanketed the neighborhood. The storm had arrived, but it sure didn't seem too bad, no worse than what I'd seen before—more like a lamb than a lion. We stayed indoors the rest of the day, just in case the weather turned suddenly violent, and I told my mother I would wait until tomorrow to check the area.

The next day I arose with the sun, showered, dressed, and, skipping breakfast, anxiously explored the neighborhood for damage from the storm. As soon as I walked out the door, I noticed fallen tree limbs lying in the street. I jogged to Myrtle Avenue expecting to see more devastation, but things did not look too bad. I headed to Dick's Luncheonette to get the newspaper, pulling the New York Daily Mirror from the rack, its headline screaming "400 Dead!" I wondered where all that destruction was. Standing by the rack, I scanned the front-page featured article. The headline: "Charles Pierce, a junior meteorologist with the National Weather Bureau in Washington, D.C., reproved his colleagues saying the hurricane would land at the end of Long Island and cross over the Sound into New England." Veteran forecasters were skeptical as a major hurricane had never struck that region before, so the official forecast made no mention of a hurricane-strength storm. By the time the forecasters realized the true path and power of the storm, the brunt of it slammed the East End of Long Island, with the eye making landfall in Bayport. The late-breaking forecast gave no one time to evacuate, leaving millions of people in the hurricane's path with no option but to ride out the storm. The paper dubbed the hurricane, "Long Island Express" because it appeared without warning. With a name, the hurricane's stature grew. Storms that had names were the deadliest ones.

I left Dick's with the paper, intending to read all the stories on the hurricane when I arrived home. Before that, though, I crossed Myrtle Avenue into the cemetery to survey the damage. It appeared the storm had spared Glendale from most of its wrath. It passed through our neighborhood with little damage other than a downed utility line here and there, along with an errant broken tree limb and occasional uprooted tree. Some of the older headstones in the cemetery were toppled by the gusting wind, I guessed, and would wait for the groundskeeper to return them to their sentinel positions. Yesterday everyone was in a panic about the destruction we would experience when the storm hit, and today the weather was calm and serene and the damage minimal.

When I walked in the door, my mother was still sitting in her favorite chair beside the radio. Her brow furrowed, she exclaimed, "John, the latest report said the death toll from the storm has risen to over seven hundred people, making it one of the deadliest hurricanes in history. We were lucky to be on the fringe of it and not near the shoreline where the tidal surges caused the most damage."

"You're right."

"What did you see on your exploration of the neighborhood?"

"Well, not much really. Some downed trees and limbs on the street and toppled tombstones in the cemetery."

According to the newspaper, the hardest hit areas were along the coastline.

It said, "The full moon, with the autumnal equinox, created winds of 120 miles per hour, with gusts reaching 185 miles per hour, causing thirty-foot tidal surges from Manhattan to Montauk that swept houses to sea and downed utility lines, leaving thousands homeless or without power."

After I finished reading the Mirror and listened to the latest radio news, I said, "I'm going to see if Howie and Gus want to venture to Rockaway Beach to see the damage left by the storm and maybe test the ocean's waves." While the hurricane's aftermath lingered, temperatures were warm and summerlike. With the sun struggling to emerge from the slightly overcast sky, most people would say it was a great day for the beach.

"Be careful if you go into the water. There could be a strong undertow. You won't see it, but it would make it difficult for you to get out of the water. People have drowned before the lifeguard ever reached them."

"I know, Mom. I'll be careful. I promise."

I walked two houses down and knocked on the door. Howie answered almost immediately. He must have seen me through the window. His mom called from the kitchen, "Howie, who's at the door?"

"It's Ridge."

"Hey, man," I greeted Howie, "now the storm has passed, I'm thinking we could go to Rockaway Beach to see what damage it caused. I already walked along Myrtle and through the cemetery, but not much to see there, only a few uprooted trees and toppled tombstones. The tidal surges probably destroyed the boardwalk. I can't imagine what that looks like. Interested?"

"Yeah, I'm up for that. I heard on the radio that hundreds of people died. The devastation must be unbelievable."

"Yeah, my mom said the death toll reached 700. Based on the weather today, you'd never have believed such a violent storm passed through yesterday."

"You're right. Not in a million years."

"Wear your swim trunks under your duds in case we want to test the waves—they should be killer. I'm sure Gus will want to go since he's the best swimmer. He has no fear of the ocean, but maybe he'll feel differently once he sees the waves."

"Okay then, let's not futz around. You get Gus, and I'll go home for my trunks and meet you guys outside my front door in a half."

We arrived at Rockaway to find the wooden planks and iron railings of the boardwalk strewn along the beach, heaped in a jumbled mess of twisted wreckage, and when we looked to the ocean, we knew why. The waves were gigantic, the biggest we had ever seen. What the waves must have been like at the height of the storm, near the eye. Looking toward the water, I said, "The eye hit the Hamptons, so the waves were bigger there than here, and this looks scary."

As we walked amid the rubble, we encountered other curious people with astonished expressions on their faces, awestruck by the destruction and enormity of the waves crashing onto the beach. The turbulent surf of white-capped waves bubbling like a cauldron of boiling water challenged us to enter. Gus pointed to a nearby sign lying among the splintered boardwalk planks. It said, "Swim at your own risk, no lifeguards on duty." That sign, posted Labor Day, had nothing to do with the hurricane, but its words were prophetic.

Peering over his shoulder at the water's edge, Gus said, "Well, are you two chickens ready to take a dip? Shouldn't be afraid of some little waves." Howie and I looked at each other in dismay but realized Gus wasn't kidding.

"I'm game," I said, "if you guys are."

With fearless abandon, not grasping the hidden danger of the strong undertow that my mother warned me about, we walked toward the water.

Clearing debris to make space, we placed our towels on the damp sand and shed our street clothes to our swim trunks, ready to enter the water. The waves, probably twelve to fifteen feet high, were the largest I had ever seen. I noticed some old bitty nearby looking at us like we were crazy. Maybe we were.

I stepped in the turbulent surf, glancing over my shoulder to see if Gus and Howie were following. Unaware of the danger coming at me, a tremendous wave erupted, hurling me end over end. I was tossed head over heels under the water, tumbling—I thought—toward the shore. But I was wrong. The receding wave, with its gripping undertow, like the suckers of a giant octopus, swallowed me into the dark void, drawing me back into the ocean. Desperate, arms and legs flailing in a frenzy to escape, my feet struggled to find firm ground to keep my head above the water before the next wave barreled in. Shoulder-deep, I attempted to wipe the briny water stinging my eyes with the back of my hand. Blind to the action behind me, I leapt in the direction I thought I needed to go to reach safety. Spitting water, I can see I'm heading toward the shore hoping to reach the safety of the wet, sandy beach before the next wave surges forward. I was close because the next crashing wave propelled me onto the beach, where I landed unceremoniously in a heap on my stomach. Once I gathered my bearing, I rose to my knees and look up to see Howie, Gus, and a crowd of others watching with relief etched on their faces. They ran to me yelling above the roar of the ocean, pulling me up from the sand. Gus said, "We saw you swallowed by that monster wave and jumped back before it sucked us in too! When you disappeared, we thought we would have to come in after you, but thank God, you made it back."

"I thought I was going to drown," I said. "The pull of the undertow was almost more than I could overcome, like a powerful magnet. If another humdinger of a wave had erupted, I wouldn't be talking to you two knuckleheads now. I'll never do anything that dopey again, that's for sure."

A man in the crowd in a white naval uniform stepped forward. He said, "You went into the water before I could warn you not to. Never challenge a hurricane, even its aftermath. You won't win. You were fortunate not to have drowned. Let that be a lesson you never forget."

"You're right, sir. I should have listened to my mother. She warned me." Standing together by our towels, mesmerized by the crashing waves still pounding to shore, we agreed our swimming expedition in the wake of a hurricane was foolhardy. We left the beach with a newfound respect for the power and fury of a hurricane, even though we caught only the last vestige. When I am older, probably joining other fuddy-duddies scurrying for food and other supplies for another hurricane, I will undoubtedly tell my children how I almost drowned at Rockaway Beach in the famous Long Island Express of 1938, a hurricane that left an impression I'll never forget.

My eyes opened when a swell washed over, slapping my face. "Lieutenant, are you okay? Your face is quite swollen. You passed out when we pulled you onto the raft."

"I'm not sure. My head is pounding. I smashed against the bulwark and might have a broken jaw or concussion. I lost some teeth and felt a large bump on the back of my head. Do we have any medical supplies?"

"Nothing that will relieve pain."

"Okay. Let me think about what we need to do."

"Yes, sir."

I closed my eyes, hoping the rest will give me strength, and my story the reason for survival.

6

LOVE AT FIRST SIGHT?

NEW YORK WORLD'S FAIR, 14 JUNE 1939

After working full-time during the day while attending college at night, I felt I earned a few days' rest before embarking on my career in banking. The New York World's Fair, several years in planning, would be the perfect respite. Situated on 1,216 acres of land in Flushing Meadows and built atop an ash dump, the fair opened to great fanfare on April 30 with a dedication by President Franklin Roosevelt. The organizers hoped the fair, an exposition of countries from around the world, would lift New York City, and the country, from the depths of the depression that plagued our nation for the last decade. Most people, barely eking by, were starving for a sign of better times to come. The fair's "Dawn of a New Day" theme promised a bright future so I was anxious to see what it would be. I did not know that day at the fair would forever change my life.

Relaxing at the kitchen table with a cup of coffee in hand after finishing breakfast, I was reading the Daily News article about the growing crowds at the fair when there was a loud knock at the front door. My mother was at an early cleaning job so I wondered who could be calling at this time in the morning. When I opened the door Gus pushed in front of Howie, greeting me "Hi-de-ho Ridge, happy birthday."

"Thanks guys. You're both out early." Puzzled, I asked, "All to wish me a happy birthday?"

"Well, kind of." Gus explained, "Howie and I thought with all the hoo-ha about the World's Fair and the weather being so ideal today, we could celebrate your twenty-first birthday having a killer time at the fair. It has been open for a month, so the glitches should be ironed out. Who knows, maybe we'll be lucky and meet some babes. What d'ya think?"

"You two lugs read my mind. I was thinking the same thing about going to the fair today after I peeked out the front window and saw how nice it is. Temperatures are forecasted to be in the seventies all day, with no chance of rain."

"This nice weather will bring out the people," Howie said. "The crowds are growing and will be larger when the public schools break for summer vacation next week."

"Well, my birthday aside, it is a perfect day to hit the fair. Does that mean you two are paying for my ticket?"

"Yeah, man," Howie said, "We've enough moola between us to pay your entrance, plus spring for a couple of beers and a hot dog. You're only twenty-one once!"

"Thanks, guys. There may even be some special events since it's Flag Day, and if we happen to meet some babes, I'll mention it's nice to have a national celebration when it's your birthday."

"Good luck with that humdinger line," Gus quipped. "It would be a real stretch if some gal took you seriously, but I want to hear you give it a try."

"Let's get a move on then," Howie said, "if we want to beat the crowds."

We walked to the Myrtle Avenue subway, paid the five-cent fare, and rode the new IND Line to the fair, exiting the turnstiles at the last stop adjacent to the park entrance just as the gates opened. As we hurried toward the ticket booth, Gus said he read the IND was built expressly to transport fairgoers to

Flushing Meadows and would be dismantled after the fair closed.

"That seems like a waste of a lot of dough," I proffered, "but I guess that's government bureaucracy. The politicians always know how to squander taxpayer dollars."

"You're right, Ridge," Howie agreed. "Their plan might even be to return the site to an ash dump after the fair closes. Wouldn't that be nuts?"

"I wouldn't be surprised," Gus added. "The politicians are crazy."

We stood on a prolonged line before reaching the ticket booth. So much for getting to the fair early to beat the crowds. Howie and Gus paid the seventy-five-cent admissions into the fair and, with programs in hand, we ventured into the first stop of the World of Tomorrow, the 610-foot spire-shaped Trylon and the adjacent 180-foot diameter Perisphere, connected to each other by the world's longest escalator. Those colossal structures were the symbols for the fair's World of Tomorrow theme, with the exhibit inside depicting the utopian city of the future. Those incongruous edifices, casting long shadows across the open plaza, seemed oddly out-of-place with the surrounding exhibits.

"Hey, you lugs, look over there," I said pointing to the statue of George Washington. "I wonder why he's here in the middle of the world of the future." I pulled the program from my back pocket and read aloud, "It says 'the statue commemorates the 150th anniversary of George Washington's inauguration (in 1789) as president.' I venture the fair was planned with the past in mind, with the attractions showing the way to the future."

"That must be the reason," Howie agreed.

"You know, a plaque on Wall Street commemorates the spot where he was inaugurated that I pass every day at work," I said. "I wonder what good old George would think today if he saw the skyscrapers where he once stood taking his oath as president?"

"He'd be amazed for sure," Gus said.

"The clock is ticking," Howie reminded us. "The lines are surely building at the most popular attractions so I don't think we'll be able to hit all the top spots today. Let's decide which ones we really want to see and get moving."

"Yeah," I concurred, leading the way to a concrete bench by the base of Washington's statue where we spent several minutes planning our itinerary. Even though it was a World's Fair, the most popular attractions had nothing to do with visiting foreign lands (except for maybe the German beer garden, where we'd be sure to stop) but rather the rides, the aquatic show, and new inventions on display at the various kiosks sprinkled throughout the fair.

Howie urged, "GM and Ford are attracting the largest crowds because they're killer, so let's head there first. It helps they're located next to each other."

"Howie's right about General Motors and Ford, but let's make sure to see RCA's television invention," I said. "The paper said it's a small movie screen that you can have in your home. I wonder what you'd be able to watch on it. How does a movie magically appear on the screen?"

"GM, Ford, RCA are bonkers," Gus chimed in, "but we absolutely, positively, cannot miss Life Saver's parachute jump and Billy Rose's Aquacade. I'm not leaving the fair today until we see those. And more importantly, if we don't end up meeting some glams, we can at least ogle the bathing beauties in the Aquacade. That alone is worth the price of admission right there."

"Yeah," Howie agreed, "I'm with you on that. Life magazine had pictures comparing ladies' swim attire from the 1890s—you know, a black knee-length, puffed-sleeve dress worn over bloomers, which looked like something my grandmother would wear—to the bikini, a two-piece bra-and-panty outfit that shows the belly button and a lot of thigh and cleavage."

"If we're lucky, the girls in the aquatic show will be wearing bikinis," I gushed.

"I sure hope so," Gus said in an approving voice. "I can't say I saw any chicks at Rockaway Beach last year wearing a bikini, but I wouldn't have minded if I had. The trend this summer might be spurred by a little promotion from the Aquacade."

"Now that you mention it, Gus," I said, "I don't recall seeing anyone at the beach in a bikini last year either. You two lugs would have been the first to know if I did, and we would have been talking about it all winter. How about you, Howie?"

"Same here," Howie said. "But we're always together, so if one of us had seen a bikini, all three of us would have."

"Yeah, you're right," I confirmed.

"The photos in Life," Howie drooled, "show almost everything, the curve of the breast, the rounded hips, tight thighs, and belly button, everything I dream of."

"It must leave little for the imagination," I added.

"It must sure be easy on the eyes," Gus sighed. "Well, here's to the bikini and a great summer at the beach this year.

With our itinerary for the day planned and already at the first stop, we entered the Trylon where we viewed, from an overhead moving sidewalk in the Perisphere, a diorama depicting the utopian city of the future. When we exited the exhibit, Howie urged us on to the General Motors pavilion to experience Futurama, the fair's most popular attraction. Its 36,000-square-foot exhibit had the longest wait times, and this proved to be true when we approached the building to be greeted by a snaking switchback line of people a mile long. The daunting crowd made no difference to us, though, as we raced to the end of the line, falling in place behind three girls. *Gus may be right about meeting some dolls*, I thought.

As the serpentine line inched forward toward the entrance, a natural back-and-forth banter with the girls in front of us developed. I presumed they were working girls in their mid-twenties based upon their dress. Contrary to the seeming age difference, though, we actively chatted with them about the various attractions and exhibits we most wanted to see. I took note when I heard the blonde say she wanted to see the Westinghouse Time Capsule that wouldn't be opened until the year 6939. She said it contained writings by Albert Einstein, a Mickey Mouse watch, and copies of *Life* magazine. I wondered if that included the issue with the bikini, and what people five thousand years from now would think of these items when they found them—that is, if they find them. Who would know where to look then?

The longer we talked, the more I snuck furtive glances at the blonde. We hadn't introduced ourselves to each other, so I listened intently as they spoke, learning that her name was Ellen. While her looks were my first attraction, it was her personality that captured my attention. She was quiet but not shy, deferring to her friends who did most of the talking, and that impressed me for someone so beautiful who was not seeking to be the center of attention. I couldn't avert my eyes from her, even though I willed myself to do so. I didn't want her to catch me staring. I loved listening to her speak in her soft voice. She was beautiful, for sure, dressed in a black crepe skirt that fell an inch below her knees, topped by a white silk blouse cinched at the waist by a black leather belt with a silver buckle, and black heels that accentuated her shapely, toned legs. Her attire provided a striking contrast to her lustrous long blonde hair under the black beret she wore that framed her bronzed, rounded face and slightly upturned nose. She had a sultry aura, but I don't think she realized how beautiful she was, and her modesty and self-effacing demeanor made her even more appealing to me. She stood about five feet three inches and her petite figure, I thought, would look great in a bikini.

Although attracted to her looks, the more I listened to her speak, the more I realized there was more substance to her than that. And that made me wonder how she—or her friends, for that matter—could be interested in us guys. The only reason we were conversing, I thought, was the circumstances of being next to each other on the slow-moving line, seeking ways to amuse ourselves until we entered the ride. We were flirting, and they were receptive, but maybe only in a cute, sisterly way. No matter the reason for our connection, though, I was elated for the opportunity to speak to a beautiful woman. It felt good to have the attention of three pretty girls. Our conversation continued uninterrupted for an hour while the line slowly inched toward the entrance, and I wondered if she would say yes to a date with me if I asked.

Before I knew it, and with regret our conversation was ending, we entered Futurama, the long wait passing in a satisfying blur. I looked at Ellen and thought, *I'm more attracted to her demure personality than her beautiful looks.* Her maturity and self-assuredness were attributes I had never encountered in a girl before. She was a person with a "good head on her shoulders." A girl, I thought, worth knowing better.

At the last moment before entering the ride we hastily agreed to pair-up so no one sat alone in a seat for two. Absorbed with Ellen, I had not been paying too much attention to Howie and Gus and how they were getting along with her friends, but I hoped it was going as well for them as it was for me. I sensed Ellen might be as interested in me as I was in her. I just hoped my intuition was right. I took her by the arm and with all the moxie I could muster said "Ladies first!" as I guided her into the lift seat, adding as I followed her, "By the way, I'm John."

"I'm Ellen."

"I know," I smiled knowingly, with assurance.

"I thought your name was Ridge. How did you know my name is Ellen?"

"I'm a good listener. What about you?"

"So am I," she responded with the emergence of a grin, her brown, almond shaped eyes crinkling at the edges. "Your name is not Ridge?"

"No. I mean, yes, Ridge is my nickname. My name is John Ridgeway. My mom and relatives call me John, but friends, and sometimes my mom, call me Ridge."

"Well, I thought Ridge was unusual for a first name. I'm glad to call you John. I'm Ellen Curran. I have no nickname, but my mom called me Bean when I was small. I've outgrown that name, so please don't tell my friends about it."

"Your secret is safe with me. It has been my greatest pleasure meeting you, Ellen."

"I might say the same, John," she blushed in response.

We had no sooner sat and buckled in before the ride took off, sweeping us in a whoosh twenty feet into the air above a huge diorama of the world as it would be in the 1960s, encompassing a vast array of miniature towns, houses, roads, and cars that grew larger in scale as we passed through the various sections of the exhibit so that by the end of our journey everything was scaled life-size. When we hopped off the chair lift at the end of the ride, Ellen's heel caught on the platform and she stumbled forward. Luckily for me, I caught her by the waist as she was falling, affirming my intuition she had a figure for a bikini. When she straightened up, she looked into my eyes and, with a seductive wink, said, "Thanks, John. Great catch."

"You're welcome." Without thinking, I said, "Since I caught you, I was wondering if I may have a date?"

"Yes, of course, especially since you saved me from landing flat on my face. These heels were not a good idea for walking around the fair. I don't know what I was thinking."

I watched with curiosity as she rummaged in her purse. She retrieved the fair ticket and a sharpened eyebrow pencil and printed on the ticket: Ellen Curran, PR 5-9538, and presented the stub to me with a smile, "There you go. Call me."

Looking into her eyes that moment, I thought, *could this be what people refer to as 'love at first sight?'* I placed her ticket stub in my wallet to make certain I would not lose it.

The others left the ride right behind us and we gathered at the exit to decide upon our next attraction. Paired off and holding hands—me with Ellen, Howie with Jane, who said her last name was Killorin, and Gus with Kitty, who said her name was Katherine Hughes—we strolled to the nearby Ford Motor pavilion to take its ride that rivaled General Motors Futurama. None of us cared about the large crowd as it provided the opportunity for everyone to converse more. After another lengthy but satisfying wait, we entered the lobby underneath a stainless-steel sculpture of Mercury where we viewed the automobiles on display comparing Henry Ford's Quadricycle and 1903 Model A with the new Lincoln-Zephyr, opining how streamlined the Zephyr was compared to those early models.

Admiring the Zephyr's sleek lines, Gus sighed, "I wish my father would trade his old jalopy for this."

"Dream on," Howie said, "This car costs a small fortune."

"Yeah, you're right," Gus sadly agreed.

"Come on, let's shake a leg," I interjected, "The 'Road of Tomorrow' beckons."

We climbed the stairs to fall in at the end of another long line for the main attraction, a ride in a Lincoln-Zephyr on a curving, half-mile-long track that transported us along the highway of the future. The ride was not as exhilarating as Futurama, which caused your stomach to drop when it lifted into the air, but the privacy of the Zephyr's darkened space afforded the opportunity to kiss Ellen—if I had the nerve to make the move. We sat in the back seat and as the car moved along the track, I peered into her eyes, searching for an indication, and when her lips parted and her eyes closed, I acted on my intuition. I placed my lips on hers, and she returned the kiss. I'd never felt such a strong attraction to a girl before, one I wanted to explore further. I grasped her hand as we exited the car and, with a smile on her face, she gave my hand a squeeze as we walked toward the others.

"My stomach's grumbling. Do you guys and gals want to head to the Food Zone for something to eat?" I asked. "I'm thirsty from the long waits standing in line and dreamed of having a juicy tube steak washed down with a nice cold larger beer. How about everyone else—hungry?"

Howie and Gus knew about it, but Ellen asked, "What's a tube steak? I'd love to taste something from Europe?"

"It's one of my favorite foods," I said. "A hot dog drenched with A. Bauer's horseradish mustard topped with sauerkraut."

Ellen laughed again. "I don't know anyone, John, who elevates the stature of a frankfurter to that of a steak."

Howie said, "Then you don't know Ridge. Let's scoot to the Schaefer Center for some brews and dogs. Their 120-foot-long bar is one of the longest in the world. I want to see that."

"Now you're talking," Gus said.

A crowd three-deep at the bar blocked the entrance when we entered the pavilion, but Gus quickly spotted two empty tables we pushed together to accommodate the six of us. Howie and I then went to the food counter for the hot dogs and beer while Gus entertained the ladies with his knowledge of the latest female swimwear. We returned to the table with the food and drink to find the girls laughing uproariously as Gus explained to them the benefits of wearing a bikini to the beach as "all that sun would be good for your skin."

The conversation while we ate allowed everyone to get to know one another better. The girls, we learned, graduated from Jamaica High School two years ago. Ellen said she's a secretary at Manufacturers Trust Company at their City Hall branch in Manhattan; while Kitty, a blonde, with a nice figure, who spoke in a very refined voice that hinted of an Irish accent, was a receptionist for a ladies' coat manufacturer in the textile district; and Jane, the one with black hair and a boisterous personality, was a bookkeeper at a lighting manufacturer in Ridgewood, Queens. The fact they were working girls gave them a maturity, I believed, that made them seem older than us. Ellen, to my delight, said she had no steady boyfriend. Jane and Kitty also shared they had no boyfriends, although Kitty said someone at work asked her out several times, but she was not interested. That particular news brought a smile to Gus's face.

After finishing lunch and the last of our beer, we headed to the amusement area.

On the way, Jane proposed visiting the British Pavilion to view an original copy of the Magna Carta. "That document, believe it or not," she said, "was written in the year 1215—just think of that! That's over five hundred years older than our own Declaration of Independence." When Jane told us that, we all agreed we had to see that ancient paper.

While we waited our turn for a close view of the parchment, I wandered into the next aisle where a glass cabinet held crowns, rings, and scepters. "Ellen, look at this," I said, pointing to the glass case. "It says these are replicas of the Crown Jewels. I wonder what the real ones are worth, and if King George wears them for special events. He must have a phalanx of bodyguards to protect him if he does."

"You know John, the real jewels may be worth a 'king's ransom,' but I'm not impressed. They look heavy and are rather gaudy. I'd rather wear a nice Southsea pearl necklace—that would make me happy." I envisioned a string of Champagne-colored pearls around her inviting tanned neck, just as Gus beckoned us to view the Magna Carta.

On the path to the Aquacade, we passed a large crowd elbowing each other to inspect an object in the middle of a kiosk. Curious as to what was attracting such a horde, we moved toward the crush of people, gradually worming our way into the center as those, satisfied with what they saw, struggled back to the path and freedom. As we neared the item causing such a stir, we saw it was RCA's television invention. Once we maneuvered so the sunlight was not cast across the screen, we watched a newsreel of President Roosevelt's speech that he made on the fair's opening day. None of us had seen anything like this, a miniature twelve-inch movie screen encased in a large wooden cabinet. I wondered about its practicality since there are twenty-four hours in a day, and the president's speech was only two-and-a-half minutes. "How do you think they'll fill the rest of the day?" I said to those standing there. "No one will be satisfied watching the speech for hours on end."

"I agree," someone said. "It's a novelty only the rich will be able to afford."

"Yes," Gus also agreed, "only for those with moolah to burn. Not too many of that class of people after the Depression."

With the sun high overhead in a cerulean, cloudless sky and temperatures climbing we continued our trek to Billy Rose's Aquacade, where a large throng crowded around the entrance for the next performance. The doors opened just as we reached the gate, and the ten-thousand-seat Art Deco amphitheater rapidly filled. We grabbed six seats together and waited for the show, featuring a swimming exhibition by Johnny Weissmuller, Tarzan himself, to begin in fifteen minutes. Gus told Kitty he was really looking forward to seeing Weissmuller in the flesh since swimming was his sport.

Jane, hearing Gus, interjected, "While it will be great to see Tarzan in person, to see how his live persona compares to the one on the movie screen, I'm especially interested in the acrobatic swimmers and their synchronized water dancing. I've tried to duplicate their moves at the YWCA pool and know how extremely difficult they are to do. They make it look effortless! They're amazing."

"I totally agree," Gus added, "and if they're wearing bikinis, which would be bananas."

Ellen and Kitty laughed at that, but then Kitty said, "I'd like to see how the bikini looks. I wonder if I would look good wearing one?" Gus looked at Kitty and nodded yes, giving her a thumbs-up. Kitty demurred, obviously pleased Gus thought so.

I whispered to Ellen that I was anxious to see the bikini as well, saying, "You'd be a 'knockout' in one—the envy, I'm sure, of other gals and a delight to the guys."

Blushing, Ellen softly said to me, so only I would hear, "I don't have the figure for such a swimsuit. My bust is too small and my hips too narrow, and even if I did have a figure for it, I'd be too shy to wear it in public at the beach." Her modesty was very appealing for a girl so pretty, I thought, but I knew she had the body for such a swimsuit and she had no reason to be shy at all.

As we were leaving the amphitheater after the show, Gus said, "Let's get off our keisters and move into high gear. The amusement area beckons."

"Yeah," I said, "That'll be a wonderful place to end the day. We'll have to check out the Parachute Jump."

"Oh!" Ellen reminded us, "We forgot to see the time capsule. Well, next time."

"Yes, next time," I said. "We have to come again."

With the afternoon sun ebbing in the west, its golden glow lighting the horizon and the warm temperatures abating, we hurried to the Amusement Zone, the fair's most popular venue, vowing to risk our lives on the parachute jump. That ride would require all our courage, but the thrill, we agreed, would be worth it, providing a harrowing tale of our bravery to tell others. Life Savers Candy Company sponsored the ride, a mushroom-shaped tower with eleven brightly lit candy-colored rings with parachutes. One ride on the jump cost forty cents—a lot of money, considering the admission price to the fair was seventy-five cents.

As we stood by the entrance to the ride, both Howie and Jane and Gus and Kitty, after seeing its height up close, refused to risk their lives, making their case: "What if a cable snapped?" "It's a long way down!" "We'd surely be killed."

Ellen, however, showing no fear, whispered to me, "John, I'm game if you are."

I did not want her to know I had my own fears, so I loudly boasted, "Well, Ellen and I are going up. You chickens have no cojones." I purchased two tickets and while outwardly crowing that I wasn't afraid, I grasped Ellen's trembling hand and we approached the ride. Once we were seated, the operator instructed us to pull the rip cord when we reached the top. He then strapped us in the canvas seat for two beneath the chute and snapped the buckle secure. Before we had a chance to change our minds, the breeze was blowing through our hair as the cable lifted us over the next minute 250 feet into the air. On our ascent I confessed to Ellen I was afraid of heights, and she admitted the same.

We nervously marveled at the panoramic view as we headed toward the zenith—the vast layout of the fair coming into perspective, with twinkling lights and bustling crowds below and the breathtaking skyline of Manhattan beyond.

When we reached the top, my voice trembled as I told Ellen, "I've never been so high in the air before."

"Me neither," she said with a shiver.

"Just don't look down when I pull the release, and we'll be okay."

I grabbed the rip cord as the attendant instructed and pulled, praying the chute would not plummet us in a free fall. We floated to the ground in several seconds, the warm breeze blowing in our faces. I looked at Ellen holding on to her beret; her windblown hair framing a contented smile, a vision of beauty I'd never forget.

Safely reaching the bottom, where pole-mounted springs cushioned our landing, we quickly unbuckled, jumping from the platform seat. We ran to the others, telling them the thrill was unbelievable, the scariest part being the slow ascent to the summit praying the cables wouldn't snap. I chided the others for chickening out but quickly admitted to them that we were scared to death. I confided, "Ellen and I admitted our fear to each other only after we were strapped in and on our way up, when it was too late to back out." That admission brought a hearty laugh from the group.

With the fair near closing for the day, we savored our last moments together before saying goodbye. Howie and Gus raved about the wonderful time they had, as did Jane and Kitty, and they exchanged phone numbers, borrowing Ellen's handy eyebrow pencil, promising to see each other again.

I'd forgotten about Flag Day and that it was my birthday, but said to Ellen, "I expected a more of a show for my birthday."

"Today was your birthday?" she asked. "Why didn't you mention it, John? We could have celebrated."

"Ellen, we did celebrate," I told her.

"When? I missed it."

"You didn't. Meeting you was my gift."

She blushed, an embarrassed, dimpled smile brightening her face.

Walking to the IND for the journey home, I asked Ellen, "Will I be seeing you next weekend?"

"I'll be upset if you don't call me, so yes, the answer is yes. You have my number."

"I do. It's snug in my wallet."

Mom was asleep in her favorite chair in the parlor when I walked through the door, music from Martin Block's Make-Believe Ballroom playing on the radio while an open book rested in her lap. She opened her eyes and looked up when she heard the door shut. "I thought you'd be home earlier. I must have dozed off waiting for you. I made your favorite BBQ chicken dinner for your birthday, and baked a strawberry shortcake for dessert, but we can celebrate tomorrow. You must be exhausted."

"No, I'm wide awake. I met a girl at the fair and lost track of the time. I'd still be there if the park hadn't closed."

"Tell me all about her. How did you meet?"

"Howie, Gus, and I agreed to visit General Motors first since it's the most popular attraction. The line was long, and slow moving, but to pass the time, we began talking to the girls in front of us. They were older—at least we thought so—but we enjoyed talking to them about the different attractions. The more we talked, the more I found myself drawn to one of the girls. Her name is Ellen, and she is beautiful and has a great personality. She's an only child too and is a secretary at a bank in the city near where I work. We spent the rest of the day with them."

"Sounds like you boys had a great day."

"Yeah, unbelievably, Howie hit it off with Ellen's friend Jane, and Gus the same with her friend Kitty. The fair could not have been better. I even kissed her when we were in the Ford exhibit, and she returned the kiss. She may like me. I thought about her all the way home. She gave me her phone number so I can call her. Do you believe there's such a feeling as 'love at first sight'?"

"She must be special. She seems to have made quite an impression on you. With your father that's how I felt when I first met him. So, yes, I do think 'love at first sight' is possible."

"I've never met anyone like her, not even Cheryl Nolan who I thought was the one."

"Anything is possible when it comes to love. You will know soon enough if it is."

"I hope so."

That night I dreamt of Ellen and tomorrow's call to make plans for that first date.

7

THE FIRST DATE

Cinema, Three Days Later

"Good morning, Birthday Boy, you're up early," Mom said as I walked into the kitchen.

"I couldn't sleep. I've been thinking of Ellen and about making that phone call to her. I've got nervous butterflies in my stomach."

"Why? She's expecting your phone call!"

"You're right."

"So, what's your plan?"

"I thought I'd take her to the cinema and to Jahn's after the show."

"That sounds nice. What movie are you planning to see?"

"I'm not sure but thought she might enjoy Wuthering Heights. It's showing at the Orpheum and has received rave reviews for Best Picture and Best Acting for Olivier and Oberon."

"That's a good choice; a movie that would appeal to a young woman."

"I thought so. Oh, I didn't mention, Ellen lives in Jamaica so I'll need the car?"

"Okay, but you may want to clean it up before you go. It hasn't been washed in a while."

We didn't have a telephone, so I told Mom, "I'm going to Dick's Luncheonette to call her. Before I go, though, I want some of the Strawberry Shortcake you baked for my birthday. It looks too good to resist."

"Sit at the table. I'll serve you a nice big slice. Do you want a glass of milk to wash it down?"

"Sounds good."

Fortified by the two slices of cake I ate, I trekked to Dick's rehearsing, on the way, what I'd say to Ellen. I hoped she'd feel the same today as when she said yes to the date at the fair.

The bell on the door jingled as I entered Dick's, and the person in the telephone booth looked over as did the soda jerk behind the counter. I ordered a chocolate egg cream to drink while I waited for him to finish his call and retrieved the fair ticket with Ellen's phone number from my wallet. When he finished his call, I entered the booth, inserting a nickel into the slot. My stomach was a bundle of nerves as I dialed the number. The phone rang several times before a booming male voice answered, "Hello."

"Mr. Curran, this is John Ridgeway. Is your daughter Ellen in?"

"Yes, she is. Hold a sec. I'll get her. You must be the young man she met at the fair."

"Yes, sir."

Clunk. Mr. Curran laid the receiver down, calling "Ellen, telephone for you. It's the young man you've been telling us about." That was good to hear.

A few seconds later, Ellen's lovely voice answered, "Hello, John, I'm so happy you called. I'm looking forward to seeing you this Saturday."

"I'm looking forward to seeing you too. I thought we could take in a movie and go to Jahn's Ice Cream Parlor after the show."

"That sounds swell to me. What movie will we see?"

"I thought you would enjoy Wuthering Heights. It's showing at the Orpheum."

"I haven't seen that movie, but Jane saw it with Kitty last weekend and they both said it was terrific."

"Great. Previews start at 5:00 p.m., so I'll pick you up around 4:00. I'll have my mom's car, so we don't have to bother with the bus or trolley."

"Then we're all set. I'm looking forward to seeing you John, even more than movie."

"Ellen, you sure know how to boost a guy's ego. I can hardly wait until Saturday."

"Me too. Before you get off the line, let me give you the directions to my house."

"Thanks. Let me get a pencil to write it down." The fountain clerk heard me and passed over a pencil and paper. After I hung up, looking at the directions, I savored her words: *She's looking forward to seeing me more than the movie. Wow.*

I spent Saturday morning washing the car and applying polish to revive the faded green paint. No matter how hard I rubbed the polish to restore the luster nothing could be done to disguise the corrosion on the fenders of the 1928 Ford Model A. The car ran well, but rust spots showed her age. Most of the time she sat in the driveway as Mom and I never ventured anywhere where we needed a car. Food and other necessities were easily purchased in the stores along Myrtle Avenue using my mother's wheeled shopping cart. My date with Ellen was the best reason for getting the car out of the driveway and onto the road. Satisfied the car looked as good as I could get it, I swept the floor of the interior, and then went inside to shower and dress.

When I came into the living room, Mom smiled approvingly, "You look handsome, John. Ellen will think so too, and I'm not saying that because you're my son. It's true."

"Thanks. I splashed on the Old Spice cologne you gave me for my birthday. How do I smell? Good enough to kiss?"

"I always loved that scent on your father, and now you. Yes, I would say you're good enough to kiss. Here are the keys to the car. Have fun."

"Wish me luck."

"You don't need it, John. Believe that."

I kissed Mom on the cheek and eagerly left for my date with Ellen, the anticipation of seeing her evoking the nervousness I felt the other day when I called her.

My nerves settled as I concentrated on the drive to her house. She had given me excellent directions and I arrived at her home in Jamaica–a white, two-story colonial on a shady tree-lined street of mature Maple trees a few minutes early. I parked at the curb and walked to the front door, which opened just as I reached the bottom step. Ellen, wearing a navy-blue dress with a cinched waistline and a parade of white buttons up the front, greeted me with a wide smile, inviting me in to meet her parents.

Mr. Curran entered the foyer and introduced himself with a firm handshake while Mrs. Curran invited me to sit in the chair in the living room opposite the sofa where she and Mr. Curran sat. I sank into the cushion and thought Ellen's father did not fit the image I had from the phone call. He was about six feet tall with wavy black hair that belied his Irish heritage and had the good looks of Tyrone Power while Mrs. Curran, with chestnut hair and olive skin, reminded me of the actress Sidney Fox. Ellen had the blended looks of both parents, but I wondered where her blonde hair came from just as she said, "I'll be right back," and slipped from the room.

"She must be getting her purse and applying fresh lipstick," Mrs. Curan said.

"I understand, John, that you just graduated from St. John's?" Mr. Curran asked. "You know, I'm a graduate of St. John's. What are your plans now that you're entering the working world?"

"Well, sir, I've accepted a credit trainee position at Bank of Manhattan," I answered as Ellen returned to the room and interjected, "We'll be late for the movie if we don't scoot." Mrs. Curran said we should hurry so not to miss the coming attractions, and, with that, the conversation ended. We quickly said our goodbyes and I escorted Ellen to the passenger side of my car, opening the door for her before going around to the driver's seat. Mrs. Curran, out the door, hollered from the top stoop, "Enjoy the movie."

"We will," Ellen shouted back over the sound of the engine as I started the car. I pulled away from the curb and the wind moved through Ellen's long blonde hair. She leaned back and shook her head once I had gained some speed, exclaiming, "This breeze is wonderful." I looked at her contented face and thought, *you look wonderful.*

On the drive to the Orpheum, we passed the Trylon Theater in Rego Park where Ellen noticed on their marquee The Hound of the Baskervilles showing at 5:20 p.m. "Would you be disappointed if we saw that movie instead?" she asked. "I loved The Triumph of Sherlock Holmes starring Arthur Wontner, and this movie with Basil Rathbone might be even better."

"I don't mind at all. I saw that movie also and really liked it."

"How funny! We've the same taste in movies. I love Holmes' deductive reasoning to uncover clues leading to the murderer. Another Sherlock Holmes movie (The Adventures of Sherlock Holmes) is coming to theaters soon. Let's see that one next."

"Sounds like a second date."

"It does," she smiled.

The giant banana split we shared at Jahns' was more than one person could consume but for two people, who knows. We would soon find out. As we tackled the giant dessert Ellen commented how much she enjoyed Basil Rathbone's banter with Nigel Bruce, saying "They were perfectly cast for Holmes and Watson, even better, I feel, than Wontner and Fleming in those roles."

"I couldn't agree with you more."

Eating the last of the melting ice cream, I said, "Well, we finished that banana split. It didn't have a chance against us."

"We make a good team," she said.

I peered toward the register looking for the waitress for the check noticing the time on the wall clock. Almost midnight. Sad the night was over, I said, "It's late. We should be going. I don't want your parents to have a bad impression of me."

On the drive to her house, Ellen said how much she enjoyed the evening and was looking forward to our next date.

I pulled to the curb in front of her house. The porch light was off and the leaves on the maple tree by the sidewalk enveloped us in darkness. I wanted to kiss Ellen in the movie but was unsure of myself. Our conversation at Jahn's, though, gave me the confidence I needed, so I embraced her, placing my right hand on the nape of her neck, gently turning her face to mine. A glimmer of light from the moon revealed her expressive brown eyes which widened and then closed as her luscious lips parted, inviting my kiss. Time escaped us and, after about a half-hour of necking, looking toward the front door of her house, Ellen noticed the porch light was now on. "My mother is at the front window. I should go in. You smell so good."

"It's Old Spice cologne. I'm glad you think so. It was a gift from my mother. I'll walk you to the door."

When we reached the top step, I swatted away the ticking moths circling the light bulb over the front door. "I'll call you tomorrow."

"I'll be disappointed if you don't," she said. "I had a wonderful time."

Walking to the car, I glanced back. Ellen, still standing on the stoop, waved goodbye before turning to enter the house.

I hopped in the driver's seat and thought, *I'm really falling for this girl. I can't wait to see her again for our date next week and the ones after that.*

8

DINNER WITH THE PARENTS

I phoned Ellen to confirm our date for Saturday, but she apologized, saying she had to cancel. She forgot her family was going out for dinner for her grandmother's birthday. I was disappointed, but she surprised me with an invitation for a spaghetti dinner on Sunday at her house.

I readily accepted, looking forward to seeing her again. "What time should I arrive?"

"Around 2:00 p.m. Bring a hearty appetite; my mother makes the tastiest meatballs and gravy. After dinner we can play a game of Monopoly. I'm undefeated in my family."

"Mom, I'll be missing dinner this Sunday with the family."

"Oh, what's up?"

"Ellen invited me to her house for dinner with her parents. Her mother is cooking spaghetti and meatballs."

"Well, pursuing your relationship with Ellen is a good reason. You should bring a gift. A bottle of wine to go with the meal would be appropriate."

The next day I asked the proprietor of Myrtle Avenue Wine and Liquor for a wine recommendation to complement a dinner of spaghetti and meatballs. He suggested Chianti and led me to a shelf with several choices. The bottles that were encased in a straw basket immediately caught my attention. He noticed my attraction and explained the wicker casing is fiasco, or flask in Italian.

I thought Chianti would be the perfect choice, so I purchased two bottles. Placing the bottles in a brown bag and separating them with a cardboard strip, he handed me the package saying, "Most people use the empty bottle as a candle holder to add romantic atmosphere to their next dinner." I thanked him for the tip.

I arrived at Ellen's house ten minutes early. She must have been peering out the window when I parked at the curb as she met me at the door when I ascended the front steps.

"John," she greeted me with a wide smile that fit the sunny weather, "I hope you like spaghetti and meatballs with caprese salad, focaccia bread, and cannoli for dessert."

"Sounds delicious. I love spaghetti." I know what cannoli is, but not caprese salad and focaccia bread? I hope I eat everything on my plate. I want to make a good impression on her parents. "I have two bottles of Chianti that will go well with meal."

"I think so, too," Ellen said as she called, "John is here. He brought wine."

Mr. Curran entered the parlor from the kitchen, drying his hands on a towel before extending his hand in greeting. I shook his hand and gave him the wicker-wrapped wine bottles. "Glad you could join us for dinner John. This wine goes perfectly with the meal Mrs. Curran prepared. I hope you're hungry; my wife's meatballs are hard to resist so don't be embarrassed to have more than one."

"I told John to bring an appetite, so he's probably starving about now. Will we be eating soon?"

"In about fifteen minutes. The water is boiling, so I'll cook the spaghetti while your mother finishes with the meatballs and gravy."

"Call us when it's ready, Dad. We'll be on the front stoop enjoying the sunshine."

As we sat on the top step, Ellen told me, "My mom comes from an Italian family where cooking and a love of food at Sunday dinner is their bond. I've asked for her meatball recipe, but she said there isn't one. She learned by observing her mother who cooked using a little of this, a little of that, tasting as she went along."

"I guess all good cooks have their methods."

"You're right. I do know the most important ingredient in a meatball is the breadcrumb mixture. Breadcrumbs, I learned, retain the juices from the meat. But, as important is the ratio of lean-to fat meat, as fat adds flavor."

"I never realized making meatballs was so complicated. Your dad said it takes ten minutes to cook the spaghetti. How long does it take your mother to make the meatballs and gravy?"

"I never kept track of the time, but it seems like a couple of hours. Maybe I'm exaggerating, but it's longer than you would think."

"Well then, this will be a spaghetti meal I'll remember. What is caprese salad and focaccia bread?"

Before Ellen could explain, her mother appeared at the front door to say dinner was ready. As we followed her inside, Ellen whispered to me, "Don't worry. You'll love everything, I'm sure."

Place settings at the dining room table were arranged with Mr. Curran at the head of the table, Mrs. Curran on the side by the kitchen door, and Ellen and I seated together opposite her mother. Salad and bread were on the table, along with the uncorked bottle of wine and four goblets.

Mr. Curran came from the kitchen carrying a large ceramic bowl filled with steaming spaghetti while Mrs. Curran entered with a tureen of meatballs and gravy.

Mr. Curran passed to me the bowl of spaghetti, "Help yourself." I took Ellen's plate and loaded it with a good serving before serving myself. I repeated the process with the meatballs and gravy. Mrs. Curran gave an approving glance to Ellen and said, "John, you're a gentleman. Your mother raised you well." Ellen smiled with pride at her mother's remark.

"Now, what does everyone want to drink with the meal?" Mr. Curran asked. "We have Chianti John brought, Trommer's beer, or ice water. John, what's your pleasure?"

"Sir, I'm normally a beer drinker, but considering the scrumptious meal Mrs. Curran prepared; I believe a glass of Chianti would be most appropriate."

"Good choice. Ellen, how about you?"

"Chianti for me too."

Ellen's mom said, "Same for me."

With the libations served, I took a bite of the meatball and said, "Mrs. Curran, the meatballs are delicious. Ellen shared the secret about the breadcrumbs, I hope that's okay?" She glanced toward Ellen and smiled.

"Certainly, Ellen is learning to be a good cook."

While eating our dinner we discussed the latest happenings at the fair and Ellen recounted our death-defying ride on the Parachute Jump to the astonishment of her parents and reminded me of her desire to return to the fair to see the Time Capsule.

Mr. Curran removed the cork from the second bottle of wine and refilled our glasses, pouring the last vestige into Mrs. Curran's goblet. Ellen told her father, "Save the empty wine bottles, Dad, I want to use them as candle holders the next time we have spaghetti to add atmosphere."

After the table was cleared, Mrs. Curran served cannoli and coffee for dessert, and Ellen suggested we play a game of Monopoly. I hadn't played that game in quite a while, having forgotten how much I enjoyed it. Ellen, with bold moves and a little luck, won the game easily.

While we were playing, Mr. Curran inquired about my plans now that I had graduated from St. John's. I explained to him that I worked at Bank of

Manhattan while attending college, and that when I received my degree, the bank offered me a trainee position in corporate lending which I accepted. I said the bank, founded in 1799, unlike many businesses, emerged from the Depression stronger than ever, and was as solid as the bedrock of lower Manhattan where it is headquartered.

He seemed impressed with my comments and offered that he was a partner of the esteemed accounting firm of Lybrand, Ross Brothers and Montgomery. "You know," he said, "developing contacts with accountants is a key source of obtaining new business for bankers."

"I heard that, sir."

"It's true. Clients often ask for a banking recommendation when they're seeking a loan, and that's when we can direct business to a lender that we have a relationship with. You'll find mutual referrals are the lifeblood of both professions."

"Making good loans, I see, is only half the story for a successful banker. Bringing in new clients for the bank to grow is equally important, and a referral from an accounting firm such as Lybrand is highly valued."

"That's right, John."

"My first day of training is next Monday at the 40 Wall Street office."

"Well, when you get settled let Ellen know and I'll take you to lunch. That will show your supervisor that you know the value of cultivating a relationship with an accountant. I've a client who banks in your office, W.R. Grace, so I've been to your building numerous times for meetings. Did you know there's a plaque in the lobby that proclaimed 40 Wall Street the world's tallest building when it was dedicated in 1930?"

"Yes, sir. I've seen the plaque. Someone told me 40 Wall's title was short lived, though, falling several months later when a stainless-steel spire was installed atop the Chrysler Building, so it could claim the title. And Chrysler's title, amusingly, fell shortly thereafter to the Empire State Building. There's a competition in New York City for the title of 'World's Tallest Building.' I wonder how long it will be before the Empire State loses its crown?"

"You're right. Well, New York is the world's financial center and towering skyscrapers signify that. You know, Ellen works in the Woolworth Building?"

"Yes, I know. We plan to meet for lunch when our schedules permit."

"What you may not know is that the Woolworth Building was once the tallest building in the world until it lost the title in 1930 to 40 Wall Street."

"How funny is that. I didn't know."

After that Sunday spaghetti dinner, Ellen and I were inseparable. Our relationship began to grow, I hoped, to love.

9

THE PROPOSAL

Ellen and I saw each other every weekend for picnics and concerts in Forest Park. If the weather was hot and humid, we spent the day at Rockaway Beach. Our nights were spent seeing the latest movie at the cinema or visiting Coney Island for its rides, amusements, and arcade games. We even returned to the World's Fair to view the time capsule Ellen wanted to see as well as risking a second plunge on the parachute jump. Howie, Jane, Gus, and Kitty often joined us, and we almost always landed at Charlie McGrath's Tavern for beers and the comradery of our friends.

During the week, when our work schedules permitted, Ellen and I would meet at the coffee shop for lunch. If the weather was nice, we'd grab a "dirty water" hot dog from a street vendor, strolling to the tip of Manhattan to enjoy the harbor and raised torch of the Statue of Liberty from a bench in The Battery, or feeding pigeons in Bowling Green, the city's oldest park. Several times we ventured to Trinity Church at the end of Wall Street to study the ancient tombstones in the surrounding cemetery where Alexander Hamilton, Robert Fulton and other well-known people are buried. On one excursion there, I recall Ellen challenged me, "One of the first people to be buried in the cemetery in 1746 was John Zenger. Bet you don't know who he is."

"No, and I won't take that bet. You are too smart for me. I'm sure you'll tell me, though."

Ellen relished her knowledge, responding with a little suspense, "Zenger was a newspaper publisher involved in a libel trial that established the right to a free press."

"I'm impressed. You always amaze me with your knowledge. How do you remember such obscure facts?"

"Easy."

"It is? Teach me your method so I can use it in my course work at the bank."

"Easy, like I said. But my technique will not help you, sorry. I read about him in this pamphlet," she winked as she waved the paper in my face, "I plucked from the rack when I entered the church while you were getting our hot dogs."

"You're a sneak, you know that, but I love your teasing sense of humor. I sure would've considered new study techniques, though."

We were at Charlie McGrath's Tavern enjoying burgers and beers with Howie, Jane, Gus, and Kitty, lamenting that the lazy days of summer would soon cede to the crisp, cooler weather of autumn.

"You know, the Schuetzen Park Oktoberfest is next weekend. That would be a great way to usher in the fall season," I said, "and celebrate our summer adventures."

"I love fall, but I'm not much of a beer drinker," Jane said. "For me, it's the best time of year, not for the Oktoberfest but for the trees that are ablaze in a colorful array of russet, orange, and gold, the air filled with the musky-sweet aroma of fallen leaves."

"And I love the acrid smell of the leaves my father rakes into the street and sets aflame," Ellen chimed in.

"Well, I'm not a fan of raking leaves," Howie opined. "That's extra work on the weekend I don't need. Anyway, you don't have to drink beer to have a good time at the fest. Just watching the people after they've had too much to drink is entertainment enough."

"Well then," I said "let's plan on going to the Oktoberfest. It will be crowded if the weather is nice so, if we want to go, to ensure we get a table, we should plan to be there when the park opens."

"Count me in," Ellen said. "That will be a perfect way to usher in the Fall season even though I'm not a big beer drinker either."

The weather on the day of the Oktoberfest was ideal for those inclined to serious beer drinking. Temperatures were summerlike in the high-70s; hot enough to make a person sweat and drink that beer. Despite our best intensions to arrive at the park early, we left later than planned, only to be greeted by a long line at the entrance. Luckily, once inside the park, Gus spotted an empty, overlooked table by the fence that could accommodate the six of us. Row after row of tables surrounding the band and dance floor were already filled to the brim with people talking loudly over the music that spewed from the stage. Most of the patrons I surveyed, even the ladies, held liter-sized mugs of beer that they were sloshing about or tipping back for a deep drink with the beat of the oompah band playing Bavarian folk music. Anxious to join the festivities, Howie, Gus, and I bee-lined to the bar to retrieve glasses and pitchers of Würzburger Hofbräu beer, salted peanuts, and bags of pretzels, while the girls safeguarded the table. We returned with the refreshments and after the beer was poured, Howie toasted the friendships we'd made since our meeting at the fair. Gus, on a different note, after a couple steins of beer, proposed one last visit to the fair, vowing he would ride the parachute jump even if it killed him. The beer went down smoothly, and soon we were making another trip to the bar.

Around noon, the bandleader introduced Schuhplattlers (men in feathered felt hats wearing lederhosen and women with braided hair wearing dirndl dresses), who performed German folk dances on the wooden platform surrounded by a string of lights that shuddered and clinked in the breeze. The choreographed dancers stomped, clapped, and struck the soles of their shoes, thighs, and knees with the palms of their hands, while the high energy of the music and the fervor of their dance kept the throng of people in a joyous, festive mood singing along with the songs they knew. Almost every song ended with the deep-pitched buzz from the brass tuba, the bandleader, sweat pouring from his brow exhorting the crowd, "*Eins, zwei, drei g'suffa,*" whereupon everyone guzzled and slurped the remaining beer in their stein, crashing the empty glass on the wooden picnic table in a satisfied thud.

After slurping the last of my second liter of beer, I turned to Ellen, and over the sound of the lively polka music, said loudly, "We should eat something more substantial than pretzels and salted peanuts. Are you hungry? It's almost time for lunch."

"I'm famished. What do you suggest? I've never had German food before unless a frankfurter qualifies."

"I'm having knockwurst, with sauerkraut and a side of German-style potato salad. I think you'll like it."

"Sounds delicious. I'll have the same as you. My mom's always cooking Italian, and sometimes she'll make corned beef and cabbage for my dad, so I'd love to try something new."

"Okay, stay at the table with Jane and Kitty while Howie, Gus and I go for the food, and don't accept any dances from strangers."

Ellen laughed, "I won't move. You've made me hungry so hurry with the food, please!"

We returned to the girls after a lengthy wait on the food line and ate while the Schuhplattlers performed their second set. Ellen, with a clean plate and a satisfied grin said, "The knockwurst was wonderful. It's shorter, plumper, and juicier than a regular frank, and has a slight smoky flavor. I would describe it as a fancy hot dog."

"That's a perfect description. I'm glad you enjoyed it."

"Well, I like it and can't believe I've never tried it before."

The Schuhplattlers left the stage, leaving the space empty for dancing, as the bandleader announced, with great fanfare, "now the Chicken Dance. Let's see everyone on the dance floor." The platform quickly filled, gyrating couples moving in sync with the music like chickens. Ellen, eyeing their moves and grasping the beat, grabbed my arm, urging, "John, get up. We must dance to this song."

"I don't know the 'chicken dance.'"

"Neither do I, so we'll learn together."

I gulped the last of my beer, emitting a satisfied belch which I tried to muffle, placing the empty stein on the wooden picnic table. I reluctantly followed Ellen to the dance platform as she pulled me along by the elbow in a hurry to get me there before the song ended. Immediately picking the steps, she motioned for me to copy her moves. Not much of a dancer, especially after consuming three liters of beer, I gave it my best effort placing my hands into my underarms and flapping them like a chicken like the others I watched next to me while Ellen wiggled her shoulders and hips in sync with the music.

"I'm hopeless," I shrugged.

Ellen laughed and leaned into me, hollering over the loud sound of the brass instruments, "That's okay. Look by the band stage, Gus and Kitty are on the floor, so you're not alone, and Gus looks as befuddled as you. Besides, the floor is so crowded everyone is bumping and falling into one another. No one will know you're not a good dancer."

"I guess you're right."

"I am. This is so much fun. I'm so glad you suggested coming to the Oktoberfest."

I savored the joy on her face as we stumbled through the dances, remembering the laughter and music; and the band playing songs we'd never heard before but dancing anyway.

Ellen, over the din, yelled, "We'll have to make this an annual tradition."

"Yes." Sweat pouring from my brow and the back of my shirt soaked from perspiration, I exclaimed, "I'm thirsty for another beer. How about you?"

I'd known Ellen for almost four months and enjoyed the times we spent together. I wanted to tell my mother how I felt. Get her opinion. Sitting in the parlor reading the day's paper, while she listened to the news, I uttered, mumbling in a low voice beneath the sound on the Radiola, "I'm in love with Ellen. What do you think?"

"What?" She didn't hear me.

Louder, I say, "I'm in love with Ellen. Is it too soon to feel this way?"

"John, I've seen your relationship blossom. Have you told her how you feel?"

"No, I'm looking for the right moment. Maybe tonight, after the movie at dinner, I'll tell her."

We saw Mr. Smith Goes to Washington and went to Triangle Hofbräu, an historic hotel/restaurant with the ideal ambiance for a romantic dinner after. Many famous patrons enjoyed the place from Babe Ruth and Mae West to Ernest Ball, the vaudeville-era pianist, who wrote the song "When Irish Eyes Are Smiling" in one of the guest rooms.

The maître d' greeted us when we walked through the door, and I slipped him fifty cents, requesting a cushioned booth in the tap room wanting its cozy atmosphere and subdued lighting. He must have guessed my intent for privacy, as he seated us in a quiet corner. Live music from the trio on the small stage added to the aura.

Once we settled into the booth, Ellen declared, "Jimmy Stewart was perfectly cast as Jefferson Smith and, after seeing the movie, I see a lot of you in him. "

"What do you mean? I don't look like him, do I?"

"No. Not in looks, but in the type of characters he portrays in his roles, that of a person who is hardworking, dedicated, and loyal. I see those qualities in you."

59

"That's a comparison I like."

Seizing the moment, and changing the subject with a shy grin, embarrassed by Ellen's compliment, I said, "We've been going steady for several months, but what do we really know about each other?"

A question knitted in her brow, Ellen, with a bemused expression, asked, "What do you mean?"

"Well, I posed the question, so I'll answer first. I know your favorite color is green. Your middle name is Marie, and your birthday is May 29—which makes us both Geminis."

"All true, but superficial. You don't know any of my deep, dark secrets. I have some, you know."

"Everybody does, even me."

"Oh, yeah. Tell me one."

"I'm not proud of myself. It happened after my father died. Life was difficult for my mom and me. There were days we barely had enough money to buy food for the table, and a few times we even went for a day without eating. I was fifteen and working after school at Bill's Grocery stocking shelves so I could earn money to give to my mom for expenses. On one of those days when we had no food, tempted, I stole some food which I stuffed in my pants pockets. I didn't notice him nearby, but Mr. Bill saw me steal a package of cheese and several candy bars."

"What did he do to you? Were you arrested?"

"He didn't fire me or have me arrested. He said he knew my circumstances and understood how desperate I was. He let me off with a stern warning after I promised to never steal again. And I never did. His compassion made me ashamed of what I did. He never told my mother and I vowed to be the best worker he had. And I was until the last day I worked there."

"Well, that's a story with a happy ending and a life lesson well learned. Since you shared, it's only fair I do so too. When I was around thirteen, I was hanging with a bad group of kids. I desperately wanted to fit in, to be a part of the group, but I was a follower. We'd go into the stores along Jamaica Avenue and shoplift small items, stuffing them into our coat pockets. I was caught stealing lipstick. I was so afraid my parents would find out. The store detective let me go with a warning because of my age. I decided after that incident to make new friends, people with higher moral values. Luckily, I met Jane and Kitty while working on the school newspaper, and we've been best friends ever since."

"Ellen, what I do know about you, the kind of person you are, far outweighs that one incident. You're honest, smart, and loyal. That's the person I know."

With raised eyebrows and a wide, satisfied smile, Ellen teasingly retorted, "Is that all?"

"No, there's more."

Intrigued as to what I might say next, she asked, "There is? Tell me."

"You're confident and not afraid to be vulnerable. You're adventurous and willing to experiment and take risks, like the parachute jump. You make time and don't rush. You enjoy giving pleasure as much as you enjoy receiving it. You're supportive and not judgmental. And you're a willing learner, playful and passionate, and I know one more thing."

"Oh! What might that be?"

Emboldened by the strength of my feelings, and scanning the tap room to see who might hear me, I snuggled closer to her in the banquette, our legs touching, and whispered, "I know I love you, Ellen, more than anyone else in this world. I've felt that way since the day we met at the fair. It was 'love at first sight.'"

"Oh, John, I love you too," Ellen beamed. "I've wanted to say it to you ever since your clumsy chicken dance at the Oktoberfest. I knew in that moment on the dance floor you were the person for me." She drew my chin to hers and gave me a soft, passionate kiss. When we separated, she used her pinkie finger to wipe the smudge of red lipstick at the corner of my mouth.

"Mom, it's time you meet Ellen."

She looked up from her mending and smiled. "I've been waiting for you to ask. I didn't want to rush you because I knew you'd know when the time was right."

"Thanks for understanding. I told Ellen last night I loved her, and she said the same to me. I was hoping to invite her for Sunday dinner for your amazing sauerbraten, potato dumplings and red cabbage."

"That would be lovely. Are you sure, though, she'll like sauerbraten?"

"I think so. She loved the knockwurst at the Oktoberfest, and I told her sauerbraten is even better. She is adventurous when it comes to trying new food."

"Well then. Sauerbraten it is. Tomorrow I'll buy a nice rump roast and the other ingredients I need. The meat needs to marinate for several days so we should be able to have dinner this Sunday if that is your plan."

"Thanks, Mom. Is 3:00 p.m. good?"

"Yes. That'll give me ample time after church to prepare everything. I can't wait to meet her."

"You'll love her as much as I do."

Sunday arrived before I knew it, and I drove to Ellen's to pick her up and bring her to my house. Sitting in the parlor looking out the window, mother saw us when the car pulled up, and was at the door to greet us. Ellen handed me the black forest cake she baked and stepped forward to shake hands with my mother. "So nice to meet you Mrs. Ridgeway."

"The same. John has spoken so much about you that I'm delighted to finally meet. Please come in."

I handed the cake to Ellen who gave it to my mother, who said, "Black Forest cake will be the perfect dessert with our dinner. I've cooked sauerbraten, a traditional German dish. Don't be alarmed by the name, it's not sour but rather sweet and spicy and, if I don't say so myself, utterly delicious. I hope you'll like it."

"That sounds scrumptious, Mrs. Ridgeway. John said you were a great cook."

"Oh, well, that's nice to hear," Mom said, as she looked at me. "He usually eats whatever I place on the table in front of him."

Ellen offered to help in the kitchen, but Mom said to relax in the parlor as the meal was almost ready. While we sat on the sofa, I tuned the Radiola to The Jack Benny Program and we listened to his comedy until Mom called us to the dining room a few minutes later.

The table, set with my mom's best chinaware plates and silverware on a linen tablecloth, sunlight shimmering through the window on the vase of fresh magnolias in the center of the table, gave the room a posh restaurant ambiance. While Ellen helped my mother bring the food from the kitchen to the table, I sat there quietly taking in my surroundings. When Ellen and I were sitting in the parlor listening to the radio, I surveyed the room, ashamed of the shabby run-down appearance of our house, but when I looked at the meal on the table my mother prepared and her smiling face, I realized she did everything possible to ensure the dinner was extra special for me and for that I was ashamed of my earlier thought of embarrassment. As far as I could discern, our meager abode was of no concern to Ellen.

After the first bite of sauerbraten, Ellen marveled, "I've never tasted meat so sweet and tender. What's the secret, Mrs. Ridgeway?"

"Well, the ingredients vary depending upon personal preference. The key is the rump roast must marinate for several days. My marinade consists of red wine vinegar, dry Riesling wine, nutmeg, peppercorns, juniper berries, salt, cloves, and bay leaves. All these ingredients make the meat so tender you can cut it with a fork. I strain the marinade into a saucepan to make the gravy and thicken it with crushed gingersnap cookies, flour, sour cream, and brown sugar, which I pour into a gravy boat for ladling over the meat."

"Mrs. Ridgeway, that's the most complicated recipe I've ever heard of."

"It does sound intimidating. The real secret, though, is to marinate the meat for at least three days, longer if you can, and use plenty of gingersnap cookies in the gravy—that gives the sauce its sweetness."

"How do you keep track of all those ingredients; what amount and when to add?"

"I cook by feel, a little of this, a little of that. I'm guided by the aroma and, of course, I taste as I go along."

"That's funny, Mrs. Ridgeway, my mother makes her meatballs the same way. A good cook works on instinct and a good sense of taste. I hope to be as good a cook as my mother when I have my own home."

"Ellen, I'm sure you'll do just fine. And please call me Anne. Now, let's enjoy that black forest cake you baked. It looks delicious and is the perfect way to end the meal."

Over dessert, Ellen and I talked about our jobs in the city and our frequent sight-seeing excursions during lunch to local landmarks. My mother was amazed at all the history that was shoe-horned in that small area of lower Manhattan.

After we cleared the table, I showed Ellen the basement to obtain her opinion about decorating the space into a socializing area. We shared the space with the Conrad's, our neighbors on the second floor, and except for the furnace, coal bunker, and some odds-and-ends, it was empty.

When we entered the darkened basement, I turned on the overhead light. "I know it doesn't look like much," I said, "but I can brighten the walls with white paint and if I put in a bar and pool table, it'd be a great place to hang with our friends when winter settles in."

"I see your vision," Ellen said, "but aren't pool tables expensive?"

"They are, but I found a used one—in poor condition because of a car battery that leaked acid on the felt playing surface. The owner doesn't play anymore so he said the only cost to me would be removing the heavy slate-covered table from his basement. Once it's fixed up, the bar and pool table should ensure everyone will want to come."

"That's a great idea, John, and a good use of vacant space."

With the Christmas holiday season upon us, I told Mom, "I'm going to ask Ellen to marry me."

Pleased, she said, "So much has happened this past year. You've matured from a responsible but carefree young man into an adult ready to tackle the next challenges in your life. You put yourself through college with no financial help from me, earning a college degree that led to a job with a prestigious bank and, most importantly, you met a beautiful young lady who brings out the best you. You and Ellen are meant for each other. I'm so happy for you."

"Yeah, but what if she doesn't say yes? I believe she will, but you never know until you put it out there."

"She will. I see the way she looks at you."

On Tuesday, December 19, 1939, I asked Ellen to leave work early as I had a surprise for her. We met outside the Woolworth building where I hailed a taxi to take us to Midtown. Curious about the surprise, she implored me during our ride uptown to tell her what it was. "You'll find out soon enough," I said, "but first we have to attend evening mass." Bundled in overcoats, with scarves around our necks and woolen gloves on our hands to fend off the winter chill, we exited the cab and walked up the steps into St. Patrick's Cathedral. It was crowded with people in prayer, as well as with tourists marveling at the grand interior of marble columns, buttresses, arches, naves, transepts, and altars, and stained-glass windows. We lit two votive candles at the entrance before sitting in the nearby pew to pray while the chorus sang Ave Maria to the haunting sounds of the pipe organ.

Following the rush of people out the church door after mass, we crossed the street to view the holiday window displays of Saks Fifth Avenue. Appreciating the creativity of what we saw, Ellen suggested we cross Fifth to compare them to those of Bergdorf Goodman. I thought the displays of both stores were amazing. Ellen agreed, "It takes a lot of creativity to produce a new theme every year. Now, you've kept me in suspense long enough, tell me, what's the surprise?"

"You'll see soon enough."

"I know, but when?"

As we turned the corner at Bergdorf, I guided Ellen through the throng of people clogging the Channel Garden leading into Rockefeller Center, the Art Deco building project that opened earlier in the year to view the lighted Christmas tree. The crowd, three deep, elbowed and nudged each other to glimpse the skaters on the ice-rink below while shoppers on the perimeter, washed by the glow from the surrounding window displays, scurried with bags full of presents. Nearby, Salvation Army volunteers rang bells seeking donations for the needy. We watched the activity for a while, Ellen's arm through mine, her head resting against my chest. We stood next to the decorated fir tree that stood above the statue of the Greek legend Prometheus in the fountain beneath us.

Feeling the passion of the Christmas season and my love for Ellen, I removed the sapphire engagement ring from my vest pocket, the ring given to me by my mother to place on the finger of the person I would marry. Enveloped by the sounds, smells, and goodwill of the holidays, I screwed up my courage, while knowing, deep down, what the answer to my question would be. Shivering from the frigid temperature—and maybe a little nervous anxiety—I turned to Ellen, taking her gloved hands in mine. The black Garbo slouch hat she wore, pulled down to shield against the wind, framed her face and accentuated her expressive brown eyes and wind-blown hair. With a deep breath, peering down into her eyes, I asked, "Ellen Marie Curran, will you marry me?"

The happy tears that welled in her eyes gave me the answer before she exclaimed, "Yes, absolutely. Yes!"

Those people around us noticed her fervor, and watched as I removed the glove from her left hand and slipped the engagement ring on her finger. The crowd chanted, "Kiss her, kiss her, give her a kiss."

Not realizing my marriage proposal attracted so much attention, and blushing with embarrassment, I pulled Ellen to me and gave her a long, warm kiss to the satisfied cheers of the onlookers.

"When you said to leave early from work, and we attended mass at St. Patrick's," Ellen said, after the crowd went back to watching the skaters on the rink below, "I wished this proposal might be the surprise, at least I hoped so. And my wish came true. I can't wait to get home to tell my parents. They'll be very pleased—they've been impressed with you ever since that day you came for my mother's spaghetti and meatball dinner."

"That's nice. I wasn't sure what they'd say. Because you were pestering me so much about the surprise, I forgot to mention that I read in the paper this morning that the New York premier of Gone with the Wind is tonight. Do you want to see the Red Carpet, the theatre is only three blocks from here? We'll see some of the stars."

"That would be a great way to end the most amazing evening. Maybe Clark Gable and Vivien Leigh will be there?"

"They should be. Let's take a quick look before we head home."

As we neared the Astor Theater on Broadway, we encountered a phalanx of New York's Finest in blue blocking the surrounding street, providing crowd control for the throng of people crushing each other to see the stars. Inching our way toward the door, we settled into a spot that offered a good view of the red carpet with the surrounding crowd buffering us against the chill wind. We waited for what seemed an eternity, only to learn to our disappointment that Vivien Leigh and Clark Gable would not be attending. Ellen seemed satisfied to see Olivia de Havilland, escorted by Jimmy Stewart, saying, "I adore James Stewart; he reminds me so much of you, John, in personality and goodness."

"I know. You already told me, remember? What about looks, who do I remind you of? Clark Gable?"

"Heavens no. Some people think he's handsome, but not me. I think he looks like a monkey, and you certainly do not. I'd say you're closer to Leslie Howard, but he's an English actor. To me, you've a striking resemblance to Gary Cooper. Jane and Kitty even think so. Not just his looks, but his mannerisms, the way he talks and moves. The strong, silent type. A man of few words, but when he speaks everyone listens. That's you John if you didn't know."

"Wow, I must be a real catch!"

"You are."

That holiday season was the best of my life, the happiest I'd ever been. I was floating on Cloud Nine with joy. Ellen and I celebrated our wedding engagement the following Sunday hosting a Christmas Eve dinner at Victor Keonig's, to which both families attended, meeting each other for the first time. Mom was overcome with the cordiality of Mr. and Mrs. Curran and their comments about the fine upbringing she gave her son as a single parent.

Bubbling below the surface of our consciousness were events taking place in other parts of the world that would impact my relationship with Ellen. Their significance would soon come to fore. However, during that joyous period, we felt untouchable.

10

STORM CLOUDS

Shortly after I met Ellen and began courting her, events in Europe occurred that dampened my outlook for a bright future. I always pushed those thoughts to the back of my mind, but couldn't quash the foreboding sense our idyllic life would be disrupted.

Germany's aggression in Europe in the later part of 1939 threatened world peace. When they invaded Poland in September, Great Britain and France responded two days later with a declaration of war. That didn't stop the inevitable. Within a few weeks, Germany conquered most of Europe, driving the British from the continent at Dunkirk.

Ellen and I were mostly oblivious to the happenings in Europe. Maybe we didn't want to think too much about them. We read the accounts in the morning newspaper on the way to work and listened to the radio broadcasts in the evening. However, most weekdays we were hard at work, and we spent our nights and weekends socializing with our friends. The war in Europe was far away, across the Atlantic Ocean. Out of sight, out of mind, they say. On those occasions when I did ponder what was transpiring in Europe, I concluded that we would eventually be drawn into the conflict just as we were in World War I. If that occurred, I wondered what my options to serve in the military would be. I decided to find out.

I usually met Ellen for lunch. One day, when she couldn't meet, I stopped in the nearby naval recruiting office to gather information. The recruiter gave me a friendly greeting when I walked through the door, and asked if I wanted an application.

"Not yet," I answered. "I'm looking for information on what the Navy offers as compared to the Army. I'll have to speak to my fiancée before I decide."

Noticing my business attire, he said, "I should've realized you weren't ready to sign up. Most people coming in aren't wearing a pin-striped suit and a tie."

"Like I said, I'm looking for information. What can you tell me?"

"If we enter the war in Europe, and it looks like we might, we'll have a great need for officers. The Navy is building its fleet and will need people at all levels to fill the ranks. If you're a college graduate, we've created a Reserve Midshipmen's School, known as V-7, to train additional officers to complement those from Annapolis."

"V-7 would be what I'm interested in."

"Okay," he said, "If you enlist in the program as an apprentice seaman, and serve the length of the war, assuming we are in one, plus six months, you'll graduate as an ensign, which is a 'commissioned officer of the line.'" He handed me a large envelope. "Here's information on the program."

"Thank you, sir. You've been very helpful. I've some thinking to do, and a talk with my fiancée."

"If you've any questions after you review the material, contact me at this number and I'll be happy to answer them." He handed me his card which I tucked into the envelope.

I kept the visit to the naval recruiter to myself while I mulled over what I should do.

Conditions throughout the world were growing worse daily. By May 1940, I feared our entry into the war would soon be a reality. If that happened, our wedding plans would surely be interrupted. I had to act on my gut, and that required a serious conversation with Ellen. It was a conversation I had been hesitant to have until I was sure of what I must do.

After we finished Sunday dinner, Ellen offered to help my mother wash and dry the dishes. Mom called from the kitchen, knowing I wanted to speak with Ellen, and said, "You and John enjoy the cinnamon crumb cake and coffee. I'll be with you in a moment as soon as I put these dishes away."

Ellen sliced the cake into three squares, placing them on the plates my mother left on the table. Offering me the first slice, her smiling face changed to one of concern. "John," she said, "you have that look. I've noticed it a lot lately whenever you seem to leave the conversation and stare off in deep thought. Something is weighing on your mind, and I've been nervously waiting for you to tell me what it is. I pray it's not about the wedding and second thoughts about getting married."

"Oh no, Ellen, never think that. I love you so much, you know that."

"Well then," she said with an inquiring expression, "What is it?"

"It's about the war in Europe. I believe our entry into it is inevitable, and I've been thinking about what I—er, I mean we—should do, since we're in this together. I don't believe we'll be able to avoid the war. It is turning into another world war. I've spoken to Howie and Gus, Johnny Faeth, and several of our other friends and, while they agree with my assessment, they said they would wait for the draft rather than enlist, hoping, I'm sure, by some miracle we will not enter the war."

"That makes sense. Don't you agree?"

"Not exactly. I've a different thought about it, and I've been dreading telling you, but I think it's the right decision for both of us."

"Tell me."

"I believe the Navy offers the best option if you must serve in the military."

"Why the Navy?"

"Well, I'm sure it will be the same today but soldiers in the army in

World War I fought in terrible conditions, living in muddy, wet trenches, eating cold reserve rations from tin cans, while sailors in the Navy ate cooked meals in a mess hall, slept on clean bedsheets in a bunk, had their uniforms laundered, and bathed in showers with soap. Officers in the Navy have it even better, with semiprivate staterooms and waiters serving them their meal in the Wardroom."

Ellen, always practical, said, "John, that's a lot to absorb. I want what is best for you and the safest place for you to be when we enter the war and, from what you've just told me, the choice is easy. It's the timing that concerns me. Should you enlist before we declare war, or should you wait and take your chances with the draft?"

"We're not even married yet, and I can't imagine living apart from you, but if I enlisted now, at least I'd be sure to be in the branch of service I want."

"Don't make me cry. I cannot bear the thought of being apart from you. But, most importantly, I want you to be safe wherever you are and, if signing up now will do that, then I'm on board. What's the next step?"

"Well, earlier this year the Navy created a school to train officers to supplement Annapolis graduates. If I make it through the program, I'll be an officer."

Trying mightily to contain her emotions, Ellen, with a steady voice, said, "Then, the decision is made. Please tell me the naval school is nearby and that we will be able to be married this December as we planned. Oh, what about your job at the bank, and your mother? I've so many questions."

"I'm not sure how fast this process will be or when it will begin. I first must be accepted into the program and, if I am, I'll speak to my supervisor at the bank to make sure they'll give me a leave of absence."

"You'll be accepted, I know it. And you'll do well, I know that too, you always do when you put your mind to the task at hand."

"I hope so. But there is one thing, though, that worries me," I said, in effort to lighten the mood.

"What?"

"I've never been on a ship before, other than the Staten Island Ferry, and I'm sure that doesn't count for someone joining the Navy. What if I become seasick when the time comes to be on a ship at sea? That would be embarrassing for a person in the Navy, especially for one who enlisted."

"I'm sure everyone in the Navy, at one time or another, has been seasick. You will be okay. I'm sure of it."

With Ellen's support, I was ready to make my application.

The next day, on my lunch hour at work, I walked a block to the Third Naval District Office of Naval Officer Procurement at 33 Pine Street to complete an application for the V-7 program. A new recruiter at the reception desk handed me an application and instructed "Complete this at one of the desks in the adjacent room and when you're done, return it back to me. I'll give it to Lieutenant Stone, who will review it while you wait. He'll let you know where you stand."

There were several people wearing suits in the room when I entered. I assumed they had the same idea I had. After I filled out the paperwork, I returned to the recruiter, giving him the completed application along with a transcript of my grades from St. John's. While he scanned the form to ensure there was no missing information, he advised, "Our goal is to train thirty-six thousand reserve officers as quickly as possible as there's an urgent need to fill the command ranks of our rapidly expanding fleet."

"I hope to be a part of that buildup."

The recruiter told me to wait in the lounge by the front door while Lieutenant Stone reviewed my application. I had today's New York Times with me in the event I had to kill some time, so I opened to the partially completed crossword puzzle. When the recruiter returned a few minutes later, he waved his hand for me to follow him. I tossed the completed crossword and newspaper into the wastebasket by the door as he escorted me to Stone's office.

Standing behind his desk when I entered, Stone offered his hand and told me to take a seat. "I reviewed your application, Mr. Ridgeway, and the transcript of your grades at St. John's and from what I see you are exactly the caliber of candidate we want for the program. I've therefore approved your acceptance to our first class on Monday, July 8. You'll need to complete these documents," he handed me a stack of paperwork, "to finalize your acceptance. You will also have to take a physical, but you'll take that when you return with the signed paperwork. You are in good physical shape, from what I see, so I don't think you'll have a problem passing."

"Sir, that's exactly what my fiancée said, about being in shape that is," I replied as I took the package from him. "I'll return with the completed paperwork by the end of the week. Do I need an appointment for the physical?"

"No. I'll review everything while you see the doctor. That shouldn't take more than an hour. See you Friday."

"Yes, sir."

I returned to work to finish the day, elated about my conditional acceptance into the V-7 program but also apprehensive about what it may do to my relationship with Ellen and our wedding plans.

Ellen, waiting with my mother in the parlor, sprang from the couch when I walked through the front door, both anxious to hear how my application went. "It went well," I said. "I've been accepted into the program subject to completion of the paperwork in this folder and a physical exam. Assuming I pass the physical, the first class starts on the Monday after July 4th."

"Oh, John, I knew you'd be accepted. You're the quality of person the Navy needs."

Mom asked, "Do you know where the school is that you'll be attending?"

"I forgot to ask. There are several locations on different college campuses, and Columbia is the closest, so it makes sense that would be the school."

"I sure hope so," Ellen said. "Maybe you could commute to the school from Glendale."

"That's not an option. You're required to room and board to receive the 'Full Navy treatment.'"

"Oh," my mom said as she went into the kitchen. "I'll percolate the coffee to enjoy with the cheesecake Ellen brought."

I turned to Ellen, "We should be able to see each other often if I'm boarding at Columbia. But, if that doesn't work out, the program is only four months. It should go quickly enough."

"You're right, but I have bad news."

"You do, what?"

"You know what boarding means?" Ellen said, trying to lighten the mood.

"No, what?"

"No visits to Rockaway Beach this summer to work on your tan."

"You know I don't tan. That's a sacrifice I'm willing to make. Although I'll sure miss seeing you in a bikini."

"Oh, don't be silly. You can see me anytime you want, without the bikini," she whispered in a low voice just as my mother entered the dining room with the cake and coffee on a tray. "I just thought of something," Ellen said, "What about our wedding in December? If I figured correctly, you'll graduate around the end of October, so we should be good, right?"

"I don't know, but I'll find out. The school starts soon and once I'm there, I'll have a better feel for the lay of the land."

11

COMMISSIONED OFFICER

July 8th was here before we knew it. I arrived for my first day of naval training with a suitcase full of clothes in hand. I boarded *Prairie State*, formerly the turn-of-the-century battleship *Illinois* that was part of Teddy Roosevelt's Great White Fleet. Moored in the Hudson River on the Upper West Side of Manhattan, *Illinois* was decommissioned in 1920, where she served as a floating armory until her conversion last year to a naval training facility. The *Prairie State* moniker was adopted so *Illinois* would be available for an Iowa-class battleship being built. The ship, to my amazement, no longer resembled a battleship. The big guns and imposing main deck superstructure were gone, replaced by a light-gray, three-story clapboard wood barn-like structure that had fire escapes on each end of the building, fore and aft, and a railed catwalk on the roof where security guards roamed, armed with Springfield rifles. *Illinois* was faintly visible on the bow under the coat of gray paint that failed to hide her prior identity.

Everything aboard my new home was denoted in Navy jargon. I shared a room with three mates on the second floor. It was a cabin on deck two, and my bed was a bunk. Instead of a window, I had a "port." The stairs were "ladders," and the elevators were "hoists." The bathroom was "the head," and the dining room was "the mess."

Soon after we deposited our suitcases in our cabins, we were led to the gymnasium where we found tables piled with clothes in various sizes. Our new naval wardrobe consisted of blue wool shirts, skivvy shirts, bell-bottom trousers, navy-blue topcoats, undershorts, black leather shoes, and visor hats with a strip of gold braid on the brim. The chaotic process of getting out-fitted took over an hour, everyone jostling among the various garments, seeking the best fit. Once we made our selections, we returned to our assigned cabin to don our new duds. Civilian clothing, no longer needed, was boxed, and mailed home. I later learned my mother was surprised when she received that package with all my clothing, except for my pajamas.

That first day ended with all the recruits reporting before mess to the medical office for vaccinations (smallpox, tetanus, typhoid, and yellow fever), two in each arm, along with another routine physical exam.

Despite the chaos of that first day, I was confident I'd made the right decision to join the Navy.

The next day, and every day thereafter, we adhered to the following routine: wake to "Reveille" at 0530 (5:30 a.m.) to shave, shower, dress, and make our bunk before marching in formation to the mess for breakfast. After that, our day was filled with lectures, study halls, close-order drills, and seamanship training aboard the yacht moored next to *Prairie State*, while evenings were spent in our cabin studying material that would be taught the next day in class. Officers patrolled the halls to ensure no one was wandering about except to use the head. "Tattoo," the signal to get ready for bed, sounded at 2155 (9:55 p.m.) followed by "Taps" five minutes later signifying "lights out."

The day of my first liberty, Ellen took an extended lunch break to meet me near the ship in the luncheonette at Whelan's. I got there early and settled in the booth at the end of the counter, hoping the seats would afford us privacy to talk. Figuring I'd have some time while I waited, I grabbed the Daily News from the rack by the door, intending to work on the crossword puzzle. I didn't get far with the puzzle. I was too anxious for Ellen's arrival, glancing at the door every time someone entered. Although it had been only three weeks since we had seen each other, that short time seemed like an eternity. I looked up from the puzzle just as she entered, the patrons at the counter turning around as she passed by their stools, the sound of her high heels clicking on the marble floor, announcing her arrival. She wore a stylish black business suit that accentuated her shapely figure. I rose from my seat in the booth so she'd see me. "Ellen, you don't know how much I've missed you," I said as she neared. "These past three weeks seem more like three years."

"I know," she smiled. "Not seeing you every day has been torture, and riding the subway to work by myself has been so lonely. Luckily, it's not forever, I keep reminding myself. Only two more months before you're done. By the way, John, you look smart in your uniform. I'm glad you're all mine."

"Thanks. Now give me a kiss and then tell me what I've been missing at home besides you."

"How's this?" she said, standing on her tippy-toes and giving me a long kiss. Those at the counter, witnessing the reunion, clapped and whistled.

Red-faced with embarrassment, we took our seats in the booth, and Ellen calmly said, "Not much, really. Just work, and last Saturday I went to a movie with Jane and Kitty, and on Sunday I visited your mother who made sauerbraten. I keep saying it, but I really want to make that with my mother. I know she'll love it as much as I do."

"I know about your dinner with my mother. She sent me a note that she was going to write her recipe for you. What movie did you see with the girls?"

"Rebecca, an Alfred Hitchcock psychological thriller starring Olivier and Joan Fontaine."

"Was it good?"

"Yes, but not as good as the Sherlock Holmes movie. Just so you know, I can't wait for V-7 to end. I miss you so much. We still must complete our wedding plans. Victor Koenig's would be a good venue for our reception. The food is good and the prices reasonable. My parents like it, and I think your mother does too."

"Koenig's sounds good to me. I've been so busy learning seamanship and navigation that I almost forgot about the wedding plans. Whatever you decide. I'm on board. You know that. I'll be more helpful to you when I complete V-7. Let me work on the honeymoon. I want a nice place to take you so that I can bring you into my bedroom laboratory for some experiments."

"That sounds naughty, but I'm open to anything, even one of your 'experiments.'" Ellen glanced at her watch. "Wow, I lost track of the time. And we didn't even have lunch. I'll grab a coffee and buttered roll to go. I told them I was taking an extended lunch, not the rest of the day, although I'd like to. It took longer than I thought to get here from Lower Manhattan."

Ellen stood and I followed as she grabbed her "to go" order and hurried out the door to look for a cab. We walked to the end of the block where I hugged her, kissed her on the lips, and said, "I'll be dreaming of you again tonight."

"Me too, about you that is. When will I see you again?"

"I'm not sure. I'll call you at work as soon as I know."

"Hopefully, we'll have more time. We didn't even talk about what you've been doing these last three weeks. Next time I want to hear all about it."

I hailed a passing taxi, and Ellen hopped in the back seat, and as the cab pulled away from the curb, she turned to the rear window and waved goodbye.

When we received our midshipmen dress-blue uniforms, a twenty-four-hour regular liberty was granted that extended from early Saturday afternoon to late Sunday afternoon, when we had to be back at *Prairie State*. Most of the men from out of the area headed to Times Square seeking entertainment and the company of women, while those having difficulty with the course material were restricted to the school to study.

Fortunately, I made it home to see my mother and spend time with Ellen. I also enjoyed the privacy of my bedroom, even though it was for only one night.

Mom was expecting me and opened the door as soon as I appeared on the front steps. "John, you look handsome in your uniform," she greeted me, wrapping her arms around me in a hug. "The Navy agrees with you. You've gained weight."

"I did. We work hard all day long and I always have a huge appetite when the meals are served. I eat everything on my plate, even the beets and lima beans they give us on occasion."

"Well, I hope you have an appetite for the sauerbraten I made."

"Always for my favorite."

"No need to call Ellen. She'll be over shortly. I invited her to dinner. After dessert I'll be going to the movies with May Conrad so you and Ellen will have the place to yourselves."

"Thanks, Mom. You're the best."

"I know."

When Mom left for the movies, we went into the parlor, and I tuned the radio to Make Believe Ballroom. Sinatra's rendition of "The Way You Look Tonight" filled the room. "Listen to the words," I said, clasping Ellen's hands. "This song says everything that I cannot find the words to express on my own." I kissed her, my arms wrapping around her waist, drawing her into me. She returned the kiss, reaching up, placing her hands on my neck. "You smell so good," I whispered in her ear.

"Thanks to my new perfume, Tabu by Dana. The creator of the scent was tasked with making a fragrance that was sensual and shocking."

"Well, he achieved his goal. I want to ravage your body so badly." We were alone, and my bedroom was steps away. I lifted Ellen's blouse from her skirt and touched her bare back reaching to the clasp on her bra.

She wriggled away before I could unclasp the snap, saying "John, stop it. We have important work to do."

"What's more important? I've missed you so much."

"I feel the same, you know I do. But we must finish our wedding plans. Time is running out."

"You're right. I apologize for being so horny, but I can't help myself when I'm alone with you and the bedroom is steps away, I love you so much."

"Apology reluctantly accepted. I've spoken to my parents about booking the reception at Koenig's. The restaurant requires a non-refundable deposit so if we cancel for any reason, the deposit will be lost. It's a risk we'll have to take."

"Okay. How much is the deposit?"

"It depends on the number of people. I made a list of those we should invite from the names your mother gave me, the list from my parents, and all our friends."

"How many people are there altogether on all those lists?"

"Well, if you agree, there would be one hundred and thirty-eight."

"Wow, that's a lot of people. This reception will cost a fortune."

"John, the bride's parents traditionally pay for the reception, and if we lose the deposit for any reason, so be it. They can afford it. My parents said paying for the wedding is the least they can do since you'll be taking care of me for the rest of my life after we're married."

"Well, just so you know, there's no one on earth I would rather provide for more than you. Please tell your parents I want to share the cost with them. More than half the people on the list are my friends and relatives."

"I will, but they won't take your money. They'll be suitably impressed with your offer, though. My parents think so highly of you."

Tired from all the planning, I muffled a yawn. "I should drive you home before I fall asleep where I sit. I need a good night's sleep before I go back."

Midway through V-7 we were given a two-hour seamanship test. I completed the exam in about forty minutes, turning my papers over on the desk, sitting silently while the others continued working. Noticing that I had finished the test, the instructor came down the aisle to my desk, turning over my papers. He began checking my answers, finding that I scored a high mark. "Where did you attend college?" he asked.

"St. John's in Brooklyn."

"You know your stuff, Ridgeway. Did you grow up around the water?"

"No, sir. The training on the yacht in the Hudson River has taught me a lot."

"I'm glad to hear that."

When the class standings were posted on the bulletin board, I ranked first in seamanship and, as a result, several classmates came to me for tutoring during the evening study periods. One person I helped, John O'Shea, a graduate of Boston College, was close to bilging, but I developed a liking for his friendly "luck of the Irish" personality, so I made him a project. I wanted him to make it through the program, so I gave him extra tutoring, and by explaining concepts over and over, I also became more confident in my knowledge and grasp of the subject matter. I hoped if the time came in a "real-life" situation where I had to apply what I learned, I would be able to translate my classroom learning into practice and action. My class of 300 apprentice seamen produced 264 officers commissioned as ensigns in the United States Naval Reserve. I graduated near the top of the class and was awarded a gold watch for seamanship. To my satisfaction, O'Shea had the distinction of being the "Anchor Man," number 264 in our class.

After graduation, I was assigned to Fort Schuyler in Bronx, New York as an instructor teaching a refresher course in seamanship to commissioned officers who were recalled to active duty. When I learned of my assignment, nervous anxiety surfaced that I had not felt since I was a child. Cdr. F. Brian Quinlan, the executive officer at Fort Schuyler said I would be teaching officers from ensign to lieutenant commander. He advised me not to be concerned with the fact that everyone in the class outranked me as that had no bearing on my role as an instructor.

Quinlan, after reviewing my personnel record, said, "I'm confident you'll do fine. You'll be teaching people who have been away from active duty for a while, and this is a refresher."

"Thanks for your confidence, sir. If I may, I have one request."

"Yes?"

"I'm getting married on Saturday, December 7th and, if possible, would appreciate if I could get leave the week following for a honeymoon."

"Ensign Ridgeway, I won't stand in the way of love so I'll arrange for a substitute instructor so that you can have your honeymoon. My best wishes on your nuptials."

"Thank you, sir."

The weekend before I reported to Fort Schuyler, Ellen and I visited the friendly confines of Charlie McGrath's Tavern to review our final wedding plans, taking a table in the corner where we could enjoy a beer and talk. Charlie saw us settling in the booth and came over, "What brings you two in so early in the day?"

"Hi, Charlie," Ellen greeted him with a broad smile. "We're here to review our wedding plans, and thought this would be a nice, comfortable spot to do that. Everything was topsy-turvy because of the uncertainty surrounding John's next assignment in the Navy."

"So, Ridge, where are you off to? Close to home, I hope."

"Yes, I'm happy to say. I'll be teaching seamanship at Fort Schuyler in the Bronx, so the wedding is moving ahead as planned. It will be on December 7th, and you will be receiving an invitation."

"Thanks, I look forward to being there. Where are the festivities?"

"The wedding ceremony will be at Ellen's church, St. Bonaventure in Jamaica, with the reception at Koenig's."

Ellen looked at me and said, "Everything is set then. We have the church, the hall, and I'll mail the invitations later today. There's nothing more to do."

"I envy you Ridge to have a girl like Ellen," he said with smile to Ellen, "who knows how to get things done. You must be proud of her."

Ellen blushed, and then frowned as I said to Charlie, "I am. But there's one more thing to do that she forgot about."

"There is?" she said with a pout. "What did I forget?"

"Only one of the most important things."

"Yeah, what?" she asked, unsure of my answer.

"The honeymoon, but I'll work on that."

"That's right," she said, as my promise to manage the honeymoon dawned on her. "That was your 'to do' item, remember?"

"Oh yeah," I sheepishly apologized. "Ellen, do you forgive me?"

"Yes, of course. Now let's celebrate!"

"Charlie, please rustle up two draught beers and a bowl of salted peanuts and pour a beer for yourself and join us."

"Coming right up."

While Charlie went for the beers, Ellen said, "I forgot to mention that Kitty might have found us an apartment in Glendale near your mom. Here's the advertisement for it. We should make an appointment to see it tomorrow."

"I agree, otherwise, we might be sleeping at your parents' house. I don't think your bed is large enough to accommodate the two of us, and even if it was, we'd make too much noise before going to sleep."

"It's a twin. You would have to sleep on the floor, and I wouldn't want that."

When I walked into the classroom that first day, my stomach was a bundle of nerves. I had no idea what to expect and shuddered at the people sitting quietly before me waiting for me to speak. All of them were measurably older than me and as we went around the room to introduce ourselves, I learned they were an elite group of businessmen, professional athletes, and politicians. The entire first session was spent on introductions, each person telling a little about themselves.

When I returned home that evening Ellen was with my mother to greet me, "John, how was your first day?"

"Nerve wracking. Everyone was much older than me, and all outrank me. I knew that would be the case, but when the time came to walk into the classroom, I was intimidated. I expected to be nervous but hoped it didn't show. I asked each person to introduce themself to the others and give a little background on what they were doing before being called back to duty. That worked to calm my nerves. You couldn't guess who was in the class. Walter Peck, owner of the ladies' apparel chain Peck and Peck."

"I wouldn't have guessed," Ellen said. What 's he like?"

"Can't say yet, but he seemed friendly and was rather talkative."

"John, you'll do fine, no matter who's in the class," my mother interjected.

Ellen added, "It's not hard to believe. You're very smart, and you're a hard worker, and that sets you apart from others who don't put in the effort you do."

"I guess you're right. It's a refresher course, so that should make teaching the subject matter easier. Seamanship is really an art and involves many skills, from navigation, weather, meteorology, and forecasting to ship handling; from the operation of deck equipment, anchors, cables, and lines to communications, cargo, and munitions storage; and dealing with emergencies, survival at sea, search and rescue, and firefighting. And so much more—too many things to mention them all."

"Amazing," Ellen said, "I never realized how complicated being a Navy officer was."

"I know. There was a lot to learn in a short period of time, but somehow, I survived. I think the tutoring helped to reinforce my knowledge. I should be able to teach the course once I get over my nervous jitters."

"John, I don't see how anyone could learn all that you did in fifteen weeks, and do it with excellence, but if anyone could, it would be you." Ellen always knew how to make me feel good about myself.

The wedding was fast approaching, and I had to finalize my plan for the honeymoon. Afterall, that was the least I could do since Ellen took care of everything else.

12

TRAGEDY to WEDDING BELLS

On a Sunday afternoon in mid-November, temperatures delightfully in the high sixties, Ellen and I trekked into Manhattan. We rode a horse-drawn hansom cab and strolled the barren pathways of Central Park, past the Bethesda Fountain, stopping to view the ice skaters at Wollman Rink. We walked through the Artisans' Gate exit, a block from the Plaza Hotel, where we went for cocktails. We entered the hotel through the main entrance on Fifth Avenue and passed through the palatial lobby to the Oak Room, settling in a booth to order drinks. "I love this room," Ellen remarked.

I hadn't been there before, but looking around, could see why. The atmosphere was cozy, with the crystal-grape-laden chandelier casting a warm glow on the walls of English oak and frescoes of Bavarian castles.

Spotting our arrival, a tuxedoed waiter approached to take our drink order. "Miss, what may I serve you?"

Ellen responded, "I'll have a Between the Sheets cocktail to remind me why we're here."

"Certainly," he blushed in response. "Sir, what may I serve you?"

"Between the Sheets, what's that exactly?" I asked Ellen as I turned to the waiter, and said, "I'll play it safe and have a Rheingold, draft if you have it on tap."

Before the waiter could respond, Ellen explained, "John, I've never had one, but I've read it's also called a Maiden's Prayer and is made with brandy and rum. I thought it would be the appropriate cocktail for today since we are finalizing our plan for the honeymoon. If I don't like it, I'll just join you with a beer."

"Brandy and rum," I snorted. "I bet you'll end up having a Rheingold."

"You're probably right, but, as they say, 'you only live once.'"

After discussing various honeymoon options over a couple of glasses of larger beer (Ellen found the Between the Sheets too strong), we narrowed our choices to either Atlantic City or Niagara Falls. Since we are both beach lovers--even though the winter chill would be upon us—we chose Atlantic City for the opportunity to crack the window in our room to enjoy the soothing sounds of the ocean surf while making love.

"The Claridge Hotel is the best hotel in Atlantic City, so I'll book a room there," I said.

Ellen protested, "That would be too expensive; you needn't spend that kind of money to impress me, you know that. Let's save our money for a house."

"Okay, you're right. I'll check less expensive options," I promised.

So, the next day, breaking my promise and hoping to surprise Ellen when we arrived in Atlantic City, I booked a suite on the top floor at the Claridge. *You only marry once*, I thought, *This extravagant expense is worth it, especially for her.*

The Sunday after Thanksgiving, Jane Killorin held a bridal shower at her house. Ellen received many thoughtful gifts that any newlywed would desire for their first home. To my dismay, the day's happiness ended in tragedy. My mother was walking home from the shower with her dear friend, Louisa Hartmann.

After hopping off the Myrtle Avenue trolley, she fell to the sidewalk, dying from a massive heart attack before she even landed on the pavement. Louisa said bystanders, including a doctor on his way to a house call, tried in vain to save her life, giving chest compressions, but to no avail. Complete shock rocked me when I learned of her death. She was only fifty-six years old, trim and in good health. At least I thought so. That's the thing: a person can appear outwardly healthy, but inside their core there's a problem that can't be seen until it's too late, and nothing can be done to fix it. Suffering from the loss of my father when I was ten, and now my mother, made me realize my marriage to Ellen was meant to be. She was there to fill the massive void. I was alone, except for her.

Ellen pleaded with me to delay the wedding, saying, "It would be the proper thing to do under the circumstances," she sobbed.

"Ellen, I appreciate your concern, but I'm certain, like I've never been before, that my mother would've wanted us to move forward with the wedding. She loved you so much and knew you made me happy and a better person, and that made her happy. I know she's smiling on us from above."

"John, are you sure?"

"Yes, absolutely."

Tuesday the wake for my mother was held at George Werst Funeral Home. Family, friends, neighbors, and acquaintances filled the parlor to capacity, the overflow spilling out the door onto Cooper Avenue. I was overwhelmed at the massive outpouring of love for my mother, and that brought tears and rekindled the memory of my father's wake years ago, when the same outpouring was displayed. She was as beloved in the neighborhood then as now, and I swelled with pride that she was my mother.

We buried her the next day in All Faith's Cemetery beside my father. The graveside mourners braved the gray sky and strong wind gusts that echoed the somber, depressing mood of the day.

Knowing mother would have wanted to see the bright side of things with my upcoming marriage, I invited family and close friends to a buffet lunch of sandwiches, salads, and drinks. We turned the sad occasion into a celebration of her life, one that was well lived and respected.

Ellen and I were married on December 7, 1940, on a mild, sunny, clear blue-sky day, reflective of the joyous occasion.

Standing at the altar with Howie next to me, nervous sweat pooling on my brow, I peaked at my watch, 3:00 p.m., and looked to the rear of the church just as Ellen appeared in the entrance at the appointed time. Her father was dressed in a black tuxedo by her side to escort her down the aisle. Overcome with emotion, tears filled my eyes as I thought of my mother, wishing she had lived to see the moment. She would have been so happy for me. Radiant in her white dress with a sweetheart neckline and fitted bodice, her face covered by a lace veil, Ellen proceeded slowly toward me with her father as the organist played the Bridal Chorus. The ambient sunlight filtering through the stained-glass windows added a warming glow to the vision. When she neared, I saw the smile on her face and thought, *I'm the luckiest man in the world.*

The marriage ceremony passed in a blur, and we left the church for Koenig's in a shower of white rice and well wishes. The reception was a gala affair. Howie Dehls, my best man, gave a funny toast, interjected with stories from our childhood, while Jane Killorin, the maid of honor, offered several amusing tales about Ellen. I remember the emcee introducing Mr. and Mrs. Ridgeway and dancing to our song, Irving Berlin's classic "Always." The festivities ended late, and Ellen and I returned to my house in Glendale, exhausted, where we slept for a few hours before rising early the next day for the drive to Atlantic City for a four-night honeymoon.

A uniformed bellhop greeted us at the curb when we arrived, welcoming us to Jersey's "Skyscraper by the Sea" as he took our suitcases from the trunk and placed them on a rolling cart, which he wheeled into the lobby. With happy tears in her eyes, Ellen smiled as I signed the register for Mr. and Mrs. John Ridgeway. I told the valet who parked the car in the hotel's garage we wouldn't be needing it for the next four days as everything we needed was right there at the hotel. I think he knew my meaning.

Surveying the posh surroundings in the lobby, Ellen was dismayed when she realized we had checked into the Claridge, having assumed we were staying somewhere more modest. She was even more shocked when we entered our opulent suite on the top floor, 370 feet above sea level. The bellhop placed our luggage on the upholstered bench at the end of the luxurious bed and asked if there was anything we needed as he handed me the room key. I said we were fine, tipped him generously, and he closed the door behind him as he exited the room.

Ellen kicked off her heels and moved to the window, pulling the curtains aside to view the garden, boardwalk, beach, and ocean below. She turned to me, "John, come look. The view is amazing." As she shifted back to the window, I moved behind her, wrapping my arms around her slender waist and nuzzling the nape of her neck with kisses.

"Well, honey, what do you think?" she asked.

"Of the view? I think you're amazing."

She turned around and peered into my eyes. I raised my hands cupping her chin, and with parted lips, gave her a long, lingering kiss. The thin straps of her dress slipped from her shoulders, the dress sliding gently to the floor, pooling by her bare feet. She stepped forward, and I reached behind, unclasping her bra. She leaned back, and the bra joined the dress on the floor. I gently touched her, and she responded. We removed the rest of our clothes and facing one another in a naked embrace, moved to the bed, where we made love to the sound of the crashing waves below.

"I love you so much," Ellen panted.

"And I love you. Only you." With that declaration, she trembled in orgasm, and together we climaxed.

The honeymoon passed in a whirlwind. During the days, we took barefoot walks in the sand. In the evenings, we visited the Steel Pier with its human cannonball and diving horse. We ended our nights making love in our penthouse to the sound of ocean waves.

After we returned home from the honeymoon, Ellen spent a couple days adding her own touch to my mother's house, seeking my consent for the changes she wanted to make. She displayed the gifts from the bridal shower and wedding so visitors would know of our appreciation when they visited. Our search for an apartment was unsuccessful. It seemed moving into my mom's place was meant to be. I asked Ellen if she minded, and she readily agreed it made the most sense. She loved the homey atmosphere and the added benefit of the basement entertainment space.

I resumed my teaching duties at Fort Schuyler nine days after the wedding. Even though I was teaching, I was also gaining valuable experience as a leader. Commander Quinlan observed my authoritarian voice in the close-order-drill of my platoon and made me his adjutant. That meant I gave the commands for 792 men when the battalion was formed.

After the completion of my first training class, bolstered by the command experience as battalion adjutant, I was confident in my ability as an instructor and a leader of men. Subsequent classes went smoothly, and the year passed uneventfully. The tension I first experienced from having people of stature in my class faded as I discovered everyone, no matter their social status, has insecurities to overcome. Some of the more notable people I taught in addition to Walter Peck were Bill Dickey, catcher for the New York Yankees; Lee Artoe, tackle for the Chicago Bears and a key member of their "Monsters of Midway" line; and Harold Stassen, governor of Minnesota.

That first year of our marriage passed in a blink of the eye. While conditions in Europe were worsening, I wanted to celebrate our first anniversary experiencing the festive atmosphere of the season in New York City. We attended mass at St. Patrick's Cathedral, lighting two votive candles when we exited the church, one in memory of my mother and the other a prayer for peace, before walking a block to Rockefeller Center to view the lighted tree. We watched the skaters on the rink below from the promenade for several minutes, observing one dressed as Santa Claus, who attracted a crowd, before the chilled air enveloped us and I hailed a cab to take us downtown.

"Where to now?" Ellen asked. "Not to Macy's, I hope. It'll be jam packed with hordes of holiday shoppers."

"Not shopping. I'm taking you to dinner."

"Where?"

"You'll see."

"Another one of your surprises?"

"Yes, and I'm sure you'll like it." I thought of the sauerbraten meal my mother prepared the first time she met Ellen and decided I would take her to Luchow's, the famous German restaurant, a city landmark since 1882. When we exited the taxi and entered the restaurant lobby for our 6:30 p.m. reservation, we were greeted by the pine scent of a towering Tannenbaum decorated with festive ornaments, nuts, candies, and wax candles. We were right on time, so the hostess seated us promptly in the Heidelberg Room featuring the massive painting Potato Gatherers by Swedish artist August Hagborg. Despite the room's grandeur, the colorful Bavarian beer steins and mounted animal heads that hung on the walls gave the space the feeling of a cozy German hunting lodge. We loved the festive atmosphere of the strolling accordionist, and when he played "Beer Barrel Polka," Ellen said, "This song reminds me of the Chicken Dance at the Schuetzen Park Oktoberfest. That's when I fell absolutely, totally in love with you. This is the perfect place to celebrate our anniversary."

"I'm glad you're pleased. I have a gift for you at home, something of my mother's that I know she would have wanted you to have."

"Oh, John, you're making me tear up. I need my hankie. What is it?"

"You'll see, another surprise. Now, what shall we eat?"

"I'm not looking at the menu," she said. "I know what I'm having, Sauerbraten."

"Me too. No need to look at the menu. I'll order two Wurzburger's so we can join the party."

The next day, after we returned home from dinner with Ellen's folks to celebrate our anniversary, I flipped on the radio. The newscaster announced that our Navy was attacked in Hawaii. It was surreal. We stood there for a moment in shocked silence.

Ellen came to her senses first, alarmed about what this would mean for me. She asked, "Will you be called to sea duty?"

"I don't know," I answered, "but I'll soon find out."

Stunned, she added, "Did you expect us to be at war with the Japanese? Now, it truly is a world war."

"No. I'm as shocked as you are."

The next morning, Commander Quinlan announced to the instructors that our jobs would be vital to the war effort as it was even more imperative now to have fully trained officers for the fleet which was adding new ships every day. Ellen, I knew, would be relieved with that news, but I was not sure how I felt about it. Only time would tell.

Our inevitable entry into the war happened as I predicted, though the destruction of our naval fleet in Pearl Harbor was not what I ever expected. President Roosevelt proclaimed, "Yesterday, December 7, 1941, a date which will live in infamy the United States of America was suddenly and deliberately attacked by naval and air forces of the Empire of Japan." That early morning attack by the Japanese had taken us by surprise. Hundreds of their fighter planes, bombers, and torpedo planes launched from six aircraft carriers delivered a staggering blow to our fleet in the Pacific. All 8 of our battleships were damaged, with 4 sunk, along with 3 cruisers, 3 destroyers, an aircraft training ship, a minelayer, and 190 aircraft. Even more devastating was the loss of 2,403 men and another 1,178 wounded.

Although we were at war, I wanted to focus on uplifting the spirits of our families and friends.

"Ellen, I'm thinking we should host a New Year's Eve party. We have the basement with the bar and pool table. Everyone could use a little cheer about now. This Christmas has been such a downer and the coming year will be difficult as the nation goes to war. What do you think?"

"That's a terrific idea since a lot of people are still home."

We invited everyone who hadn't left for military training, and their girlfriends or wives. A festive atmosphere greeted our guests when they came through our front door to the lighted balsam pine in the parlor decorated with tinsel, garland, and my mother's treasured Christmas ornaments. The party quickly got into full swing as people drank glasses of beer from the half-keg of Rheingold on tap which I had delivered. The pool table was a popular attraction, drawing those who thought they were hustlers. I believe everyone, for a while, forgot we were in a war. Ellen hung mistletoe from the ceiling rafter in a prominent location, and almost everyone made several visits to stand under it for a kiss with their sweetheart. The music playing from the Radiola was drowned out by lively talk, but when the clock struck midnight, everyone joined in to sing "Auld Lange Syne" to the sound of Guy Lombardo's Orchestra that permeated the space. Everyone cheered in the New Year, bidding farewell to 1941, blowing paper horns, clanging metal noise makers, and tossing party hats in the air, and kissing whoever was nearest mistletoe or not. Ellen and I viewed the action from behind the bar and smiled at the joy on the faces before us, forgetting in that moment all the terrible events taking place throughout the world.

The next day, the reality of war sank in. We were in it now, whether we wanted to be or not, and that created new challenges for Ellen and me.

13

WAR CALLS

My duties at Fort Schuyler allowed plenty of time to ponder my situation relative to that of my friends, especially on those occasions I was on the base overnight as duty officer. I used that quiet time to catch up on correspondence with my buddies in the service like Johnny Faeth, a Marine in the Pacific; Artie Hagenlocher, a Merchant Marine in the Atlantic; Howie Dehls and his brother, Warren, in the Army in Europe; and Georgie Beck, in the Coast Guard. I became a "clearinghouse," for lack of a better term, for their correspondence. I condensed the letters I received into a general newsletter that I distributed among the group. I provided each person's address, so if anyone wanted to correspond directly with someone else, they could do so. I believed writing a letter was half the pleasure of correspondence—the other half, receiving a letter.

While teaching seamanship to higher ranking officers was empowering, something was missing. I should have been ecstatic with my situation, being close to home with Ellen, out of harm's way, but I wasn't. Deep down, in my gut, I believed I was shirking my duty as a man, and that feeling weighed on me, bubbling in my subconscious. It surfaced every time I mailed a newsletter from my friends, filled with their stories of the horrors and dangers of war.

I had to address it.

Ellen and I returned home from Sunday dinner with her parents. I had been anxious to initiate that difficult conversation, waiting for the opportune moment to broach the subject, but there never seemed to be a good time. She was quietly sitting on the couch in the parlor, thumbing through the Sunday newspaper circulars, searching for coupons for items we needed. I admired her thriftiness.

"Ellen," I interrupted, standing by the couch.

She looked up with a smile. "Yes?"

"I have something important I need to discuss with you. Something that's been weighing on my mind for some time." Her smile disappeared, changing into a look of trepidation, reluctant to hear what I would say.

"I've been pondering this for quite a while, but before I make a decision, I want your feelings, and opinion."

She nodded, sensing what I was about to say. Her worried expression turned to one of support and understanding.

"The war will not be ending soon," I pushed on, "and since the attack on Pearl Harbor, the Navy is more involved than ever, especially in the Pacific."

I cleared my throat and forged ahead. "Our friends have put their lives on the line in Europe and the Pacific, and I feel it's my turn—actually, my duty—to do the same. I need to be on the front line, not in a classroom, and for me that would be aboard a ship at sea. I've spoken to Captain Stottlemeyer, the base commander at Fort Schuyler, and he's given me insight on what to expect. He served on the battleship *Idaho* in World War I and has a wealth of experience. What do you think? Before you answer, I know it'll be hard on you, but I can't live with myself if I don't do this."

Ellen sighed heavily, but her eyes showed me she agreed. "You think I didn't know how you felt?" she said. "I could tell every time you mailed a newsletter that being home while everyone else was 'over there' fighting the battle was eating away your insides. John, you must follow your gut. I'll support your decision whatever it may be. I'll manage all right. I have my parents and friends for support, and Jane and Kitty both told me what to expect."

When I reported to Fort Schuyler on Monday, I submitted a transfer request for sea duty aboard a battleship. Because I volunteered, and had the recommendation of Captain Stottlemeyer, my request was granted. I was assigned to the recently launched battleship *USS South Dakota* in Pearl Harbor, Oahu.

A few days later, Commander Quinlan handed me the train ticket for my trip west to California. My departure was just around the corner: September 6, 1942. Ellen's eyes welled with tears when I showed her the ticket; overwhelmed by the reality of my imminent departure—I would be away for a long time. I weakened when I saw the agony on her face, but she noticed my reaction and quickly regained her composure, saying her supervisor at the bank gave her the day off to see me to the train. A pang of regret surfaced about my decision, but Ellen's strength reassured me I was doing the right thing.

"Well," I said in resignation, "there's no going back. It's what anyone in my circumstances would do. It has just taken me a little bit longer to get there—mainly because of my reluctance to leave you."

Trembling, Ellen embraced me. "I love you, John. No matter how hard this is for the both of us, you're doing the right thing. I just worry about your safety."

"Don't worry about me. I know how to take care of myself, I've been doing it since I was ten. And *South Dakota* is our newest, and best battleship."

"I wish I could do more. I know what I'll do. I'll start by taking over your newsletter. I learned from you how important a letter from home is. Jane and Kitty will want to help. That's it, that's what I'll do."

Dressed in my khaki uniform and with my seabag strapped over my shoulder (packed by Ellen, so I wouldn't forget a thing), we walked hand in hand down Myrtle Avenue to catch the subway into Manhattan. A half hour later we exited into Grand Central, the largest train terminal in the world. Almost an hour-and-a-half early for my train's departure, we went to the terminal's main departure board at the south entrance to confirm the track location. The posting said the train was on time scheduled to leave at 1:00 p.m. from Track 61. The terminal is a labyrinth with over forty platforms on two levels, so unsure of the location of Track 61, we trekked to the information booth in the center of the main concourse to ask for directions. When we approached the booth, the agent looked up from the book he was reading, saw my naval uniform, and automatically explained my train was a military troop transport leaving from a platform underneath the rest of Grand Central, a special platform—unknown to most, he confided—used by President Roosevelt when he visited the city because of its private elevator access directly into the Waldorf Astoria. He turned and looked at the massive four-sided brass clock behind him and said I had over an hour before boarding. He suggested we relax in the lounge on the mezzanine. We thanked him for his courtesy, and as we headed into the concourse, I told Ellen, "I'm impressed that I'll be departing from the same platform used by the president of the United States. I never knew there was a special track. Must be a secret."

"That's the least you deserve," Ellen said, "for volunteering for such a dangerous mission."

"I don't know about that. Hey, since we've plenty of time before the train leaves, let's spend the rest of the hour in the lounge the agent mentioned. We can get something to eat. I'm hungry. How about you?"

"Sounds good. Our last meal together."

"That is, until next time. Hopefully in the not-too-distant future."

The lounge was well appointed with game tables, easy chairs, a player piano, and a snack food counter. We grabbed a couple of hot dogs with mustard, relish, French fries, and Cokes. We settled into two chairs overlooking the bustling crowds racing through the main concourse from arriving and departing trains, and others entering and exiting the terminal at the corner of Forty-Second and Park.

I devoured my frank in three large bites, impatient to find Track 61. "Ellen, are you almost done? I want to make sure I'm at the train early."

"John, you're always in a hurry. Slow down. You didn't finish your fries. You'll end up with an ulcer. The clock says 12:30. We've plenty of time."

Pacing while she ate, unable to contain my anxiety, Ellen acceded to my impatience, "Let's go," she sighed. "I'll finish my hot dog as we walk."

We proceeded down the marble stairs from the East Balcony that spilled into the Grand Concourse and threaded our way through the scurrying throng of commuters, dodging people left and right, toward the elevator that would deliver us to Track 61. When we reached the Grand Central Terminal Restaurant on our way, I grasped Ellen by the elbow and gently guided her into the corner of the vaulted, ceramic-tiled arch in front of the restaurant's entrance.

"Wait here," I instructed, as I crossed thirty feet to the opposite side of the ceramic arch. I peeked over my shoulder to see the puzzled look on her face, when Ellen exclaimed, "John, what are you doing? I'm confused."

"Stay there a second, you'll see," I implored.

I waited for a lull in the foot traffic and when it was quiet, turned into the corner and, with my back to Ellen, spoke into the arch, "Ellen, I love you and will miss you more than you can imagine."

I spun around to find a surprised, teary-eyed smile on her face. She moved quickly to me, and we embraced. I hugged her tightly and enjoyed the fresh, lemony smell of her hair and the hint of Tabu on her throat, scents I would soon miss. Over the din of the new rush of people passing by, I whispered, "Many marriage proposals and expressions of love have been made on this very spot. Ellen, you know how I feel."

Anxious about the passing time, with my departure rapidly approaching, we re-entered the Grand Concourse and wove our way through the horde of people toward the elevator that would take us to Track 61. Midway across the atrium, I paused pointing out to Ellen the constellations on the ceiling and noting the apparent mistakes they contained, knowledge gained from my celestial navigation course. "It will not be obvious to you, but Orion is correctly rendered, while Taurus and Gemini are reversed and not in the right orientation to Orion."

She was impressed, I could tell from the expression on her face, when she replied, "It's hard to believe with thousands of people passing through the terminal every day, no one has mentioned the mistakes, at least I hadn't heard about it." She considered that and said, "The reason must be because most people are in such a hurry they never look up, rushing through life on a human treadmill, heads down, focused only on what is directly ahead." I looked around us at the people whizzing by and thought she was right.

We resumed walking toward the elevator, and I confided to Ellen, "When I first noticed the mistakes, they seemed too glaring to be an error, so that led to some research. I learned the mural was the vision of a painter by the name of Paul Cesar Helleu, whose artistic idea was to depict the ceiling from God's view, that is, God's view from above, looking down on those below." Ellen loved that explanation, that the mistakes were not mistakes at all but merely the work of a very creative artist.

As we neared the elevator, the door, sensing our arrival, opened as if it were expecting us. We rode down with another couple, exiting into the labyrinth on the lower level, a long subterranean platform with a makeshift kiosk selling newspapers, magazines, snacks, and sundry items. I purchased the Mirror, the latest issue of Life, and two bags of pretzels to sustain me to dinner that I tucked into my seabag.

We walked down the platform toward the waiting train, the whirring sound of the diesel locomotive drowning the chatter from the uniformed passengers bidding their farewells to loved ones and friends.

When we reached the last Pullman, I turned to Ellen, put my seabag down on the platform, and bent to hold her. Taking her in my arms, I said breathlessly, "It's almost time to board the train." I straightened up, lifting her off the floor, bringing us face to face. I peered into her large brown eyes, welling with tears, and gave her a long kiss knowing the memory would have to last—creating a vision of what I would be missing and the reason for returning home. "I'll miss you more than you'll realize," I whispered in her ear.

I lowered her to the platform, and, on tippy toes, trying to maintain her composure, she said, "Promise me you'll do whatever it takes to stay safe. We have our whole lives ahead of us, and kids to rear. Promise me this is our future?"

I nodded, with a lump in my throat and an ache in my heart, unable to mutter a word. After another embrace, I grabbed my duffle and said, "I'll write soon." Holding in my emotions, I walked resolutely toward the train. Before I stepped up into the Pullman, I turned around for one last look and saw the welling tears that now streamed down her cheeks in a torrent. I blew a kiss, boarded the train, and walked quickly down the aisle to my assigned berth where I laid the seabag on the bed and looked out the window to see Ellen still standing where I left her. I tapped on the window to get her attention, but she didn't hear. I rapped on the glass with more force and Ellen searching for the noise, saw me, and hurried down the platform. I slid the window open, and we exchanged one final goodbye as the conductor leaned out the door, hollering a final call, "all aboard."

After one last announcement from the platform speakers, the doors closed, the whistle sounded, and the train started to move slowly down the track, gaining speed as it entered the black tunnel to begin the journey west. I couldn't see Ellen waving any more, the image of her beautiful smile and expressive brown eyes fading into the darkness. I took writing paper and a pen from my seabag, turned on the overhead light above the small desk, and began my first letter to Ellen, telling her how much I missed her.

September 6, 1942

My dear sweet Ellen,

We parted moments ago, and already my chest aches for your embrace. I watched you on the platform from my window as the train left until your image faded from view. That made me realize I do not have your picture to look at in those times of loneliness. When I get settled in Hawaii, I'll send you my address where you can mail a picture, send several as one is not enough. Know you will always be on my mind and in my heart.

Love, John

The New York Central diesel locomotive and its ten cars filled with servicemen hummed over the tracks on its way to Chicago where I would transfer to Northern Pacific for the final leg to Oakland, California.

Somewhere in Pennsylvania, near Ohio, around six o'clock that first evening, having eaten the pretzels, I left my Pullman berth searching for the dining car. I saw Myron Dallen there, sitting alone.

I walked to his table, "Myron, I didn't know you were called to sea duty."

He looked up from the menu. "John, what a surprise to see you! I guess our luck of being instructors at Fort Schuyler ran out. I've been assigned to the *Adroit,* a minesweeper stationed in Pearl Harbor. How about you?"

"I've been transferred to the newly launched battleship *South Dakota.* Mind if I join you? I was just coming for dinner."

"Please, I would enjoy the company. We can commiserate about our current assignments," he said as he returned to studying the menu.

Sitting in the chair opposite him, I admitted, "I finished the snacks I brought, but I'm hungry for something more substantial. I didn't feel I could wait until breakfast.

He glanced back at the menu, "I'm having Grandma's meat loaf, with Garlic Mashed Potatoes, French green beans, and brown gravy, washed down with a Rheingold beer. A battleship, huh? That sounds like it could be dangerous, but I guess we don't have much say in where we are appointed."

I didn't mention that I volunteered and requested a battleship. "Yeah, a battleship, how about that? Meat loaf sounds good. I wonder if I can get it with fries, though? I'm not much for garlic on my mashed potatoes."

The waiter took our orders and returned shortly thereafter with two ice cold Rheingold beers. We conversed about the war and the unknown of what we would soon encounter as we ate our meatloaf. Lingering over coffee, we agreed it was a long day, so we finished and returned to our respective berths for the night, making a date to meet tomorrow morning for breakfast at seven.

It was dark outside when I returned to my Pullman so I searched for the light switch on the desk, turned it on. I completed the envelope for my letter to Ellen which I hoped I could mail tomorrow when we pulled into Chicago. The sound of the wheels rumbling over the tracks was soothing. I dressed for bed, flicking off the desk lamp, and laid in the bed with the shade raised, watching the countryside pass by in the enveloping night. The gentle hum and rocking motion of the train lumbering along the tracks lulled me to sleep. I dreamt of Ellen and what I'd left behind.

We arrived in Chicago the next morning at 11:00 a.m. and had a two-hour layover before transferring to Northern Pacific to continue our journey west. There wasn't time to explore during the layover, so Myron and I opted for burgers and fries in a coffee shop in the terminal, and I mailed my letter.

The Northern Pacific departed on schedule at 1:00 p.m., steam billowing from its wheels and black smoke belching from its stack, signifying the switch from a diesel to a coal locomotive. Soon we were moving, pushing westward, through flat, fertile farmland bursting with wheat, corn, and livestock before traversing the majestic snow-capped Rocky Mountains. The train windows offered a kaleidoscope of our land's beauty. The ever-changing panorama made it hard to imagine we were at war. Soon I would be in California, though, halfway to Pearl Harbor and another day closer to fighting in that war.

Myron and I spent the journey reminiscing about our time at Fort Schuyler and V-7 before that, hoping we were prepared for the challenges sure to come.

Aside from the awe-inspiring, scenic beauty of our land, the most interesting stop enroute was North Platte, Nebraska—an agricultural town of less than fifteen thousand people 275 miles west of Omaha. It was a water-replenishment and refueling stop for our coal-fired steam locomotive. It turned out to be a memorable hour-and-a-half layover. As soon as Myron and I stepped off the train to inhale the fresh country air after sitting for hours in the smoked-filled lounge car, we were greeted by ladies of the North Platte Canteen offering free soft drinks, sandwiches, chips, and homemade donuts. It was their way of saying thanks to the members of the U.S. Armed Forces. *What a wonderful and unexpected gesture by this small, rural farming community*, I thought.

While walking along the platform with Myron, munching on a ham sandwich, he pointed to the billboard in the train depot proclaiming: "North Platte, home of Big Band leader Glenn Miller, and legendary Wild West showman Buffalo Bill Cody."

"Myron, who would've believed such esteemed people, come from this small farm town in the middle of nowhere?"

"Great people," he said, "can come from just about anywhere, even here."

The train arrived in Oakland on September 9 at eight o'clock in the morning. After our last breakfast together, I told Myron I'd look him up in Oahu. Then I grabbed my seabag and hopped the ferry for the jaunt across the bay to San Francisco where I hailed a cab to take me to California Hall. I would be staying there until the ship sailed for Pearl Harbor. The hackie told me the building was a YMCA before the Navy acquired it to house personnel passing through the city. He dropped me at the Polk Street entrance, where the adjutant at the reception desk greeted me when I walked through the door. He checked me in, saying orders would be forthcoming about my transfer aboard *George Clymer*, a newly launched attack transport, to Pearl Harbor. After settling into my room, I spent the remainder of the afternoon exploring the city. I rode the Powell-Hyde cable car to Ghirardelli Square on the western edge of Fisherman's Wharf, catching a glimpse of Lombard

Steet on the way, the crookedest street in the world, while amazed at the bell-ringing antics of the conductors as they traveled along their route. At the end of the line, I helped spin the cable car on the turntable for its return trip and then, for the exercise, walked back to California Hall stopping atop Nob Hill at the Mark Hopkins Hotel for a drink in its famous Top of the Mark to enjoy the city vista. I decided on more exploring tomorrow if *Clymer* was not ready to board.

The next morning, with no word yet when I was to leave, I boarded the Gray Line bus for a tour of the city that included a trip over the Golden Gate Bridge to Muir Woods where I walked among the towering redwood trees. I had seen pictures of these trees but stepping among them was awe-inspiring. I marveled at the cross-section of a fallen tree over 1,000 years old that denoted prominent dates in history marked by its rings including Columbus' arrival in America in 1492, the start of the American Revolution in 1775, and the Magna Carta, that I saw at the New York World's Fair, written in 1215. At the end of the tour, I meandered to Fisherman's Wharf hungry for a fresh seafood dinner. The Grotto looked inviting, so I entered. The hostess sat me near the expansive window overlooking the fishing boats. I ordered grilled swordfish with French fries and was not disappointed with the food or the atmosphere. I only wished Ellen were there to enjoy it with me. After that satisfying meal, I strolled along the wharf taking in the hustle and bustle of the area and watching several returning fishing trawlers unload their day's catch.

When I returned to California Hall, the adjutant noticed me crossing the lobby to the elevator and called me over, handing me my transfer orders. *George Clymer* was sailing tomorrow afternoon. I accepted the orders and suddenly felt my heart racing, a rush of pent-up nervous energy that I carried around for the past month. Seeking fresh air, I left the stuffy lobby through the door on Polk Street where I leaned against the building until my racing heartbeat subsided. *I'm going to war, and only God knows if I will return home in one piece to Ellen, but I'm ready for what is to come.*

Early the next morning, I took a taxi to Treasure Island Naval Station where *George Clymer* was docked, leaving my seabag at the pier to be loaded aboard the ship. I then ate a late breakfast at a nearby diner before returning to California Hall to check out. Women from the Ladies Naval Auxiliary marshalled several station wagons to transport those of us leaving that day to the pier.

The dock swelled with a horde of people queuing alongside the 491 foot long, 9,000-ton ship. Boarding was slow and methodical, but before I knew it, I was shown to my berth where my seabag was waiting for me hanging on the jackstay. Looking around, I thought, *this is what it means when someone says, "like a sardine in a can."* The space was claustrophobic, jammed with canvas hammocks stacked four high down aisles three feet wide. Luckily for me, I was assigned rack 2, the best one to have—if you could choose—as it was the easiest to climb in and out.

A loud blast vibrated the space. Someone said, "The ship's horn. We're leaving." Everyone raced from the room, seeking to get on the deck to view our departure from San Francisco and catch a glimpse of the infamous Alcatraz Prison before passing under the Golden Gate Bridge on the way to the open sea.

Once we cleared the bridge, the captain forecasted smooth sailing, saying the voyage would take six days to cover 2,100 nautical miles to Pearl Harbor. That gave me plenty of time to contemplate what I was about to encounter on *South Dakota* and write a letter to Ellen.

September 14, 1942

Dear Ellen,

Well, I'm aboard my first ship. We left San Francisco several hours ago and so far, so good. I've no feeling of seasickness. Maybe I'm meant to be a sailor.

I'll add to this letter as I have more to say. Just know I love you so much.

September 16

There are several hundred officers on the ship heading for various assignments in Pearl Harbor. Just know, bunking with that many men is not something you'd want to do. The foul odor from hundreds of sweaty bodies crammed in a space meant for less than half that number is the real problem. There is no air flow circulation and the space reeks so much I decided, along with some others with the same idea, to spend the remaining days of the voyage sleeping outside on the deck. Some of the men doused the sleeping quarters with their cologne, and one person even used bleach to combat the stench, but nothing worked to ameliorate the rancid smell. Even the deck has its pitfalls, though. One sailor, rather than going to the head, peed over the railing, and a gust of wind blew it back onto the person sitting next to him, who was not happy with the golden shower.

September 20

We're almost to Hawaii and I'm on the fo'c'sle (the deck at the bow of the ship) looking off the starboard (right) side for the first signs of land. It's around 0545 and the rising sun will soon extinguish the night horizon. I see faint, dull-gray outlines of small buildings along the coast. There are no visible lights one would normally see at night, so blackout conditions must be in effect.

We're passing Diamond Head, the remnant of a dormant volcano, which is yielding to larger buildings, probably the hotels on the sands of Honolulu's Waikiki Beach.

The sun has finally broken the horizon, bathing the palm-studded beach with a warm golden glow. This looks like paradise.

We passed the last of Honolulu and are entering the passage into the Naval Base at Pearl Harbor. It's a vast area, sectioned into three distinct anchorages, with Ford Island smack in the middle. That's where we lost the battleships from the Japanese attack. It's hard to believe the piers have been reclaimed, filled again with battleships and aircraft carriers.

We're at the pier, so I'll close here. I must retrieve my seabag and contend with *the pandemonium associated with five hundred men trying to leave the ship at the same time. I hope there's an organized method for disembarking.*

You'll be glad to know I was never seasick. I must be a true sailor.

Your loving husband, John

P.S. I'll write when I'm aboard South Dakota.

George Clymer wended her way into Pearl Harbor at 0645 and everyone aboard was on deck, straining for a good look at the damage inflicted by the Japanese. Most of the devastation, to my amazement, had already been removed and repaired. The ruined remains of the battleship *Arizona* were clearly visible, though, a stark reminder of why we were there. As we approached the pier in the East Loch where we would dock to off-load our human cargo, salvage crews working from platforms straddling the *Arizona* were dismantling and removing the superstructure with solemn respect for the remains of the sailors entombed in her hull.

When *Clymer* tied down at the pier, the captain announced debarkation would be alphabetically by the first initial of the last name, starting with A. When my turn came, I saluted the OOD on the quarterdeck, "Permission to leave the ship, sir, to report for duty aboard South Dakota."

"Permission granted," he replied.

I saluted the flag, stepped down the gangplank to the pier, where I laid my duffle down on the ground and stood for a moment to steady myself and gain my land legs. After I rid myself of the swaying motion, I hefted the duffle, filled with clothes ready for the laundry, and trekked to the end of the pier where I boarded the bus going to ComDesPac—short for commander, destroyer forces in the Pacific Ocean—to report for duty aboard *South Dakota*. I arrived at ComDesPac to be greeted by a long que of people trailing out the door to the curb seeking their orders. When it was my turn to speak to the adjutant, he informed me *South Dakota* was not in port and that I would be billeted in the barracks at Hickam Field until her return. He said the ship would be in drydock in Pearl Harbor for repairs of a hole in her hull caused by a coral reef. I didn't realize a coral reef could cause such damage to a thick, steel-clad battleship.

14

WAR IN PARADISE

After settling into the barracks at Hickam and stowing my seabag and unpacked belongings in the footlocker, I left for Ford Island wanting to gain a closer look at the sacred remains of *Arizona*. I decided to launder my dirty clothes later.

When I saw the outline of the ship's hull just below the water's surface, knowing it was the final resting place for almost 1,200 souls, I was sobered. Over half of the fatalities from the Japanese surprise attack were officers and crew from the *Arizona*. A salvage worker taking a water break told me the ship sank in a matter of minutes after a fourth bomb hit the forward magazines, sparking an explosion that resulted in most of the fatalities when the gun turrets, conning tower, foremast, and funnel collapsed, toppling onto those below. Numb from what I saw, I returned to the barracks to pen a letter to Ellen to tell her how much I missed her and that, even though Hawaii may be a tropical paradise, my first glimpse made me sad to be there.

September 20, 1942

Dear Ellen,

I miss you. Words cannot express how much. I'm not on the ship but in the barracks at Hickam Field. When I reported for duty earlier today, I was told South Dakota was at sea, but returning to Pearl for repair of an accident caused by a coral reef that ripped a hole in her thick steel-clad hull. I was told it may take a few weeks for the repair so I'll have some free time to explore this tropical paradise. I'll tell you all about it.

Coming into Pearl we passed the hulking remains of the battleship Arizona. It was a somber experience knowing men are trapped in her sunken hull, that space being their final resting place. After I stowed my gear in the barracks, I returned to Arizona for a closer look. Salvage teams were dismantling the superstructure and, aside from that, most of the damage from the attack has been cleaned up and the anchorage is once again full of ships.

I look forward to your letter. Include a nice picture from our wedding that I can frame and display in my room on the ship. I want to make my roommates envious. Ha-ha. You can address it to me at Hickam Field.

Love always, your husband, John

Hungry, I headed to the Officer's Club for dinner, mailing my letters to Ellen on the way, where I bumped into Myron Dallen, who was just leaving. What a surprise to see him again! He said *Adroit* was on a mission, so he also was rooming at Hickam until her return. We spoke for a moment and, since we both had nothing planned for the next day, agreed to meet for breakfast at 0730, followed by sightseeing to Pearl City.

The next morning, Myron was sitting at the table when I arrived for breakfast, reading the paper. When the waiter saw me sit down, he came over with two menus saying he would be right back with a carafe of fresh coffee. After a quick scan of the menu, we both ordered scrambled eggs, with diced potatoes, white toast, and orange juice. Most of our conversation centered on the odds of both of our ships not being in port at the same time but grateful that we would have a couple of days to check out the sights. We finished our coffee, hit the Men's Room on the way out the door, and trekked to the base entrance, where we told the sentry at the guard booth we just arrived from San Francisco and planned to go to Pearl City to do some exploring.

"There's not much to see in Pearl City," the guard advised. "It's about four miles from the base, and too far to walk in this humidity. I recommend you grab a hack, take a quick look around, and then hop the train to Honolulu where there is more to see and do." The weather was hot and muggy, the temperature rising with the sun. Already the sweat on my brow was running down my face and soaking my shirt. We thanked the sentry for his advice and proceeded to the taxi stand across the street where we caught a cab for the short ride to Pearl.

The cabbie sensed we were new to the base, so he proudly boasted, "You'll love Pearl City for the many stores that sell fine handcrafted souvenirs made by the local natives." He took us to the edge of town and said he would come back for us when we were finished with our jaunt. We thanked him for his courtesy but said that, after Pearl City, we would be taking the train into Honolulu. "That's a good idea," he said. "You'll love Honolulu even more than Pearl City as there is more to do there. You will see girls in bikinis on Waikiki Beach while listening to relaxing Hawaiian music when drinking your beer under the banyan tree at the Moana Hotel. I'd be there now if I didn't have to work. This heat and humidity is unbearable."

"Thanks for the sightseeing tips," I said as I paid the fare.

We hiked a short distance to the stores, walking along the main street for several minutes before we encountered anything worthwhile investigating, and by that time our shirts were soaked with perspiration, clinging to our bodies like sodden towels. Sweating profusely, I mopped my brow with the handkerchief pulled from my rear pocket and repeated the process several more times as we walked about, wringing the sweat. Soon my handkerchief was a wet rag, no longer useful. The sentry was right, there was nothing much to see in Pearl City. It was a small village of honky-tonk bars and run-down stores devoted to selling—mostly to new servicemen to Pearl like us, trinkets made by the locals. In one shop, though, I became intrigued by a small wooden outrigger canoe model sitting on the shelf, scrutinizing the intricate detail of its construction. The store proprietor noticed my interest and immediately came over, hungry for a sale. He enthused, making his pitch, "Handcrafted by a native Hawaiian and an exact replica of what you will see on Waikiki Beach. It will make a great memory of your time here for only three dollars U.S."

I appreciated the quality of the workmanship and countered, "Two dollars and you got a sale."

He quickly accepted, and Myron and I watched him as he carefully wrapped the outrigger in old newspaper that he pulled from under the counter and tied with heavy twine. He handed the package to me with a delighted smile, his yellow stained teeth showing, obviously satisfied with the sale. That made me think, to my chagrin, I paid too much. Worse, though, I regretted I would now have to carry the package around for the day in the sweltering heat.

With the wrapped outrigger package tucked under my sweaty arm, Myron and I crossed the street to a food stand selling native cuisine. The vendor approached us, shoving a bowl of poi in my face, urging me to try it. He said poi is made from brown taro root, whatever that is, and is a food staple of the natives.

"I'm not hungry," I said. "I just finished breakfast on the base."

He turned to Myron, who said, "We ate breakfast together."

Persistent, the vendor insisted I try it. "No one ever said no to a free taste," he exclaimed. "You can't be in Hawaii and not have poi. You'll love it. I promise." Hoping to satisfy his urging, so that we could leave, I sampled a small mouthful. It had the texture of mashed potatoes but resembled wallpaper paste in appearance and, I thought, *probably tasted like it too*. I thanked him, lying, "It's delicious. Maybe I'll have more of an appetite later in the day."

He smiled, satisfied, "I knew you'd like it."

With nothing more of interest in Pearl City, we trudged to the train station, passing a grocer with a skinned goat carcass hanging from a hook outside its door. Without refrigeration and in the stifling heat and humidity, the large slab of raw meat was covered by hundreds of large, black flies. Myron joked, "This is not the prime aged meat they serve at Peter Luger's when you order a filet mignon."

"You know, Myron," I chuckled, "I've never eaten in Peter Luger's, but I'm sure you're right. The locals must not mind the flies with their meat, especially when you consider they like poi."

We continued to the train station, where we purchased tickets for the ten-mile trip to Honolulu and waited on the rickety old wooden platform outside the terminal with others in uniform from the base. Several minutes passed before a vintage steam locomotive, circa 1870, with several passenger cars, akin to what I'd seen in a western movie, pulled into the station, white fumes billowing from its wheels and coal-black smoke belching from its stack. The train quickly filled, all those aboard anxious to get going and into the breeze. Myron and I grabbed two seats next to an open window hoping the wind would dry our sweat-soaked uniforms. The engineer, leaning his head outside the cab, surveyed the passenger cars, receiving the signal from the conductor that all were aboard. He clanged the bell a few times to signal our departure as the train moved away from the station, black smoke from its stack filling the air as she gained speed on the rails on her way to Honolulu. The warm breeze blowing through the open window provided some relief from the humidity, drying our sweat soaked shirts by the time we reached Honolulu thirty-five minutes later. On the way, we passed acres of pineapple and sugarcane growing alongside the tracks in the red Hawaiian dirt.

When we reached the station in Honolulu, a person attired in beach wear told us Waikiki Beach was a ten-minute walk, or an even quicker mule-drawn trolley ride away. Since a gentle breeze was blowing off the bay, and the humidity was not as stifling as it was in Pearl City, we decided to walk along Kalakaua Avenue, Honolulu's lively main street. The Royal Hawaiian Hotel, a pink Moorish-style structure situated in a lush garden directly on the beach, was our first landmark.

"Myron, this place looks like paradise. Let's check it out." We entered the bustling tropical lobby packed with naval servicemen. "I wonder what it takes to snag a room here," I said, "instead of the barracks at Hickam." So, we inquired of the clerk at the reception desk, who told us, "The Navy requisitioned the entire hotel to provide R&R for its submariners." Myron and I looked at each other dumbfounded, and Myron aptly noted, "It sure beats Hickam, but the price for a room could be worth your life." The scuttlebutt was submarine mortality rates were the highest in the Navy.

Enthralled by the luxuriant surroundings, we meandered through the lobby overflowing with scattered planters filled with moth orchids, yellow plumeria, and pink ginger. We exited on to the rear patio allured by the fragrant aroma of the lush garden, coconut palms, and faint hint of Hawaiian music. I quickly noticed the panoramic view was marred by concertina wire strung along the beach as far as the eye could see, probably all the way to Diamond Head three miles away. I overheard someone say the barbed fencing was installed after the Japanese attack to protect against a land invasion. I looked around and thought it was hard to believe this could be a place of battle, but nobody knows where one could break out.

The soft white sandy beach beckoned us, so Myron and I decided to find a store that sold swim trunks. We figured this might have been our only chance to swim on Waikiki Beach. We headed back to the reception desk to inquire if there was a store selling beach attire and suntan lotion. He said the hotel gift shop was closed, but a retailer nearby on Kalakaua sold beach items. We left through the palatial front entrance, waiting at the curb for a horse-drawn trolley full of rowdy sailors to pass before crossing the street to the store recommended by the hotel clerk. "I wonder where they came from," Myron mused. "It appears the alcohol is flowing freely. Probably submariners letting loose having just returned from a patrol."

"Yeah. I'm sure their nerves are on edge. They just need to let off some steam and pent-up tension."

When we entered the clothing store, it was obvious the assortment of swimwear was limited. After rummaging through the shelves, each of us found trunks that looked halfway decent—not that we intended to attract the attention of any girls in bikinis, but we surely didn't want to be laughed off the beach by our compatriots. I grabbed a bottle of Gaby Suntan Lotion to go with my purchase, and we returned to the hotel where the reception clerk directed us to the men's locker room. An attendant rented us a locker for a small fee and gave us two beach towels. We changed into our new swim attire, storing our clothes and my souvenir outrigger canoe in the locker, and stepped onto the patio. We crossed to the sand, ready for our debut on Waikiki Beach.

It was close to noon, and the midday sun, directly overhead, created bands of heat waves rippling across the hot sand. Myron and I applied a liberal dose of Gaby cream to our face, arms, and shoulders to protect against the sun's rays, and maybe induce a tan, and walked on the hot sand toward the teal-blue water. The beach was crowded with sunbathers, swimmers, and uniformed servicemen walking along with beers in hand. A cluster of people about a hundred yards away near the water's edge in the direction of Diamond Head caught our attention. Interested about the commotion, I asked a fellow walking toward us if he knew what the fuss was about. "Yes," he said. "Everyone is watching a surfing demonstration by Duke Kahanamoku."

Vaguely familiar with the name, I inquired, "I've heard that name before. Is he a famous surfer?"

"Only the best. He's considered the 'Father of Surfing,' but you probably heard his name in connection with the Olympic Games. In his youth he gained fame as a swimmer, setting the world record in the one-hundred-yard freestyle here in Honolulu Harbor, followed with a gold medal in the one-hundred-meter freestyle in the 1912 Summer Olympic Games in Stockholm and again in 1920 in Antwerp. Duke is Hawaii's most notable ambassador to the world."

"You sure know a lot about him, especially his swimming records," I said.

"I do," he responded, "because I swam in college and always measured my performance against his Olympic records in the hundred-meter freestyle which I bested by a full second. I'm too old now for competitive swimming so I took up surfing like Duke. There's no greater thrill than catching the perfect wave and hanging ten riding the curl onto the beach."

"Thanks for the info. I think we'll check Duke out."

Blending with the civilians on the beach in our swim trunks, we walked among the sunbathers laying on towels and under umbrellas to the Moana Hotel where Duke, big as life, was holding court. He grasped a twelve-foot board planted on end in the sand, explaining surfing techniques to the crowd surrounding him. In his early fifties with the toned body of a world class athlete, Duke was about my height, six feet tall, and had a full head of shocking white hair atop a bronzed muscular build. His black swim trunks contrasted strikingly with the highly lacquered red surfboard he held that had a black vertical stripe down the center bordered in gold with his name stenciled in script under the words "The Maui" above a small crown. Duke and his surfboard presented a very impressive image, one I won't forget.

Myron and I mingled with the onlookers as Duke boasted, "I once rode a series of waves from Kalehuawehe Beach for more than a mile to Canoes Beach. This beach (Waikiki) is good for beginners, a place to practice technique before tackling the larger waves on Oahu's Haleiwa's Ali'l Beach or Maui's Ho'okipa Beach." Myron and I professed to each other that even though we lived near some of the finest beaches in the world neither of us had ever attempted surfing in the waves of Jones Beach or Rockaway Beach; nor could we recollect anyone else doing so. It must be that those beaches were always too crowded with bathers. I told Myron about the waves I saw at Rockaway Beach in 1938 after the hurricane passed through, telling him, "I'm sure they would have been a challenge, even for Duke."

After listening with fascination to Duke speak for several more minutes, native Hawaiian music, probably the faint sounds we heard earlier, lured us to the expansive patio of the Moana Hotel. The space was aptly named the Banyan Courtyard. Spotting an empty table near the sand's edge, we plunked down into the white wicker chairs to order two beers. I had stuffed money in my trunks just in case we became thirsty in the heat.

Waiting for the server to come to our table, I closed my eyes and attuned my senses to the paradise that surrounded me: the shade of an enormous banyan tree nestled in a cocoon of bougainvillea and coconut palm, buffered by a sweet hibiscus scented breeze, the soothing melodies of Hawaiian music, and the sound of gentle waves rippling to shore. What more could one ask for? *If only Ellen were here with me now and there was no war, that would be heaven.*

My reverie ended abruptly, "Gentlemen, what may I serve you?" the waiter standing at the table in a flowered Hawaiian shirt asked.

"We'll have two beers and some salted peanuts," I answered.

The waiter returned several minutes later placing a tray with two bottles of ice-cold Coors on the table, pouring the contents of each bottle carefully into a tall, iced Pilsner glass. *This,* I thought, *is how beer should always be served.* Myron and I clinked our glasses, toasting each other, "Life is great," but we knew otherwise. We had seen the sunken remains of *Arizona* and knew war was raging in the Pacific. We'd be in that war soon enough—just not this day.

We finished our beers and the waiter, passing by the table seeing the empty glasses, returned to see if we wanted refills. "We're from New York," I said. "We've never heard of Coors, but it's a mighty fine beer. We'll have two more in the iced-Pilsner glass."

"Coming right up. Coors, so you know, is brewed in Golden, Colorado," he said. "It's the most popular beer throughout the Islands. I've never served anyone who left after only one Coors, especially when you have the sweet sounds of Hawaiian music to relax to while drinking your beer. Hang around, there will be a show later with hula dancers that you will enjoy."

"I'll drink to that," Myron said.

Stirred by renewed commotion on the beach, our attention diverted to a large red surfboard wending its way toward the water. Duke Kahanamoku had been coaxed by the crowd on the beach into giving a demonstration. We hurried to watch, telling the waiter we would be back. With beers in hand, we arrived at the water's edge just as Duke entered the small cascading waves, settling prone on the board and paddling away from the shore. Three Hawaiians pushed a nearby outrigger canoe (like the model I purchased) nose first into a tiny swell and jumped in, rowing furiously to catch Duke for a ringside seat.

Duke and the outrigger crew paddled about one hundred yards from shore, where they rode steadily in the water, waiting, I believed, for the perfect wave to bring them back in. Duke went first, catching a nice curl of a developing wave. He glided effortlessly on its crest, the crowd anxiously awaiting his return. To everyone's amazement, he bent forward and rose into a headstand that he held for a second or two before settling back into an upright standing position, riding the last of the curl onto the beach, where the spectators screamed, "Duke, Duke!" I looked for the outrigger, catching sight of it just as it tipped sideways, flipping the three riders into the surf. No one else noticed their mishap. All eyes were on Duke, the crowd chanting, "You're the greatest."

Dripping wet and holding the massive red board upright in the sand, Duke asked if anyone was interested in trying their hand at the surf as the three riders righted their capsized canoe. They returned to shore, no worse for wear.

"Myron, too bad that person we spoke to earlier isn't here, he would have jumped at the chance to surf with a legend."

"You're right. That would have been the thrill of a lifetime for him."

Thinking it couldn't be too difficult to stand on a board, I raised my hand to Myon's dismay, and stepped forward.

Myron looked at me and said, "Hot-damn, John. Do you know what you're doing? He's an Olympic champion and the world's greatest surfer."

"Myron, it looks easy. The hard part would be doing a headstand. The worst that can happen is I'll fall off, but at least I can say I received a personal surfing lesson from Duke Kahanamoku, and to me that is worth the embarrassment."

"Okay then. Good luck. You'll need it."

Duke saw my raised hand and nodded his approval, motioning me forward with a wave of his arm as no one else volunteered. I handed Myron my glass of beer and followed Duke into the water as he put the board down instructing me to lie on it flat on my stomach. He waded into the surf and guided the board through a couple of small waves. When we were far enough out, he swiveled the board around, pointing the front edge toward the beach. He coached me to stand by kneeling first with my hands gripping the sides and then gently rising. He pushed the board forward with the first good wave and hollered, "Forget the headstand. That maneuver will be in the next lesson." I thought surfing would be easy, but before I knew what happened the curl vanished and another small wave coming across caught me by surprise and I toppled sideways off the board into the water. Embarrassed by my quick exit, I confided to Duke as we waded back to the beach that riding the board was more difficult than I thought it would be. He said, "It took me a while to master the board. You've nothing to be ashamed of." Red-faced, I returned to Myron in the crowd of onlookers, who handed me my beer, saying, "Good try, you need this. Surfing must be harder than it looks because Duke makes it look so easy."

"You're right. It's not so easy to maintain your balance, especially when you're hit by a surprise wave." We both laughed at my lame joke as Hawaiian music lured us to the Banyan Courtyard for another round of Coors. We returned to our table, greeted by the waiter who delivered two ice-cold Coors. "I knew you'd be back, so I figured you'd want the same. More peanuts?"

"Thanks, you're a mind reader," I said, "But do you have burgers on the menu? I've developed an appetite since my surfing expedition. How about you Myron, hungry?"

"Yes, I'll have a juicy hamburger, grilled medium well, with French fries and a dill pickle."

"Make that two. And bring ketchup and mustard. Thanks."

"Coming right up."

Waiting for our food, I thought of Ellen again and wished she were here. I closed my eyes to the music, knowing this may be the last time for quite a while. Then the bandleader announced through his microphone, "Aloha, everyone, welcome to the Moana Hotel where you'll enjoy an exhibition by these beautiful native Hawaiian girls who will perform several traditional hula dances for you." He waved his hand toward four barefoot young women in grass skirts, covered from the waist up with flower leis of purple, green, and white orchids, crowned by a white hibiscus pinned to their long, flowing black hair. "Hula dancing," he explained, "is a complex art form. The movements of the dancers' hands, feet, and hips tell a story, with each motion representing a word in the song. The grass skirts, known as pa'u, are made from the fronds of a palm tree. For those with a camera, the dancers and band members would love to pose after the performance with those wishing a souvenir photo to remember your visit to the Moana Hotel. On behalf of myself, the dancers, and the band, enjoy the show. Aloha and mahalo."

The performance lasted about forty-five minutes, and when it ended, a line of civilians and sailors sought to capture some Hawaiian magic in a picture. Myron and I, without a camera, settled our bill with the waiter, thanking him for the superb service. The afternoon heat had dissipated and the last rays of daylight were vanishing behind the fuchsia cone of Diamond Head. It was time to head back to Hickam. We ambled along the beach back to The Royal Hawaiian, where we showered and changed into our khakis. Refreshed, and with the sun fading into the horizon, we relaxed on the patio with one more beer to savor the sunset before heading to the train.

Our return trip to Pearl City was in the dark—the full moon erasing the stars from view. The only sounds were the train's wheels humming along the rails in concert with the snores of sleeping servicemen in harmony with the chirping crickets and croaking frogs alongside the tracks.

When the train pulled into the station, we scrambled to the transfer hub where we waited for about twenty minutes in the queue before boarding the bus back to the base. On the short ride we decided to meet again tomorrow for breakfast at 0730 to make new exploration plans.

During my walk to the barracks, scattered clouds rolled in, releasing a light rain, reminding me someone said, "you can usually count on rain every night in Hawaii, nature's air-conditioning to wring out the humidity of the day."

I settled into my room, stowing the outrigger into the footlocker, thankful I didn't have to tote it around anymore, but glad I did because of its unique workmanship. As soon as I undressed, I fell into bed and went right to sleep. I was exhausted from the heat, humidity, beers, and surfing expedition.

The humidity on the base was unbearable the next day so Myron and I returned to Waikiki Beach, venturing into the water while enjoying ice-cold Coors again at the Moana Hotel. Duke was missing, but I noticed oil sludge on the beach that I hadn't noticed yesterday, an indicator of war put there by our ships filing past Honolulu to Pearl.

21 September 1942

Hi Honey,

I miss you so much, and wish you were here. Waikiki is a tropical paradise as you imagine but barbed-wire-fence strung along the beach to protect against an enemy invasion detracts from the view. Once you get past that, though, and step onto the sand and into the water, it is very relaxing. Much nicer than Rockaway Beach. The water is aqua-blue and the sand white and soft except for the occasional bit of oil sludge that washes ashore from our passing ships heading to Pearl. You can wade quite a distance without getting in over your head and knocked over by a wave.

I know you'd enjoy lying on a blanket in the sand, soaking up the sun's rays, working on your tan, with the scented ocean breeze caressing your skin while sipping a tropical drink and Hawaiian music serenading your ears. Sound like paradise? This could be a place to visit for a second honeymoon although it may not be practical as it would take as long as a vacation to get here from New York.

I've been to the beach a couple of times with Myron Dallen, who I ran into on the train when I left New York. You don't know him, but he was an instructor at Fort Schuyler who has also been re-assigned to sea duty. When I'm with him and Hawaiian music is playing in the Banyan Courtyard at the Moana Hotel, I close my eyes and dream of you. When I open my eyes, there's Myron, and back to reality.

South Dakota is due in Pearl tomorrow, so I'll have more to say once I'm aboard.

I almost forgot to mention, I tried surfing on a surfboard on Waikiki Beach. I received a lesson from Duke Kahanamoku. He is world famous; an Olympic swimming champion and considered the "Father of Surfing." To my embarrassment, I fell off the board before I could stand up. Maybe I'll do better next time with some practice. You should have seen Duke, though, he did a headstand without falling off.

I'll write soon, Love always, John

15

THE STORM RAGED

Atlantic Ocean, 13 September 1944

A bolt of lightning pierced the low-scudding rain clouds. I was startled awake by the following thunderclap. My eyes opened as a bracing cross swell nearly flipped the raft; the needle-like spray of the saltwater stinging my eyes shut. I was surrounded by people bouncing in huge waves that resembled rolling pewter hills. Groggily, I lifted my head. Over someone's shoulder, a dark, heavy cloud blackens the horizon, its upper reaches tinged with a dull, reddish cast. For a moment, I was confused, my mind still clinging to the memories of the past. The throbbing pain in my head brought me back to reality. Just before the ship spiraled into her death roll, I stared through the window at a titanic wave, the largest I'd ever seen. Beneath its foaming white crown, the sky was as black as a rolling Saharan Desert sandstorm, and when it collided with *Warrington*, the ship shuddered, lifted, and descended the face of the wave, landing on her starboard side, spume surging through the superstructure. Lying at the bottom of the trough, ocean foam bubbling over her midsection and through her bowels, she fought to bounce back, but it was not to be. She turned under, the next deluge engulfing her like the whale that swallowed Jonah. Propelled overboard a step outside the bridge my last remembrance.

A faint voice against the roar of the ocean asks, "Lieutenant, can you hear me?"

I opened my eyes to see who is speaking, just as a giant comber breaks across the raft, wiping the sting of the driving rain from my face but smothering me in spume. I cough another mouthful of briny water. "Did I pass out?" I asked.

"You've been in and out of consciousness since we pulled you in."

The raft waffled, water cascading through the webbing. "How long?"

"An hour or so. You mumbled about trying to remember how you got to this place. You've one hell of a bump on your head and your cheek is swollen."

"I'll be okay," I uttered through the pain in my head, my senses returning. "I knew what was coming," I muttered. "Just my bad luck to crash into the bulwark when I was flung overboard."

"Schultz pulled you to the raft. You're safe now. Close your eyes and rest," a voice said. Suddenly the float turned sideways, surging up the face of an enormous swell, threatening to flip over. We rode to the foaming crown, where we dropped precipitously. The raft smashed into the trough with a jarring thud, the force of the smackdown throwing two men without life vests into the waves. Surrounded by suffocating walls of black water, efforts to rescue them were futile. A cross swell swept them away. I blinked and they were gone, lost to the sea's clutches.

There's nothing that can be done to change our situation other than to hold tightly to the float and ride the swells until the storm passes, I thought. *Hopefully, our SOS calls will bring rescue.*

"Ridge, it's Cole. Can you hear me?"

"Barely." The sound of the thunder and waves was overpowering.

"There're eighteen of us on the raft. You're senior, so we'll be taking orders from you if you're up to it."

My head was pounding. I recalled Captain Gatch on *Arizona*, seriously wounded, but remaining in command of the ship until the end of the Battle at Santa Cruz. "I'll grin and bear it. No choice. Just give me a few more minutes."

We rode the undulating waves through the afternoon, rain spouts drenching us, the wind howling, and the swells still huge. The whitewater at their crests, though, seemed to be abating, or was I just wishing that were so. A good sign if true, but it was hard to discern after the last vestiges of daylight ebbed behind a gray sky into the darkness of night.

Greene hollered, "A shark just smashed into the raft!"

That caught everyone's attention.

"I felt it too!" Tuttle yelled.

"Where?" Arbogast demanded.

A weak voice in the water mumbled, "I'm glad to see you guys. I almost lost all hope." It was Arel Smith drifting alone in the darkness, a lucky swell whooshing him into the raft.

Greene and Hart each grabbed an arm and hoisted him onto the raft.

Pack asked, "Weren't you with others?"

"No. I was seasick in my bunk, puking my brains out, but that feeling went away when I was tossed from my rack into the bulkhead."

"What happened?" I asked.

"I landed on the floor in several inches of water," he explained in a cracked, raspy voice. "The room was pitch black, but I could tell no one was there. That's when fear took over. I realized the ship was in danger of sinking."

"How did you get off?"

"I was tossed around a bit, like a pinball. When I was thrown into the jack stay, a kapok from the overhead knocked me down. I grabbed it, fumbled to get it strapped on in the dark, and struggled to the door and up the ladder sideways looking for where everyone went."

"Who'd you find?"

"No one. Everyone was gone. The ship was listing so sharply I wasn't sure I'd be able to get off. I said a Hail Mary, crossed my fingers for extra luck, climbed over the rail, and slid into the water. Just in time. The ship turned under. I was sucked under the water a few feet but scissor-kicked to the surface, when a wave hurled me into a lifeline that smashed into the middle of my back. It has been hurting ever since."

"At least you're alive. We're not sure how many others made it."

"I've been scanning the swells but couldn't see a thing because of the stinging rain. My eyes hurt like hell, like someone threw sand in my face."

"Well, Smith."

"Yes?"

"At least you're alive. Welcome aboard."

"Thank you, sir."

"The swells should ease as the trailing edge of the storm passes." I said to the group over the whipping sound of the waves. "Try to get some sleep. Most of us have been awake for over twenty-four hours."

Pack uttered, "It will be impossible to get sleep. Every time we hit a cross swell; the raft feels like it's going to flip."

"Try," I asserted through the pain in my jaw, "We'll need our energy tomorrow to search for others and to watch for sharks that are likely to show up when the ocean settles."

"Yes, sir," everyone on the raft replied in unison.

Don led a prayer for those who were lost and for those still alive, wherever they might be, hoping for a miracle.

Hunkering down, we clung to each other like leeches sucking blood, trying to gain warmth from one another. Still, we shivered uncontrollably from the cold water splashing on our skin.

16

NEW CHALLENGES

Atlantic Ocean, 13 into 14 September 1944

The wind subsided in the small hours. Sunny skies greeted us the next morning, although the sea remained high. If I hadn't experienced it myself, I would have never guessed a hurricane roared through the day before to claim a Navy destroyer and most of her crew.

"Men," I hollered as loud as I could through the throbbing pain of my head, "we made it through the night. Until we're rescued, we'll be faced with new challenges. The unrelenting rays of the sun and the likelihood of circling sharks are our new enemies. I believe we all know one another, but let's introduce ourselves anyway. Don, you first."

"Yes, sir. Don Schultz, assistant gunnery officer."

"Larry Allphin, torpedoman."

In a raspy voice, "Paul Klingen, radioman."

A wave splashed across the raft, turning it sideways. Everyone tightened their grip on the rope loops strung around the edge. The raft settled into the swell.

Spitting a mouthful of water, "Bill Greene, quartermaster."

"John LaTronica, machinist mate."

"Coleman Pack, gunnery officer."

"Gene Arbogast, seaman."

"Dan Berman, seaman."

"John Richards, boatswain's mate."

"Bill Sapp, water tender."

"Charlie Everts, chief torpedoman."

"Jack Tuttle, fire controlman"

"Mel Smelesky, seaman." Another large swell unsettles the raft.

Spitting water, "Layton Strong, seaman."

"Glenn Melson, ship's cook. I hate to say it guys, but there's no dinner being served tonight." A laugh or two followed his remark, from those still able, with a sense of hope.

"Perley Boyd, stewards' mate. I guess I have the night off." That brought a laugh from everyone despite our dire circumstances.

"Arel Smith, radarman, late arrival to the raft, thank God."

"Hart, communications officer and mailman. You all know me. Let's pray my SOS calls were heard by someone who can save us."

"Greene, what do we have in the way of supplies?" I asked.

"Sir, someone thought to stow extra cannisters of fresh water on the float. We have six five-gallon kegs of potable water, twenty tins of hardtack, a couple dozen packs of malted milk tablets, and several tins of Spam. Good thing I thought to take my knife. Melson will need it to open the Spam."

Hart interjected, "Glenn, you'd have to be a magician to create a tasty meal from hardtack and Spam."

"You're right, but it will taste good when we get hungry, you can count on that."

"Thank God for whoever thought about the water," I said, "they deserve a medal. Fresh water is life over all else on this raft. There are nineteen of us so we'll have to ration our consumption to ensure it lasts for several days, at least until we are rescued. Melson, what do you recommend for each serving?"

"Sir, we'll start with one biscuit, a little Spam, and a cup of water three times a day to start if you agree."

"Okay. Let's start with that. No matter how tempted you are, do not swallow the seawater. It will kill you, that's a fact. If we run low on potable water, take a malted milk tablet to slake your thirst. What about medical supplies?"

"Sulfa powder and burn ointment," Greene reported. "That's it."

"The sulfa powder," I said, "was useful when we were in the Pacific, but it's of no use here. The burn ointment may be of value, though, to protect against the sun's rays. Okay, then, let's set a system of watches to look for other survivors. And, as the swells subside, keep an eye for shark fins."

Tuttle cursed. "Sharks! That's all we need after the hurricane."

"Try to get some sleep if you can. John, Charlie, and I will take the first two-hour watch. Anyone have a watch that works?" I asked. "Mine's broken."

"I do. My wife gave me this waterproof watch for a Christmas present last year and it's still working," Don said as he took off his watch and handed it to me.

"Thanks, Don. I promise not to lose it. It is now 1030. We'll take the watch to 1230, then Greene, Smith, and Klingen, you'll be on."

My watch over, I closed my eyes to escape into the past. What else was there to do? The raft rose and settled in the easing swells.

17

WELCOMED ABOARD

USS South Dakota, 22 September 1942

I found it hard to comprehend the Japanese attack was less than a year ago—our resilience to recover from such destruction was remarkable. Pearl Harbor brimmed with over a hundred ships, and our big guns, on the battleships *West Virginia, Pennsylvania, Colorado, California, New Mexico, Idaho, Mississippi, Maryland,* and *Tennessee* would soon be joined by my ship, *South Dakota.*

Sunlight streaming through the barracks' window was my signal to get out of bed. It was 0630. I had slept fitfully, tossing, and turning, anxious for *South Dakota's* arrival later in the morning. Most of the night I laid in bed thinking of Ellen and about what would transpire today–a day a long time coming but finally here.

I quickly showered, shaved, and dressed, and at 0655 walked to the Officer's Club for breakfast. Grabbing the Hawaii Times from the rack by the door as I entered, I skimmed the major headlines while waiting for my breakfast of scrambled eggs, toast, pineapple juice, and a cup of Kona coffee. I'd never tasted that coffee before but liked its flavorful blend of brown sugar, milk chocolate, honey, and a hint of fruit. The waiter told me the coffee comes from beans grown on the slopes of the volcanos on the Big Island where the mineral-rich soil coupled with the changing weather of sunny mornings and rainy afternoons gives the bean its unique taste. After a second cup I folded the paper under my arm and trekked to the pier, where I boarded a tender for the short trip to Dry Dock 2 in Pearl City where *South Dakota* would be repaired for the gash in her hull. I jumped from the tender as it pulled alongside the dock and walked along the pier, taking in the bustling activity. The area was alive, humming with laborers moving about with purpose, determination etched on their faces. Great battles, I knew, must still be fought, and won. The sooner the better, so we could all return home to our loved ones.

I had such an adrenaline rush about *South Dakota*'s impending arrival. My heart was racing so much that I hadn't noticed how delightful the weather was for the first time since I'd been in Pearl Harbor. The temperatures were in the mid-seventies, fifteen degrees cooler than the day before when Myron and I were in Honolulu. The cooling change in the weather must have been due to yesterday's heavy rain, which lasted longer than usual, aided by the winds that swept across the water to shore. I thought, *I could take this climate year-round when it is like this—and trade it for the snowy, frigid winters of New York.* The Christmas holiday season, though, wouldn't be the same, substituting a decorated blue spruce for a decorated palm.

I found a comfortable spot near the dock to sit and opened the newspaper to the sports pages, which covered the results stateside because of all the servicemen stationed here. I was able to keep an eye on the activity on the pier while reading the paper. The Dodgers split a double header with the last place Phillies taking game two 4-2 after dropping the opener 7-3. I was happy to see my team doing well, two games out of first place behind the Cardinals, with Pee Wee Reese looking like a future Hall of Famer. Maybe the Dodgers would make it into the World Series—that would be something for me to cheer about in this world of misery.

I glanced toward the water and looked at my watch. Almost 1030. A large ship faintly visible on the horizon was coming; it must have been *South Dakota* scheduled in port at 1130.

I had another hour before she arrived, so I tackled the crossword puzzle featuring points of interest in the Hawaiian Islands. I enjoyed the challenge of the New York Times crossword puzzles when I rode the subway to work, finding them to be a stimulating way to pass the time after reading the financial news. I was having difficulty with this one, though, as I was not familiar with many of the sights, customs, and native terms that were its theme.

Absorbed trying to complete the puzzle, and to my surprise more than half finished, I looked back to the water to gauge *South Dakota*'s progress. Her silhouette was growing larger and more defined as she loomed closer. I lost my concentration on figuring out the crossword clues, and instead watched the ship intently searching for the damage that brought her back to Pearl Harbor, but nothing was visible.

I tore out the crossword so I could complete it later and tossed the rest of the newspaper in a nearby trash barrel. I jumped from my perch to move closer to the pier to observe the ship as it glided into the dry dock. A worker nearby said the repairs would take at least several days, maybe a month depending upon how serious the damage.

Despite all the battle wagons in Pearl Harbor, *South Dakota* was magnificent, even with a gash in her hull. Maybe I was biased. Maybe because she was our newest battleship commissioned earlier in the year on March 20th. One thing for sure, she was a far cry from the turn of the century battleship *Illinois*.

I observed the berthing process, anxiously awaiting the last whoosh of water from the drydock that would expose the reason for her return to port. Sitting away from the dry dock entrance were two navy tugs that took a position on each side of her bow, where they cautiously guided her forward. The tugs pulled away when the bow entered the open lock. A crane with two winches sent down guide wires that workers attached to each side of the forward end of the ship as she floated slowly ahead into the dock. Once the bow was situated all the way forward in the lock, another set of wires were attached to the aft end of the ship to position her in the exact spot where she would be laid to rest on the keel blocks. The mooring lines were tightened to secure the ship and when that was done, the caissons (gates) closed. A loud whirring sound grabbed my attention, and I realized that it was the pumps spewing the water from the lock. Several minutes passed before the keel settled onto the blocks sitting in the concrete bed. When all the seawater was emptied from the lock, the gaping hole was clearly visible. The gash was so large I reasoned that the watertight compartments and secondary hull layer kept water from flooding into the rest of the ship. I couldn't believe a coral reef could cause so much damage to a thick steel hull. I wondered what damage an enemy torpedo could have done. Sink the ship?

South Dakota was more enormous than I thought when I viewed how much of her was below the waterline. That unseen area housed the four massive General Electric steam turbines, boilers, screw propellers, storage for over two-and-half million gallons of fuel, and sleeping quarters for most of the crew, and perhaps—as it was for the men of the *Arizona*—their final resting place.

I waited on the pier until the gangway was lowered to the dock and crew members began disembarking. Then I returned to the tender for the trip back to the barracks at Hickam to retrieve my seabag and other belongings. After I emptied the contents of my footlocker, I returned to *South Dakota* to report for duty.

I walked up the gangplank with my shouldered duffle and the outrigger canoe I purchased in Pearl City under my arm. It was surreal. I reached the railing, lowered my bag and parcel on the deck, and saluted the flag, requesting permission from the OOD to board the ship to report for duty.

"Permission granted," he saluted in return.

"I'm to report to Lt. Cdr. Jason Collins," I said.

He beckoned a nearby mate, who was swabbing the deck, instructing him to direct me to the Combat Information Center (CIC). When we entered, he pointed to Collins, a dark-haired man in a khaki uniform I reckoned to be several years older than myself. I stepped over to him, gained his attention, and saluted, "Lieutenant Ridgeway reports as ordered." Collins returned the salute and told me to stand at ease.

"Welcome aboard Lieutenant. We've been short one man in the CIC since the ship left Philadelphia, and with your addition we are up to full complement. A full staff will be needed once we return to sea as I expect we'll see battle action." Collins told the sailor next to him, "Take the lieutenant's gear to his stateroom and then return to your post." He then looked at his watch and said, "It's 1300, and my stomach tells me it is time for lunch. How about you? Are you hungry?" Before I answered, he suggested we dine in the Crew's Mess as it would give us an informal opportunity to get to know each other.

The Mess was noisy and crowded when we entered with a couple hundred crew there eating lunch. Collins searched around and found us seats in the corner where we could talk. Over a lunch of hamburgers, fries, and lemonade, I told him, "I graduated from college and with our entry into the war almost a certainty, rather than wait for the draft to get me, I applied to V-7 as I believed the Navy offered the best living conditions and potential for advancement." He nodded in agreement. "This may sound funny," I continued, "especially since I volunteered, but this will be my first time at sea. My time in the Navy thus far has been as an instructor at Fort Schuyler teaching a refresher course in seamanship to officers recalled to active duty. Before the voyage from San Francisco to Pearl, I'd never been on a vessel larger than the Staten Island Ferry. My biggest fear, I'll be honest, is getting seasick. I don't know what I'd do if that happened."

Collins chuckled, "Don't worry about getting seasick. I've seen veteran sailors sick, but everyone survives—to their dismay. Although now that I think about it, there was one person I remember who could never recover whenever the sea became choppy, so I arranged for him to be released to shore duty. He was one happy sailor when he got off the ship."

Finishing lunch over a cup of coffee, Collins confided, "I'm an Annapolis graduate and expect to make the Navy my career, following in my father's footsteps. He's a retired rear admiral who served on a battle wagon in World War I, although he may be recalled to active duty to an administrative position in planning and logistics." Collins explained, "Let me show you to your stateroom. You'll be bunking with three others; Connolly will be working with us in the CIC. I'm not sure if anyone will be in the room now, but, if not, you'll meet them later."

We left the Mess, and Collins brought me to my sleeping quarters saying he would return in half an hour to give me a tour of the ship. My seabag and parcel were lying on an upper bunk, which I assumed was my assigned bed. He began to leave, but before he was out the door I said, "I'm pleased with the accommodations as compared to my trip to Pearl on *George Clymer* where I was crammed with five hundred others in a space meant for half that number." He emitted a small laugh, and said, "I'll be back shortly."

My bunkmates weren't there but I noted their names on the lockers: Patrick A. Davis, John M. Connolly, and Robert X. Timmons. I wondered what the "X" signified, Xavier? The room, while compact, had two double-deck bunks with overhead fans to circulate air, cabinets, storage lockers, and a desk. I grabbed my duffle and unpacked the contents, stowing the items in the empty built-in bureau, placing the empty seabag, outrigger canoe, and holstered .45 automatic I'd been issued when I boarded, into my locker. On the small desk was a coconut carved to make it into an ashtray—I assumed for my roommates who smoked.

While I waited for Collins to return, I retrieved the folded crossword puzzle from my pocket but put it down and decided to start a letter to Ellen. I found writing paper and a pen in the desk drawer, turned on the overhead light, and put pen to paper just as Collins knocked on the door and entered the room. "Ready for the tour?"

I slid the paper and pen into the drawer and said, "Can't wait. She's an impressive ship."

"She sure is, as you are about to see."

18

COOK'S TOUR

We walked along the passageway, Collins saying when we exited midship on the main deck, "*South Dakota* is the flagship for a new class of fast battleship designed to provide protection for carriers from enemy warships, carrier planes, and submarines, but you already know that. We carry 2,364 men, including 114 officers. You are the most recent addition."

"I'm glad to be aboard. It means a lot to me to serve on a vessel such as this."

"You saw the damage?"

"I did."

"Let me fill you in on the cause. After we transited the Panama Canal, we sailed to Nuku'alofa in the Tonga Islands, where we refueled and took on additional ammunition for our antiaircraft guns. Two days later we struck an uncharted coral pinnacle in Lahai Passage, suffering extensive damage to the hull on the portside, as you saw. The key point to what I'm telling you is that we didn't steam over a coral reef, but rather a pinnacle outcropping. That has been a frequent problem in these vast uncharted waters."

"How unfortunate, especially since the ship is so new."

"Yes, in our investigation of the accident we learned an error was made in the weight calculations for the added ammunition. That added weight caused the ship to ride lower in the water. Even so, the uncharted pinnacle was the main factor."

"I see."

"When new coral reefs or pinnacles are found, usually when there is an accident, its location is reported so our navigation charts can be updated. There is endless uncharted water in the Pacific, only now being discovered and plotted."

"Sir, when I saw that hole, I'd never have believed a coral pinnacle could've caused such damage unless I'd seen it myself—ripping a hole in the hull as large as it did."

"You wouldn't think coral could do such damage to a thick steel hull. I spoke to an officer who was in the Engine Room when we struck the pinnacle. He told me the hull plates reverberated so loudly he thought the ship was hit by a torpedo. Divers inspected the damage but couldn't see much in the murky water, other than a large gash, due to leaking oil. Our engineers were able to contain the damage, enabling us to limp back to Pearl at fourteen knots. On our return to Pearl, the captain adopted a zigzag course, for extra precaution, to reduce the risk of an enemy torpedo."

"That was a hard way for the ship to start her tour in the Pacific."

Collins nodded, "I'll say. We look forward to a new beginning."

I followed Collins along the main deck to the forward sixteen-inch turret, where he turned to me and said, "A bit of technical background, no need to remember the specifics, but it will give insight about the ship and how she is different from the other battle wagons here in Pearl. She's 680 feet long at the waterline, that's 50 feet shorter than the *North Carolina* and *Washington*, but our beam is the same, at 108 feet, so we can transit through the Panama Canal. Our shortened length was for a purpose. It allowed for more armor cladding which overcame the main deficiency of *North Carolina* and *Washington*."

"I wasn't aware of that difference."

"You'll find her impressive," Collins said, as he continued the tour, offering more facts about the ship. "Our shorter length, though, presented design issues. Since she is less streamlined than the other ships, she requires a more powerful propulsion system. We're packing 130,000 horsepower to achieve our top cruising speed of twenty-eight knots, which, believe it or not, is fast enough for waterskiing."

Collins continued, "Although that coral pinnacle revealed a weakness on our underside, the egg heads who designed the ship analyzed numerous scenarios of bombs and torpedoes hitting the ship determining that sloped armor cladding thicker in those places where strikes are most likely to occur provides sufficient protection. Our belt armor is over twelve inches, would you believe, and the angle of its sloping makes it equivalent to over seventeen inches. That's thick enough, the experts determined, to protect the ship against the shell from a sixteen-inch gun."

"That's amazing how engineers' figure all of this out on paper," I commented. "I just hope they're right about their assumptions."

"You and me both," he laughed.

With all that armor-cladded protection, I thought, *the ship's first significant damage was caused by a coral pinnacle, and not an enemy torpedo. How ironic is that?*

Collins must have read my mind by the expression on my face because he said, "Although the underside of the hull that was damaged has the least amount of armor, it's not likely to take a direct hit there from a torpedo as that would come closer to the waterline. That's what someone who knows told me."

"It's reassuring to know the engineers took that into account when calculating the ships' armor cladding."

"I agree."

Standing outside the forward turret, Collins peered up at the massive guns, saying, "These, John, are the main attraction. The reason we are called a battleship."

I squinted into the sun at the imposing barrels. "They're enormous. How big are they?"

"Over sixty feet in length. They weigh nearly two hundred thousand pounds each with the breach, and fire armor-piercing projectiles, known as APCs, which weigh twenty-seven hundred pounds. Those shells can carry almost twenty-three miles. You'd need radar to sight a target that far away. And a lot of luck to hit it."

"Impressive," I nodded. "I've been to the Picatinny Arsenal in Staten Island where the sixteen-inch shells are manufactured, and I saw *North Carolina* when it was being built in the Brooklyn Navy Yard but never had the opportunity to board her for a tour."

"Well, today is your day to see a battleship up close. This turret operates with a crew of seventy-nine, and each barrel in the turret can be fired and elevated independently of the other. The entire turret rotates all the way down to Deck 3, just above the projectile and powder magazines, where the food that feeds these monsters is kept. These guns, like I said, are the main attraction, so let me explain to you how they work."

Collins opened the hatch. I peered in from behind him, and despite the gun's massive size, it was a tight fit to enter, room for only one person to pass at time. He ducked his head and stepped inside. I followed. "The APCs are stored below Deck 3 in a projectile magazine. A block-and-tackle type system moves the shell on a hook along a ceiling-mounted trolley to the lower handling room. From there the shell is moved to the upper handling room via a hoist, where it is either stored in a circular room that can hold thirty shells or transported via another hoist to the gun house, where we are now. The shell, when it arrives here, is tipped onto a transfer tray, and moved forward onto the loading tray for insertion into the gun's breach by an electrically powered arm. After the gun is fired, it returns to a 'gun-ready' position, ready for the next shell to be loaded. That whole process of firing the gun, from start to finish, believe it or not, is about thirty seconds, much faster than you would think."

"That's amazing. I had no idea it was that quick."

"I'll take you into the gun pit."

Collins headed for the door. I followed. He turned unexpectedly, and I bumped into him as he added, "I should mention, also beneath Deck 3, adjacent to the projectile magazine, is the powder magazine. A similar process, as I explained for moving the APCs, moves the powder bags, which are stored in metal containers known as powder tanks. The people handling the powder bags are the strongest people on the ship. It's a sweaty, backbreaking job. They must jam six hundred pounds of powder explosive into the breech. That's enough charge to propel the shell over twenty miles. Luckily, they're not doing it all day long. Only during gunnery practice and, hopefully soon, firing upon the enemy. It's incredibly hectic when the guns are firing, and the deafening noise and vibration add to the mayhem. You'll see what I mean the first time you experience guns going off. Make sure to have your earplugs in."

"I can't imagine what the noise is like when all nine guns are fired in sync. I guess I'll find out soon enough."

"I hope so."

"The biggest gun I heard fired at Fort Schuyler was a five-incher, and that was plenty loud. In addition to the noise, the vibration must be enough to knock you over."

"You're right. Hold on tight to the chart table or bulkhead railing when the guns are firing or you'll either land on the deck or be propelled into the wall. Someone I know broke his arm when he was thrown to the floor."

"I'll remember that. Earplugs and a firm grip on the railing required."

"Yes. Don't forget."

"By the way, who directs the gun when it is fired?"

"Good question. The turret officer uses a rangefinder to ready the gun into the approximate position, but the actual aiming and firing of the gun is done from the CIC where we'll be working."

We exited the turret onto the main deck and walked aft along the rail to the stern as Collins explained, "In addition to the sixteen-inchers and the smaller five-inch guns, we're heavily armed with antiaircraft weapons, as you can see," he said, pointing to a nearby battery. "We have sixty-eight

40 mm guns and seventy-six 20 mm guns. Antiaircraft capability is vital to the defense of the ship and the aircraft carrier assigned to us. The enemy has been using suicide bombers, known as kamikazes, to crash bomb-laden planes into our ships. That makes it imperative we shoot them down before they reach us or our carrier."

Standing on the fantail aft of the sixteen-inch turret, Collins pointed to the catapults at the very rear of the ship, one on the starboard side and one on the port side. "Those platforms," he said, "launch Curtis SO3C floatplanes, whose mission is to scout beyond our radar range. They can fly over eleven hundred miles round-trip at an altitude of around sixteen thousand feet."

"Do they have any weapons?"

"Yes, but limited combat capability. They have a forward-firing .3 caliber Browning machine gun, operated by the pilot, and .5 caliber Browning, operated by the tail gunner. Depending upon their mission, they carry two 100-pound drop bombs or 325 pounds of depth charges."

"Where do they land when they return to the ship?"

"That's always the first question."

"I thought so."

"The pilot, on his return, lands in the water as close as possible to the ship, which slows to receive him. That crane," he points to the one sitting between the two launching catapults, "is swung around to pluck him from the water. That's when the fun begins, especially if the sea is choppy. I've seen practice drills where it has taken quite a while to get the plane back on board. That's one job I wouldn't want."

"From what you said, me neither."

Collins ended the tour in the Combat Information Center, where he introduced me to the crew and said, "Take the rest of the day to get settled and poke around the ship. You'll have plenty of time in the coming days to learn everything you need to know in here."

I returned to my stateroom to find John Connolly sitting at the desk where I sat before the tour writing a letter. He stood, "Hi, John Connolly. You must be the new man?"

"Yes. John Ridgeway, but friends call me Ridge. I'm glad to be aboard the newest ship in our fleet. Collins gave me the tour--she's very impressive."

"She is. I'm also in the CIC so we'll be seeing a lot of each other, maybe too much since we're rooming together. We were short a man. I guess he told you that?"

"He did."

"I just finished a letter to my wife telling her about our accident with a coral pinnacle, and that we'd be in dry dock for several days for repairs. She'll be happy to hear that. She worries about my safety, and if I'm in port, she knows I'm safe."

"My wife's the same, about safety."

"I was just going to the Wardroom for dinner, dropping this letter at the mail room on the way. Want to join me?"

"Sounds good. I'll follow you. It will take me a day or two to find my way around on my own. I hope to be up to speed before the ship leaves port."

"It may take you longer than you think. I'm still finding new places and I've been aboard for a month."

We entered the Wardroom, taking two seats at the vacant table in the corner. The room had four large rectangular dining tables, two lounge chairs next to a magazine rack, a table with a phonograph and a variety of records, and a radio tuned to the latest news from the mainland. As soon as we sat, a waiter approached, handing us menus. I was surprised to see the Wardroom was serviced by black stewards' mates. The menu had a choice of meat or fish for the main entree, and John and I both selected roast beef, with mashed potatoes and green beans, with iced tea, and apple pie for dessert. The food was served on China plates with silverware, a white linen cloth covering the table. This was better than I thought it would be.

After dinner we returned to our stateroom where John introduced me to Timmons and Davis who were getting ready to head out for the evening.

Connolly decided to join Timmons at the movie on the fantail while Davis said he was going into Honolulu with someone from the radio room for some libations. I begged off the movie saying I wanted to write a letter to Ellen telling her about my first day on the ship when I noticed a large manila envelope lying on my bunk. It was from Ellen addressed in black script to Lieutenant John Ridgeway with a notation underneath my name: Do not bend – photos. I opened the envelope along the edge with the letter opener I found in the desk drawer, carefully removing the contents, two 8 x 10 photos, and a letter. The black and white photo was from our wedding, a picture of us on the steps of St. Bonaventure exiting the church in a shower of rice. The other one was a colorized photo of Ellen with a radiant smile, her straight blonde hair resting on her shoulders of a navy-blue blouse. She was beautiful. My heart ached to hold her and tell her how much I loved and missed her.

Dear John,

I miss you so much. You've been away for less than a month, but it seems like an eternity. How will I survive without you until you return? Make sure you stay safe. I don't want anything to happen to you.

The Schuetzen Park Oktoberfest was cancelled. I think because of the sentiment against those of German heritage in the community. I thought of you, though, with a smile, being dragged to the dance floor by me to do the Chicken Dance. How much fun we had.

I may look for a job closer to home as it is very lonely traveling by myself into the city. When I mentioned that to Jane, she suggested I apply for an opening in the accounts receivable department at the McDermott Lighting Company where she works. She said their business is booming due to the tremendous increase in the sales of lighting products to the various branches of our armed forces. She said you can find their lights on the decks of our naval ships. Maybe you'll find them on your ship. I have an interview next Monday, and the pay is equal to what I'm making at the bank, so I'll be making more take home because of the savings on commuting expense. Wish me luck.

I went to my parents last Sunday for the usual spaghetti and meatball dinner and brought a bottle of Chianti in the wicker basket. My parents now have a collection of candle holders. I'm taking one home for us.

Hope you like the colorized picture. I wanted to surprise you with something special, so I went to a professional photographer someone at work recommended. Kitty said my glamour shot makes me look like a movie star. What do you think? Miriam Hopkins with straight hair?

I miss you so much John. Please write soon.

Your wife, Ellen

P.S. I almost forgot to mention. Everyone says hello, even Charlie McGrath, who I bumped into in Bill's getting fresh lemons for the bar while I was getting a couple of apples to bring to work.

I wanted to properly showcase the pictures Ellen sent so on my next trip to Honolulu I searched for a store that sold frames, but with no luck. I ended up buying two frames from a souvenir shop in Pearl City. I placed the colorized picture by my bunk and stored the other one in my locker, since there wasn't enough space to display both.

19

READY FOR THE ENEMY

SOUTH DAKOTA, AT ANCHOR IN PEARL HARBOR, OCTOBER 1942

During the repairs to *South Dakota*, I learned the operation of the instruments and equipment in the CIC as well as making several more forays to Honolulu to enjoy the Hawaiian music, Coors beer, and sandy beaches of Waikiki and Hanauma Bay. I even gave Myron the "cook's tour" of *South Dakota* which he said was "night and day" compared to his measly little minesweeper.

The repairs were completed on October 9th, and loading of ammunition and stores began the very next day as we prepared to sail. All the activity on the pier was invigorating and made my adrenaline flow. We would be seeing action soon, and I'll admit, I was fearful about what was to come, of the unknown and how I would react to it. The enemy had large guns and planes that dropped bombs, but so did we. I just prayed our armor cladding would protect us; and that the engineers who designed *South Dakota* were right in their assumptions.

The scuttlebutt was we would be leaving Pearl Harbor soon with *Enterprise*, but before that occurred, I had to send a letter to Ellen telling her not to worry about my safety.

15 October 1942

Hi Honey,

The repairs were completed last week, and we went to sea for a couple of days just to make sure there were no leaks. Scuttlebutt around the ship is we will soon join a task force to engage the enemy. Don't worry about me. The ship is well protected with thick, armor-cladding in all the right places to protect us against enemy bombs. I will be safe. I'm sure of it.

This may interest you. The ship's store—besides selling the usual shaving supplies, toothpaste, and soap—has perfume and silk stockings, which they picked up in Colon, Panama when the ship passed through the canal. Who would've thought we had such items in our inventory. There's a choice of perfumes, Mais Oui, Plantino Dano, and Tabu, which I know you like, and so do I, so I purchased two bottles to keep you in supply. Just don't attract too many men at work. You're mine. If you want one of the other perfumes, or stockings that you can't get at home, let me know. Jane and Kitty may want something.

I've been aboard the ship long enough to fall into a routine. Our day is divided into seven Watches. Most of the time I've been on the Morning watch from 0400 to 0800 (that's 4:00 a.m. to 8:00 a.m.) after which I'm off for eight hours before my next watch, the First Dog watch from 1600 to 1800 (4:00 p.m. to 6:00 p.m.). I usually have dinner in the Wardroom after that and then head to the fantail to see that night's movie. Tonight, it was "Sergeant York" starring Gary Cooper. It was a great war movie, about a real hero fighting in the trenches. It made me think that my decision to join the Navy was the right one. You'll find this funny. I was sitting next to my bunkmate Timmons during the movie and couldn't resist. I had to get an independent opinion, so I asked him if I reminded him of Gary Cooper. He laughed; thought I was kidding. Are you sure about my resemblance to him? Before I forget, you do vaguely remind me of the actress Miriam Hopkins, but you're much prettier. Even my bunkmates think so.

Most of my free time is spent penning letters to you and my friends or working on the accounting correspondence course. My schedule is full but, believe it or not, leaves plenty of time for sleep.

You'd like this. I don't have to worry about oversleeping. There are no alarm clocks on the ship, so when it is my turn for watch, the ODD (officer of the deck) sends a messenger to my stateroom to shake me awake if I were asleep so that I'd be on time. Thus far, though, I'm always ready to go when the messenger arrives, and sometimes I arrive on duty before I'm due. You know, I've always been early to arrive before the appointed time. Also, you'll like this, if it's the Morning watch, breakfast is brought to me from the Crew's mess. Almost as good as breakfast in bed. Life aboard the ship is pretty good, no complaints.

Well, the messenger sent by the ODD just arrived. I wasn't early for duty today because I was writing this letter to you. I'll say goodbye here, and like I said, don't worry about me, I plan to stay safe.

Love always, John

We left Pearl Harbor with *Enterprise* and several destroyers to meet on October 23rd with *Hornet*; heavy cruisers *Portland, Northampton,* and *Pensacola*; light cruisers *San Juan, San Diego,* and *Juneau*; and several destroyers. The combined force, designated TF 51 under the command of Rear Adm. Thomas Kinkaid, was tasked with stopping Japanese troop landings seeking to reclaim Guadalcanal.

20

NAVAL TRADITION

Even though we were enroute to engage the enemy, an important naval tradition had to be honored before that happened. Navies mark the first time a sailor crosses the equator in a "Line Crossing" ceremony. Portuguese explorer Ferdinand Magellan created the passage rite to test a sailor's seaworthiness when he circumnavigated the earth in 1522. Sailors ever since have endured the ceremony, transforming from a "Slimy" Pollywog to a "Trusty" Shellback.

Thomas Gatch, captain of *South Dakota*, set aside time before our looming date with the enemy to ensure the ritual continued. This was a good thing because it broke the tension mounting among the crew. The ritual began the evening before we crossed the equator on "Pollywog Day." Our executive officer Ben Gerwick played King Neptune, "visiting" the ship with his lovely, but hairy queen, Amphitrite; and his first assistant, Davy Jones. They were to judge the charges against the Pollywogs posing as sailors.

The festivities commenced in the crew's mess with the Pollywogs providing entertainment for the pleasure and amusement of the king and his court. The program contained comedy, song, and dance, and ended with an impromptu beauty pageant. Most of the performers had theatrical experience gained from high school plays, marching bands, and dance combos. Since I had no talents in those areas whatsoever, I volunteered to direct the show but was told that Pat Rohan had that job, having experience before the war managing his hometown theater. That left me to assist with the costumes as I was not so good at telling jokes. The comedian job, anyway, was already filled.

With the lights dimmed, the show began. Emcee Warren Yates approached the center stage spotlight to introduce Don Kelly, a professional comic who had performed at various venues in the Catskills. With sweat showing on his brow, from the realization he was facing a tough audience, Kelly took the microphone, opening with this joke:

Having passed the enlistment physical, John was asked by the doctor: "Why do you want to join the Navy, son?"

"My father said it'd be a good idea, sir."

"Oh! And what does your father do?"

"He's a general in the Army, sir."

Muted laughter (from the Pollywog performers standing in the wings) was drowned out by the groans from the Shellbacks. King Neptune's frown of disapproval, and thumbs down motion, said more was expected.

Undaunted, Kelly—the professional I'm sure he was, playing to an openly hostile crowd—pressed on.

"Well," snarled the tough old Navy chief to the bewildered seaman. "I suppose after you're discharged from the Navy, you'll be waiting for me to die so you can piss on my grave."

"Not me, Chief," the sailor replied. "Once I'm out of the Navy, I'm never waiting in line again."

That joke was an icebreaker; laughter was heard throughout the mess. King Neptune tried to hide a smile.

With more confidence, Don continued.

A Navy chief and an admiral were sitting in the barbershop. They were both finished with their shaves when the barber reached for aftershave to put on their faces.

The admiral shouted, "Hey, don't put that stuff on me! My wife will think I've been in a whorehouse!"

The barber turned to the chief, who said, "Go ahead, splash it on. My wife doesn't know what the inside of a whorehouse smells like."

That joke, I was glad to see, brought the house down; roars of raucous laughter erupted. Kelly pulled off a strong performance. But would it be enough to gain us some relief from tomorrow's hazing?

One day while on leave the lonely Navy sailor went to a bar. He began talking to the beautiful woman sitting alone next to him and, after a while, asked her to his hotel room. She agreed.

During the sex, the sailor looked down at her and proudly asked, "How am I doing?"

She looked at him with a bewildered face, and said, "Are you kidding me? I'll give it to you in nautical terms that you'll understand."

Anxious for the compliment about his sexual prowess, he replied, "Great."

"You're doing about three knots."

Puzzled, the sailor asked, "What do you mean?"

"You're not hard, you're not pleasuring, and you're not getting your money back. Is that clear enough, sailor?"

The crowd was in stitches, clambering for one more joke. He finished with this:

A captain notices a light in the distance, on a collision course with his ship. He turns on his Aldis lamp and sends the signal, "Change your course, 10 degrees west."

The light signals back, "Change yours, 10 degrees east."

The captain gets a little annoyed. He signals, "I'm a US Navy captain. You must change your course, sir."

The light signals back, "I'm a Seaman First Class. You must change your course, sir."

Now the captain is irate. He signals, "I'm a battleship. Out of my way. I'm not changing my course."

The light signals back a final message: "I'm a lighthouse. Your call."

Kelly stepped from the stage to rousing applause. Captain Gatch, standing in the rear of the mess, appeared to be laughing the hardest.

Next up, Yates introduced The Pollywog Dance Band, who opened with Glenn Miller's theme "Moonlight Serenade," transitioning to Tommy Dorsey's "I'll Never Smile Again," followed by "I've Got a Gal in Kalamazoo," and "Chattanooga Choo Choo." The atmosphere was lively until seaman John Sinclair sang with feeling Vera Lynn's hit "Till We Meet Again," the room turning eerily quiet, everyone wishing they were home with their loved ones. I closed my eyes and thought of Ellen and our strolls through Forest Park, the camaraderie of our friends at Charlie McGrath's Tavern, and Sunday dinners with her parents. Sinclair, coaxed for another song, sang an emotional rendition of "I'll Be Seeing You," which led to the whole room joining him in chorus. I believe a few tears may have been shed.

The upbeat mood returned when the band struck up Glenn Miller's "In the Mood" to close the show, and several sailors in drag jumped on the floor to Lindy Hop as if they were at the Glen Island Casino. King Neptune, seizing the opportunity for some impromptu fun, told those in female drag to go on to the stage to compete for the title of Miss *South Dakota*. Needless for me to say, the sailor with the biggest boobs won. He was quite fetching, I'll admit, wearing a grass hula skirt with a yellow and white plastic flower lei around his neck. The long, dark-haired wig he wore (who knew where he got that) and his shaved, nylon-covered legs added to the illusion of a beautiful, barefoot native Hawaiian girl. "You're prettier than Hilo Hattie," someone yelled, at which point I thought that sailor had been at sea too long (I later found out he wasn't kidding).

Despite the king's obvious enjoyment for the night's performances, the

Pollywogs were ordered to report the next morning after breakfast to Davy Jones to receive their subpoena and stand before the court to answer the charges brought against them by the Shellbacks. No one was spared, not even Kelly for his stellar comedy routine or Ken Peterson for winning the Miss South Dakota title.

22 October 1942

Ellen,

There's a naval tradition hundreds of years old that I wasn't aware of until we were at sea. It's known as Crossing Day. That's the day when a sailor, called a Pollywog, crosses the equator for the first time to become a Shellback. No one is spared from this ritual, not even an admiral.

The weather for our ceremony was sunny and cloudless, with temperatures in the mid-80s. "Perfect weather," I heard one Shellback remark, "for the tortures we have planned." I knew what to expect—at least I thought I did based upon the continuous taunts from the Shellbacks after we left Pearl. I'll admit, the whole ceremony, now that it's over, and I look back, was a real gasser, despite being on the receiving end of the hazing.

Although the day began normally enough, I had an uncomfortable feeling something was about to happen soon, but when? How do you know the events of the day are underway? Well, I soon received the answer to my question. Just as a group of us sat down in the mess hall for breakfast, the Shellbacks appeared, ordering us back to our cabins to redress with our uniforms worn inside out and backward. Try doing that with your clothes. Easier said than done. When we returned to the breakfast table, unbeknownst to us, the cook, while we were redressing, added a heavy dose of chili sauce and jalapeno pepper to the egg omelets, making them so hot to the tongue that everyone scrambled to the water cooler for a drink to extinguish the fire in their mouth. The Shellbacks stood over us to make sure we ate our eggs, all of them. And that was only the beginning.

After breakfast we marched to the fantail to appear before King Neptune and his Queen, Amphitrite, both wearing elaborate crowns of seashells (trinkets purchased in Pearl City). Davy Jones, with a leering smirk, stood astride a long canvas chute filled with rotting garbage, where he read the charges against each Pollywog. I forgot what my offense was but remember he handed a paper to the judge, who intently reviewed it for several seconds before pronouncing, in a bellowing voice, "Guilty." With a thunderous pound of his gavel on the table, which shook from the blow, he loudly said, "Give him the works." I thought, what will that be? The last time I heard that phrase was for the toppings on my hamburger. Well, I soon found out.

After my guilty verdict was called out, my punishment was administered. I bent down on my hands and knees and entered the chute of garbage while the Shellbacks spanked my butt as I crawled through the tunnel of waste. When I exited the chute, I was tossed into a canvas tub overflowing with axle grease, cigarette butts, gray paint, and other garbage of unknown origin, to "cleanse" the dirt on me from the garbage chute. Once I finished my swim (King Neptune called it a "refreshing dip in the pool"), I received a haircut from the Royal Barber, who gave me a short, uneven trim. I'm sure I no longer look like Gary Cooper. Anyway, I was now deemed suitable to be received by King Neptune and his lovely queen, who thrust her smelly foot in my face for me to kiss. I almost puked, but luckily that concluded the ceremony. I'm happy I earned my Shellback certificate, which I'll make sure not to lose so that I have proof of what I endured.

I had to go to the Engine Room for diesel oil, which I applied to a rag and scrubbed all over my body. That was the only way to remove the grease and paint. After that, I took a shower for about fifteen minutes before I felt clean enough to put my uniform back on.

A photographer took pictures, so I'll make sure to get a set to send to you. Despite all the hazing, it was good natured, and I must say a lot of fun.

I'll write again soon.

Love you, John

With my letter written, ready to be mailed, I returned to the reality that we were on our way to engaging the enemy. I hoped I was ready for what was to come.

21

BATTLE AT SANTA CRUZ

CORAL SEA, 25 OCTOBER 1942

One of our scout planes spotted a Japanese carrier in the Coral Sea north of the Santa Cruz Islands about 350 nautical miles from our position. That was beyond the reach of our carriers so Kinkaid ordered *Enterprise*, *Hornet*, and the rest of the convoy to steam toward them at flank speed hoping to get within striking distance for our planes. When we neared the presumed enemy position, *Enterprise* dispatched twenty aircraft, but the Japanese, having sensed the intended strike, turned north out of range. Our planes returned without finding or engaging the enemy and the day passed waiting for the enemy to reveal its next move.

I had an inside view of the activities taking place in our cat-and-mouse game with the enemy while on Middle watch in the CIC. I monitored the radar screen closely for any hint of their position. I knew they were out there, somewhere. Bleary-eyed from watching an empty screen for over two hours searching for tell-tale blips without luck, the grit of tiredness quickly evaporated when I noticed a mass entering the screen, moving our way. The time 0250. The Japanese had reversed course and were steaming toward us. I beckoned Collins over, "Look at this, Jason," pointing to the screen. "The Japs have changed course. They're coming for us."

"Seems they're looking to engage," he said. "I'd guess that by 0500 they'll be 200 miles from our position, close enough for them to launch their planes and for us to launch ours."

"Your right based upon their present course and speed."

"I'm going to alert Gatch. You pass this information to the bridge so they're up to speed when the captain joins them."

"Aye, aye, sir."

Suddenly a ringing alarm broadcast throughout the ship: "This is not a drill. This is not a drill. General Quarters. General Quarters. All hands man your battle stations. All hands man your battle stations."

An adrenaline rush from the announcement spurred me to monitor the radar screen with heightened scrutiny, issuing updates on the enemy's changing position as they approached.

I hoped we would surprise them by launching our planes first, reaching their carriers before they'd launched their strike force and reached us. That was wishful thinking. As Captain Gatch explained to those in the CIC, "The element of surprise is very limited, probably nonexistent. It would be a success if we reached them before they launched most of their planes. But I don't see that happening. If we can inflict damage to their flight decks to thwart their returning planes from safely landing, that would be a victory for us."

"Yes, Collins?"

"Captain, when will *Enterprise* and *Hornet* launch?"

"I'm sure Kincaid will pull the trigger soon as both sides are almost within striking distance of each other, if not already there. If we see a mass of blips coming our way before we launch our planes, we will have waited too long. Bottom line, the Japs will be awaiting our arrival as we will be awaiting theirs. It'll take time for the planes of both sides to reach their targets so each side will be closely tracking the radar blips."

"Jason, look. *Hornet* has been attacked. I'd say fifty to sixty planes based upon the myriad streaking images."

"You're right. They're hitting them with everything they have, dive bombers, torpedo bombers, and fighter planes."

"When do you think we'll get hit? I don't see anything coming our way or towards *Enterprise*."

"The only reason we haven't been attacked yet is due to the rain squall we're in."

"What squall?"

"Take a look outside."

I walked to the door and exited the passageway for a quick peek. Collins was right; we were in a heavy downpour surrounded by cover of low-lying funnel clouds. The storm was clearing, evident by the blue skies on the horizon, and soon its protective canopy would no longer conceal us.

I hurried back to the CIC and resumed monitoring the radar screen, intent on determining the enemy's position and whether a strike force was coming for us. Taking in a wider view, I was puzzled by what I saw. The radar showed several distinct clusters, which I believed could be four enemy carrier groups—an armada larger than we thought, and certainly more than we could throw at them. That was a terrifying thought. Fearful of that prospect, I beckoned Collins back to the radar screen to confirm my analysis. "Sir, I'm seeing four distinct battle groups. What do you think?"

Collins, surveying the clustered blips, with a thoughtful hand on his chin, nodded agreement, but before he could utter a word, thunderous noise and vibrations shook the room. "Shit, we're being hit!" The lights shuddered, and the radar screens blinked. We were under heavy enemy fire. The screens flickered back to life, filled with streaking comets flaring in every direction. Dive bombers and fighter planes were attacking from every angle, swerving in and out, over and across–dropping bombs, and firing machine guns and torpedoes. Unable to follow what I was seeing on the screen now that the enemy was directly upon us, I left the CIC and went to the bridge to observe the action. No sooner had I entered the room to see *Enterprise* launching the last of her planes while under attack by a squadron of fighters that emerged from the cover of a blinding sun. The Japanese were shooting the planes on her deck, resulting in the loss of two Avenger torpedo bombers and three Wildcat fighters as well as two Avengers and a Wildcat that just lifted off but forced to return.

Cheers on the bridge erupted when we learned our two scout planes landed bombs on the deck of the carrier *Zuiho* that prevented her aircraft from taking off. Carriers *Junyo, Shokaku,* and *Zuikaku,* though, were still in business, having launched approximately 110 aircraft seeking our utter destruction.

Enterprise and *Hornet* began their attack at 0820. They launched over seventy aircraft, an array of dive bombers, torpedo bombers, and fighters, streaking toward the enemy 150 miles away. Had they inflicted damage to add to that administered by our two scout planes? We were awaiting word.

Ten miles from our position, *Hornet* was the first to take it on the chin, coming under heavy attack when two large bombs ripped open her flight deck, killing ninety. Engulfed in flames by the time the enemy departed at 0920, she was in serious trouble. Her returning planes had to divert to *Enterprise,* but those landings were abruptly halted when another wave of enemy aircraft arrived at 1000, causing all our fuel-depleted returning aircraft to ditch in the ocean, the pilots hoping for rescue by our escorting destroyers.

The battle was in full swing by 0900 and with *Hornet* out of action, the Japanese concentrated their attack on *Enterprise.* At 1005, I counted over twenty enemy dive bombers emerging from the scud clouds that moved in. They swarmed from all angles, dropping bombs and firing torpedoes. It was a fury of aggression I never could have imagined; the blast sounds louder than a hand grenade exploding in one's ear. The ship shuddered like a 9.0 earthquake as our antiaircraft guns returned fire. Despite our efforts, some of the enemy penetrated our defenses. Two five-hundred-pound bombs dropped on *Enterprise's* flight deck, causing significant damage, killing forty and injuring scores more.

We steamed parallel to *Enterprise*, separated by two thousand feet, defending her from the enemy onslaught. Taking advantage of our closeness, a Japanese fighter emerged from the low-lying clouds, flying several feet over the water between our two ships. If we shot at him, the fire from our 40 mm guns would have torn into *Enterprise's* port side. He was one clever kamikaze that escaped.

Another wave of enemy torpedo planes broke through the low-lying clouds, around 1010, sixteen in all. They splintered into two groups, half attacking *Enterprise* and the other half attacking us and *Portland*. Our sleeping antiaircraft guns sparked back to life upon their return, spraying a hail of bullets at the invading planes. One plane dodged the unrelenting maze of fire from our guns, coming straight for the bridge. He was so close I could see the white of his eyes and his yellow, cigarette-stained teeth below his mustached manic grin. Our gunners, by the grace of God, hit him just before he reached the tower. I could read the screaming words on his lips, *Tenno Heika Banzai*, "Long live His Majesty, the Emperor," just before the nose of his plane swept upward ninety-degrees from the barrage of bullets, the tail tipping back to reveal the lethal torpedo strapped to the underside. With a chorus of cheers from those on our bridge, he dropped into the ocean like a dead weight, the burning hulk vanishing in a wisp of black smoke that bubbled from the water's surface.

Seconds later, another plane careened toward us from the starboard side, following its comrade's path. It was taken out just before it reached the bridge. The wing tip hit the water, causing the plane to cartwheel like a dancing gymnast across the water. It crashed with a jolting thud against the side of the ship.

From my view on the bridge, I could see our tower being ripped to shreds by the steady stream of fire from the enemy's invading guns. Their bullets ignited clumps of our protective armor plating, producing sparks and flying shrapnel that ricocheted in every direction imaginable. The thunderous return of our antiaircraft guns lit up the sky like Fourth of July fireworks.

When a third plane came swerving toward the bridge through the hail of our antiaircraft fire, I remembered my promise to Ellen to remain safe. I quickly ducked back into the CIC for its protection from the flying shrapnel and ricocheting bullets.

Then, suddenly, it became eerily quiet. For a split second, I wondered if it was because I moved inside, away from the loud blast of the gunfire. That wasn't the case. The Japanese had departed, leaving us no one to shoot at. The attack was over. The enemy, depleted of ammunition and low on fuel, returned to their hornet's nest.

My ears were still ringing with the noise of battle, despite the lull in action. I ventured back on to the bridge to survey the damage. The silence broke when a third enemy strike of dive bombers and fighter planes suddenly emerged at 1130.

Captain Gatch left the bridge and moved on to the wing to observe the action. Unsure why, I followed in his footsteps. Maybe I was trying to get close to him, to see what he was seeing. Our antiaircraft guns came back to life, seeking targets. Despite the torrential rain of bullets they fired, one enemy dive bomber, shearing sharply to the right, miraculously barreled unscathed through the hail of bullets, coming straight at us. Too stunned to move, I stood petrified, watching the five-hundred-pound bomb attached to his underbelly drop onto our number 2 turret. Shutting my eyes, both hands over my ears, I braced for the impact. A deafening explosion erupted, shaking the bridge. The thick armor plating of the turret withstood the blast but shed shrapnel in all directions. Two of the barrels of our sixteen-inch guns were bent–not that it mattered in this cat-and-dog fight between planes and antiaircraft guns.

A wave of blood splashed across my face, the metallic taste dripping from my lips. Stunned, I dropped behind the bulwark, seeking the protection of the steel plating. A loud moan followed. Next to me, the captain is splayed on his back where he fell, lying in a mushrooming pool of blood. *I'm okay,*

I realized. *The splatter on my face must be from him.* I used my shirt sleeve to wipe the blood from my eyes. Then I quickly ripped my shirt off, the buttons popping. I frantically wrapped it around the gash on the captain's neck to staunch the bleeding. Looking for help, I yelled over the thunder of the enemy planes and exploding bullets, "Zeigler! The captain has been hit. We have to move him to safety!" He heard my call and crawled over. Together, crouching low along the bulwark, we dragged the captain inside the bridge. I leaned him upright against the wall to stem the flow of blood. Anxious that he may die from his wound, I implore Zeigler, "Get the doctor, right away. Tell him the captain is seriously injured and may be dying. We need to get his wound closed before he bleeds out." With sweat pouring profusely from his forehead, Zeigler raced to the door, stumbling into the passageway in search of the doctor. I turned back to the captain, who was conscious and moaning in great pain. I applied pressure on his wound to stem the gushing flow, the entire front of his shirt red with blood. Despite his serious injury, he groaned, "What's the status?"

"Sir, you were hit by shrapnel from a bomb that hit the number 2 turret. The doctor is on his way. Just hang in there."

"I'm sure it looks worse than it is. Who am I talking to?"

"Lieutenant Ridgeway, sir, from the CIC. I was next to you when the bomb hit. You're wearing my shirt." That brought a grimaced smile to his face. *I don't know what made me say that. Nervous energy, I guess.* Somewhat revived, despite the shock, as the blood loss stemmed. He regained his senses and, with authority, assumed command of the ship, issuing orders to those officers on the bridge while propped against the bulkhead until the doctor arrived. He kept command until the battle was over as the doctor sutured the wound. After he finished sewing him up, the doctor told him, "Captain, you were very lucky. The shrapnel just missed your carotid artery. The quick thinking of the lieutenant stemmed the flow of blood. I sutured the wound, and the bleeding has stopped. It will take a few days before the pain lets up. I can give you pain killers to make you more comfortable."

"That's okay, Doc. I'll live with the pain," he moaned. "It'll remind me to return the favor the next time we engage the enemy."

The doctor, turning to me, said, "I think he'll survive. You saved his life."

The battle spanned almost three hours from beginning to end, from when the first enemy assault arrived to when the third enemy assault departed. However, the actual combat amounted to about only one hour of intense fighting. Within that one hour, there was unlimited fury and destruction. Our gunners shot down many of their planes, evidenced by the black balls splashing into the water all around us, disappearing in a smoky fizzle.

South Dakota acquitted herself well in her first battle encounter, credited with downing thirty-two enemy aircraft in three waves of attack. After the captain was taken to medical for a closer check of his injury, I walked along the main deck surveying the damage. A couple hours had passed since the last enemy plane left, but the aftermath reeked of the acrid smell of spent gunpowder. I swore I could still hear the deafening sounds of the enemy's guns and bombs and the return fire from our antiaircraft guns. I closed my eyes, willing the relentless pounding in my head to fade away. The destruction that surrounded me was a sober reminder of the hell of war. I thanked God I was in one piece, having been close to the specter of death when that lump of shrapnel tore into Captain Gatch.

A crewman who saw me standing next to the captain when he was hit, came over. He recounted a story about a piece of shrapnel that hit the alidade and deflected into the charthouse, where a small sliver pierced the heart of one of the people working in the room, who fell mortally wounded onto the floor with seemingly no external wound. I was glad to be alive.

Because of the damage we suffered at Santa Cruz, *South Dakota* was dispatched to Noumea (New Caledonia). It was the nearest port where the bullet holes and shrapnel punctures that permeated our main deck superstructure like Swiss-cheese could be repaired.

★

I was returning to my stateroom after dinner with Collins, when I bumped into Davis just walking out the door. "Connolly and I are going to tonight's movie, This Gun for Hire. Want to join us?" he said.

"No, thanks, Pat. I saw that movie on Clymer, so I thought I would use this time before my watch later to write a letter to Ellen."

"I just finished a letter to my old lady, so now the movie. By the way, is it any good? — Not that it makes a difference."

"I liked it. Alan Ladd plays a sadistic killer-for-hire who goes crazy when he learns his latest hit was paid off in marked bills, while Veronica Lake, the movie's 'eye candy,' tries to calm him down. She's easy to look at, even prettier than our own Miss South Dakota."

He laughed at my comparison. "Sounds better than some of the other movies we've seen. I'm not sure I know who Veronica Lake is but if she's prettier than Miss South Dakota, which isn't saying much, I'll take it."

Davis headed off to collect Connolly from the Wardroom, and that left me alone in the empty stateroom. Turning on the overhead light, I sat at the desk, gathering a pen and writing paper from the drawer, thinking about what I would say.

29 October 1942

Dear Ellen,

By the time you receive this letter, you will have undoubtedly read about our encounter with the enemy in the newspaper. I haven't a scratch, so don't worry about me. While the battle spanned three hours from start to finish, the actual fighting was only an hour or so, but it was intense. The ship's armor cladding did the job and believe it or not, the most serious damage we sustained was from an accidental collision with one of our own ships after the battle was over. We are heading to the nearest port where the repairs can be made. It will probably take several days to patch all the holes we have but, when they're done, we *should be as good as new.*

There were casualties, but they were from the aircraft carriers who were the main targets of the enemy.

You never know what the future holds, but rest assured I'll do my best to play it safe. If anything ever happens to me, though, please know you have my blessing to start a new life with someone else. You deserve that happiness without regret.

Your loving husband, John

I wanted to tell Ellen more, much more. I wanted to tell her about the destruction and death suffered by both sides from the exploding bombs, ricocheting bullets, and flying shrapnel. I wanted to tell her about the captain and how I was standing next to him when he was hit by shrapnel. But I couldn't. I promised her I would stay safe, so I didn't want her to worry needlessly when nothing could be done to change things. *Someday*, I thought, *after the war is over, and I've returned home, I'll tell her all about it. Just not now.* Finished with my letter, and with the grit of tiredness in my eyes, I climbed into my bunk. I reflected again on the battle at Santa Cruz. My head still ringing, I hoped a good night's sleep would make it go away.

22

LICKING OUR WOUNDS

Vestal, a tired and weary repair ship–by all appearances–greeted our arrival. An onslaught of workers clambered over our main deck like a colony of ants patching and welding bullet holes and puncture wounds. The repairs would take days as the damage was extensive. With regards to our two big warped sixteen-inch guns, Captain Gatch (recovering from his neck injury but still in command of the ship), determined their lack would not hamper our readiness for the next assignment. He must have based his decision upon the battle at Santa Cruz where those guns were never fired. Our antiaircraft guns were the main combat weapons that day, against the enemy's fighter planes and torpedo bombers.

I bumped into Jeffrey Robertson, one of our gunnery officers entering the Wardroom the same time I was meeting Collins for supper, so I asked him if we would be handicapped by the loss of those guns.

"Not really," he answered, "even though they're the main guns on the ship and the reason we're called a battleship. We still have plenty of firepower with all the antiaircraft and five-inch guns, and don't forget, we still have seven working sixteen-inchers."

"Yeah, you're right."

"The action at Santa Cruz centered on our antiaircraft guns against enemy planes, and that fight is not accomplished with sixteen-inch guns, or even five-inch guns for that matter. Those guns may be obsolete in today's warfare of planes and aircraft carriers."

"That's what I was thinking," I agreed.

"Yet, in the event we do need our sixteen-inch guns in a showdown with another battleship or heavy cruiser, I believe the training our gun crews have received using the latest equipment gives us the edge. We will be ready for them, I'm sure of it."

"I assume that's why the captain is willing to forgo those gun replacements, opting to be ready for the next assignment."

"I'm sure that's his reasoning. I do have one concern, though, but it's based upon rumor. The scuttlebutt among those in the gunnery unit is the Japs prefer fighting at night and train for it, so if we were to engage them, I hope it's during the day."

"That rumor aside, the capability of our men at Santa Cruz shooting down so many enemy planes demonstrates our skill. That gives me comfort."

"Me too."

Noumea was not a tropical paradise like Honolulu, with luxury hotels on white sandy beaches, but from where we just came from, it would do. Rich in mineral deposits of nickel and chromium, the island had been an important source of raw material to Japan before the war, but those days were over. The island, convenient to Guadalcanal, was an important naval base for us.

While our repairs were underway, I went ashore, intending to do a little exploring. I soon discovered there was nothing worth seeing, so I didn't venture too far from the pier. The natives, known as Kanaks, spoke what sounded like French to me. Their women, wearing only grass skirts, approached those who appeared interested in buying a souvenir and appeared quite proficient in selling their goods despite the language barrier. I resisted purchasing another native-made craft, content with my outrigger canoe. If I looked hard enough, I was sure I could have purchased a shrunken head from the local witch doctor. That would have made a great conversation piece for the coffee table in my parlor at home. The Kanak men were scary in appearance, another reason I stayed away. They were the last sort of person I'd want to run into alone in a dark urban alley. They wore what looked like war paint on their faces and carried sharp spears. Quite intimidating, for sure.

When the repairs were completed, we left Noumea with *Enterprise* to rendezvous with the battleship *Washington* and destroyers *Walke, Benham, Preston,* and *Gwin.* A new task force was being formed under the command of Vice Adm. Willis Lee aboard *Washington.* The mission: prevent Japanese troop landings from recapturing Guadalcanal.

We were to intercept and engage the enemy on Friday the thirteenth of November. I prayed that superstitious day would be a bad omen for the Japanese, not us.

It took several days to reach our target after leaving Noumea on November 7th. Activity on the ship was eerily quiet, everyone going about their jobs, the days passing without incident. If one didn't know better, one would've thought we were on a routine shakedown cruise–but I knew better and felt the undercurrent of tension that simmered below the surface. The shock of Santa Cruz made everyone aware of the danger, fearing the next battle could be much worse.

After dinner on the twelfth, trying to wring the nervous tension from my system, I went to the movie to see The Maltese Falcon starring Humphrey Bogart and Mary Astor. Even though I'd seen the movie with Ellen at the Orpheum, it was such an excellent detective yarn I was glad to see it again. When a good movie comes along, everyone shows up even if they'd already seen it. I especially enjoyed the interaction between Sydney Greenstreet and Peter Lorre, having forgotten how good those two supporting actors were. Their chemistry with Bogart made the movie. I wasn't a big fan of Mary Astor, though, and would have preferred Miriam Hopkins in that role. I figured I was just partial to blondes. The movie helped me to forget for a while our expected date with the enemy tomorrow.

When the movie ended, I returned to my stateroom for some shut eye before my watch. Tomorrow promised to be a big day, and I needed to be clearheaded and alert. I went to pull the blanket down when I noticed a letter sitting on the desk. It was for me, from Ellen.

November 7, 1942

Dear John,

I received with joy your letters of October 15th and 22nd, but I'm worried about the outcome of the rumored battle engagement you mentioned. Please tell me everything is okay, and that you are safe and unharmed.

I can't wait to see those pictures of the Line Crossing ceremony. Sounds like it was a lot of fun, that is, for those administering the punishment. Well, you only must do it once. I'll get a frame for your Shellback Certificate so you can hang it next to your diploma from St. John's.

I know you are interested in my daily routine. Well, it will be changing. No more lonely subway rides into the city to Manufacturers Trust. I was offered a position in the accounts receivable department at McDermott Lighting Company where Jane works, and the pay is more than I earned at the bank. I gave my two-week notice and will start my new job Monday, November 23rd. The bank didn't want me to leave, and offered a raise, but I said I already accepted the job and didn't want to backout on it. They understood. They are giving me a farewell party before I leave.

So, you know, I buy the newspaper at Bill's in the morning

on the way to work to learn whatever I can about the war in the Pacific, and when I return home from work in the evening, I listen to the news on the radio for the latest war updates. Thankfully, I've heard nothing to give me concern about South Dakota, so I pray that I'm right and that you are safe. I cannot imagine you not returning home to me from this war and a life without you.

Usually on the weekends, I see Jane and Kitty, and we talk about what's going on in the war with our men, trading stories. Everyone says they miss your newsletter, so I plan to carry on with what you started. Jane and Kitty offered to help with the typing.

Sunday afternoons, I've been going to my parents for dinner. They always ask about you. I mentioned to them that you even thought about my well-being for perfume and nylons from the ship's store. My father was surprised that these items were in the store of a battleship. I told him it must be the new Navy. I would love another bottle of Tabu, and if you can still get several pairs of nylons, that would be great. I want to give a couple pairs each to Jane and Kitty. You know, us working girls must look good for the job.

I pray this letter finds you safe.

Your loving wife, Ellen

23

BATTLE AT SAVO ISLAND

*B*ong, bong, bong echoed loudly throughout the ship. I looked at my watch: 1100. The announcement over the speaker system blared, "General Quarters, General Quarters, all hands man your battle stations!" A mad scramble by the crew to their assigned stations followed, and then we waited. Nothing happened. It was a false alarm, determined to be an errant torpedo from a lone Japanese submarine. There was no enemy armada in sight. The afternoon passed without incident.

Finished with dinner, I walked into my stateroom to find Timmons at the desk penning a letter. "Bob, sorry to interrupt, but do you have a minute? I want your opinion."

"Sure, I was just addressing the envelope. What's up?"

"It was so quiet today. Where do you think the Japs are?"

"Not sure. My watch this morning started with that alert from *Trout* about a massive Jap naval force heading to Guadalcanal, but no carriers were sighted, which is telling. Where they are now, we don't know."

"I heard that," I responded.

While we were pondering the enemy's whereabouts, an announcement was broadcast to the crew. Our mission changed from preventing troop landings to that of defeating a Japanese naval force seeking to recapture Guadalcanal.

"Sounds like we'll be going against a large naval force, warships as compared to troop transports. And, if they've no carriers, this battle will be different than the one at Santa Cruz. It'll be fought with the sixteen-inchers, and that could prove dire for us with those two sixteen-inchers out of commission. You agree?"

"I hate to say it, but yes. Our armament is less than full strength and we might be outnumbered."

The rest of Friday the thirteenth passed without incident. No enemy was found. Nothing happened.

I awoke to Reveille the next day at 0515, and while getting dressed, General Quarters boomed throughout the ship at 0535. There was no time for breakfast, but I had no appetite. My nerves were raw, and I was on edge, anxious for what would transpire. I was sure we'd be engaging the enemy today (just a day later than we were told), and against a force much tougher than we thought.

The waiting game began. Tensions among the crew were high because of the frequent sounding of General Quarters intermittently throughout the day, spurred by on-and-off alerts about enemy aircraft. When we neared Guadalcanal, the entire crew sat permanently fixed at their battle stations ready for action, anxious to unload their ammo at the enemy when given the order.

With the sun fading into the sea, dipping below the horizon, word passed to the crew that we would be in attack position at 0000 (Midnight). I was on Middle watch, but with too much nervous energy to wait until then, I reported to the CIC after dinner just as General Quarters sounded again at 2100. Most of the men were still in battle position from earlier soundings, having never left their station.

I went over to Connolly, who was peering intently at the radar screen.

Interrupting his concentration, I asked, "What do you see?"

"Nothing. I'm glad you're here. Watch the screen for a minute while I rub the tiredness out of my eyes. I need to be alert when the action starts."

"Catch some air on the bridge wing," I said. "I've got you covered."

"Thanks, Ridge."

"Well, if we're still on for midnight, we have another three hours before the action starts, so take your time." Adding silently, *I hope we deliver the first blow*. It will be pitch black then, the only light from that of the moon. Then I remembered the scuttlebutt that they prefer fighting at night, and that worried me.

Returning to the radar screen, Connolly exclaimed, "There's a concentration of blips moving into view! It must be the force *Trout* saw yesterday. They're about fifteen miles away and heading towards us. Ridge, look!"

I moved next to him to study the mass of blips on the radar screen, and looking at my watch, noted the time, 2200. *Maybe we'll engage them before midnight*, I thought. Then I noticed a change on the screen.

"John, the mass is breaking up. I see two clusters. What do you think?" I asked.

"Yes, their force is splitting into two groups."

"I'd say the larger mass is the main group while the smaller one is a sweeping group that appears to be setting up to attack our flank." After an analysis of the movements on the screen, we determined the main force centered around the battleship *Kirishima,* with Admiral Kondo aboard, sailing with heavy cruisers *Atago, Takao*, and *Nagara*, and destroyers *Asagumo, Hatsuyuki, Inazuma, Shirayuki, Samidare*, and *Teruzuki,* while the smaller force centered around the light cruiser *Sendai* and destroyers *Ayanami, Shikinami*, and *Uranami*.

Connolly called Collins to the screen, and after reviewing the movement for a few minutes, he agreed with our assessment. "I'll bet their flanking unit will be the first to attack," he said. "If we take the bait and turn toward them, their main group will be in position to give us a broadside. I'm going to the bridge to explain this to the captain," He raced out the door while we kept our eyes on the screen.

"They're slowly moving closer to our position," I said to John. "We'll have to attack soon, I would think well before 0000, or else they may strike first."

It was almost time for me to be on duty. To settle my nerves, I stepped onto the foredeck for fresh air before I took over from Connolly. The sea was calm, barely a ripple, and the slight breeze on my face came from the ship's movement. The fragrant, citrusy aroma of the flowers on Savo Island wafted over the water across our deck, and someone standing next to me in the dark said, "That Island is bursting with orchids." Inhaling the sweet smell, I closed my eyes and envisioned making love to Ellen in the moonlight on the white sand beach of Waikiki. That idyllic thought faded when I opened my eyes realizing the sky was clear, earlier clouds having evaporated into the night. The waxing gibbous half-moon shimmering across the ocean's surface was a giant flashlight, providing excellent visibility. *Ideal weather for a battle*, I thought.

Collins, having returned to the CIC after informing Captain Gatch on the enemy's movements, popped his head out the door, breaking my reverie, "Ridge, it's almost showtime. We'll be attacking momentarily."

I stepped to the radar screen, relieving Connolly, who stayed by my side, and began analyzing the blips. The excellent visibility afforded by the moon was a godsend for us, but maybe not; neither side, I reasoned, had an advantage over the other, that is, if I didn't discount the size of their armada, and the fact we were short two sixteen-inchers, and the rumor they preferred night fighting.

Nervous chatter sounded throughout the CIC, wondering if we would fire the first salvo, and when that would be. The waiting was exhausting, evidenced by the sweat dripping from everyone's forehead, and the perspiration mushrooming under their arms. The tension was unbearable.

Shortly after 0000, the tower phoned the bridge with a physical sighting of the enemy, which we confirmed in the CIC by radar. *Sendai, Ayanami, Shikinami*, and *Uranami* were nine nautical miles away. Not sure why, but I needed visual proof they were there. I stepped outside to confirm the tower's sighting, looking in the direction I saw on the radar screen. There they were.

Small smudges, likes clumps of dirt, on the horizon backlit by the light of the moon. I quickly returned to my radar screen, and Lt. Cdr. Collins, standing aside me and Connolly, phoned Gatch to advise of the enemy's position. General Quarters rang out, everyone waiting the order to fire.

Washington sighted the enemy the same time we did, and Vice Adm. Lee, in command of the TF, ordered a starboard side salvo of her nine sixteen-inch guns at *Sendai*–the ship with the largest silhouette six miles from her position. The thunder from her guns caused my adrenaline to rush. *Washington*'s secondary battery of five-inch guns fired on *Shikinami*.

When will we fire? I wondered, just when we blasted a starboard-side volley at *Ayanami*, the ship nearest to our position. I thought I was ready–plugs stuffed in my ears to eliminate the deafening sound of the guns when they fired–but I wasn't as prepared as I should have been. The plugs muffled the roar, but not much. The jolt of the ship from the blast of our guns caught me by surprise, the reverberation and aftershock throwing me backward hard against the bulkhead. Collins, noticing the pain on my face as I rubbed the back of my head, came over to me, yelling over the din, "I should have warned you about the recoil. It's worse than the noise of the guns if you're not prepared. You can break a bone. Get ready for another salvo."

Still rubbing the back of my head, with a hand grabbing tightly to the rail on the bulkhead, I grimaced. "You did warn me when you gave me the 'cook's tour.' I remembered the earplugs but forgot to hold on to the table." The next salvo fired just as I regained my footing with a grip on the rail.

"Take a minute on the wing bridge to shake it off."

"Yes, sir. That should clear the cobwebs."

As soon as I exited onto the deck, I became enthralled with the action taking place in the distance. I watched *Washington*'s salvos hit their targets (discovering later *Sendai* and *Shikinami* both escaped to safety in the dark night shadow of Savo Island). With a lingering pain in my neck and a growing bump on my head, I returned to the CIC.

★

Our gunnery batteries were spot on, their calibration on *Ayanami* so precise that the third salvo struck her. I took the night-vision binoculars Collins left on the shelf and said, "I'll be right back," while Connolly watched my screen. I went on the foredeck to gain a better look at the damage. She was in flames, smoke billowing from her deck. I could see her crew jumping over the side into the water, trying to escape the fiery inferno. Plumes of black smoke spiraled upward, forming dark clouds in the clear moonlit sky. The fragrant aroma of orchids I smelled earlier was washed away by the acrid smell of gunpowder and burning oil, which hung heavy in the air. I re-entered the CIC just as we steamed through the disintegrating ship, splintering what was left of her in two like a snapped tree twig. The captain gained his retribution, I thought, for the injury he suffered at Santa Cruz.

While monitoring the radar screen, I discovered *Sendai, Shikinami,* and *Uranami* emerging on the north end of Savo Island at 0030, obviously having escaped *Washington's* volleys. *Walke,* our nearest ship to their position, launched simultaneous assaults against all three ships. While her attack was courageous, I deemed it foolhardy—to David taking on Goliath, but with the opposite outcome.

We were trailing *Washington's* wake, so I left the CIC with the binoculars to observe the action on the foredeck, wanting to see the Japanese's reaction to *Walke's* attack. I found out soon enough. I saw it with my own eyes. The rumor about Japanese proficiency in night fighting was confirmed. *Sendai* zeroed in on the muzzle flashes from *Walke's* guns for perfect aim for the return fire of her five-and-a-half inch guns. That barrage, together with a well-aimed torpedo from *Uranami*, ripped into *Walke's* starboard bow, and that was all that was needed to sink her. Less than ten minutes later, *Walke,* hit by a fireball, upended, and disappeared bow-first. I could see her crew scrambling to escape the flames, jumping over the rails into the fiery, oil-slicked water while depth charges rolled off their racks into the water and exploded on impact. No one had a chance.

With the quick disposal of *Walke,* I shifted the night-vision binoculars to *Preston* for her reaction to *Walke's* sudden demise. I prayed she wouldn't make the same mistake, but it appeared her captain was unaware of *Walke*'s fate.

Mesmerized by the action unfolding before me, I watched *Preston* fire upon *Atago*'s moonlit silhouette. Her initial salvo landed close; *Atago*, to escape the fire, moved toward the dark shadow of Savo Island. Before she could make her getaway, *Preston* adjusted her aim such that the next volley hit *Atago* causing her stack to catch fire. The flame flickered against the dark backdrop of the island. Bolstered, by her success against *Atago*, *Preston* aimed her guns at *Nagara*. Before she could fire a volley, *Nagara* (having homed in on *Preston*'s muzzle flashes when she was firing on *Atago*), landed a salvo from her five-and-a-half inch guns on her starboard side, causing explosions and fire to erupt on the main deck. In the mayhem and confusion of extinguishing the fires, *Preston* didn't notice *Sendai* stealthily moving in on her port side. I raced into the CIC to tell Collins so that we could send a radio alert to *Preston* to warn of *Sendai*, but we were too late. *Sendai* delivered a fatal volley from her five-and-a-half-inch guns that demolished *Preston*, causing her to roll on her side. She dipped back on her stern, the bow pointing to the moon, and sank like a dead weight, swallowed by the sea. She was yet another addition to "Iron Bottom Sound," the name given to that stretch of water at the southern end of The Slot between Guadalcanal, Savo Island, and Florida Island by our seamen because of the ships and planes it claimed since the war started. *Walke* and *Preston* were the latest additions to that ocean graveyard

Collins joined me on the foredeck, and I handed him the binoculars saying, "I can't bear to look any longer." I told him what I saw. "Most of the crew, those that made it into the water," I said, "were engulfed in flames. I heard their screams to be rescued. Some were struggling to survive by clinging to wreckage or an errant life raft, anything to escape the fire-slicked water. I saw flashlights by those able to get far enough away signaling in morse code for help."

Having witnessed the quick demise of *Walke* and *Preston*, I turned my attention to *Benham*. I was glad she wisely retreated, escaping unscathed while *Gwin*, having taken a couple of hits but not crippled, also retreated. Both ships would be around to fight another day, just not this one.

Saddened by what we witnessed, Collins and I returned to the CIC. It was heartbreaking watching the swift demise of our ships, so close to us, yet we couldn't help to save their surviving crew in the water. We couldn't have prevented what happened. We tried to warn *Preston*, but we were too late.

Suddenly we were under attack, surrounded by the enemy. We fired back, our forward turrets honing on a ship dead ahead until she vanished from view–either sunk or hidden in the safe shadows of Savo Island. Our aft turret fired on a ship directly astern; the muzzle blasts from our guns setting the fantail ablaze, igniting our Seagull search planes.

The room rattled, followed by a deafening blast. I was knocked to the floor. A bomb must have landed just outside the CIC. I get to my knees, hollering to Collins, "My screen is out. That five-inch shell must have jostled and loosened a wire."

Craning around, he yelled back, "You're not alone. All the screens are blank."

Then, in an instant, the entire CIC was enveloped in darkness except for the soft glow of the red auxiliary lights.

"Ridge, get several flashlights so we can see what we're doing." Collins went to grab the phone to tell the captain we were disabled, but before he could pick it up, a call from the bridge informed us that electrical problems and power failures were rampant throughout the ship affecting our radar, communications, fire-control, turret motors, ammunition hoists, and gun batteries. *South Dakota* was defenseless. The power outage made us an easy target, so Lee ordered us to vacate the battle. He told Captain Gatch to use the flaming waters from the debris of *Walke* and *Preston* as a buffer, so we zigzagged past *Preston* on our port side as her crew—what was left of them—screamed for help, pleading to be saved. We were ordered to leave them behind. There was nothing we could do.

Collins, Connolly, and I left the CIC, as there was nothing to do in the darkness, and went on the foredeck for the light of the moon while the engineers grappled with fixing the electrical problem. Without the benefit of our radar, unbeknownst to us, the enemy moved near our position undetected. Suddenly a powerful searchlight illuminated our starboard side. It was the cruiser *Takao* lighting us up. Shielding our eyes from the blinding light, we ducked below the bulwark. Collins exclaimed, "That light makes us a sitting duck!"

"Just like a target in a Coney....," before I finished the sentence, we were under fire from *Kirishima* on our port side, *Takao*'s light making us an easy target.

"Look!" Connolly screamed, pointing to the streaming wake on the starboard side.

"*Takao* fired a torpedo," Collins said, "and it's coming right at us. Brace yourself!"

My body tensed for the impact and explosion, but nothing happened. The torpedo missed.

More torpedoes followed. We counted thirty-four in all.

I watched in terror as each streamlined wake of white water surged toward us wondering if that would be our end. To our sheer disbelief, they all missed. Amazing. God was with us.

The relief, though, was short-lived. *Kirishima* had us in her sights, firing unchallenged–inflicting serious damage to our superstructure, foremast, fire-control, and communications. She administered to us a real school-yard shellacking.

The damage to the ship was the least of it, compared to the number of dead and wounded we suffered. Their blood ran like water over our decks, spilling over the side through the scuppers. Some died where they sat in their gunnery battery, while others succumbed to lethal wounds from ricocheting shrapnel. Death was in an instant for many of them, no chance to even say a prayer. The wounded were brought to the Crews' Mess that served as a triage area, operating room, and recovery bay. The floor there was slippery from their blood and the ship's surgeon needed someone to hold him steady as he furiously administered treatment. The dead, what remained of them, were left where they fell, to be claimed when the fighting stopped.

Though hard to comprehend, God did watch over us. It could have been worse—much worse if not for *Washington* coming to our rescue. She inflicted multiple salvos on *Kirishima* from her sixteen-inch guns, enough of them hitting their mark to set her on fire.

We watched the action from the foredeck, mesmerized by what we saw.

"What do you think about *Kirishima*?" I asked.

"What do you mean?" Collins asks.

"Well, she's in flames, not defending herself against *Washington*, yet still bent on attacking us. We're not a threat, but *Washington* is. I wonder why. Her captain must be crazy."

"You're right," Collins said. "Doesn't make sense, but let's thank her captain for being nuts."

Washington fired seventy-five APCs at *Kirishima*, enough of them landing to take her out, reducing her to a ball of flames, steaming in circles like an out-of-control mad man just like her captain. She was so badly damaged she capsized and sank around 0330, making her the newest addition to Iron Bottom Sound.

Early the next morning, I awoke to the ambient light peeking through the porthole; the stateroom was empty except for me. The horror of last night flashed in my mind as the smell of battle pervaded the space, hanging in the air. I dressed and walked onto the deck. The smell was thicker outdoors. The acrid scent of gunpowder and the metallic stench of blood was on my clothes, on my skin, and in my hair. And inside me too; it had become part of me. I hadn't eaten breakfast but threw up the last meal I had eaten as I surveyed the devastation: bodies, and pieces of bodies, strewn across the deck that was stained red with their blood. Volunteers solemnly collected the remains, whatever was left of them, for burial, but not quick enough to allay the miasma of rotting flesh being baked into the deck under the beating sun. That foul smell of battle and death would stay with us for days; a constant reminder of war, and the ultimate price we paid.

Forty of our men died in the battle.

They were committed to the sea in a ceremony on the fantail presided over by Captain Gatch, still bandaged and healing from his neck wound. Slowing to five knots, the service began when the OOD intoned, "All hands bury the dead."

The chaplain read scripture followed by the committal and the benediction. Standing with our heads bowed, the captain concluded the service with a prayer.

Each of the dead, wrapped in a sailcloth sack containing a five-inch shell, shrouded in an American flag, was carried to the rail on a plank by six side boys. With the signal from the chaplain, the plank was tipped on the rail, and the body slid into the water, creating a small splash as it was committed to the sea to its final resting place. Taps solemnly filled the air.

As I surveyed the carnage and witnessed the burials at sea, I thought, *these men gave their lives for their country in a war they did not start but one they were sent to finish, leave nothing to mark their existence on earth, or the deeds they accomplished yesterday. How very sad.* The ceremony was one I will never forget.

I went for a drink of ice-cold water after the burials were concluded, although something stronger would have been more appropriate. I entered the Wardroom as the radio crackled, "The sea battle of the fifteenth was the greatest the world has ever seen." *South Dakota* was credited with sinking a battleship, three cruisers, one destroyer, and causing heavy damage to another cruiser and destroyer as well as several troops' ships in defense of Guadalcanal. The island, under Japanese control before August 1942 after their attack on Pearl Harbor, bolstered their strategy, until we took it from them, to build a defensive ring around their conquests and threaten the lines of communication from the United States to Australia and New Zealand. It was through a reconnaissance mission we learned of the enemy airfield on Guadalcanal at Lunga Point and realized the critical importance of the island. Our Marines easily took the island and renamed the airfield Henderson Field but holding it since had been hotly contested by land, sea, and sky. Our victory yesterday at Savo Island saved Guadalcanal from falling back into enemy hands.

Heavily damaged, we returned to Noumea where we were greeted by *Prometheus*, another World War I repair ship. The damage this time, reflective of the death toll we suffered, was too extensive to be repaired in Noumea. A return to the Navy Yard in Brooklyn, New York, would be required for the major repairs. *Prometheus* was tasked with fixing just what was needed to ensure we were seaworthy for the trip. With their work completed, we sailed for Nuku'alofa, Tongatapu, arriving November 27th, where we weighed anchor to wait for our destroyer escort to the Panama Canal.

I wrote a letter to Ellen to tell her I would be home for Christmas; a surprise I was sure she was not expecting so soon. I purposely glossed over the battle at Savo Island, not wanting to tell her about all the death we suffered—though I was sure she'd read about in the papers and have plenty of questions upon our reunion.

28 November 1942

Hi Honey,

You may have read about our battle at Savo Island near Guadalcanal. Admiral Halsey said it was the greatest sea battle in history. I'm okay, not a scratch. The ship took a lot of hits and is heavily damaged, but the armor-cladding did the job. Still, the repairs are more than can be handled here so we will be back in New York.

That means I'll be home for the Christmas holiday.

We're anchored in Nuku'alofa on the island of Tongatapu, having arrived early yesterday from Noumea where repairs were made to ensure we are seaworthy for the cruise to New York. We're waiting for our destroyer escort to the Panama Canal before we leave for home.

Not much to see here. I bummed a jeep ride with a couple of Marines for a tour of the island, which is about nineteen miles long and less than ten miles wide. The roads are poor but getting better due to the work of the U.S. Army, who are improving the existing roads and constructing another sixty miles of coral surfaced highway. With all the ongoing roadwork, it took quite a while to navigate the island which is volcanic in origin, but you wouldn't know it from the surrounding coral reef formations, lush vegetation, and coconut palms. There are many caves on the island's east coast, but most are inaccessible to explore because the entrances are forty to fifty feet above the water. The white sandy beaches are strung with barbed wire, just like Waikiki. Other than the harbor, there is nothing here worth fighting over.

On my jaunt with the Marines, we stopped at the cemetery to pay our respects for our war dead from the Coral Sea battle that are buried here. The graves are decorated with flowers placed daily at the direction of Queen Salote, who is the ruler of Tonga. She is very tall, and towers over the men.

I'll close here. Watch duty calls. Can't wait to hold you soon. I'll give you more details about when we should arrive in New York when I learn them.

Love, John

Our sister ship *Indiana* arrived on November 28th to relieve us for our return to the New York Navy Yard in Brooklyn. We transferred our 20 mm guns and ammunition to *Indiana*; while Captain Gatch conferred with Captain Merrill of *Indiana* to share his experiences with the Japanese, giving him the benefit of his knowledge. I was sure he distinguished between the two types of battle engagements we were involved in. One that centered on antiaircraft guns, carriers, and fighter planes and the other one on the sixteen-inch and five-inch guns on the battleships, cruisers, and destroyers. The transfer of our antiaircraft guns would shore up *Indiana*'s defenses against fighter planes and dive bombers.

With the lines hoisted on November 30th, *Warrington,* our destroyer escort, accompanied us 5,952 miles to Balboa—the small town adjacent to the Panama Canal's entrance. We had been in the Pacific for just a few months but, in that short period, fought two major sea battles, suffering heavy damage and significant casualties. I had been aboard for two months and experienced all of it, enough I'd say, to last more than a lifetime. *It'll be nice to get back home, back to Ellen.*

24

A PROMOTION

7 December 1942

Dear Ellen,

A short note so I can get this letter in the mail to you while the ship is in Balboa. Disregard my letter of November 28th. I received a big surprise when we arrived in port, a promotion to First Lieutenant with orders to report immediately to Commander Harold Demarest of the destroyer Warrington. Warrington escorted us to Panama from Nuku'alofa. You know what this means, though, I won't be home for Christmas, and that breaks my heart. Oh, how I'll miss seeing you.

This should be a safe assignment compared to South Dakota. Although some destroyers that are screens for carrier and battleship groups have been easy targets for Japanese submarines, Warrington, thus far, has escorted troop and cargo transports, which has proven to be safer duty.

The boys in South Dakota are giving me a farewell party this afternoon, and after that I'll transfer to Warrington. More to come.

Love, John

P.S. I just realized when I dated this letter that today is our second wedding anniversary. Happy Anniversary. I miss you so much, and I'm so disappointed I won't be home for Christmas to celebrate with you.

Before I transferred to *Warrington*, my bunkmates—Davis, Connolly, and Timmons—along with Lt. Cdr. Collins and other shipmates from the CIC, congratulated me on my promotion, giving me a farewell party in the Wardroom. Collins arranged the celebration with cake, ice cream, cheese and crackers, mixed nuts, cola, lemonade, and Kona coffee.

He gave a speech about my short time aboard, and toasted to my dismay and embarrassment, "Best wishes, John, on your promotion. At the rate you are progressing, Admiral Halsey should look out for his job." I smiled at his remarks, my face beet red, thanking him for the nice words and, looking around the Wardroom, realizing what a great group of people I had the honor and privilege of working with under the most severe circumstances. I wished everyone Godspeed and told them I regretted having to leave the ship—not just because I would miss them, but because I wouldn't be able to see Ellen when the ship returned to New York. That brought laughs from everyone.

Davis said, "You'll be home soon enough, before you know it."

"I hope so. I really miss her."

We had grown very close over the last three months. War will do that, especially with the life-and-death experiences we shared and the friends we buried at sea.

The transfer to *Warrington* was an adjustment. She paled in comparison to *South Dakota* in terms of size and armament, but my duties were so much greater.

After the farewell party, while I was in my stateroom gathering my gear before disembarking the ship, Captain Gatch stopped by to wish me luck. He was wearing his khaki uniform and holding a pipe in his hand that had a sweet cherry aroma. I hadn't noticed his moustache before which gave him a distinguished look akin to General Douglas MacArthur. Maybe it was the pipe that did it. He thanked me for a job well done, "Although your stay was brief, it personified excellence in the performance of your job and continues the outstanding reviews you had while at Fort Schuyler and V-7."

I thanked him. "Sir, I hope I can be half the man you are. Your strength in commanding the ship after being wounded was truly inspiring."

He nodded his appreciation and issued a final salute, which I returned with a snap—my farewell to *South Dakota* and the man who commanded her.

I walked the gangway, saluted the flag, and requested permission to board. Cdr. Harold Demarest, a strongly built man about my height with neatly parted blonde hair and a slender face, responded, "Permission granted. Welcome aboard, Lt. Ridgeway. I'll show you to your stateroom so you can unload that duffle and then I'll fill you in on this ship."

As Demarest led me down the companionway to my quarters he boasted, "Although *Warrington* is a fraction of the size of *South Dakota*, she's still plenty of ship as you'll find out." We entered my stateroom and I immediately noticed there was only one bunk.

"I didn't realize I would have private sleeping quarters with the promotion," I confided. "I'm pleased having spent the last few months with three others, no matter how well we got along."

"I'd forgotten what it's like to room with others. This perk goes with being the number three officer on the ship. Let me give you some background. *Warrington* is one of five Somers-class destroyers built between 1935 and 1939 based upon a Gibbs & Cox modification to the Porter-class destroyer, which she succeeded. Somers-class ships were added to the eight existing Porter-class vessels to reach the London Naval Treaty tonnage limit of thirteen ships of 1,850 tons."

"I'm aware of the London Naval Treaty. It was an extension of the Washington Naval Treaty of 1922. Our enemies have violated the agreement, specifically Japan with *Yamato* and Germany with *Bismarck*."

"I'm impressed. Most people are not familiar with these treaties and the restrictions they placed on size and armament."

I thanked him for his compliment, and he continued.

"When *Warrington* was being built, new high-pressure, high-temperature air-encased boilers, like those on the battleship *New Mexico*, became available, and the class was built to a modified design, which created the *Somers* class. This allowed a single stack and eliminated reload torpedoes, leading to weight savings that allowed for an increase in the quadruple, centerline torpedo tube mounts from two to three. Despite the weight-savings measures, my feeling, from having handled the ship for the past year, she is still overweight and possibly top-heavy, and, although I haven't experienced bad weather with her, like a gale or typhoon, I wouldn't want to discover then she doesn't perform well in such conditions."

I didn't comment but thought Demarest's observation insightful.

"When's the season for typhoons?" I asked. "I'm familiar with hurricanes in the Atlantic, but while I was aboard *South Dakota* we had no foul weather to speak of. The Japs were the problem."

"Yes, them! Worse than a typhoon for sure. Luckily, we're through the season which runs from mid-May to the end of November."

"Well, sir, we'll have to wait until next year before we're likely to encounter a typhoon to test the ship's stability. Who needs that problem, anyway, on top of fighting the Japs."

Demarest nodded. "Join me for dinner in my stateroom. We'll talk about your duties, the ship, and what I expect from you as a senior officer."

Sitting down over a steak dinner in his stateroom, Cdr. Demarest said, "I'm the fourth captain of *Warrington*, assuming command from Cdr. Harold Fitz a year ago. Before that, I was the captain of the USS *Colhoun*, a vintage World War I destroyer laid down in 1917. I'll admit, I thought I went to heaven when I was assigned to *Warrington*. I realize there's no comparison between a battleship and a destroyer in terms of size and fire power."

"Yes, sir, that's obvious. But every ship has a purpose."

"You know, John, I'm glad you said that. You're very perceptive."

"Well, every class of ship is different for a reason. Also, my friends call me Ridge, rather than John. It's a nickname since I was a kid."

"Okay, Ridge. But address me as captain in front of the crew, Harold when it's just you and me."

"Understood, sir."

"Okay, then. You should know I believe the destroyer is the most versatile ship in the fleet and is called upon to do the most dangerous and high-risk jobs, from laying minefields outside of enemy harbors to transporting troops and supplies in enemy-controlled waters, escorting convoys or screening a task force to provide air and gunfire support, bombarding invasion beaches, and scouting enemy naval forces, fighting submarines and other warships, pretty much a jack-of-all-trades. You name it, the destroyer is asked to do it."

"The destroyer really is the glue that holds things together. I never fully appreciated all they do, but I'm proud to serve aboard *Warrington* to continue that tradition of service."

"I'm glad to hear that, Ridge. Captain Gatch gave you high praise and said your quick thinking saved his life. Consider yourself, along with XO Williams, my alter ego in running the ship, which is a 24/7 job. I'll seek your counsel when I think I need it, although the final decision on matters concerning the ship will be mine alone."

"Aye, aye, sir. I'll do my utmost to live up to your standards."

Demarest handed me a sheet of paper, saying, "I received this from Fitz when I assumed command, and he said it was passed to him by his predecessor. I believe Leighton Wood, *Warrington*'s inaugural skipper, prepared it when the ship was commissioned."

<u>USS Warrington (DD-383)</u>

<u>History</u>

Builder: Federal Shipbuilding and Drydock Company

Laid Down:10 October 1935

Launched:15 May 1937

Commissioned:9 February 1938

Captain: Commander Leighton Wood

Shakedown: April 1938 to May 1938

<u>General Statistics</u>

Class and Type: Somers-class destroyer

Displacement:1,850 tons standard; 2,905 tons fully loaded

Length:381 feet

Beam:36 feet 11 inches

Draft:14 feet, fully loaded

Power:4 Babcock & Wilcox boilers, 2 General Electric

Geared steam turbines, 52,000 shaft horsepower

Propulsion:2 shafts

Speed:39 knots

Range:7,020 nautical miles at 12 knots

Complement:294 (16 officers, 278 enlisted)

Armament:8 Mark 12, 5-inch guns in four Mark twin mounts

8 1.1-inch antiaircraft guns, two quadruple mounts

12 .50-inch machine guns

12 21 Mark 15 torpedo tubes

2 depth charge racks

1942:12 X 4 1.1-inch guns, 6 0.50-inch machine guns and 1 torpedo *bank removed, replaced by 2 X 2 40mm Bofors AA guns and 5 X 1 20mm Oerlikon*

AA guns; 6 depth charge throwers installed.

Demarest noticed the puzzled look on my face as I read the handwritten comment at the bottom of the page, probably thinking I couldn't read the script, and said, "I updated the sheet for armament changes that were made since she was launched. My script is not the neatest."

"Same for me. That's why I print most everything. I found I don't have to explain my sloppy writing. I could read yours though."

"Well, if you ever need clarification on something I write, just ask. Basically, more antiaircraft guns were added to defend against kamikaze pilots. Although our weapons to this point have only been fired in practice, we've had a lot of training, so when the time comes to engage the enemy, we'll be more than ready, I can assure you of that. Hearing the guns go off is good for morale, even if we're not shooting at the Japs. The crew is anxious for the opportunity to administer some tough payback for the losses of *Walke* and *Preston*."

I nodded in agreement. "I watched from the foredeck as both ships went down, the surviving crew in the flaming water, screaming for help, pleading to be rescued, and there was nothing we could do to save them. It was horrible. A great loss of good men."

"I know," Demarest said glumly.

"Sir," I said with vengeance, "I hope we'll have the opportunity to exact retribution."

We were both silent for a moment, and then Demarest asked if I wanted a coffee and some dessert. "I had the cook bake an apple pie, and we have vanilla ice cream," he said.

"You've tempted me. Thanks."

The next day was sunny. The cloudless sky, cerulean. Temperatures were mild, aided by the prevailing trade winds blowing from the southwest. I decided to walk along the pier and view the ship from land before she headed to sea. *Warrington* had a trim line, but after five years traversing the Pacific, she appeared tired and worn weary, the saltwater and humidity imbedded in her bones. Several years sailing the open seas will do that.

When I reboarded the ship, Captain Demarest greeted me, asking, "So what do you think? I watched you walking the length of the ship along the pier."

"Honestly, sir. She looks like she could use an overhaul."

"You must be a mind reader," he exclaimed. "I've submitted two requests for the same, and authorization finally came through this morning. Drydock space in Pearl is available and we're to report there. We'll be leaving Balboa tomorrow at 0900."

"That's good news, sir."

"Yes, it is. I'm giving liberty to half of the crew tonight while the other half will get the first leave in Pearl."

"Sir, I haven't been to Balboa before, but my *South Dakota* bunkmate gave me this tip sheet. Should I post it in the crew's mess?"

Demarest took the paper, scanned it quickly, and handed it back, saying, "Good idea, although, most of them have been here before and undoubtedly learned from their mistakes. Nevertheless, it's a good reminder."

Things you should know in Balboa:

1. The French perfume sold in the shops is nothing more than scented water.

2. Rum is produced in the West Indies and is the best liquor to drink. Bourbon and scotch are imitation and will make you sick. The beer is good.

3. The hostesses in the dance halls and bars will dance with you if you buy them a "Blue Moon" drink for a dollar, which is nothing more than Coca-Cola.

4. Over half of the hostesses are prostitutes and have venereal disease so, if you must, use a condom.

5. Drink water only at American-run hotels, navy and military stations; otherwise, you may get dysentery.

6. No alcohol is allowed to be brought back on board the ship.

7. Shore leave ends at 2200 for enlisted crew and at 2400 for officers.

8. Have fun. You deserve it.

9. We weigh anchor tomorrow at 0900.

★

Shore leave went without a hitch except for a couple of returning crew who were drunk and caught trying to smuggle small flasks of rum taped to their legs, hidden by their bell-bottom pants. The OOD confiscated the alcohol and poured it over the side into the water in my presence. I overlooked the infractions as I didn't want my service on the ship to start with the reputation of being a "hard nose." Although I was sure some bottles of rum probably slipped through the inspection and made it on board for the cruise.

The voyage to Pearl Harbor was uneventful, taking six days through calm seas. I was on the bridge when we arrived off the coast of Oahu at 1100, the distinctive volcanic tuff cone of Diamond Head signifying our return to paradise. I took the binoculars from the shelf and turned toward the land, focusing on the hotels on Waikiki Beach, trying to discern the banyan tree of the Moana Hotel, a place of personal enjoyment. Maybe I would see Duke with his large surfboard surrounded by a crowd of fans. People were visible swimming and sunbathing on the beach. It was going to be a great day.

When we rounded Waikiki Beach heading into Pearl Harbor, Navy Port Control directed us to the West Loch where we moored alongside *Helm*, a Bagley-class destroyer. *Helm,* someone told me, was the only ship to get under way when the Japanese attacked Pearl Harbor, her antiaircraft credited with downing a Zero. Our date with the dry dock was postponed a couple days because the ship already there needed additional repair on her keel for damage caused by scraping a coral outcrop.

John Hart, our communications officer; Coleman Pack, our gunnery officer; and Don Schultz, assistant gunnery officer, and I took the tender to Pearl City where we caught the train to Honolulu. We hopped off at the first stop on Kalakaua Avenue and walked past The Royal Hawaiian on our way to the Moana Hotel. The grounds were well-manicured, the front courtyard dominated by two large Royal Palms on either side of the main entrance. We entered the lobby and passed directly through to the patio where we grabbed a table near the beach in the cooling shade of the enormous banyan tree. It was just after noon. Time for refreshing Coors beer to quench our thirst.

Don hailed the waiter, who, when he neared the table, remembered me from my visits with Myron Dallen. He asked if I tried surfing since my lesson with Duke Kahanamoku. I told him no, "I don't have a surfboard. It wouldn't fit in my locker." He laughed.

That query brought interest from Hart. "What was that about? A surfing lesson with Duke? Who's Duke?" I told them the story, and we all had a good laugh. I thought they were envious when they found out how famous Duke was.

The waiter returned with four bottles of Coors and iced Pilsner glasses and slowly poured the beer creating a nice, foamy head. That first sip went down smoothly.

"It's almost 1300. How about lunch?" I asked.

Don told the waiter, "I don't need a menu. I'll have a burger, cooked medium, with fries, onions, and a dill pickle. And Ketchup."

Hart, lighting a cigarette he took from the pack of Camel's in his pocket, said, "Make that two. I'll have the same, minus the onions."

I looked at Cole, who nodded, and I said, "Make mine like his." Pointing to Hart.

"Before you go," Hart said, "we'll have another round of Coors."

While we waited for the food, we enjoyed the soft breeze coming off the white sandy beach and the Hawaiian music from the trio that was playing. I closed my eyes, envisioning Ellen with me as I always did when I was at the Banyan Courtyard.

The beer flowed easily and after a couple hours on the patio we were all in a good mood. The emcee announced a special treat, a performance by Hilo Hattie.

"I can't wait to see her," I said. "Someone said Ken Peterson, who won the title of Miss *South Dakota* in our Line Crossing Ceremony was prettier." I knew Hattie was a favorite among the military and, although we listened to her music on the Webley Edwards radio broadcast Hawaii Calls, none of us had seen her in person, or even a picture of her. She was always just a voice. In my imagination, I always pictured Loretta Young, the beautiful raven-haired actress who appeared opposite Clark Gable in Call of the Wild.

Well, now I know. When she appeared on stage, Schultz likened her to Marie Dressler, the frumpy actress who played Annie Brennan in the movie Tugboat Annie opposite Wallace Beery. Although Hilo was not young and slim, I had to admit she was a great performer—hence the reason for her popularity. Hattie closed her show to rousing applause dancing the hula to her signature song "When Hilo Hattie Does the Hilo Hop." Shouts from the audience for an encore brought her back to the stage to sing "The Cockeyed Mayor of Kaunakakai."

The crowd started to leave when the song ended. Hart took a last deep draw on his cigarette, stubbed the butt against the bottom of his shoe, put the stub in the ashtray, and said, "Is everyone up for one last Coors for the road, or should we head back while we can still walk straight?"

Pack groaned, "I'll be soused if I have another beer. I have an early watch."

"Yeah, we've had a lot to drink, and it'll be getting dark soon," I said, laying a ten-spot on the table to settle the bill. "Let's shuck off our shoes and socks and trek along the beach to The Royal Hawaiian. We can get a cup of java there to sober up before catching the train back." I noticed on the way that Duke was not around; perhaps he was tackling the large waves on Oahu's North Shore. The concertina wire was still strung along the beach though, marring the idyllic view. If I looked away from the beach to the hotel and surrounding gardens of palms and bougainvillea, it was impossible to tell we were at war. It was still paradise.

Warrington entered the dry dock two days later and was there for ten days while they scraped the barnacles from her hull and applied a fresh coat of gray paint. Most of the rehab was cosmetic, so I hoped there wasn't a serious problem lurking below the surface that needed attention and went untouched. Only time would tell.

25 December 1942

Hi Honey,

I was elated to hear your sweet voice yesterday. It has been too long. I miss you so much. I know you'll be spending the day with your family while I'm here with the boys. We did our best to create a little Christmas spirit. A string of lights has been strung from the bridge tower fore and aft, as with almost all the ships in the West Loch. The wardroom and crew's mess have small fir trees decorated with candy canes, tinsel, and handmade ornaments the natives sell in the shops in Pearl City. It will have to do.

I'm in my stateroom but will be leaving in a few minutes for Christmas dinner. The menu is Virginia ham with pineapple slices, mashed potatoes, green string beans, and garden salad. There is apple pie a la mode for dessert (the captain's favorite). The cooks are excellent, and I must say I've never had a bad meal.

They even bake all the breads, cakes, and pies, and make the ice cream.

I forgot to mention when we spoke yesterday, the last time going into Honolulu, several of the guys and I visited the Dole pineapple plant. After the tour we were served all the fresh pineapple and pineapple juice you could eat or drink. The pineapple with today's meal reminded me. I never realized how much I like pineapple. It must be expensive in New York if it comes all the way from Hawaii.

I hope the Christmas presents I sent have arrived by the time you receive this letter. There was not much of a selection of gift items, other than the usual souvenirs, but I did find for you a hand carved wood perfume bottle in the shape of a hibiscus. I thought it was quite unique. The one shaped like a monkey pod is for your mother, unless you want to switch them. Couldn't find anything for your father. I hope he understands.

Well, Cole just knocked on my cabin door to tell me dinner will be served. We have Bing Crosby's recording of White Christmas to play on the phonograph while we eat. I think it'll become a holiday classic. Just wondered if they ever have snow here, probably not, although maybe they do on the island of Maui on the volcanic summit of Haleakala which is 10,000 feet above sea level.

Wishing you a Merry Christmas and a Happy New Year. Give my regards to your parents, and to Jane and Kitty, and Charlie McGrath the next time you see him.

I hope to be home next Christmas to enjoy the holidays with you.

Miss you and love you. John

January 9, 1943

Dear John,

I miss you so much and was terribly disappointed to learn how close you were to being home for Christmas, but it was not meant to be. I guess your phone call will have to hold me until you return.

Your package of presents arrived today. The hand carved perfume misters are beautiful. I think I like the monkey pod so I'll give my mother the hibiscus. I'm sure she'll love it.

Now that I'm working in Ridgewood, I haven't been into the city much, although Jane, Kitty and I went to Rockefeller Center the Saturday before Christmas. We went late in the afternoon hoping to see the lighted tree in all its splendor, but the lights weren't lit. We walked down to Times Square, and all the neon billboard lights were dark, as were the marquee lights on the theaters and the restaurants. It was very eerie, and sad. I guess the effects of the war have finally hit home. It seems the joy of the season has been deflated. Even the Horn and Hardart automats had minimal lighting. They're calling them "dim-outs." I hope everything is back to normal by the time you come home.

My job at McDermott Lighting is great. It is so much more interesting than what I was doing at the bank, typing correspondence for the officers. The "man overboard" lights we manufacture are on most of the US Navy ships. Maybe you have them in Warrington. I was told the lights are fastened to the bulwark at internals along the open decks.

My parents say hello, as do Jane and Kitty. We have been working on a newsletter but have not found the time to sit down and finalize our first issue. Jane volunteered to sort through the letters that we have received for interesting details to share among everyone. I'll send you our first issue before we send it out so that you can give us your stamp of approval.

I'm looking forward to hearing about your new position. You're sure moving up the ladder quickly. I knew you would.

Love always dearest, Ellen.

25

HO-HUM

Warrington left Pearl Harbor just after the New Year, spending the next several months escorting cargo transports throughout the war zone. In all that time, we never experienced a military threat from the Japanese. The routing, while safe, was monotonous, nothing but endless green ocean. When we arrived at our destination, we were usually in port just long enough to refuel the ship before returning to sea to escort another cargo transport going the other way. Boredom was our enemy, not the Japanese. Each day was the same as the last one, and the next day the same as today. I never had much new to write Ellen but asked her to keep sending letters with news of home—savoring the smallest details as they brought me back there. Most of my letters spoke about the movies I saw or the cook's creative attempts to prepare new dishes. I asked him if he could make sauerbraten, but he'd never heard of it.

★

To boost morale and relieve pent-up frustration among the crew from the boredom of our day-in-and-day-out routine, Robert Kennedy, our medical officer, an amateur boxer in his youth, approached Demarest for permission to stage a boxing tournament for the enlisted men on the ship. The captain was receptive, so Kennedy established five weight categories and had a ring with posts and ropes constructed on the fantail. Kennedy provided the gloves. One bout developed into the main event. A seaman in the Engine Room, a raw-boned sailor of slender build who weighed 160 pounds dripping wet, wanted to box the boatswain mate, who was entered as a heavyweight and was considered a bully among many of the crew. The heavyweight match usually drew the most attention, but this one more so due to the weight disparity between the two fighters. When the fighters touched gloves in the center of the ring and the bell sounded for round one, the Engine Room seaman took a stance akin to the famous John L. Sullivan. He moved to the bully and with a flurry of left jabs, which astonished him with their ferocity, stunned him with a right uppercut to the jaw. It brought the tough boatswain mate to his knees and then to his keister in a daze. He groggily struggled to his feet, but Kennedy, seeing the glaze in his eyes, stopped the fight, declaring a TKO for the seaman. Everyone cheered his victory, not sorry to see the bully get his due.

Finally, I had something new to write Ellen, at least I thought so. Our first visit to Bora Bora. We sailed there, thousands of miles from Balboa, many days at sea. The excited anticipation of a new port among the crew was palpable, especially since they believed Bora Bora to be a tropical paradise better than Honolulu. The elation of a new port, though, quickly evaporated when we learned the layover would be only for a few hours, just long enough to refuel and take on provisions before returning to Noumea. No one debarked the ship. The crew was terribly disappointed. The only bright spot was the movies we swapped with another ship for films we hadn't seen.

29 May 1943

Hi Honey,

It's your birthday today, Happy Birthday. I wish I were there with you to celebrate and give you a great big birthday kiss. Hopefully, I'll be home for your next one.

I thought I would have something new to tell you. We're in Bora Bora, the main island of the Society Islands of French Polynesia. It's in the center of a lagoon surrounded by a thin strip of land, encircled by a barrier reef. It looks quite beautiful from what I can see, but we'll only be here for a few hours, leaving no time to go ashore. The men are terribly disappointed as they were so looking forward to a new port to explore.

Please know when I'm in bed I often lie awake thinking of you and what you are doing before I fall asleep. I think of many things I would like to express in my letter about how much I miss you and what you mean to me in my life but when I start writing the next day my well-worded thoughts have disappeared. I never seem able to say what I thought the night before. Simply, I love you so very much and miss you a lot. Again, happy birthday.

Love, John

P.S. Your newsletter was smashing. You girls have the knack for sharing the most interesting details. It's the best way to stay in touch with everyone.

The next several months were spent escorting convoys between Noumea, Guadalcanal, and the New Hebrides Islands–always returning home to Noumea. We were never in a port long enough to debark the ship, always leaving as soon as we had refueled. The crew felt like prisoners in a floating penal colony. That monotonous routine had everyone on the ship in a trance, hypnotized by boredom. Some crew openly expressed the hope we would encounter the enemy while others asked for more target practice just to hear the thunder from our five-inch guns, the loud noise from the blast cathartic.

I had a good sense of the crew's mood, overhearing the griping and minor flareups from men getting on each other's nerves, so I went to the captain.

"The boredom of our daily routine and the absence of a decent port for shore leave is taking a toll on the men. They're fatigued, and tempers ignite over the most trivial things. Something must be done to relieve the stress."

"I'm as concerned as much as you are, Ridge, probably more so, since I've been living with this dilemma before you even came aboard. I'll give more thought as to what I can do. I've been mulling the idea of requesting a change in assignment, maybe ask to be a part of a destroyer screen for a carrier group. The scuttlebutt is the men would welcome an engagement with the enemy."

"You're right about that, sir."

"That may be the solution. I'll make some inquiries."

Upon our umpteenth return to Noumea from another routine convoy, Commander Demarest informed me, "I'll be getting away from this drudgery soon."

"How's that, sir? That's great news."

"Yes, for me. I've been in command of *Warrington* for almost two years, which is a lifetime in the Navy for a command, as you know."

"Yes, I know."

"I've received orders to report to ComDesPac operations in Pearl to cede command of *Warrington* to a new skipper at the end of August, and you, with my recommendation, are being promoted to XO (executive officer) to replace Wesley Williams who will get command of his own ship. I'll be returning to Annapolis to serve on the staff of the Postgraduate School in Electronics, Engineering and Physics department. Quite a change in duty, but I'm okay with it."

"That's great, sir."

"Yes, I guess so. I put an evaluation in your personnel file stating you warrant your own command if that's what you want—and if this war doesn't end soon. But the war may be over before you must make that decision. We're winning most of the battles these days, closing in on Japan."

"Well, sir, it's been a privilege serving under you. I've learned a lot about seamanship and command. At least you'll be able to escape the monotony."

"Yes, Ridge," he laughed. "But not in the manner I was planning. I was hoping to find a way for the entire crew. Now it's in your hands to find a way."

On 30 August 1943, Chief Boatswain Mate Johnson piped aboard Cdr. Robert Dawes, our new skipper who stepped onto the ship's deck and exchanged a salute with Commander Demarest. Dawes appeared about ten years younger than Demarest and his round face with closely cropped black hair hinted at a jovial personality when he smiled. I knew instantly I would like to report to him.

The relief of command routine normally takes a day, but before the process even started, we were caught in an electrical storm while patrolling our station in the screen that day. The disturbance, we surmised later, caused our radar antennas to go haywire. The malfunctioning equipment led Robert Reville, the operator in the Radar Room, to erroneously report an unidentified ship to Demarest. He was still in command and probably anxious for combat activity before he relinquished control to Dawes, decided to pursue and investigate. The unidentified ship turned out to be a false reading and in the process of searching for the target, with eyes in the Navigation Room averted from the fathometer, our propeller scraped on a shoal.

"Shit," Demarest exclaimed under his breath to Williams and me, standing aside him on the bridge. "Just what I need when turning over command. Wes, report the mishap to the commander of ComSoPac, and check the charts to make sure this outcropping is new. Ridge, have a diver inspect the damage. I hope it's minor."

"Aye, aye, sir," we both responded in unison.

Such mishaps were a normal and frequent occurrence, and the damage to our propeller was minor. ComSoPac–short for Commander, South Pacific Ocean–ordered us to Noumea for the repair, which delayed transfer of command to Dawes until after the repair was completed on September 8th.

During the week Dawes was aboard before Demarest transferred command, he observed the crew and how the ship handled. I also had my "sit-down" with him, and he told me he had reviewed my file, commenting that my performance was comparable to Regular Navy. I assumed he was referring to a comment Commander Demarest must have placed in my file. I was pleased since Dawes said he was a 1933 graduate of the U.S. Naval Academy. His last duty before taking command of *Warrington* was Executive Officer (XO) on *Converse,* a 2,100-ton Fletcher-class destroyer.

Our first dispatch under Dawes was an escort screen for a night convoy of merchant ships to Guadalcanal. From there we escorted another convoy back to Noumea. That was the same boring routine we'd been following for the last several months. Everyone on the ship, me included, hoped for some excitement with the new skipper, even if it meant transferring to a battle group and potential engagement with the enemy.

Then one day, what do you know? While I was in the CIC, I got a call from Julian Ahlers, our sonarman, who detected an echo, the metallic ping of a submarine. I immediately phoned Commander Dawes on the bridge with the news. He said we would attack since if it were one of our subs, they would have made their presence known.

I agreed. "I'll sound General Quarters," I said.

"No, hold off until we drop our first depth charges."

"Aye, aye, sir, but why?"

"I want to see how the crew reacts in an emergency and how quickly they man their battle stations once General Quarters is sounded."

"Sir, based upon our training—and we've had a lot of that to add excitement during our never-ending routine patrols—I'm confident the crew will perform well, up to your standards."

"Well, Lieutenant Ridgeway, we'll soon find out. I'm sure your assessment is right, but there is a difference between practice and the real thing. Nothing beats a good test, wouldn't you agree? Although, this may well be the real thing."

When we neared the suspected target, Dawes ordered the depth charges dropped, and General Quarters sounded. I thought, *I'm impressed with his means of testing crew.* Once the first can was dropped, all battle stations were manned within two minutes. Dawes, in a low whisper, said, "Excellent." He later confided to me he never doubted the crew's ability. To our chagrin, we didn't find the enemy submarine, the sonar ping disappearing. If there was a submarine lurking, she made a silent getaway.

1 October 1943

Hi Honey,

Today we're leaving Espiritu Santo to escort Prince William (one of our aircraft carriers) to Samoa. Mark that down on my list of exotic places I will have visited. I'm hoping the crew will have liberty, they really need it, and that we're in a civilized port.

8 October

Well, we're in port but learned it will only be long enough to refuel and then we're headed back to Espiritu Santo. There will be no leave. The crew is so disappointed, but "orders are orders." I'm not sure who's in worse shape, the ship or the men. I wouldn't want to pick one over the other; both are at their breaking point. I believe this is even worse than fighting the Japs. At least that would make your adrenaline flow. Commander Demarest was sure lucky to escape this monotony.

I never mentioned this before, but the thought just came to me. Last night's movie was one I'd seen at least three times, so I went on the foredeck to enjoy the night sky. When we're sailing at night, it is so dark—almost pitch-black, in fact—the only light that of the moon. Since it was a crescent moon, the smallest sliver casting light, it was especially dark. The heavens were magical, better than any movie. Shooting stars flamed through the sky, dropping like lighted raindrops into the black sea. The sky was a sparkling dome of shooting stars. It's incredible. Breathtaking, I would say. You must see it to believe it really happens in nature. Someone described it to me as a "reeling chorus of persistent, piercing lights." I wish I had a camera that could capture the spectacle. We could never see this at home. Too much light from the skyscrapers in Manhattan.

I thought of something else I never mentioned that you may find interesting. At the dining table in the Wardroom, the stewards mate brings the dinner to the table on a serving tray, and you take as much as you want, and then he goes to the next officer, and the next, until he has gone around the table. Instead of starting at the same officer at each meal and giving that person first choice at the meats, and so on, we have a small wooden Indian head which we call the "Buck." Before the meal starts, the steward places the "Buck" alongside the officer's plate who will be served first. Then, at the next meal, the "Buck" is moved to the officer at his right, and that officer is served first. We always sit in the same seat at the table for dinner. Also, at the end of the meal, the steward passes cigarettes and cigars. I was finally tempted and tried a cigar but tossed it over the side after a few puffs. Too strong for me. The captain, though, certainly enjoys a good smoke. I think he brought with him a good supply of Cuban cigars.

I forget if I mentioned this before, but I had a craving for sauerbraten and the cook is so good, so I asked him if he could make it. He said he doesn't have the recipe and I couldn't help him other than to say there are a lot of ingredients and that it takes three days to make. He looked at me like I was crazy for asking him. I guess I was. Just wishfully thinking about that dinner at Victor Koenig's with potato dumplings and red cabbage washed down with a large stein of Trommer's beer. That would be heaven. I can smell that sweet aroma.

I am making a quick dash to the PO in Samoa while we are refueling to mail *this letter. We have only an hour or so before we weigh anchor.*

Love always, I miss you so much, John

Despite the new skipper, nothing changed. We were relegated to the same boring routine. In my downtime, I decided I would read the ship's log from the beginning, hoping to find some interesting facts that I could write to Ellen about. I wasn't expecting much, just the usual boring journal entries.

13 October 1943

Dear Ellen,

You won't believe this. Aside from reading and re-reading your letters and the newsletter you prepare to relieve the monotony of our daily voyages; I've been reading the ship's log. I began at the beginning from the day she was launched and believed like our monotonous cruises, that most of what I would read would be the usual dull entries. But I hit paydirt, you might say, right at the start. On her shakedown cruise to Cuba in 1938 she ran head-on into the Long Island Express hurricane that I've told you about, where I almost drowned at Rockaway Beach in a foolish attempt to challenge the waves in the storm's aftermath.

According to the record, when the ship hit the heavy weather, Commander Wood, who was the captain, reduced speed to about 6 knots and headed the ship's bow into the wind and seas. That maneuver eased the situation, but only for a half-day, as the weather grew worse. The ship by that point was ensnarled in the hurricane, battling the storm for two days before she reached New York.

The log entry said the wave heights, when the ship was in a trough between two waves, were higher than the foremast. That's over 100 feet compared to the 15-foot waves I experienced at Rockaway Beach. It says when the ship crested one wave and started down the other side, the screws either came out of the water and raced or the ship picked up speed down the face of a wave with the bow digging into the bottom of the next wave so deeply the ship would come back out of it stern first. The crew must have been terrified the ship was going to break apart and sink.

The captain saved the ship by flooding the empty fuel tanks with seawater. He wasn't trying to scuttle the ship as the seawater added ballast that gave the ship the stability needed to ride out the storm.

One interesting fact I noticed was the absence of a weather forecast for the voyage. I assume that was because back then there was no system for storm warnings, so the captain had no way of knowing where the storm came from or where it was headed. The ship had weather instruments, but by the time they were able to assess the readings, it was too late. The ship was already ensnared in the throes of the hurricane. All they could do was pray, hold on, and ride it out.

In evaluating what I've read in the log, I believe the ship only gained the stability she needed to ride out the storm when her ballast tanks were full. That is something I will make sure to remember if we ever encounter very heavy seas. I don't think consideration has been given to the modifications to the ship since she was launched. Antiaircraft guns and ammunition bunkers on the deck have been added for the needs in the Pacific to combat enemy planes. Guns were added in 1942 and more guns this year. I'm sure this extra weight had made the ship top-heavy and has raised the center of gravity. That would add to the ship's instability in a bad storm.

I apologize if I'm boring you with this, but it is exciting to me to learn that the ship and I both experienced the Long Island Express hurricane and survived.

Your loving husband, John

26

SOME EXCITEMENT, MORE BOREDOM

PACIFIC OCEAN, 1943

Our only battle "engagement," (if I stretch the definition) happened when we were at anchor in Guadalcanal. A lone Japanese plane would fly over in the middle of the night, causing everyone to scramble from their bunks when General Quarters was sounded. Our land-based antiaircraft batteries fired on him, trying to knock him out—always to no avail. Because his plane sounded like a vintage World War I biplane, he was quickly given the name "Washing Machine Charlie." After several nighttime flyovers, we realized he was more of a nuisance than a threat, his forays intended to disrupt sleep. To rid the problem, once-and-for-all, we dispatched a fighter plane who delivered "Charlie" to the Promised Land. That ended the problem as none of Charlie's comrades "raised a hand" to take his place.

November 8, 1943

Dear John,

How are you? I miss you more than you know. It doesn't look like you'll be home this Christmas and that leaves me blue with a feeling of emptiness. On the bright side, though, it sounds like your life at sea is monotonous drudgery, but from where I sit that makes me happy (don't be mad) because I know you're safe and that you'll return home to me when this war ends.

It's amazing what you learned from the ship's log about the connection that you and the Warrington had with the Long Island Express hurricane. Maybe it was your destiny to be on that ship, what other explanation could there be for such a coincidence?

A little news about what I've been doing. I went to the RKO cinema in Richmond Hill with Jane and Kitty, but the movie was so awful we left after the first half hour and went to Jahn's for some solace. You're not going to believe what we had. It was a new item on the menu called The Kitchen Sink. It featured 18 scoops of ice cream. The server gave us three spoons and, I must say, we did a good job devouring it. But never again. I was sick to my stomach by the time I walked in the door at home. I couldn't even make dinner. But I made up for it the next day for breakfast with a triple egg cheese omelet.

All is well at work at McDermott Lighting. I enjoy the work so much more than the bank, and the company is really contributing to the war effort with the marine lights they manufacture.

My parents say hello and wish you a happy Thanksgiving. I'll be at their house for dinner after Jane, Kitty and I go to the city to see the Macy's Parade. I hope the weather is nice that day, I hate the cold and rain as you know.

Oh, I almost forgot. The girls and I have plans to go into the city this month to see the Christmas tree in Rock Center, which will be lit this year. I guess we're not afraid that we will be bombed. We are winning the war. The lights on Broadway are already shining again. Slowly we are getting back to normal. The latest newsletter is almost finished. From what I've read, everyone is safe and doing well.

Looking forward to your next letter, even if there is not much to say,

Loving you always, Ellen

18 November 1943

Hi Honey,

Greetings from the Pacific. I'm glad to hear everything is going well at home with your family and job. Thanksgiving is almost here. I guess you'll be helping your mom with the turkey dinner. Boy, do I wish I could be there with you. Well, I'm here on an island in Papua, New Guinea, at the northeast end of the Solomon Islands, and near the Japanese naval base of Rabaul—not a place that harkens Thanksgiving.

Since Commander Dawes assumed command, most of our activity was the same as before under Captain Demarest, escorting supply convoys between Espiritu Santo and Guadalcanal and patrolling the war graveyard of Iron Bottom Sound. The monotony of these continued runs, the sameness of them, the green water, drab sky, and humid weather, nothing different from one day to the next, is creating tension among the crew. The boredom and absence of shore leave is demoralizing to a point where I have serious concern for the crew's mental safety. I know Captain Dawes shares my sentiment. Something must give. I hate to say it. Even battle action against the Japs would be welcomed.

The closest we've come to an enemy engagement, and nothing for you to worry about, was from a lone Jap plane that flew over at night while we were in port anchored and asleep. Whenever he appeared, General Quarters sounded with everyone scrambling to battle stations. We soon discovered he was just a nuisance, his flyovers designed to disrupt our sleep. A fighter plane was finally dispatched to take him out and Washing Machine Charlie, as we dubbed him, was no longer disturbing our sleep.

There is not much for entertainment in Espiritu Santo even though the harbor and dock facilities are vast. The Canal du Segond Anchorage can accommodate forty to fifty ships, and many more can be handled at the anchorage in Palikulo Bay. The island is the largest in the New Hebrides, about 109 miles wide and 25 miles long. It was never a tourist destination before the war, so there are no civilized amenities other than what the army has constructed. Most of the island is covered with coconut plantations and inhabited by those scary-looking natives I've mentioned that look like cannibals. I would guess the natives throughout most of these Pacific Islands have a similar ancestry.

I just thought of something I've never mentioned before. I've seen plenty of flying fish and some porpoises, but no whales or turtles. What brought this to mind? Yesterday I was looking over the side of the ship, trying to find a breeze, and there were two large manta rays, each about six feet wide and five feet long with bony tails four to five feet in length, sunning themselves on the water's surface. No war for them. Not a care in the world, other than to work on their tan. At least they seemed to be enjoying themselves.

The daytime temperatures here are brutal, routinely exceeding one hundred degrees, with almost 100% humidity, which causes sweat to gush from your body in torrents. I drink gallons of water to stay hydrated. The heat and humidity sap your strength. Couldn't live in Florida. Wouldn't mind visiting there, though, for the palm trees, sunshine, fresh squeezed orange juice, and sandy beaches.

We received orders to replace another destroyer as part of a screen for troop transports and cargo ships coming into Empress Augusta Bay. The ship we're replacing damaged a propeller on a coral pinnacle (what else is new?) and was sent to Noumea for repairs. We are now patrolling her station seaward while the transports land their troops and supplies on the beaches southwest of Cape Torokina.

Oops. Must go.

Our radar detected Jap aircraft heading our way. General Quarters sounded for an impending attack. Fingers crossed all goes well.

I'm back. All in one piece, so you know.

After General Quarters, the ships in our convoy ceased unloading and hurriedly steamed around the troop and cargo transports. We took a position on the port (left) side of the screen, where we awaited the arrival of the enemy aircraft.

This was the first true battle action for the crew of Warrington, including Commander Dawes, but I knew what to expect. Most of the incoming Jap aircraft came in low, just above the water, attacking from our starboard side and opposite of our position, bent on making torpedo attacks. They never got the chance.

We encountered a couple of planes approaching our position at around noon from our stern and one of our 40mm guns hit the tail of one, causing it to nosedive, crashing into the water. The other plane also crashed, taking fire from us as well as from the destroyer astern. We even fired several rounds from our five-inch guns, but to no avail. Even if we had hit one of their planes with a five-incher, it would have been pure luck. It was a quick skirmish, lasting no more than five or six minutes, and then we were back to unloading troops and supplies, finishing just after sunset. I'm not surprised about the attack as there was fighting near Cape Torokina about a week ago. The conversation at dinner about today's attack lasted a lot longer than the actual attack. Everyone, though, had the feeling they were making a difference in this war. That was important for morale.

We are heading to Guadalcanal with the empty transport ships, so I'll finish here so I have this letter ready for mailing tomorrow.

Love you so much. I wish I could be home for Thanksgiving, Christmas, and New Year's holidays. I already missed Halloween. Ha-ha. Maybe this war will be over soon so that I'll make it home for all the holidays next year. It seems we are winning most of the battles, the tide turning in our favor. The Marines are taking one island after another, closing in on the island of Japan itself.

Love, John

With the skirmish at Empress Augusta Bay a faded memory, we slipped into the same old grind of shuttling troop transports and supply ships between Espiritu Santo and Guadalcanal.

Dawes, in his sea cabin on the bridge, answered my knock on the door. "Come in." Looking up, "Ridge, anything happening I need to be aware of?" He was at his desk putting an entry into the ship's log.

"I see you're reviewing the log. That's not why I came to see you, but while I'm here, to relieve the boredom," I said facetiously, "I read the ship's log since she was launched and discovered she survived the Long Island Express hurricane of 1938. I almost drowned in the aftermath of that storm at Rockaway Beach. Thought you should know."

"Well, that's a coincidence. But that's not why you want to see me."

I sat in the seat opposite his desk. "No, sir. The men are going crazy from the monotony of these shuttle runs, and I fear the crew is at its breaking point of civility. Morale is very low. Something must be done to alleviate the situation before there is a meltdown."

"I'm aware of the low morale. I've been abroad for a short time and I'm feeling the effects of the daily routine. I feel it from the men when I'm with them. I've been wrestling with ways to improve our circumstances. I think I found a solution. Not surprisingly, *Warrington* hasn't had a full ninety-day overhaul since she came to the Pacific. That's over four years! I know we're at war, but that shouldn't be. A two-week tender overhaul, scraping barnacles and slapping on some grey paint will not suffice."

"Sir, I'm glad to hear this. Do you think a lengthy overhaul in Pearl is doable?"

"I'm not sure, but I want to make a strong case that we are due. More than due. Take an inventory of the entire ship for all items needing repair, replacement, or update. No item is too small. The longer the list, the better. Once you have it, we'll go through it together. Hopefully there will be enough meat there to get us the overhaul we desperately need and deserve. In the meantime, we'll do our best to hold things together both mentally, and physically."

"Aye, aye, sir. I'll get right on it. I already have notes of things that need fixing."

Commander Dawes and I both agreed the ports we visited were unsuitable for shore leave or liberty. There were no towns or places of entertainment and recreation. The U.S. Armed Forces created whatever civilization existed in many of these islands, and the island natives—Kanaks, Melanesians, and Tonga's—primitive, scary-looking people with curly black hair standing straight up, rings in their noses and long bows or spears in their hands for hunting wild boar, came from another world. Mingling with them was not an option. Our best entertainment was a baseball or football game against the crew of another ship or a picnic ashore with Coors beer (in the khaki-colored can authorized by the U.S. government). That was the extent of our R&R, self-entertainment, at its best. Rivalries developed between the different ships and the men from *Warrington* fared well, winning most of the games we played. I managed the team and usually played right field when it was baseball and hit for a pretty good batting average.

The shuttling between Espiritu Santo and Guadalcanal continued unabated through mid-December, when we scraped a propeller on a shoal for a second time and, as fate would have it, the damage was too extensive for Noumea to handle. We were diverted to Pearl Harbor for the repair. That brought glee from the crew. Our voyage to Pearl Harbor came about not the way Commander Dawes envisioned but was nevertheless a welcomed, fortunate accident. It had one unique aspect that I couldn't wait to write Ellen about--namely, when we crossed the International Date Line on Christmas Day, it gave us two Christmas celebrations in one day. I thought this would have been a joyous event, celebrating two Christmases in one day in the middle of the Pacific Ocean. However, the opposite was true. The day was depressingly somber, reflective of the gray overcast sky and endless green ocean, but we did the best we could under the circumstances. A nice dinner was served, and some of the crew members who were theatrically inclined (probably those who performed in a Line Crossing ceremony) put on a variety show of music and comedy. The crew even sang a dissonant rendition of "Auld Lang Syne" that lifted our spirits, making it a Christmas I knew I'd never forget because of the comradery it spawned. The next day, it was evident from the chatter around the ship that everyone was anxious to return to Pearl Harbor for the bars and nightlife of Honolulu and the beach at Waikiki.

The eve before we reached Pearl Harbor, after the sun ebbed below the horizon, I treated the crew to a double feature on the fantail instead of the ship's mess. The breeze sweeping across the deck made it surprisingly pleasant. Wolfman, with Claude Rains and Lon Chaney, Jr., was followed by Boom Town starring Clark Gable, Spencer Tracy, Claudette Colbert, and Hedy Lamarr. All that was lacking was popcorn and candy. I thought of Ellen.

We arrived in Pearl Harbor on December 29th, and Commander Dawes, hoping to raise the morale of the crew, was quite generous in granting liberty. The Royal Hawaiian Hotel was still fully occupied by submariners so almost everyone drifted along Kalakaua to imbibe alcoholic libations in the bars on the strip, before congregating at the Moana Hotel to enjoy the beach and tranquil Hawaiian music in the Banyan Courtyard. By nightfall everything quieted down, with the blackout still in effect and strict curfews enforced, although the likelihood of the Japanese ever attacking Pearl again were one in a million.

As soon as we moored in Pearl Harbor, I disembarked the ship and took the tender to Hickam, where I hurried to the Officer's Club to make a phone call to Ellen. It was 1:00 p.m.—6:00 p.m. in New York—so I knew Ellen should be home from work. With a pocket full of coins, I entered the booth and inserted the proper change into the slot, hoping she would answer. The phone rang several times, and then she picked it up.

"Hello."

"Ellen, I'm so glad you were home. We arrived in Pearl today for an overhaul, and I needed to hear your voice."

"John!" she shrieked. I could almost see the smile on her face. "I can't believe we're talking. I received your anniversary letter, but this surprise is much better. The only thing that would top it would be if you were here with me now."

"Yes, I miss you so much and want to hold and kiss you and do other things I can't say over the telephone."

"Oh, why not?"

"The operator might be listening."

"You're right. But I can read your mind. I'll dream about it tonight in bed."

"This call is in lieu of a Christmas present. I couldn't buy a gift for you, not even a souvenir. I was too afraid of the natives."

"You know that doesn't matter to me. Speaking to you is all the gift I want."

"And for me, hearing your voice is music to my ears. When I get home, though, I'm going to make it up to you. Something nice. Think about what you'd like. Maybe a nice string of pearls to adorn your beautiful neck. Promise?"

"Yes, I promise. I'll find ways to spend your money on something frivolous."

"Funny. No, I mean it. You deserve something nice. Oh, I know your mother's birthday is soon, so could you buy a card for me and some flowers and a box of Schrafft's chocolate and tell her I wish her the best birthday ever, and many more."

"Gladly. Maybe you forgot, but New Year's Eve is the day after tomorrow. I've invited my parents, Jane, Kitty, and several others over to celebrate. Just a quiet evening to welcome in 1944. Hopefully, the war will end soon."

"I hope so too. Give my best to everyone. Tell them I wish I were there with them to ring in the new year."

"I will."

We'd been talking for over twenty minutes, and the operator kept interrupting for more coins to be fed into the slot. "Ellen, I've run out of coins. I'll write soon. Have a great New Year's celebration."

"You too, John. I wish you were here. Love you."

"Love you, too. Bye."

Once the repairs to our propeller were completed, we returned to the routine of screening convoys between Espiritu Santo and Guadalcanal. The enjoyment of Honolulu was short-lived, a memory soon forgotten like that brief battle at Empress Augusta Bay.

One incident that epitomized the monotonous drudgery we endured for so many months occurred in Lengo Channel near Guadalcanal. Ensign Paul Pigman was OOD on the bridge at the time. He was looking out the window, scanning the water on the port side with his binoculars when he thought he saw the periscope of a submarine so, to evade a potential torpedo strike, he ordered right full rudder. Dawes (in his cabin reviewing the log) sensed the ship was not moving forward, so he quickly went to the bridge. I entered right behind him and heard Dawes, in an angry rebuke, "Pigman, what the hell happened?" We were going in hapless circles.

Unable to explain, Pigman said the rudder jammed. Several minutes were spent feverously trying to unjam the rudder from the wheel but without success.

Dawes, still fuming, turned to me, "Ridge, take some seamen from engineering to the SER (Steering Engine Room) to manually steer until I figure a solution to this mess."

"Aye, aye, sir."

I entered the SER with four men and before we got to work, phoned Dawes on the bridge to see if the problem had been fixed as it was a clumsy arrangement trying to steer the ship manually. Every action had to be executed in reverse and required the helmsman to apply the rudder in the opposite direction from what he was used to.

"Ridge," Dawes reported, "the rudder is still jammed. We'll have to manually steer back to port. I've notified ComSoPac of our problem, and we have been directed to Purvis Bay, which, luckily, is only a few hours south of us in the Solomons." We had not been to Purvis Bay before, usually anchoring in Tulagi when in this sector, so we were surprised by the "Welcome" sign greeting us when we entered the sheltered harbor. It brought a rousing cheer from the crew standing on the deck, a sound that was music to my ears after what we had gone through the last several months. The sign on the hill near the harbor entrance said: Admiral HALSEY says "Kill japs. IF YOU DO YOUR JOB WELL YOU WILL KILL MORE JAPS!" Well, that certainly reminded us of why we were there and what we had to do. All we needed was the opportunity to contribute our share of the effort. As one marine was heard to say, "The only good Jap is a dead Jap."

Commander Dawes was told it would take the tender a week to repair the jammed rudder control, so he asked me for the list of repairs he previously asked me to compile, figuring some of those items could be fixed as well, especially the large crack in the deck along the starboard side by the stack. The crack had been patched with cement when we were in Pearl, but the fix was short-lived, and the crack reopened soon after we were back at sea.

With respect to the incident with Ensign Pigman and the jammed rudder, Dawes ordered, "Complete a report, Ridge, and cite all the particulars. Find out how it happened and who is responsible." Not thrilled with the task, in view of the already low morale among the crew, I interviewed the parties involved in private conversations in the Wardroom and concluded, after evaluating all the information, that Pigman was not totally at fault. Billy Chapman, our Sonarman, reported to Pigman an enemy submarine, and Pigman, standing on the port side of the bridge, reacted to the location of the suspected enemy sub believing he saw a periscope, thereby ordering full right rudder to evade the enemy. He then glanced down at the rudder angle indicator, misreading what he saw. Standard procedure for a full rudder is an angle of thirty-five degrees, which leaves a couple of degrees as a safety cushion. Helmsman Greene correctly turned the wheel to thirty-five degrees, but Pigman thought he hadn't, admonishing Greene loudly for all to hear on the bridge. "Damn it. I said full right rudder!"

Greene thought Pigman cursed him, saying "Goddamn you," so, in a heated reaction, he whipped the wheel hard in anger as far as it would go, and the sudden thrust caused the rudder to jam. Both men were wrong, but not because they didn't know proper protocol.

My report to Commander Dawes cited the facts as I knew them. "The underlying cause of the mishap," I said, "in my opinion, is attributed to the extremely low morale on the ship. Both men knew proper procedures. They had just reached the breaking point, tempers flared, and this was the reason for the accident. It's my recommendation, sir, that neither man be reprimanded."

"I'll accept your assessment and recommendation, Ridge, for the sake of morale. The incident will be forgotten, and no written reprimand will be placed in either man's record. I hope we don't see further incidents like this. Luckily, we weren't in a situation engaged with the enemy. That would have been catastrophic."

"Agreed, sir. I'll speak to both parties and advise them of your decision."

With the rudder incident a memory, we resumed the daily shuttling between Espiritu Santo and Guadalcanal. The routine continued until we were granted ten days of R&R in Sydney, Australia in April 1944. That welcome break rejuvenated the entire crew, and before we knew it, we were ordered to a new assignment, dispatched to General MacArthur's Seventh Fleet in New Guinea along with the destroyer *Balch*. The entire crew was looking forward to some possible battle action, having felt left out of all the successes taking place.

Enroute to New Guinea, the Seventh Fleet commander asked Commander Dawes to report repairs the ship needed. What a favorable surprise. Dawes inquired, "Ridge, give me that list of repairs you compiled. Update it for any new items that can be added."

"Yes, sir."

But when I handed him the list, we both concluded nothing was going to come of it since there was no Navy Yard near that could do the repairs. Pearl Harbor, the closest, was several thousand miles away. Nevertheless, Dawes instructed, "Highlight the major items that are readily evident, like that ugly crack in the deck that reopened after the last repair. It irks me every time I walk past it. Maybe we'll be lucky to have them tackle some of the smaller jobs. If I had one item that would be most important, and it is not really a repair, would be to see if we can get the malfunctioning TBS-TBY communications equipment replaced with something new. It never works the way it should."

"Yes, sir. You're right about that. I'll inquire." TBS was a desk top transmitter, while TBY was a portable transmitter, and together are essential for communication between ships.

Dawes was right. Nothing ever came of the list of repairs.

One of our first actions in the sector was to join *Balch* in support of a convoy of LSTs bound for Hollandia, a port on the north coast of New Guinea. (LSTs are flat-bottomed vessels, about the same length as *Warrington*, used to support amphibious operations of the Marines and Army through the transport of tanks, jeeps, armored vehicles, cargo, and troops directly onto a beachhead). That convoy was a new experience for us as LSTs cruise at around eight knots, hardly fast enough to rustle up a breeze. To say we were cruising was a stretch. To gain a little speed and prevent our boilers from overheating, we adopted a zigzag motion ahead of them. Because of their sluggish speed, like a snail crawling across a wide sidewalk, it took three days–where it would normally take one day, to reach Hollandia's large, well-protected harbor on Humboldt Bay. Our arrival was greeted by a debilitating blast of moist, humid air, heavier than a wet blanket in a Turkish steam bath. Temperatures were well north of one hundred degrees, and with no discernable breeze, someone aptly quipped, "Hollandia is a living hell. Those shuttles between Espiritu Santo and Guadalcanal weren't so bad after all." I agreed.

To escape anchoring in the bay, soaking up the sweat-drenched humidity, Dawes volunteered for patrol duty outside the harbor. "Anything," he said, "to keep the ship moving to create a breeze, even if it's a muggy one."

We were just waiting for the command to send us on a mission.

Standing watch on the bridge, I watched *Balch* pass us at high speed, and gaining momentum. Dawes was in his sea cabin making an entry into the log, so I knocked on his door to alert him. "Yes, come in."

"Captain, I thought you should know, *Balch* just passed us at twenty knots, looking to gain full steam. Something must be up."

"Thank you, Ridge. Send this message from me to the captain of *Balch* 'Where are you going, like it's the end of the world?'"

The reply, "Follow us."

Our curiosity piqued, Commander Dawes requested leave of our station, which was granted, and we quickly pursued *Balch*, steaming at flank speed to catch up. It took a while to close the gap, and when we did, we were directed to join her in assisting the Army in bombarding Japanese troops in a place called Wakde, a small island group two miles off the northeastern coast of Western New Guinea. The island was strategic because of its airfield in support of our campaign in the Pacific toward the Philippines. Nothing was visible on the island other than the dense jungle foliage, so we dispatched the captain's gig ashore to obtain directions on where to aim our guns. The Army captain on shore told us he would fire phosphorous shells as markers and that we should fire as close to the right of the white smoke as possible. When the smoke a blossomed through the fronds of the trees about two miles away, we commenced firing as rapidly as possible to launch as many rounds as we could before the slight breeze dissipated the smoke, erasing the target. We strove to maintain our fire, in concert with *Balch*, uniformly throughout the designated sector and kept firing until all our five-inch and antiaircraft ammunition was spent. With nothing left to fire, we returned to Hollandia. Hearing those guns go off, knowing we were firing on an enemy position, was therapeutic; the best morale booster we had in a long, long time.

That afternoon, upon our return to port, we rearmed our depleted ammunition anxious to go back to Wakde the next day to finish the job. The Army captain thanked us, saying our bombardment helped them to capture a Japanese supply depot. It was a modest achievement, but the war, I believed, would be won through the accumulation of many small victories such as that one. The Battle of Wakde, involving about eight hundred Japanese troops, lasted three days.

After our successful shelling at Wakde, we wallowed at anchor in the sweltering heat and humidity in Hollandia until orders were received to escort a convoy of LSTs to Biak, a small island on the western end of New Guinea near Papua where heavy land fighting was still raging. While Dawes was not thrilled with the assignment because of the slow-moving LSTs, he confided, "It's still a blessing to get away from port, even at a snail's pace." He was right about the slow pace. It took two days to make Biak with the lumbering LSTs, where we could have normally made it in half a day. When we arrived, we were elated to receive a request from the Army to deliver bombardment in support of their troops attacking the Moker Airdome.

Already in place when we arrived, inside the surrounding reef, was an LSM(R). I'd never seen that type of ship before, and I asked Dawes if he'd seen one. He hadn't, but we soon learned her purpose when she unleashed an impressive rocket attack against a cliff on the southeast corner of the island in the area we were patrolling. The Japanese, armed only with machine guns, were well entrenched in caves and, despite the rocket power of the LSM(R), could not be dislodged from their hornet's nest on the mountainside. Searching for a more effective method to unseat the enemy from their stronghold, Commander Dawes assured the army lieutenant colonel we could get it done. The Army gave the okay since nothing else they tried had worked. Under the direction of an Army major sent to us to direct the bombardment, we maneuvered *Warrington* to within two thousand feet of the cliff, at which point we commenced a focused attack of our five-inch guns, firing shot after shot with precision at point-blank range. The operation, slow and methodical, took all afternoon to complete. When we finished, enough of our shells hit the mark. The enemy streamed from the caves in a daze into the awaiting arms of our soldiers. Our crew was in a great mood. Pulverizing the enemy, seeing them in defeat, will do that. I said to Dawes on our return to Hollandia, "The credit for our success at Biak belongs to Lieutenant Pack (our gunnery chief) and Don Schultz (his assistant). They gave that Army major a demonstration in naval marksmanship. I'll admit, when I first saw those rockets launched from the LSM(R), I thought we would be bystanders, but I was wrong. An accurately placed round from a five-inch gun is more effective than a rocket."

Dawes agreed. "I'll put a notation in their files for the record," he said. "Whenever I have a chance to praise a crew member, I take it as it serves to boost morale and, God knows, we need that on this ship. Maybe we should have a celebratory dinner tonight in the Wardroom for our successes at Wadke and Biak. I'll check with Melson to see if he has enough steak for us."

Shortly after our successful shelling of Biak, Commander Dawes received an unexpected dispatch ordering *Warrington* to Balboa, Panama. He had no idea what was behind the order but was happy for it, for whatever the reason, because it brought us much closer to the United States and a possible trip to New York. A situation developed enroute that almost aborted our trip. Lt. Keppel, our Engineering Officer, came to me. "There's a weird grinding noise in the port-side reduction gear," he said, "and I haven't been able to figure what is causing it, and that concerns me." I guess my worry about a potential problem lurking below the surface had become a reality. I thought of my mother, when she died suddenly, seemingly in good health until she wasn't, and nothing could be done to reverse the outcome.

"This could be serious, Bill. We need to report this immediately to the skipper, and I want you to explain the problem to him." Reduction gears are extremely important for the operation of the ship. They synchronize the speed of the ship's turbines down to the speed of the propellers. If a foreign object got into the gears and damaged the teeth, it could render the whole engine out of commission. If that happened in the middle of the ocean, we would be a sitting duck. The repair of this problem required a major shipyard like Pearl Harbor because the deck must be opened to gain access to the gear. Since Pearl Harbor was several thousand miles away from our present position, it was a toss-up as to where to go, Pearl Harbor or Balboa, Panama (for the likely order to report to shipyard on the east coast of the States).

Commander Dawes was not happy with the news, and he was not surprised, offering the opinion that a thorough overhaul of the ship was way beyond past due. "This is the price you pay when routine maintenance is ignored and overlooked," he said. "It's not the fault of the men on this ship," he lamented. "It's the consequence and outcome of war."

The situation posed a dilemma for Dawes. Where to go, Pearl or Balboa?

I knew everyone was anxious to return to civilized port, even the skipper. Pearl Harbor was good, but New York was considered better. The men would risk just about anything, if given the choice, to get to either port. Yet, if we lost our engines on the way, it would be catastrophic. We'd be alone on the open seas, potential prey for an enemy submarine. That possibility was a greater likelihood if we went to Pearl Harbor.

27

HOMEWARD BOUND

PACIFIC TO ATLANTIC, JULY 1944

Before making his decision, Dawes asked Keppel to experiment with the engines as he expressed confidence the ship could make Panama. After trial and error, Keppel discovered that running the starboard engine at twelve knots and the damaged port engine at five knots, the vessel handled in an acceptable fashion. He advised Commander Dawes that he thought the ship could make it to Panama, and Dawes, wanting to get there as much as the crew, agreed to chance it. The commander of the Seventh Fleet released *Warrington*, thanking her for her service in New Guinea, and two days later we were in Espiritu Santo, refueling and loading food supplies in preparation for the journey to Panama.

Our voyage to Panama was uneventful, cruising at a leisurely twelve knots the entire trip. When we neared Balboa, Dawes reported the problem with the reduction gear and command of the ship transferred to the Atlantic Fleet, where we received orders to transit the canal—our destination, as Dawes predicted, the New York Navy Yard in Brooklyn for the repairs and maintenance. That was great news on the surface, but Dawes and I both knew the allotted time was not enough time to repair all of *Warrington*'s ills. Even ninety days might not be enough time. I retrieved my list of items that needed fixing or replacing, the reduction gear foremost, hoping it would be enough to warrant a long-belated ninety-day overhaul–but it was not to be. The request was denied; two weeks was all we would get.

The crew, ignorant of most of the ship's serious maladies, was ecstatic with the news of our return to New York. So much so, Seaman Charlie Hutton, the most artistic person on the ship, painted a large banner that we draped aft of the tower that declared "Homeward Bound." It billowed and fluttered in the wind all the way on our journey home.

We arrived at the mouth of the Panama Canal on the morning of July 8th, transiting that same day into the Atlantic Ocean at Colon, where we docked overnight to refuel and lade food supplies for the last leg of the cruise to New York. Once we were cleared to disembark, I headed into the Port Director's building in search of a telephone. It was easy enough to find. Several people were in a queue waiting to use the only public phone in the building. Without proper change, I placed a person-to-person call, hoping Ellen would answer. Fortunately for me, she was there and was thrilled to hear my voice as I was hers.

"We're in Colon, Panama, but will be sailing before noon today for New York. We're scheduled to arrive in Brooklyn Navy Yard at 9:00 a.m. on the 13th."

"That's great news. How did this come about?"

"I'll tell you when I see you. There's a long line of people waiting to use the phone to call home."

"Okay. I'll take off from work that day and will be waiting for you on the pier with open arms."

"I can't wait to kiss you."

I embarked on the ship after making my phone call, and shortly thereafter we took in the lines and weighed anchor for New York. We limped through the Caribbean Sea at twelve knots, anxious to reach the Atlantic Ocean and the East Coast of the States. It was July 9th, and we'd be home soon.

After several days cruising with purpose toward home, the New Jersey coast emerged, the beam of refracted light from the Cape May Lighthouse signaling the final leg of our journey. The night sky, dimly lit by a fading moon and a solid string of twinkling lights on the port side, ceded to the glow of the rising sun, which threatened to light the day. The bow of the ship cut efficiently through the dark water, slicing small, white-tipped waves. My first land marker—the drab gray silhouette of the Claridge Hotel, the twenty-four-story Jersey Shore skyscraper in Atlantic City—appeared on the horizon. The sun blossomed from the sea, exposing land, and confirming our arrival. As the flickering lights disappeared, gulls and terns moved in, circling overhead, our first welcome greeting, guiding the way home, as they always do. I left the bridge for the fo'c'sle so I could savor the experience of sailing into New York harbor from the sea, seeing the skyline of Manhattan from a new vantage point. The ocean breeze always seemed the same, but it had a special scent when returning to port.

Commander Dawes guided the ship forward from the bridge, past the Lightship Ambrose off Sandy Hook that pointed the way through the channel. The ship glided smoothly through waters so calm it reminded me of Greenwood Lake of my youth. As we passed Liberty Island, the sun was shining upon the outstretched arm of the Statue of Liberty, the hint of its flaming torch giving a warm welcome. The statue's symbolism—freedom—was even more meaningful given the world war we now fought. The jagged gray-black skyline of Manhattan was dead ahead, dominated by the Empire State Building, which glowed orange as the sun hit the Art Deco façade. As we sailed under the Brooklyn Bridge and came closer to the piers lining the waterfront, ocean smells mingled with the bustling noises and odors of life on land. *Warrington* was allocated two weeks for the maintenance repairs, even though the ship's condition begged for a more comprehensive overhaul.

Dawes granted ten-day leaves to those men whose hometowns were within five hundred miles of New York City, representing about a third of the crew. He told me that he wanted to give the men as much time as possible at home without them spending too much of their leave traveling to get there. Shorter shore passes were given to the rest of the crew so they could explore the environs of Manhattan, the beach at Coney Island and Rockway, or a baseball game at Yankee Stadium or Ebbets Field. Most of the men I heard speak said they would be making a beeline for the nightlife of Times Square seeking the company of the opposite sex. Who could blame them? Dawes gave me ten days leave to spend with Ellen, but I told him I would report back in several days to monitor the repairs, and more often if he felt I was needed.

Having been away for nearly two years, the memory of the kiss with Ellen on Track 61 in Grand Central Terminal kept me going. All I wanted was to feel her warm embrace and spend time doing the things young married couples do.

Warrington slowly maneuvered to the dock, settling into her berth next to the pier to await her date with the dry dock. It was July 13th, and we were home. On the foredeck outside the bridge, I saw Ellen standing on the pier below, dressed in a navy-blue suit, which made her long blonde tresses stand out. I went back inside the bridge.

"Skipper, I see my wife," I said, pointing to her on the pier.

"Your beautiful bride. Ridge, take leave as soon as we are cleared to debark. I don't want to keep you from her any longer than necessary. Two years has been long enough. I hope to take a couple days to go home to see my wife."

"Sir, let me know when and I'll return to relieve you."

"That won't be necessary, Pennington will be here. He's from Chicago so he won't be going home."

"Okay then. But I intend to stop by to see how the overhaul is going. I'll see you soon."

We were cleared at 0950 and with my seabag slung over my shoulder, I saluted the OOD and stepped quickly down the gangway, calling Ellen's name over the railing so she knew I was coming. Just as I stepped off the last tread, she moved into me with a hug and a kiss and whispered in my ear, "I've missed you so much. Let's go home straightaway. We have an appointment?"

"You're kidding. Where?"

"You're bedroom laboratory. Where did you think?"

"That's what I thought, but I just wanted to make sure."

I stepped back, taking in her beauty, a vision I dreamed about for the last two years, now a reality before me. "Look at you. More beautiful today than the day we met at the fair. I can't believe how long I've craved your embrace, and more, and now it's here. We have a lot of catching up to do. Where's the nearest taxi stand? I can't wait another minute to get home to explore your naked body."

"Oh, John. Let's hurry. The taxi is just outside the gate."

I had no sooner put my duffle down on the floor by the door entry when Ellen said, "Wait here. I'll only be a moment." Looking around the room, I was awed at how Ellen had made our house into a warm and inviting home, and wondered, *what is she up to?* Then I heard her call.

"John, I'm in the bedroom. You remember where that is?"

"Yes. I remember. The laboratory," I joked. "I'll be right in."

I lifted my seabag, and when I walked through the door into the bedroom, there she was, beside the bed in a sheer white negligee. Her blonde hair framed an alluring smile on red lips, and the silk bodice cupped her small, but voluptuous breasts. Her erect nipples begged my response. A vision of beauty, just as I remembered in all my lonely dreams at sea.

"Ellen, you take my breath away. You can't imagine how long I've looked forward to this moment, seeing you like this." As I moved to her, the nightgown slid from her shoulders and pooled on the floor by her bare feet. Naked, with urgent desire on her face, she stepped into my embrace with a hungry kiss, a kiss that was too long in coming. Her hands fumbled with my belt buckle, and with her help, I shrugged off my uniform and guided her onto the bed, where we coupled in rapturous bliss the rest of the afternoon.

After several more times making love, Ellen said, "I hope you're not too tired?"

"No, are you ready again? Give me another minute or two to recharge my battery."

"Good, I'm glad your battery is recharging, but that's not why I was asking."

"Oh?"

"No, there are people anxious to see you, so I reserved a table for dinner at Victor Koenig's for 6:00 p.m. My parents will be there, as will Jane, Celie, Kitty, and Gus, who is on leave."

"That's sounds great. Ellen, you amaze me. It'll be good to see everyone. After dinner, if you're in the mood, we can go back into the bedroom laboratory for some more experiments."

"That's a date I look forward to. How many experiments would that then be?"

"I wasn't counting, but not enough. There'll be more. A lot more."

We strolled from our house several blocks to Victor Koenig's, enjoying the people and activity along Myrtle Avenue. The day's warm temperatures cooled as the sun faded behind the trees. When we entered the restaurant, I was greeted with a "hero's welcome." Ellen made the right decision, as she always had. The festivities lasted several hours. I enjoyed that sauerbraten dinner with potato dumplings and red cabbage that I dreamed of, washed down by a few schooners of Trommer's White Label draft beer, and a healthy slice of Black Forest Cake for dessert. Everyone was anxious to hear about my time away, but I said maybe another time as I didn't want to spoil that joyous occasion with war stories. I believed everyone pretty much knew what I endured through Ellen, so the firsthand account wasn't necessary. The restaurant had emptied, and we realized we were the last table there, so we said our goodbyes and promised to get together again soon. Ellen mentioned having a BBQ before I leave to make up for the 4th of July.

We ambled home, hand in hand, along Myrtle Avenue, the streetlamps lighting our way in the dark.

I said, "It looks like some of the stores closed and new ones opened, but Bill's is still here."

"Yes, business was tough for some. The clothing store you patronized closed. Not enough business to stay open, I suppose, with all the men away in the service. I heard a beauty parlor will be moving in there, good for me."

Just as we turned the corner to our block, a light rain arrived, sprinkling through the rustling leaves of the trees. "This rain," Ellen said, "should cool the temperatures in the house, and if we leave the windows open, we can pretend we're on a second honeymoon listening to the waves crashing the beach."

"I've never liked the rain, until I walked through it with you. Usually, rain always meant to me that we had to stop playing baseball in the middle of a game. Now it will have a whole new meaning—back to the laboratory."

"You read my mind. Let's hurry."

Our apartment on 79th Street was a half-block from Myrtle Avenue. At the end of our street, on the opposite side of Myrtle Avenue, was a cemetery that made me reflect on those *South Dakota* crew members who lost their lives at Guadalcanal and were buried at sea—no tombstone to denote their life on earth. Glendale is surrounded by cemeteries spanning the religious gamut. Everyone whoever died in New York City, no matter what religion, faith, or nationality, probably found their eternal resting place in one of the cemeteries here—Cypress Hills; Salem Fields; All Faith's Lutheran, where my parents are buried; Mount Carmel; Beth-El; Mount Neboh; and Union Field. I vividly remember when I was a teen the Robert Moses Interborough Parkway being built through Cypress Hills, and the hundreds of caskets that were unearthed and reinterred elsewhere to accommodate the snaking road. Oddly, having seen death in battle and compatriots buried at sea, I found the solitude of meandering through the grounds of the nearby cemetery, with its birdsong and muffled noises of passing cars, serene and comforting. I strolled through the cemetery each morning after that first cup of coffee thereafter with Ellen, who appreciated walking the quiet serenity as much as I did. Out of curiosity, we even visited Machpelah Cemetery to view the grave of Harry Houdini, which attracts crowds each Halloween Day, to see if the Great Houdini would appear for one more great escape.

The ensuing days were filled with activity, half the time spent in the bedroom making up for the last two years, and the rest crammed with socializing with family and friends, visiting old haunts, and a visit to *Warrington* in dry dock to confer with Commander Dawes on the progress of the repairs.

I stopped by Charlie McGrath's Tavern early in my leave. When I walked through the door, I was greeted by my favorite song, Danny Boy, playing on the Rock-Ola juke box. Charlie was placing a Rheingold draft beer that he had just poured from the tap to the patron at the end of the bar when he saw me. "Ridge!" he exclaimed. "It's great to see you. It's been a long time. The girls occasionally stop by for drinks to fill me in on what is doing with the guys, and Ellen said you would drop by when you came home."

"Charlie, aside from Ellen and a sauerbraten dinner at Koenig's, I was most looking forward to enjoying a cold glass of Trommer's at your bar while I listened to some of your corny jokes. I'm sure you've plenty of new ones while I was away that I haven't heard." Looking around at the inviting environment, I said, "I see things have stayed the same, just as I remember, which is comforting. Except for the juke box, which is a nice addition. I guess that replaces your singing those Irish tunes."

"Well, not exactly. I can still be coaxed into singing a few Irish songs for my friends. Makes me think of home in Dublin."

"You sure look good, Charlie, and thanks for taking care of the girls while we were away."

"That was my pleasure. The girls and some of the older folks in the neighborhood were enough to keep me going. Business was slow while all you guys were away—beer sales were way down. But it's picking up. A couple of the old gang, Paul Kubik and Herman Nollenberger, have been in."

"I heard Herman was injured in France and is doing well since he returned home. I'll have to see him before I leave."

"He looked good to me. I didn't know he was wounded. I guess he didn't want to talk about it, and Georgie Beck, being in the Coast Guard, has been around the whole time. He usually stops in on the weekends for a few beers and we trade jokes."

"That's great to hear, Charlie. Hopefully, this war will end soon, and we can all stop by to enjoy a nice, ice-cold beer. In Honolulu they serve beer in iced Pilsner glasses. Really makes the beer taste good in that hot weather they have there. "

"I'll have to think about doing the same. Anything to keep the patrons content."

"Charlie, the neighborhood wouldn't be the same without your saloon. It's like a second home to us. You don't need iced pilsner glasses to attract a crowd. It's the comradery, your jokes and singing, that brings us in."

"I'm happy to hear you say that. Are you home for good? Ellen didn't say."

"No such luck. I still have time to serve before I'm out."

"Well, I'm glad you made it home safe and sound," he said, sincerely. "Ellen said you saw some brutal battle action in the Pacific. You know, when you were at Fort Schuyler, I never thanked you enough for the booze and smokes you were able to get me for the bar. Things were tight then, and getting supplies to run the business was difficult."

"Charlie, I was glad I was able to do it. Like I said, you've made this place like a second home for everyone."

"Thanks, Ridge, that means a lot to me. Now it's my turn to return the favor. Put your wallet away. While you're on leave, the drinks are on the house," he smiled as he slid the glass of Trommer's to me.

"Here's to you, Charlie," I raised my glass. "And to being back home."

While the ship was in dry dock undergoing her overhaul, I visited with Commander Dawes who expressed to me his concern about the extent of the repairs we were receiving—or not receiving, if truth be told. I met him on the bridge, and he said, "Let's go to my stateroom where we can talk in private."

As soon as the door was shut, he ranted, "Ridge, off the record, as you know, we were denied the degree of maintenance we should be receiving, and from my interaction with the 'powers that be' the last several days, I believe the reason pertains to the ignorance of the Atlantic command about the peculiarities of the war zone in the Pacific."

"I think I know what you are saying, skipper. *Warrington* operated for months on end with only superficial overhauls, scraping barnacles and fresh paint, and, I would add, the same for the crew, deprived of much-needed shore liberty for extended periods of time."

Dawes' anger flared. "Yes. Those conditions were common to many of the ships in the Pacific, and you may not have noticed, but that's in sharp contrast to how the Navy operates in the Atlantic Theater."

"Sir, I'm not sure I understand."

"Ridge, it's clear to me. Here they have major Navy yards on both sides of the Atlantic for maintenance and repairs, to say nothing about the numerous opportunities for liberty ashore for the crew in civilized ports. That's the damn difference." Dawes' face turned scarlet. "And most of the activities in the Atlantic involve training exercises and inspections, so the ships are in generally overall better condition."

"I certainly agree with your assessment, cap. We were too busy shuttling cargo convoys throughout the Pacific while others were fighting the Japs in great sea battles at Midway and the Coral Sea. The only battle we didn't face was a typhoon. I guess we were lucky on that score."

"One derogatory comment I received pissing me to no end was from Rear Admiral Jones, commander of the Atlantic destroyer fleet, who berated me," he fumed, as he paced within the stateroom, collecting his thoughts, "for the appearance of our crew. He said they looked like mates on a Montauk fishing boat. It took all my resolve to hold my temper."

"I'm with you."

"I know our crew wore dungarees while at sea, but so did all the crews in the Pacific, as the white uniforms were too visible for enemy aircraft, and we allowed the belowdecks seamen to sunbathe when off watch as it was their only chance to cool off after four hours in the sweltering heat belowdecks in the engine and fire rooms. Even then, the heat and humidity took its toll. Even on the bridge, take Humboldt Bay, temperatures, as you know, frequently exceeded one hundred degrees with one hundred percent humidity."

"Yes, skipper. Humboldt was a living hell."

"I guess I vented my frustration and anger. I had to get if off my chest, and you're the only person I would consider confiding to, aside from my wife."

"I empathize and wholeheartedly agree with everything you said. To have done otherwise would have been insanity. It's like we have two navies. One fighting sea battles in the Pacific and one conducting training exercises in the Atlantic and the occasional hunt for a U-boat. Quite a stark contrast. If our partners in the Atlantic spent some time in the Pacific, they would gain an appreciation of the circumstances we endured and had to live through."

"I couldn't agree with you more."

While the ship was drydocked, the maintenance workers swarmed over her in a whirlwind of activity; dismantling the CIC and charthouse, installing LORAN (electronic navigation equipment) and FOXER gear (a device towed off the stern of the ship designed to thwart the acoustic torpedoes from enemy submarines). Their efforts to repair the items on the list I compiled appeared commendable, but that was countered by the short time allocated for the extensive level of repairs needed. This resulted in much of the work being slipshod as we subsequently found out (especially with respect to the port-side reduction gear). There was no attempt to fix the crack in the deck on the starboard side of the stack. Surprisingly, the ship was painted camouflage, which was appropriate in the Pacific but seemed weirdly out of place in the Atlantic. Dawes was quite amused with our new look but didn't object considering the high possibility that *Warrington* may return to the Pacific.

Every day, news on the war in Europe was getting better; we were winning, though battles still raged in the Pacific. The D-Day Invasion of Normandy on June 6th was followed with Allied victories in Caen and St. Lo.

Ellen wanted to celebrate that good news by having dinner at Patsy's Italian, a new restaurant she discovered in the city that opened earlier in the year. Interestingly, it was an instant favorite of singer Frank Sinatra. Finished with our meal and lingering over coffee and a shared cannoli while listening to the mellow sound of Sinatra singing "There's No You" on the restaurant's sound system, Ellen said, "The last few days has gone by so fast and you'll be leaving in a couple of days, but I feel the war will be ending soon. The fighting in Europe seems to be going our way, and Germany will probably fall before the end of the year. That's what they are saying. If that happens, maybe the Japanese will surrender, and the war will be over. What do you think? Is that just wishful thinking, or a real possibility?"

I appreciated Ellen's optimism but knew there were battles still to be fought and won in Europe, and the war in the Pacific was still raging. "Ellen," I cautioned, "the Japanese have their own agenda. Rumors are that if we were to invade Japan, the population would be armed with small firearms, shovels, and pitchforks and would fight door-to-door to death to the last man—and woman. They have suicide pilots known as kamikaze's that purposely crash their planes into our ships screaming on their way 'Tenno Heika Banzai' which translates to 'Long live the emperor!' They're fanatical, no doubt about it."

"Wow, I didn't realize. I thought if we won in Europe, the same would hold true in the Pacific," she replied.

"Let's think positive thoughts. If I'm lucky, *Warrington* will be permanently repositioned to the Atlantic. That would probably allow me to have periodic leave until the war ends."

"John, I pray you're right. I couldn't bear to go another two years without seeing you."

Those last couple of days of leave slipped by, and I was saying goodbye to Ellen. Upon my return to the ship, Commander Dawes shocked me with the news that there would be a change in command before the end of August; his tour of duty on *Warrington* was over.

I was flabbergasted and said so. "So am I," he said. "I certainly wasn't expecting it. Maybe my tangle with the brass about our slipshod overhaul is the reason. That, and the negative comments about the appearance of our crew. I didn't say this to you before, but I was told not to criticize the quality of work from the yard. There must be some political connection I'm not aware of. Now you're 'in the know,' but keep it to yourself. Any talk about it will blow up in your face."

"What do you know about the new skipper?"

"Nothing yet, but I'll fill you in as soon as I'm informed."

The repairs to *Warrington,* such as they were, were completed on July 28th, and we departed the Brooklyn Navy Yard on a trial run to Casco Bay, Maine. Ellen took the day off from work to see me off at the pier, and I watched her waving a red scarf in the air as the ship pulled away from her berth.

It quickly became evident the ship was victim to the short time allotted for repairs relative to the level of repairs needed. The shoddy workmanship manifested itself almost immediately when live steam billowed throughout the engineering spaces. Lieutenant Keppel found the bolts on the high-pressure steam lines were only hand tight. This was a colossal and inexcusable oversight, clearly indicative of the poor-quality work in the Brooklyn Navy Yard. Dawes, when he was told, confided to me he would "fire the donkey's ass" who was managing the yard if he were in charge. It's said that "haste makes waste," and there couldn't be truer words, but this went beyond that. This was pure, unadulterated negligence. The trial run to Casco Bay was aborted before it began, and we returned to the yard for two days of bolt tightening. Despite our quick return to port, I was not able to see Ellen, but I did telephone her at work to let her know what happened and that I would be in touch soon. Dawes had me check all the work that had been done to determine if there were any more surprises lurking. I didn't notice anything awry, but who knows? Sometimes problems don't present until it is too late.

Amazingly, no report was submitted about the negligent work performed by the yard, which reinforced Dawes's claim that the brass wanted no complaints lodged about the quality of work, for whatever the reason. Curious. Real curious. With the bolts tightened, we made a successful trip to Casco Bay our second time out, and Keppel reported the noises from the reduction gear had disappeared. That was a happy surprise. Nevertheless, Dawes was furious with the quality and level of maintenance we received.

"Ridge," Dawes said, "The wear and tear of the Pacific is imbedded, still in our bones—the superficial overhaul we received in Brooklyn was but a meager attempt at correcting the deep-rooted problems that existed. I hate to turn over the ship to a new skipper in such dire condition, but all my attempts to have the proper maintenance were thwarted. I blame that, like we discussed, on the ignorance of the command here about the sharp contrast in conditions between the Atlantic and the Pacific. Loose bolts on the steam valves are inexcusable. Where is the quality control and management oversight? At least you know all the hidden dirt and can impart your knowledge to the new skipper."

"Yes, sir. I'll make sure he is fully informed."

After our successful run to Casco Bay, we were ordered to Norfolk, Virginia, to join a convoy there but, by the time we arrived on August 5th, Keppel reported the noise in the port-side reduction gear—supposedly fixed when we were in the Brooklyn Navy Yard—had returned. Dawes was furious with this news. We entered the Norfolk Navy Yard hoping to have the problem fixed, once and for all. A large section of the main deck was removed to gain access to the port reduction gear. Once the problem area was open to view, it was evident the gears were badly chewed up and needed replacing.

Keppel reported to Commander Dawes while I was with him on the bridge, saying to us, "I asked the maintenance worker what caused the problem with the reduction gear, and he handed me this," opening his fist to reveal a two-inch square chunk of steel about a half-inch thick, which he handed to Dawes.

"The only way this could have gotten meshed into the gear," Keppel said, "would be someone purposely tossing it in. In my opinion, this was not an accident but rather an act of sabotage."

Dawes replied, "That's a pretty strong accusation, Lieutenant Keppel."

"Maybe that's too harsh, cap, but certainly, at the very least, a worker with an ax to grind for some reason. Why, I don't know."

Dawes nodded. "I agree with you, Bill. It looks that way. Unfortunately, the powers that be admonished any complaints against Brooklyn Navy Yard, so we'll have to let the matter drop. Who knows the motivation behind such an act? Only the person who did it. It could have been a disgruntled worker, as you suggest, who didn't realize the magnitude or the gravity of what he caused, or it has been there all along since the ship was built, and gradually jostled around until it surfaced, breaking loose to cause the problem. I say that because this was a problem we lived with when we left Espiritu Santo on our return to New York. We'll never know for sure. The important thing is for the problem be properly fixed here."

Dawes welcomed Cdr. Samuel Quarles, the new skipper, aboard on August 15th, but transfer of command did not occur until two weeks later, after the port-side reduction gear was repaired and a successful test run completed. Quarles, an Annapolis graduate class of 1932, most recently served on the old four-stack destroyer *Babbitt* operating in the North Atlantic. *Babbitt*, a 1,211-ton Wickes-class destroyer 314 feet in length, was substantially smaller than *Warrington*. When Quarles was "piped aboard" two weeks earlier, his awe of the ship he was taking command of was evident as he scanned the length of the vessel, glossing over the imperfections visible to many of those serving on the ship. To be fair, how would he know of her imperfections unless he had served on the ship for a time? The two weeks he was aboard while Dawes was still in command before the repairs and test run were completed was clearly not enough time for him to grasp the problems that existed hidden in plain sight.

When Quarles came aboard on August 15th, Commander Dawes invited me to join them for the customary "change of command" procedure. We pointed out the ship's idiosyncrasies to Quarles as we went along. Because the ship was undergoing the repair to the reduction gear when we had that meeting, we skipped the usual fire, collision, and man-overboard drill, but everything else required by regulations was covered.

Dawes opined to Quarles, "The ship seems to be top-heavy, and I say this because of the slow-rolling motion we periodically experience in heavy seas. To me, this is an indication of low stability. This may be more of a factor if the ship remains in the Atlantic, especially with the hurricane season fast approaching. Lieutenant Ridgeway suggested to me the top-heavy conditions is probably due to the antiaircraft guns and deskside ammo bunkers that were added after the ship was commissioned."

"Commander Quarles," I interjected, "since I've been aboard, almost two years now, we sailed throughout the Pacific, and although we never encountered a severe gale or typhoon, we did occasionally experience heavy seas, which caused a pronounced rolling motion that Commander Dawes mentioned. We're already in the hurricane season here, so we should be mindful of how the ship will handle if caught in such a storm. You might be interested, *Warrington* was ensnarled in the Long Island Express hurricane of 1938 and returned safely to New York, but her center of gravity was lower then and the captain loaded the ballast tanks to gain stability."

"I appreciate your insight, Lieutenant Ridgeway," Quarles responded, "and your concerns are noted. You should know I've been serving in the Atlantic for several years since I graduated from Annapolis and I'm familiar with the bad weather and heavy seas. We won't know how *Warrington* will handle a hurricane until we're in a real-life situation. Hopefully, we won't have to find out."

"Yes, sir. I understand."

Quarles spent his first few days as captain getting familiar with the ship and her crew. On September 9th, he met with the command in Norfolk, Virginia to receive the orders for our next mission.

"Lieutenant, are you okay? Can you hear me?" someone asked. I opened my eyes. Greene was speaking over the sound of the waves that seem less ferocious, less threatening.

"I think so. My head is pounding." I reached behind the back of my head. I felt a lump the size of an orange. I rolled my tongue though my mouth and feel a gap from a couple of missing teeth. *Well, at least I'm alive.* I remembered taking the first watch, but even that simple task drained my energy.

"Sir, the storm has finally ebbed."

"I see. That's good news. I was dreaming about how I got to this place. I was home and now I'm here in the middle of the ocean. I hope we make it back to land. My wife would be disappointed if she didn't see me again, especially for Christmas. I already missed the last two."

"I hope so too, sir. We all do."

The sky loosened; and although the swells were still huge, the wind softened, and the rainspouts became less violent and less frequent. The rain tapered to soft showers below the overcast sky.

I lifted my aching head and looked around. I thought, *if I didn't know, I never would have guessed a hurricane roared through the day before, taking the lives of a ship and most of her crew.*

28

NEW ENEMIES

Sunny skies mushroomed late in the morning. As the day progressed, the unrelenting sun became our new antagonist, beating down on us. To shield against the sun's powerful rays, everyone removed their shirt from under their life vest, and draped it over their head and upper body as a makeshift coverup.

There were nineteen of us on the raft, and as senior officer I had to focus and be clear-headed to ensure I made the right decisions—if we were to have a chance to return to our loved ones.

"Men," I cautioned, "watch for the symptoms of sunstroke: headache, nausea, dizziness, heavy sweating, and thirst. That's our new enemy now that the hurricane has moved on." The sea had moved from rough to choppy, and the longer and deeper waves ceded to lots and lots of short, shallow waves.

"Sir, I have a headache," someone said.

"You and me, both." My head was pounding, the throbbing pain unrelenting.

"With the choppy conditions," I said, "it may be hard to distinguish between seasickness and sunstroke, so feel your forehead for elevated body temperature. That will be the best indicator. We have some burn ointment. Rub it on your cheeks and forehead. That may help."

Sapp said, "Don, do you have that ointment? Pass it over when you're done."

I instructed Don, "Pass it to the guy next to you and we'll go around the horn. Also, with the calming sea, keep an eye for sharks. The Atlantic is filled with makos, white tips, blues, and tigers, all of whom are partial to people, especially an arm or a leg. Make sure to keep your limbs in the float. If you get bitten, the scent of blood in the water will attract them in a frenzy. They're referred to as the 'hyenas of the sea' for a reason."

"Lieutenant," Richards offered, "I've read about various ways to protect against a shark attack."

"Share your knowledge, Richards," Schultz encouraged.

"Well, there are a few things. You can punch them in the snout, poke their eyes, roll up into a ball, remain perfectly still, thrash as hard as you can to scare them away, or grab hold of their fins and ride them until they tire and swim away."

"I'm not sure about the outcome with those various methods," I said.

"Me too, sir. I'd be too afraid to even try."

"But I do know what works," I told them.

"What's that, sir?"

"The best way to stay safe from a shark is to keep your hands, arms, and legs as high on the float and out of the water as possible. Don't tempt them."

Melson, since he was the ships' cook, assumed the job of distributing the rations of food and water. He passed a biscuit to each man, followed by a cup of water. As soon as he knifed open a tin of Spam, huge shark fins began circling the raft.

LaTronica hollered, "Melson, close that tin, we have visitors," pointing to the water next to him, a fin scraping the side of the raft.

Berman fell back onto the webbed griding to get his dangling leg out of the water and into the raft.

"They must have great sense of smell for blood and Spam. Who knew?" Klingen said.

Sapp yelled at Melson, "Toss the tin as far as you can. Maybe they'll leave."

"Everyone, get your legs in the raft. They'll leave if there is nothing for them to eat," I reiterated.

Melson, in a pitcher's windup, the can of Spam in the palm of his hand, threw it about sixty feet, almost falling over the side from the effort.

Greene said, "Good arm, Melson. When we get back to New York, the Yankee's could use you as a relief pitcher."

"Very funny. That was my fast ball. I hope they go for it."

With no food, the sharks left–at least for now.

We were totally alone once again. Nineteen people on a raft, lost on the open sea.

We drifted with the Gulf Stream, taking turns scanning for other survivors but found no one. The sea subsided as the day passed, the ocean becoming more tranquil. Battling the sun's rays, sharks, and the threat of hallucination were our new enemies.

The float was quiet, eerily so, the only sound the water slapping against the canvas covered cork siding of the raft. I assumed everyone was lost in private thoughts about loved ones, praying they would make it home to them.

I considered my words with Quarles about the weather before we left Norfolk. I should have been more insistent about delaying the cruise until after the storm passed. The sinking of *Warrington* should have never happened. It was preventable. Maybe I should have gone over Quarles's head and made a direct plea to Mayo or Wheyland, despite the consequences for me in doing so.

29

ON DEAF EARS

With the sea subsided, the water tranquil, and the hurricane behind us, I pondered how we came to this point. The sinking of *Warrington* should have never happened. It would have been preventable if only they had listened to me—and by "they," I mean Commander Quarles. My pleas to Quarles to abort the cruise landed on deaf ears. I should have argued harder with him to delay the cruise. That's what my training taught me, and what I lectured to my seamanship class at Fort Schuyler.

I lectured at Fort Schuyler about the potential impact of a hurricane on a ship at sea. I told the class how hurricanes form and the power they can unleash. A hurricane, I taught, is a tightly organized storm of furious energy in which a warm center of low barometric pressure is surrounded by gale-force winds rotating counterclockwise. Hurricanes are elliptical in shape and generally cover an average area of three hundred miles in diameter, with the curving cloud bands forming their eye wall extending anywhere from three to sixty-five miles in circumference. If Quarles knew anything about a hurricane our cruise would have been delayed. Understanding how they develop is necessary in commanding a vessel at sea.

The dilemma is not knowing what track the storm will take, and what maneuver would be needed to evade the worst of it. There's no safe basement to take shelter in until the storm passes. Guessing wrong could have devastating consequences.

Knowledge of how hurricanes behave improves the ship's odds of avoiding a fatal catastrophe. They are unpredictable. The Long Island Express of '38 is a perfect example. The storm went against the norm, stunning the weather experts by suddenly changing direction, slashing across the end of Long Island, and smashing into New England on a course never seen before. With a hurricane, expect the unexpected.

Hurricanes that form in the Atlantic, the deadly ones, are known as Cape Verde after a grouping of a volcanic islands in the Atlantic Ocean 350 miles off the west coast of Africa. The blinding rains and furious winds of a Cape Verde eye wall are the fiercest on the planet. While these hurricanes impact North America, they develop in tropical depressions in the savanna grasslands of Africa during the two-month-long rainy season. The resulting downpours swoop westward across the semiarid steppes of treeless grasslands to the Atlantic coast where the disturbances launch to sea, developing into tropical storms once past Cape Verde Islands. These hurricanes are the most lethal and unpredictable storms on earth.

The initial path of a Cape Verde storm is westward from Cape Verde Islands, but a turn to the north is almost always certain for those that last more than a few days. Once the disturbance approaches the Americas, the storm will continue to develop, growing into an all-out hurricane like what we ran smack into. We left Norfolk knowing we were sailing toward a full-fledged hurricane. We didn't know what direction the storm would take, but convinced ourselves we would pass by it to the west. That was a bad assumption.

A full-fledged hurricane will take one of three possible courses: (1) westward impacting Florida and the Louisiana Gulf Coast; (2) a path northwest along the Atlantic Seaboard affecting the coast from Florida to the Carolinas; or (3) further north picking up speed and intensity along the way to unleash its fury on New Jersey, New York, and New England. What makes these hurricanes so lethal is the inability to accurately predict which of the three courses the storm will take. This inability to predict their direction makes it imperative to avoid them at all costs. If a ship is at sea when a hurricane develops, a wrong decision on what maneuver is needed to avoid a head-on collision with it could deliver the ship into the eye of the storm and lead to her utter destruction and the lives of her crew. The best tools on the ship to avoid the worst of the storm if the ship is already at sea are the barometer and anemometer. However, if the ship is in power and has not yet weighed anchor, the best course of action is to stay in place. Postpone departure until after the storm passes. That's what we should have done. Instead, we chose the foolhardy and irresponsible course. There was no way we were going to beat a hurricane.

30

THE LAST MISSION

Quarles received orders late yesterday from the commander of Task Unit 29 for *Warrington* to escort USS *Hyades* to Colon, Panama. From there, to Trinidad to report to the commanding officer of USS *Alaska* (a battle cruiser on her shakedown cruise in the Caribbean) to escort her to Philadelphia Navy Yard for minor alterations. *Hyades*, a store ship for delivering refrigerated items and equipment to ships in the fleet and remote staging areas, was larger than *Warrington*, displacing 7,700 tons and stretching 469 feet in length.

Following routine procedure before a task unit leaves port, a conference was held between the respective parties to iron out cruise logistics with respect to course, speed, and so on. The details for this specific cruise were of utmost importance to this narrative.

Lt. Cdr. Charles Mayo, ComServLant–short for Commander, Service Force, Atlantic Fleet–operations officer in Norfolk, Virginia chaired the meeting attended by the commanding officers of both ships, Morgan C. Wheyland of *Hyades* and Samuel Quarles of *Warrington*. The agenda encompassed: (1) the operational assignment between the two ships—Mayo placed Wheyland in tactical command (even though he had seven years active duty as compared to ten years for Quarles) because he was an earlier graduate of the U.S. Naval Academy; (2) the communication protocol between the two ships--the communication officer of *Hyades* submitted a plan and voice code table for TBS (desktop talk-between-ships transmitter) and TBY (portable transmitter) transmissions between the two ships, which Mayo approved and to which the commanders of both vessels agreed, and a separation frequency of 2885 KCS in the event the ships lost contact with each other for any reason; (3) the cruise's course and speed—*Warrington* would take a station 2,500 yards ahead of *Hyades* and would patrol the station so as to be ahead of her by the time she completed her turn to each new zigzag on a course confirmed in a mimeographed zigzag plan given to the commander of each ship; and (4) the forecasted weather conditions—Mayo provided both captains with all available hydrographic weather information, including an advisory issued the day before by the Weather Bureau in Puerto Rico about an approaching hurricane east of the Bahamas.

Upon his return to *Warrington* after the meeting, Quarles shared with me the minutes of the conference. In reviewing the information with him, I noted everything was routine, except for the September 8th weather report which mentioned a hurricane-strength storm developing in the Caribbean.

"Captain, I see a hurricane advisory has been issued for a storm approaching the east coast of the Bahamas. What was the consensus about the impact of this storm on our planned course? I ask this because the track of a hurricane is one variable that cannot be planned, but how you react to the information is critical."

"Lieutenant Ridgeway, that was the last item on the agenda. The consensus was that it would not be a problem, nor would it interfere with our planned course as we'll pass west ahead of the storm center," he said imperiously.

"Sir," I proffered, "I beg to disagree on this. I'm not saying the voyage will not turn out as predicted. But you must consider that hurricanes are terribly unpredictable, and because of this, you cannot know with certainty if the assumption being made about the storm's path is the correct one. And considering the fact that hurricanes typically affect the weather hundreds of miles in all directions, we most assuredly will feel the effect of the storm somewhere in our path. Maybe not hurricane-strength, but certainly bringing heavy seas bordering on hurricane levels, and we don't know how the ship will handle under such conditions."

"Lieutenant," he churlishly responded, "the storm was considered and was not deemed hazardous to our cruise. End of discussion on the matter."

"But sir. I've read the ship's log as I mentioned to you, and *Warrington* barely survived that hurricane in '38. The antiaircraft guns and ammo bunkers that have been added since the ship was launched have raised her center of gravity, making her potentially top-heavy in severe weather. We've never been tested in such weather."

"Drop the subject, Lieutenant, I mean it. I've spent my entire career in the North Atlantic, and I'm not a stranger to foul weather. I've been in several heavy storms without a problem. These ships are built to handle it."

31

INTO HARM'S WAY

Atlantic Ocean, evening 10 September 1944

I had a disconcerting feeling about the cruise. A feeling that was rooted in my knowledge about hurricanes. I firmly believed we would be embroiled in the middle of that hurricane, and even if the odds were only one in hundred, it was still too great a risk to take. If we were wrong about our course, we could lose both our ship and our crew. I, however, was the only one who held that opinion. Precautions should have been taken considering the hurricane's unpredictable nature. The normal westerly, or northwesterly, track of a hurricane almost always changes course to the north, its speed of advance and wind strength increasing when it does. This change in course is the great unknown and is particularly dangerous because the timing of the change is random. I would bet the ranch we would be ensnarled in the storm to some degree. If the storm curved into the Florida-Louisiana Gulf Coast ahead of us, we may slide past unscathed–but if it curved up the east coast of Florida, we would be impacted to some degree because the storm front is very wide. To what degree is unknown, but I was afraid to find out. I hoped I was wrong about my intuition, but the odds were against us for a favorable outcome.

Although Commander Quarles deemed the weather component an acceptable risk, I intended to have our navigation and communications departments closely monitor the notices from the Weather Bureau in Puerto Rico so we could plot the storm's path. Based upon what I saw, I would strongly recommend to the captain a change in *Warrington*'s course should that appear warranted. I knew if the hurricane curved to the northwest, up the Florida coast, we would run smack into it, potentially placing the ship in severe peril. I also knew I would not lose my uneasy feeling about the storm until after we passed by it, if that was possible, and put it behind us.

Fueled and provisioned, water tanks full, and replacement ammunition and depth charges stowed for that expended during the Casco Bay training exercise, we departed the Norfolk Naval Base on Sunday at 1715 joining *Hyades* at 1800 at Old Point Comfort where we proceeded ahead of her into the Atlantic. The sea was calm, marking a good beginning. After clearing the swept channel, Commander Wheyland, aboard *Hyades*, gave the order to commence zigzagging according to the prescribed course and speed, heading south, at fifteen knots. *Warrington* patrolled her station, moving back and forth across *Hyades'* path, our sonar searching the water *Hyades* would sail through for an enemy submarine. Both ships adopted a safe, time-tested, back-and-forth rhythm. *Maybe everything will be okay and my sense of dread unfounded. I hoped that was so.*

As soon as we reached the open sea, I instructed Hart, our communications officer, to conduct tests with our TBS-TBY transmitters to see we if would be pleasantly surprised that they were functioning properly. Communication with *Hyades* would be critical if we were caught in a severe storm. Hart ordered his assistant, Lt. John Denny to try the ship's radio communication equipment (transmitters/receivers), which he had been testing for a good part of the day before we set sail with satisfactory results. Now that we were in the open sea, he reported the usual findings, the built-in RCA Victor

TBS system worked reasonably well for line-of-sight communication while the portable TBY radios made by Colonial Radio were still unreliable. The TBY transmitters never performed properly, always producing a continuous stream of static. Worthless equipment.

Hart later reported to me, "Ridge, the TBS-TBY tests produced the usual mixed results; TBS worked reasonably well with clear contact with *Hyades* while TBY yielded a poor, unsatisfactory outcome, just a jumbled mess of garbled voices and static."

"John, it's the same old story. There must be better equipment available. This stuff is over five years old. I never got a response about new equipment during our overhaul. I just pray we don't encounter a situation where our lives depend upon our ability to communicate with *Hyades*, and the equipment fails."

"Why is that?"

"Well, a hurricane is brewing in the Bahamas, and I hope we don't sail into it. We'll need to be able to communicate with *Hyades* if we do. When we get back to port, I'm going to specifically investigate replacing this equipment with something new. We were outfitted with LORAN, which helps with navigation, so there must have been improvements to the TBS-TBY transmitters and receivers."

"Thanks, Ridge. Even a small improvement would be helpful."

"I hear you." I then headed to the bridge.

Quarles was looking out the window when I entered. "Skipper," I said. He turned from the window.

"Yes, Lieutenant?" I felt the icy tone in his greeting.

"Hart tested the TBS-TBY and reported the usual mixed performance. When we return to port, I'll inquire if there have been upgrades. I never received an answer to my inquiry when we were in New York."

"Good idea, Lieutenant. I'm surprised this wasn't taken care of when the ship had her overhaul. Somebody should have caught this." I took his rebuke personally and knew that my relationship with Quarles was getting off on the wrong foot. It must have been my words with him about the hurricane. *Well, so be it.*

After quietly surveying the weather for a while with Quarles, I went to my stateroom to grab a quick nap before dinner.

Before heading to the Wardroom, I stopped by the CR (Communications Room) where I received a call form Machinist Mate John Latronica, who advised, "Things are going awry in the Engine Room."

"Okay, John. Put Lieutenant Keppel on the line."

"Sir, Keppel."

"Bill, what's going on? Why is Latronica calling me? I just left the CR and we're experiencing the usual poor results with the equipment. I guess your report will add to the growing list of problems."

"Nothing major, Ridge. Just the usual small problems we handle every day, all day long, but I want you to be aware, and report it to the captain if you believe it is important."

"Explain. Should I be concerned enough to tell Commander Quarles?"

"My opinion? Yes, sir. A recurring problem is the ventilation blowers. They frequently shut down and should have been looked at. The point of bringing it to your attention is the fact this should have been taken care of with the maintenance overhaul, but obviously, it wasn't."

"Bill," I moaned with pent-up frustration, "the ventilation blowers should have been fixed or replaced, but from what you say, they weren't touched. I guess that was too much to expect. What can you expect after the bolt-tightening fiasco on the steam valves and the possible sabotage of the port-reduction gear?"

"You're right, Ridge, and that worries me. That makes me wonder if there are other things lurking to flare up that we don't know about. I just hope we can fix whatever we find."

"Okay, Bill. Thanks for letting me know. I'll inform Commander Quarles."

I entered the bridge to find Quarles standing where I last saw him, quietly peering at the setting sun which was slipping below the horizon.

"Captain," I said, interrupting his reverie. "I just got off the horn with Keppel. He alerted me to some problems in the engineering spaces. Nothing big, he said. His point in bringing it to my attention was that the problem was supposed to have been repaired when we were in New York for the overhaul, and it wasn't."

Quarles, shaking his head in disgust, glumly said, "Thanks for the update, Lieutenant Ridgeway. The maintenance and repair *Warrington* received in New York was obviously slipshod either because not enough time was allocated for the degree of repairs needed or laziness and lack of pride by the people doing the work. We should have kept a closer watch as the repairs were being made. No matter what the case now, we must live with the result. I know Commander Dawes complained about the quality of work but was sternly admonished to not criticize the yard, basically sweeping the issue under the rug."

"Yes, sir. I've started a list of repairs that will be needed once we're back in port."

"You do that. Give me the list as soon as we return to Norfolk, and I'll turn it in. The work ethic there must be better than in New York, and maybe we'll get the results we need. If the reduction gear holds, that may well prove Norfolk is the better place for repairs."

With that discussion behind us, Quarles retired to his sea cabin for a quick nap before dinner. I remained on the bridge to survey the weather, looking out the window in the exact spot where Quarles just stood, comforted to see the sea still tranquil—the ocean calm and relatively smooth as seen in the dim moonlight. *Maybe the storm won't be a problem*, I thought. *That would be a welcome relief. I won't be sorry if I'm proven wrong about the weather.* Anxious for information that would confirm this, I called Hart for the latest weather report.

"I was just going to call the bridge, Ridge. Is the captain there?"

"No, he's in his sea cabin. What's the word?"

"Good news. The alerts from the Weather Bureau in Puerto Rico show the hurricane will pass eastward of our position, clear of our plotted route."

"Thanks, John. I'll tell the captain." *Well, maybe I was wrong. I sure hope so.*

That was good news, but then I reminded myself how unpredictable these storms can be. They can turn in another direction, unexpectedly. So, until we passed by it, I reserved judgment. I decided to keep a close eye on its track.

We maintained our station ahead of *Hyades*, patrolling as planned. I left the bridge around 1850 when Quarles returned and went to the Wardroom for a dinner of baked Virginia ham, string beans, red cabbage, bread and butter, coffee, and vanilla ice cream. Another great meal. I had a real appetite and that night's dinner was one of my favorites the cook prepared. Following a second cup of coffee with another scoop of ice cream, I went to the crew's mess to watch that night's movie, Casablanca starring Humphrey Bogart as Rick Blaine, proprietor of Rick's Café American; Ingrid Bergman as Ilsa Lund, Blaine's former lover; and Paul Henreid, as Victor Laszlo, Lund's husband. It was not often we received a new movie release so quickly. Maybe that was another difference between the Pacific and Atlantic theaters. Ellen and I had seen this movie when I was home on leave, and because we enjoyed it so much, I looked forward to seeing it again. I especially savored Sydney Greenstreet as Signor Ferrari and Peter Lorre as Signor Ugarte, both of whom had prominent character roles in The Maltese Falcon–another good Bogart film, as well as the pervasive theme song of the film, "As Time Goes By," when Lund tells Dooley Wilson, the piano player in Rick's, "Play it again, Sam."

I wasn't tired when the movie ended, probably due to the niggling sensation that all was not well. I headed to the CR for an update. Hart's earlier report pointed to calm weather ahead, the hurricane east of our position, and this was accurate as the night passed without incident.

32

CALM SEAS or TURBULENT WATERS?

I awakened at 0600, the ambient light leaking through the porthole rousing me from my fitful slumber. I hadn't slept well; pondering all night the hurricane in the Bahamas and where it might be headed. Anxious to survey the weather outside, I hurriedly showered, dressed, and left my cabin, stepping onto the deck. Conditions appeared unchanged from last night when I hit the sack, so I headed to the Wardroom for breakfast. I had a big appetite and ordered Melson's "Hungry Man" entree of three scrambled eggs, four slices of white toast, three strips of extra crispy bacon, orange juice, and black coffee. The ship seemed to be riding well, but I noted the fiddle boards attached to the tables to keep the plates and cups from spilling onto the floor. I wondered if this was an ominous sign of things to come, or just the practice of a new crew member in the galley who was acquainted with rough seas–perhaps they came aboard in New York after having previously served in the North Atlantic. After a second cup of coffee, I passed back onto the deck. There was still no perceptible change evident in the sea. *Maybe my concerns about the storm are an overreaction*, I thought. *I sure hope so.*

I walked along the deck toward the fo'c'sle, surveying the weather along the way, studying every detail. Maybe I was being paranoid. I was searching for the slightest evidence that would signal something was amiss, but there was nothing, except a slight breeze blowing from the southeast through the hazy, nickeled light of the morning. Everything was normal, but I knew in my gut that it shouldn't be. I climbed the ladder to the bridge wing and stood there for a while, still eyeing the weather from that slightly higher vantage point. Still no discernible change. I saw Quarles through the window chatting with the helmsman, while *Warrington* patrolled her station ahead of *Hyades*.

When I entered the bridge, Quarles greeted me with assurance, a wide smile on his face, "Lieutenant Ridgeway, the weather is cooperating. Do you agree?"

"I agree, thank God."

"You see, your concerns about the hurricane were unfounded."

"You may be right, but still I'm going to the CR to get the latest plot of the hurricane's path, just to make sure. I hope it shows the storm staying east of our plotted course. I'll report back."

"You do that, Ridgeway. Let me know what you find out."

"Aye, aye, sir."

As soon as I entered the Communications Room, Hart rushed over saying he was about to call the bridge. He showed me the plotted chart he prepared, and it indicated the storm may be turning westward and, if that were the case, it would most assuredly cross our track at our current course and speed. We would be heading straight into a hurricane.

Alarmed by what he showed me, I implored, "Hart, keep on top of this and immediately report any changes. Even the smallest ones are important. I'm going back to the bridge to inform Commander Quarles." On my way out, I checked the barometer. The readings were holding steady, which was a good sign, but I knew how quickly things could change for the worse.

When I entered the bridge, I found Quarles to be in a good mood, chatting with Coleman Pack about the calm weather. The helmsman mindlessly drummed the wheel.

"Not to interrupt, sir, but may I speak with you privately for a minute?"

With a puzzled frown on his face, Quarles motioned me to his sea cabin where we could talk. "Cap, I'm just coming from the CR."

"Yes, what did you find out?"

"Not good news. According to Hart's chart of the storm's course, it's almost a hundred percent certain we will feel the impact of the hurricane but to what degree I can't say. If we're lucky, we'll experience nothing more than a moderate tropical storm, catching an outer band of the storm, but the sea will most assuredly be heavy."

"That's nothing I haven't experienced before. *Warrington* should be able to handle it."

"I hope so. Like I said, I believe the ship is top heavy, and with a higher center of gravity, may not be able to take the swells as well as we would like. I instructed Hart to closely track the hurricane's path and to report any changes. We may have to consider a change in course to avoid the worst of the storm."

"Ridgeway, you worry too much. I've been in worse weather. I'm sure we can pass by the bulk of the storm, and to ensure that happens, I'll suggest to Commander Wheyland we dispense with the zigzag course at night so that we can make better speed. Have Hart estimate how fast the storm front is moving. I want to pass in front of it."

"Captain, I agree. Should I send a communication to *Hyades* with your recommendation?"

"No. I'll do it."

I was on the bridge with Commander Quarles when Keppel phoned. "Captain, the malfunctioning ventilation blower I reported yesterday has failed, as did one in the other Engine Room. If any of the other blowers go out, their gyroscopic action may cause damage to the ship's engine bearings. The loss of the blower, as you know, will cause discomfort to the crew in the room because of the heat buildup—but it won't affect our ability to carry on. I'll see to that. As I told Lieutenant Ridgeway yesterday, the lack of proper maintenance will plague us until a total failure requires a major overhaul and can no longer be ignored. I hope we make it to Colon without further problems."

"Keppel, do your best, and keep me informed."

Quarles filled me in on his conversation with Keppel and then advised that he had Denny send a communication to Commander Wheyland, who reluctantly agreed to cease zigzagging after the sun set while we maintained our station. "That's good news, sir," I said, "because we're only making 12.5 knots now, and this will help increase our speed such that we should be able to pass in front of the storm. We'll still feel the effects of the hurricane since the storm front is so vast but should be able to avoid the worst part of it. I just hope the ship can manage the heavy seas we're going to encounter." Quarles wasn't worried about that, but I was.

That night, we ceased zigzagging to gain speed, the day having passed uneventfully, ending on a positive note. Hart reported improvement with the TBS testing, although some problems persisted in getting clear transmissions. Suspect reliability had always been an issue, but maybe this time it had to do with the weather.

Although I had this nagging uneasiness about the storm, I put it aside and decided to skip dinner in lieu of a quick nap before the movie: Guadalcanal Diary starring Preston Foster, Lloyd Nolan, William Bendix, and Richard Conte. Having been around Guadalcanal, I was interested in how this would be portrayed. All I knew was that the movie was a story about the Marines, so there probably would be no naval battles. I returned to my stateroom after the movie, hoping for a good sleep. If the seas worsened, I knew my ability to sleep would be nearly impossible.

33

INTO THE EYE

I tossed and turned fitfully in my bunk throughout the night, waking frequently, propping on my elbow, trying to gauge the size of the ocean by the motion of the ship. The sea felt to be growing heavier. My fear was becoming a reality.

No longer able to lay in bed, nerves on edge, I arose at 0545, just before sunrise, the night sky still dark. I was anxious to go on the deck to take in the weather's effect on *Warrington*. I peeked out the porthole and saw the white capped swells smashing the side of the ship. I wondered, was the storm moving our way, or were we making a terrible mistake and moving toward it? Maybe it was a combination of both. I showered, dressed, and exited the bulkhead door onto the deck. Although the sun fought to come out, it was masked by an overcast sky, and the relative tranquility of yesterday was ceding to something sinister. The baleful swells were growing, the wind picking up, whipping into threatening, six foot white-tipped waves. I sensed the turbulence was slowly enveloping us in its briny clutches.

Instead of heading to the bridge, I scurried down the ladder-well and walked along the passageway to the CR to obtain from Hart the latest plotting for the hurricane. He was not there, but John Denny, his assistant–a bundle of nerves–handed me the weather chart he just completed. I scanned the paper, and it was clear that our current course and speed would take us into the heart of the storm, whether ahead or behind the eye still unknown, but this would be critically important to determine, if possible.

Armed with this information, I raced up the ladder to the bridge, entering to find Commander Quarles standing in the pilothouse peering morosely out the window at the intensifying weather. Quartermaster Bill Greene manned the helm, holding the wheel tightly in a white-knuckled grip, fighting mightily to maintain a course of 183 degrees at fifteen knots against the growing swells but probably making good only twelve knots on a course of 180 degrees. The wind, coming from the east-southeast at about 110 degrees, with the seas 15 to 20 degrees further south, buffeted the ship slightly forward of our port beam, throwing the bow off to starboard, which contributed to the rolling motion we were experiencing.

The rolling motion had not seemed too bad during the night because the breeze was light, and the swells, though long, were not steep. Although I wasn't consciously aware of it, that had been the cause of my restless sleep. I wasn't sure if the weather was changing or not. As the day progressed, it was evident the weather was deteriorating, and the ship began to roll more heavily. Quarles initially mentioned to me he thought *Warrington* rode well, but his opinion changed with the weather.

"Captain, as you can see, the weather is worsening. I just left the CR, and the latest tracking report for the hurricane shows our projected course will take us directly toward the eye of the storm. I urge you to consider recommending to Commander Wheyland a change in course and speed so that we can avoid the brunt of it. The part of the storm we will encounter will be bad enough. We might be too late."

"Ridgeway, I'm not blind." Quarles barked. "I can see with my own eyes the seas are heavier today than yesterday and growing worse as we speak, but it's nothing I haven't experienced before. We'll be okay. The ship seems to be handling well, despite your admonition about being top heavy, although I'll admit, not as well as I originally thought she would."

"Captain," I pleaded urgently, "we must make a change in course and speed before it's too late. Not to would be catastrophic."

"I'm not going to discuss the issue with Commander Wheyland," he snapped, "unless he raises it first. He has the authority to adjust the unit's course and speed to avoid danger if he thinks it's necessary, and he has the same weather information we do. Since he decided to do nothing, I will abide by his implied opinion that there is no real danger."

"But, sir, I question his judgment. He must have misinterpreted the weather bulletins to indicate the storm was stationary and that we would pass by it without a problem. I believe that is an incorrect conclusion. We are clearly going to collide with the storm, sooner rather than later if we maintain our present course and speed."

"Well, we'll see Ridgeway. I'll wait for Wheyland's decision."

Quarles remained on the bridge with me, intently scrutinizing the weather as it deteriorated before our eyes. The swells were growing, and the ship rolling heavier.

Soon after our talk about changing course, Quarles said to me sheepishly, "I thought about what you said. You're right. There's no sense in my being pigheaded about it or letting my pride blind me from doing what is right. I'll recommend to Wheyland that we discontinue zigzagging to gain speed to ensure we pass west ahead of the storm's eye. We'll feel the fringe but should avoid the brunt of it. I hope it's not too late. The only other alternative would be to reverse course and speed away from the storm's reach, heading northwest, and I don't believe Wheyland will be open to that suggestion."

"I'm relieved to hear you say this. I couldn't agree more. Commander Wheyland must believe the storm is not moving, so if we make good speed, hopefully we'll avoid the worst of it."

Quarles sent his recommendation to Wheyland, but the response was negative. He replied, "Our chart shows we'll pass the storm on the present course and speed, and I prefer not to deviate from Navy protocol of adhering to the prescribed zigzag course during daylight hours. Too many ships have been lost to enemy U-boats."

We were stunned by his response. What weather forecast was Wheyland looking at? It couldn't be the same one we had. It was also doubtful a U-boat could surface to periscope level with the size of the swells we were experiencing. His reluctance to see the obvious was maddening.

The sea was turbulent throughout the morning and grew progressively worse as the day unfolded. *Warrington* swayed in the heaving ocean. The swells, coming from a direction more southerly than the wind, escalated in size, fueled by steady eighteen-to-twenty-five-knot winds blowing in the late afternoon. As the ship rose and fell, the clappers on our bells swung fore and aft constantly. The clang was a constant reminder that the weather conditions were progressively worsening. This was not a good sign. Swells have a long wavelength that vary with the size, strength, and duration of the weather system causing the swell. These were the result of the hurricane growing larger and more intense as the storm moved closer to our position. No doubt, we were heading straight into the maelstrom.

With the worsening weather, Wheyland realized his mistake, contacting us to say he changed his mind, agreeing to Quarles's recommendation to forego zigzagging while maintaining the base course. Both ships ceased zigzagging around 1200 for the best speed hoping that would put us ahead of the storm front.

As the weather continued to deteriorate, I went to the CR to keep close track of the hurricane's path. The rocking motion of the ship told me all I needed to know about what was happening outside and above. Analyzing the weather bulletins confirmed the storm's approach, although the exact location and path of the eye was uncertain due to differences in interpretation of the data issued by the weather station in Miami and that of Puerto Rico. Forecasting using radar was rudimentary, and not much more efficient than sailors in Bowditch's era which relied on a good barometer, a thermometer, and a seasoned nose for taking stock of what they were seeing. The low-pressure area appeared to be southeast of us but its distance was not known. Why couldn't we get a better fix on this?

Desperate for a better handle on the situation, I instructed Hart, "Do some modeling assuming different scenarios for the storm's course as it relates to our present speed and course. I want to determine the possible impact points so I can recommend a change in course and speed to Commander Quarles, which I'm certain will be required—and relatively soon."

"Aye, aye, sir. Denny and I will get right on it. I'll be back to you as soon as I have something to discuss."

"Make it quick, John, time is running out. If we must make a change, we'll have to do it soon. Real soon."

"Yes, sir."

With every passing minute, the seas became heavier and the winds more intense. The swells grew larger and longer in duration. It started to rain. The heavy downpour was a sign we were nearing the storm front as windy rain bands dominate the fringe of a hurricane.

At 1430 Commander Quarles issued an order—passed throughout the ship by the boatswain's mates since we had no central public address system— "Make ready for hurricane weather. Batten down and secure all loose gear." The announcement was superfluous as the crew was already experiencing the worsening weather. It was common knowledge throughout the ship there was a hurricane and that we were heading toward it. From the action of the ship and the condition of the sea, everyone aboard was fully aware of the storm. There was no reason to tell them what they already knew.

I returned to the CR to see if Hart had developed the proposed scenarios for dealing with the storm, but he was still working on it and hoped to have something soon to consider. I implored him, "Hart, we've no time to waste. I need that information, and I need it ASAP."

"Yes, Ridge. We're sifting through the data and plotting alternate courses on various what-if scenarios. I should have it to you momentarily."

"Make sure you do," I snapped in frustration as a large swell rocked the starboard side of the ship to port causing me to stumble into the bulkhead.

Despite our belief the storm front was approaching, the barometer remained high and steady throughout the rest of the day. That was good news because the barometric pressure would be falling at a rate of .03 inch per hour if we were headed into the track of the storm.

I informed Quarles about the favorable barometer reading and he commented, "The steadiness of the barometer, at a time when it should be falling if we were heading into the hurricane, is good news. I believe we'll miss the most violent portion of the storm."

I didn't say anything but thought, *I think you're fooling yourself into a false sense of security. Not me, though, I'm going to watch this like a hawk.*

Throughout the remainder of the day, the unabated swells caused the ship to roll moderately with the wind and sea on our port beam. Clinometer readings that ranged between five and eight degrees earlier in the day climbed to fifteen to twenty degrees by the afternoon. The synchronized rolling motion of the ship was constant and becoming more pronounced. The long, lazy cross-swells were a harbinger of what was to come, and despite the favorable barometric reading I feared we were headed straight into the eye.

Standing on the bridge with Quarles, while anxiously awaiting Hart's report, we peered out the window at the growing swells. "Captain, you and I both know that a crew subjected to rolling motion over a prolonged period can have an adverse effect, causing crew fatigue."

"Yes, I'm aware. The crew may not even be cognizant of it but will nevertheless fall under its hypnotic spell."

"To that point, we've been experiencing moderate rolling for several hours, and based upon the rising clinometer readings, the rolling is growing steeper, and there does not appear to be any relief in sight. If this continues much longer, the crew will most assuredly wear down and may become incapacitated. The outcome would be calamitous."

Shaking his head and looking out the window at the turbulent waves, Quarles surrendered. "I agree, but what can we do? We're trapped in this situation."

Yes, we are, I thought, *but it didn't have to be this way, if only you had listened to me.*

The weather deteriorated significantly in the last couple of hours; the cross-swells now giant, rolling pewter hills. Green water sloshed over the decks, and white lather washed over the housings. The heavy swells caused the ship to yaw twenty degrees with each wave. We would soon have difficulty maintaining the station ahead of *Hyades* as the waves tossed and rolled the two vessels in the bucking seas.

As the seas became heavier and the rolling swells more pronounced, a problem surfaced in the turret handling room. Coleman Pack, our gunnery officer, anxiously reported to Commander Quarles, "Sir, the heavy rolling motion loosened the five-inch shells from their battens and they're crashing all around the room along with several gunpowder cannisters, slamming with force into the bulkheads. The fuse caps are on, so I don't think the ricocheting of shells from bulkhead to bulkhead will trigger an explosion, but I sure don't want to find out I'm wrong."

Quarles reacted quickly, "Pack, on my orders, enlist Lieutenant Pennington and all free hands nearby not otherwise occupied to assist you and Schultz, in restowing the ammunition. Be careful, you could be crushed if a 54 pound five-inch shells slams into you." Schultz later told me this was a backbreaking job as the jolting motion of the ship made it difficult to get a firm hand on the shells. And the ventilation system was not working properly, so the crew had to go topside frequently for fresh air, but only in the companionway as the developing rain and wind made it hazardous to venture onto the deck. The exertion required to secure the shells sapped their energy and most likely exacerbated their fatigue, although at the time it appeared to be a necessary precaution since an explosion would have been catastrophic.

Quarles, holding tightly to the rail on the bridge with a vise grip, lamented the pounding the ship was absorbing as she bucked the mountainous seas. A sudden cloud burst brought lashing rains and 60-knot winds that whipped the sea into a liquid palisade. Towering masses of dull, gray water rose on the port quarter, sweeping over the bow, creating swirling fingers of foam that probed as far back as the depth charge racks. The increasingly confused seas and undulating cliffs of water were beginning to take their toll on *Warrington*.

As the swells steepened, surging seas the color of nickel crashed into *Warrington*'s 381-foot length. The ship yawed in a drunken motion as she was lifted along on the crest. At times, the bow and stern were out of the water at the same time, which left our twin screws spinning free of water, the resulting vibration causing the ship to shudder like a blender at high speed.

Teetering atop the gigantic swells, the midship's section of the ship plonked down, which allowed water to flood into the engineering spaces, which became smothered in a mantle of eddying foam. Then the process would begin again. The ship would rise atop a huge swell, balance momentarily in the hellacious winds and spume, and then plunge suddenly, smashing bow-first into the next erupting wave with a jar that vibrated and shook the whole ship. Everyone was holding on for dear life, like riding the Coney Island Cyclone roller-coaster, fearing the ship would snap in half. After all, the smallest things became the biggest problems. The more trouble a ship is in, the likelier she will run into more trouble. Blown hatches lead to flooded bilges, and flooded bilges lead to electrical shorts, and electrical shorts lead to failed steering mechanisms, and that all leads to catastrophe.

Although I hadn't eaten in hours and wasn't hungry–probably due to a combination of nerves about our perilous situation and nausea from the jolting swells–I stumbled along the passageway to the Crew's Mess. I fell to the floor a couple of times on the way, as a cross-swell caused the ship to swerve. I was determined to put food into my stomach and drink plenty of water. If I started to puke, it was better to have something to throw up rather than have dry heaves which can cause dehydration. I entered the Crew's Mess around 1700, the time when most of the men would normally be at dinner. It was empty save for several hearty souls with the fortitude to eat nothing more than saltine crackers and chicken broth, a good indication that almost everyone was either too nauseous to keep down food or too frightened about our situation to have an appetite. Despite my queasiness, I forced myself to eat several bites of a tuna sandwich before tossing what was left into the garbage. That was all I could consume, with a couple glasses of water. If I did throw-up, at least I would have a little something to expel.

After I left the mess (around 1715), I clambered up the ladder to the bridge, entering just as Commander Quarles ordered Hart to send a message to *Hyades,* alerting them that we may have to "heave to." The message was sent, but no immediate response was received. Several more minutes passed, and still no acknowledgement. Quarles, clearly stressed--evident by the tight lines framing his face and the bulging veins at his temples—finally felt compelled to react to the deteriorating sea as eddies of water pirouetted upward against the windows on the bridge, wiping out all visibility. *Warrington* was riding high and struggling mightily in the brutal wash as a huge comber crashed amidships, sending the ship profoundly to starboard. She was rocking in all directions in the increasingly confused seas.

It was around 1800 when Quarles hollered loudly to overcome the roar of the crashing waves pummeling the bridge, "Helmsman, slow the ship to five knots and swing the bow to port into the wind. Signalman, send a coded message (on the Aldis lamp) to *Hyades* stating, 'It is necessary for me to heave to,' I hope they see our signal." He believed the ship would ride better settling into the trough of the swells, a canyon of forty-to-fifty-foot combers and hoped the move would ease the ship from the lashing rains and fifty-to-sixty-knot backing winds that whipped the sea into constant waves of gray-black water that defied gravity and tossed the ship like a baby's rubber duck in a bathtub.

Hyades responded immediately to our visual lighted message: "'Heave to' at your own discretion. Do you wish us to stand by you?"

I saw the response and recommended to Quarles, "Sir, it would be prudent to have *Hyades* remain close in the event we founder and have to abandon ship."

With a dour face, he promptly vetoed that suggestion and ordered the signalman to send the message: "Negative X we will overtake you after the storm." I silently disagreed with his decision and believed his pride got the best of his judgment. I prayed it was a decision we wouldn't regret.

Because our TBS radio transmission to *Hyades* seemed not to have been received, Quarles summoned Lieutenant Denny to the bridge to inquire about a radio circuit that would have the best chance of keeping us in contact with *Hyades*.

Denny told him, "Sir, the two ships are not on an operating circuit together, but as you may recall from the pre-cruise conference, 2885 KCS was the frequency agreed upon in an emergency."

"Yes, Denny, I do recall there was an agreed-upon channel. Please send the following message to *Hyades*, 'If we separate, will communicate with you over two-eight-eight-five KCS.' Let me know when you receive a response."

"Aye, aye, captain."

After we 'hove to,' Quarles set the course for 110 degrees to keep the wind and sea off our port bow. He also ordered engine speed maintained at five knots to keep steerage, which produced actual speed through the water of about four knots.

This action brought immediate relief, and the ship rode well for several hours until late in the night. With the easing, the crew felt better about our situation, having survived the earlier balancing act atop forty-to-fifty-foot swells that threatened to smash the ship into pieces.

While the ship handled the sea well, problems cropped up that needed to be addressed: a series of mechanical malfunctions were becoming a constant plague. Lieutenant Keppel was in frequent contact with the bridge throughout the day and into the night, relaying one problem after another. He advised Quarles that it was necessary to increase our speed to twelve knots to stop the main injection flapper valve from pounding. The droning noise, he said, was taking a toll on the crew in the ER. Quarles asked me what I thought, but was clearly not interested in my answer, and abruptly refused Keppel's request saying he felt the strain would be too great on the hull if the ship emerged from a swell and crashed down with force into the trough before the next swell emerged.

"Captain, I understand your thinking, but what if we lashed down the valves to reduce the banging?" He agreed this would solve the problem and told me to have Keppel get it done.

Not long after the situation with the flapper valve was resolved, Keppel requested permission to stop the port engine altogether to locate the source of saltwater coming into the ER. Quarles was amenable to that request because the starboard engine was sufficient to maintain the five-knot speed he had ordered. Keppel reported the problem fixed within an hour, and the ship resumed ahead on both engines.

Even though Quarles was mostly reluctant to heed my advice, I stayed on the bridge anyway. I intended to add my counsel so I could suggest different courses of action for whatever situation that arose. As daylight faded—what little there was—into night, the wind and sea increased in velocity and size, and the ship's rolling motion moved from moderate to heavy, with the clinometer readings frequently exceeding forty degrees. As the ship heeled and pitched through the dizzying seas, the crew below clung to handholds and wrapped their arms and legs around any available stationary object. The wind was howling, saltwater blowing in horizontal sheets at bridge level, wiping out visibility.

Loud banging noises erupted outside the bridge. It seemed the wind, along with the waves, was ripping us apart. Slamming up and over the waves tested the ship's rivets, some of which buckled and emitted a sound like popping corn. It was quite possible the repeated up-and-down pounding of the hull would create sufficient metal fatigue to cause the bow or stern to snap off. When the wind whipped into our superstructure, it hissed against the stack, forcing Quarles to shout at full lung to make himself heard to the OOD and helmsman. Deeply concerned, he instructed me to take a couple crew and investigate what was happening outside.

"Yes, sir. I think I can handle it alone." I threw on my foul-weather gear retrieved from the Pea Coat Locker. Tethered to a rope line that I attached to the rail, I exited the bridge onto the starboard side wing to inspect the damage. The visibility was so low I could not make out the ship's bow, no more than 120 feet away, and the driving rain and salt spray stung my face like a thousand needles. Giant, mottled whitecaps stretched endlessly in every direction under a black, starless dome. The gale force wind was so savage it was lopping the tops off the slate gray sixty-foot combers and driving whitewater like horizontal rain. The wind was howling, and saltwater blowing in sheets across the bridge. I looked up and saw that the anemometer had been blow away. I wasn't surprised by that, as the last reading I saw said 130 knots (a 150-mph gust), well above 12 on the Beaufort scale. The ship was the victim of ferocious swings up fluted waves and down into troughs that was beginning to tear her hull apart. Before I knew what hit, a large wave knocked me to the deck against the bulwark. I quickly recovered to my knees and grabbed the rail, pulling the rope taut to make sure it was still secure. I looked up to find the structural members supporting the bulwark clearly visible, obviously inadequate to protect against a storm of this magnitude. The ship's thin metal hull plates keened and groaned when the spouts of foaming green water snatched them and swept them over the side. The roughening seas had unmasked the fragile nature of the ship's superstructure in her battle against the storm. The pounding we experienced earlier in the day, before we 'hove to,' probably worked to loosen the rivets, which the latest wind gusts ripped open, causing some of the port and starboard bulwark plating to peel off. I looked down from the bridge wing and could faintly see that the metal gun shield on our five-incher had buckled. With nothing I could do, and with the surging pewter-colored sea engulfing me and the driving rain stinging my face, I returned to the bridge to inform Quarles of the damage. With resignation he said, "There's nothing that can be done to fix it. I pray it doesn't get worse and the ship blows apart."

Meanwhile, Keppel handled the problems that cropped up in the Engine Room, which arose from the excessive heat caused by the failing ventilation system until shortly before 2300–when his luck ran out. Quarles and I were both on the bridge when Keppel frantically reported, "Captain, the Engine Room blowers are out, and water is pouring in torrents through the vents. The problem is serious because the heat from the engines is turning the space into a scalding steam bath. I urgently need more men to work in relays because of the heat."

"Keppel, hold on." Quarles covered the phone's mouthpiece and related to me his conversation with Keppel and then said to him, "Keppel, I'm sending Davis to assist you, and I instructed him to bring some fresh help to work with you in shifts. That should alleviate your manpower problem. How are the bilge pumps working?"

"Sir, the pumps are adequately handling the water entering the engineering spaces, but the tide may be turning against us. The pumps are straining to expel the water as fast as it is coming in. Every time we slam into a swell, or a wave sweeps across the deck amidships, another surge of water cascades in. I'm afraid it will soon be a losing battle."

"Do your best. Help is on the way."

"Yes, sir."

Without the ventilation blowers, the ER seethed as the thin steel of the bulkheads grew superheated, and the space filled with steam such that the crew couldn't see a foot in front of their faces. The crew could only work for several minutes at a time in the 180-degree heat.

No sooner had Keppel hung up the phone than the ship lost electric power for a short interval, causing the main engines to vacuum, the steering and steering mechanisms to go out of commission, and the engine telegraph (the device used by the helmsman on the bridge to order the engineers in the Engine Room to power the ship at a certain desired speed) to go out of operation.

Quarles yelled, "We've lost power!" The bridge was pitch-black when the lights went out, even darker than the night sky outside, everyone blindly searching for a flashlight. The outage lasted about half an hour before power returned, and during that time, the ship laid in the trough of the sea, rolling side to side, riding up and down the side of huge fifty-foot combers. We were dead in the water, at the mercy of the wind and sea.

Davis was in the ER when the power outage occurred, and Keppel told him the loss of vacuum was caused by the stoppage of the electric condensate pumps. He said the main steam condensate pump was being warmed up, and when it could be turned on, enough vacuum would be recovered to run the engines. Electric power was temporarily restored by the number 2 auxiliary diesel generator, but that lasted only a few minutes. Keppel investigated and found the motor was ruined by the saltwater flooding into the Engine Room. Fortunately, the number 1 auxiliary generator continued delivering electrical power until the main power was restored.

Unable to establish contact with the ER and not knowing what caused the power outage, which caused a loss of steering, Quarles ordered a shift to hand steering until the electric power was restored–*if* it could be restored.

Quarles turned to me, "Lieutenant, take some men to the SER to man the rudder cranks until we regain power. I don't like bouncing around with no control over the direction we're pointed."

"Aye, aye, sir." Leaving Greene at the helm, I summoned Quartermaster John Martin and four other seamen. We struggled aft along the open deck, gripping tightly to the gunwale as huge waves of cascading water swept over us with force, threatening to sweep us over the side. We slowly worked our way along the deck, fighting the bucking seas and stinging spume to the SER, a small space about ten feet square. I pointed my flashlight at the apparatus, and Martin took hold of the rudder control while two of the seamen turned the crank, the other two seamen waiting their turn with it. I instructed Martin to set the course to 110 degrees. The process was slow and awkward, and with no engine power, the value of turning the rudder and expecting a reaction was nearly worthless. Even so, we turned the rudder to the desired course and waited for the engine power to be restored. Thirty minutes later power was regained. I told the men I was returning to the pilothouse to see if the skipper wanted to keep the steering on manual in case the power went out again. "I'll send someone back to let you know if he wants to switch to the primary steering on the Bridge. Keep the course to 110 degrees," I admonished as I left the SER through the bulkhead door.

Leaning into the wind and taking a beating from the pounding surf, I crawled slowly back to the bridge, holding on to the rail for dear life. By the time I made it back, the power was still on, but there was confusion in the bridge. Quarles was screaming at Greene, who had resumed control of the wheel, to belay steering. He evidently hadn't heard Quarles's order over the crashing swells to continue steering from the SER. I told Quarles I thought he might want to maintain control there just in case the power went out again, so I said I instructed the men to hold to a course of 110 degrees. He was relieved. While the power was out, the bow had fallen off to the south, leaving the ship to wallow in troughs of towering fifty-foot swells. When power was restored, headway was regained, and we proceeded upwind.

Keppel reported a bit of good news around 2345. "Other than the sea water that temporarily knocked out the ship's power, the bilge pumps," he said, "have been able to expel the water flowing into the engineering spaces."

While we made it through the day, we still had the night ahead of us. No one was hitting the rack until we were through this. There was no chance of sleeping anyway; the steep rolling motion of the ship had everyone on edge, terrified the ship would break apart, wondering if she would continue to roll and return to an upright position, ready to tackle the next swell, or if she would turn under into a death roll. The ferocious swings up the fluted waves and down into the troughs had everyone holding on for dear life as they listened to the groans from the ship's creaking frame reverberate through her thin metal plates. Crew thrown from their bunks landed in puddles of their own vomit and excrement as the ship bucked violently out of control. Some men prayed, dredging the bottom of their faith, while others scribbled lopsided notes to their mothers.

34

FLEE THE STORM

The timing of events is my best estimate because I was not watching the Chelsea clock (or even looking at my watch), too deeply immersed in efforts to save the ship. It was just after midnight; black as pitch outside, the moon and stars obscured by dense clouds. With absolutely no visibility due to the sheets of driving rain and combers sweeping across the decks, it was impossible to gauge the speed and magnitude of the swells. The anemometer was gone, so the only tool we had was the clinometer. It read twenty degrees, having eased from forty degrees after we 'hove to,' but as the hours passed the reading slowly ticked up. The next swell could easily be fatal.

Quarles, lying in his sea cabin just after midnight but unable to sleep, arose from his bunk in a panic and entered the bridge, "Helmsman, summon Lieutenant Hart." When Hart arrived three minutes later, Quarles instructed him to send an urgent message to *Hyades* requesting her to rejoin us as soon as possible. Hart went to leave, but a huge swell caused the ship to dip and roll to port, shuddering as it slammed into the comber. He lost his footing and crashed hard against the bulkhead, opening a gash just below his hairline, blood spewing down his face. He picked himself up, using his shirt sleeve to stem the blood, and after he regained his footing, left the bridge in a mad scramble to the CR realizing we were in a life-and-death struggle. Quarles, watching him leave the room in a panic, mumbled to himself, "He probably won't hear from *Hyades,* but the attempt has to be made."

Unable to sleep, although I tried to catch a quick nap earlier, I joined Quarles on the bridge. It was probably around 0130 when Keppel phoned about the alarming conditions in the ER, which were growing worse as he spoke. Seawater was streaming into the room through the ventilators and blowers, and the torrential inflow, he said, would soon outpace the ability of the bilge pumps to expel the water. Sounding like he was at his wits end, Keppel exclaimed, "It's out of control, Captain! I fear we'll lose full power soon." Quarles, with a deflated shrug of his shoulders, gave me the grim news.

Keppel called back minutes later informing Quarles, "The temperature in the ER has risen to a point where the men can only remain in the space for several minutes before having to go topside, and it's dangerous out there because of the list of the ship and the waves smashing across the deck. Someone could be washed overboard. The water soaking the engines has turned the entire space into a steaming inferno, even worse than it was earlier. I told the men to drape wet towels over their heads, which may help, but surely not for long."

We were desperate for a remedy to reverse our worsening situation. Quarles, hoping for a good idea—something he hadn't thought of—queried everyone on the bridge for suggestions seeking a solution that would alleviate the gravity of our situation. While ideas were tossed about, Quarles took me aside and confided, "I believe our only chance to save the ship is to reverse course, putting the stern into the sea and increasing speed to fifteen knots at a course of 280 degrees, keeping the wind and sea dead astern. Hopefully, the engines will hold, and we can race away from the worst part of the advancing storm."

"Skipper, that's worth a try, provided we're not in the eye and can keep the storm behind us. The danger lies in executing the 180-degree turn. We would be vulnerable to capsizing should a huge swell smash us amidships while we are in the middle of the maneuver causing us to capsize."

"I know, but we must try. It's our only option."

Quarles called the ER, "Keppel I'm bringing the ship around. As soon as she reverses course, I want you to increase engine speed to fifteen knots. I'll let you know when to give it the gas. We need to outrun the storm because we are heading into the thick of it. Maybe we're already there."

"But, sir, I don't think the engines can handle it."

"Keppel, do as I order. Our survival depends on it. If we don't do this, we'll capsize. Do you understand me?"

"Yes, sir."

Hopefully, we hadn't waited too long.

After Martin in the SER executed the turn, the ship came around easily, and Quarles instructed Keppel to increase engine speed to fifteen knots. The maneuver worked, and the ship's motion greatly eased, but our feeling of comfort quickly evaporated as *Warrington* began yawing, requiring increased amounts of rudder to stay on course. It was impossible to maintain steering in a following sea, but we had to make the effort. I said to Quarles, "They're blind in the SER to the wave action and cannot react fast enough to what little we can see on the bridge. The rudder's effectiveness is reduced almost to the point where its effect is the opposite of what it's supposed to be. I don't have to tell you, cap, the use of a rudder depends upon the amount of water pressure brought to bear on its forward face, and with the current conditions of a following sea, that pressure has been eliminated. Add to that, it's still too dark for us to see what we're doing. We'll have a better chance once there is daylight if we survive that long."

"I agree. I hope we can pull this off."

"Yes, our lives depend upon on it."

Quarles asked me, "Have we heard from *Hyades*? Hart left over an hour ago to send a message, and while I'm not optimistic about receiving a reply, I want to know the outcome. Go check."

"I've heard nothing, but I'll go find out." I left the bridge for the CR holding the bulkhead railing tightly to maintain my balance as the ship rocked. I tumbled down the ladder when a large swell hit amidships. When I entered the room, I saw Hart feverishly talking into the transmitter mouthpiece. He turned when he saw me and said, "*Hyades* has not responded to the captain's request to rejoin us, but I'm still trying to make contact. What if we send a radio distress message? With luck that could be picked up by anyone who was tuned in."

"Hart, that's a good idea. I'll suggest it to the captain." I phoned Quarles and informed him about Hart's failed attempts to reach *Hyades* and his suggestion about the radio transmission.

Quarles approved sending a distress signal in plain language but omitting the identity of *Warrington* by name as our identity would be evident by knowing our "call signal." He ordered, "Ridgeway, formulate and send the message, I'm too busy trying to ensure the ship remains on course."

"Aye, aye."

Hart looked at me. I told him, "Send the following transmission on all circuits: 'In distress…Need assistance…Engineering spaces flooded…Have lost power…Wind hurricane force." The message was sent, and we waited, but there was no response. Hopefully, someone heard our call. *But,* I wondered, *how will we know if they had?*

The situation was grave; *Warrington* bounced in the swells with no control over her movements or her ability to react.

With nothing more I could do in the CR after the message was sent, I left Hart and returned to the bridge, entering the room behind Lieutenant Kennedy. Kennedy told Quarles, "Captain, the situation in the ER is dire. The crew are suffering from severe exhaustion. Keppel asked me what could be done to combat the steam heat, and when I got there, I found him lying on the deck outside the room trying to recover from the effects of the intense heat inside. I revived him and told him his idea of a wet towel draped over their head was the best that could be done. I thought you should know."

"Okay, Doc. Anything you can do to help his men is beneficial. It's imperative our engines keep running. Our survival counts on it."

Kennedy—apparently intending to be helpful to Commander Quarles, who turned back to the window, watching the great waves sweeping across the bow--suggested that if anything were to happen to the ship, the crew would have the best chance of survival if they remained on board. When I heard him say that, I thought, *Kennedy has no clue. If the ship capsizes, the last place you want to be is aboard the ship when she sinks, taking you with her to her grave.* After listening to his advice, Quarles told Kennedy, "If the ship capsizes, we'll all be lost if we remain aboard. If it seems imminent the ship will sink, I'll issue the order to abandon her. We'll have a better chance for survival riding the swells in a Carley float." Quarles then ordered the boatswain's mates, since we had no Public Address system, to disseminate the following message to the crew: "The ship is in trouble. Wear your life vest. Prepare to abandon the ship when I give the order."

Kennedy, clearly not a mariner, sheepishly agreed. He said, "The ship is rolling so strongly–"

As if we didn't know, I thought sardonically.

"–it took quite a bit of effort to make it to the bridge from the ER. I had to crawl slowly along the deck, gripping tightly onto the rail to avoid being swept over the side."

Well, at least that comment made sense.

Trying to make headway on a northwest course at about fifteen knots, Quarles wondered if the ship could make it to the Navy Yard in Charleston. Unable to raise Keppel on the phone, he told me he was going to the ER to get his opinion. As he reached the door, Kennedy hollered over the din of the crashing waves, "Captain, it would be foolhardy to traverse the deck now!"

I resisted the urge to comment, *as if waiting for a while would make it safer to do so.*

"You might be swept overboard!" Quarles looked back at him with an exasperated grin but didn't answer nor heed his advice, instead beckoning me to join him. We left Hart on the bridge with orders to keep the ship to her course of 280 degrees.

Still shrouded in the dark of night, Quarles and I grabbed flashlights as we left the bridge for the ER. The huge combers sweeping across the open deck forced us to hold tightly to the deck rail. Quarles fell to his knee, and I grabbed his arm, pulling him up off the deck. It took us several minutes to make the trip to the ER as the ship was rolling so strongly, we had to proceed with snail-like caution lest we fly over the side, as Kennedy warned, and as Quarles almost experienced.

When we arrived at the Forward Engine Room, Keppel was lying on the deck outside the bulkhead door, probably where Kennedy had found him, not having recovered, in a state of total collapse. Quarles nudged him with his foot, and Keppel, seeing the captain, uttered deliriously, "The damage to the engines can't be repaired. Water is streaming into the room faster than the bilge pumps can expel it. It's hopeless. We tried our best; it wasn't enough. I'm sorry. If you don't believe me, go see for yourself."

Quarles grabbed my forearm and pulled me along behind him, uttering, "Let's check it out. We must find a way to keep the engines running."

As soon as we opened the door a blast of scalding steam spewed into our faces, but it was instantly extinguished by a torrent of water that smashed us from behind, washing over our backs, as the ship swerved into another swell.

Just as we recovered our senses, the ship juddered for a moment and then took a sudden very deep and long roll to starboard. She swerved to port with the next swell, allowing great quantities of seawater to cascade into the engineering spaces, flooding the area beyond hope–several feet deep in water. Electric power was totally lost, and the starboard engine stopped. The only light now in that pitch-black space from the weak beams of the two wet flashlights we were holding.

When the power went out, Keppel seemed to get a boost of adrenaline. We pointed our flashlights at him, still on the floor. He drew to his feet, somewhat revived, and asked Quarles, "Do I have permission to close the throttles to both engines?"

Realizing the situation was futile, Quarles granted his request, and handed him his flashlight. *Warrington* had settled in irons.

With nothing more that could be done in the ER, Quarles and I carefully wended our way back to the bridge. As soon as we entered, Hart called out, "Captain, I held the ship on the course of 280 degrees as long as I could, but once the electric power failed, it was no longer possible."

"Hart, I know you did your best. The power is not coming back on, so the course no longer matters. Broadcast an SOS in plain English and let's all pray someone receives it and responds. Give our position and heading. Have Davis provide you with our location coordinates."

"Yes, sir."

Warrington, dead in the water, languished in the trough of sixty-to seventy-foot combers at the mercy of Mother Nature.

35

LAST DITCH EFFORT

Sometime early in the morning before daylight, dead in the water, *Warrington* broached in the following sea, turning sideways in the shearing wind and giant combers. The swirling vortex of the storm had enveloped us in its deathlike grip. When the ship slapped into the troughs, she made an ear-splitting noise, like a clap of thunder. She twisted, reeled, and began the long descent, as if in slow motion, down the face of the wave. The clinometer reading of 57 degrees screamed our fate. It was just a matter of minutes before we turned into a death roll–but no one could really know with certainty as to the exact timing. The next towering swell could do it. If not that one, then the next. We had to ease the rolling or die. There was no time to waste.

Over the roar of the waves hitting the windows on the bridge, I yelled to the captain, "We should load the ballast tanks. Maybe that will ease the rolling and add stability. I'd also top off our fuel tanks with ballast since the engines are dead."

"Good idea, Ridgeway, I should have thought of that," he said.

Quarles and I both knew the risk of turning broadside when the ship was running with a high quarterly sea, but the risk seemed to be worth taking, provided we had our engines. Already shipping heavy water, the maneuver further exposed us to capsizing. It was a conscious decision, a final, futile attempt to escape the hurricane by running before the following sea. Without power, it didn't matter. Now we needed to gain stability to lessen the rolling motion.

The crew in the SER did their best to steer the ship, and while the process was cumbersome, steering without engine power was irrelevant, *Warrington* was now at the mercy of forces beyond our control. The wind and sea pummeled us relentlessly, sweeping over the deck on the starboard beam, causing the bow to fall off to south-southwest, which was probably the catalyst that led to the flooding of the ER and the loss of our engines, generators, and communications.

We operated in total darkness with flashlights, in the luminous glow of the ship's instrument dials that limned the gray ashen faces of the exhausted bridge crew. Quarles, around 0400, ordered all hands to have the ship completely closed fore and aft, using the boatswain's mates to communicate this directive to the crew as this was the only way to pass the word among the men.

The danger of capsizing was inevitable, but we had to try everything we could to keep the ship afloat until rescue arrived, if it would arrive. If the ship went under, there would be no trace; they'd never find us. Quarles, with renewed vigor, snapped back to the reality of our situation and ordered the crew to jettison as much upper deck weight as possible. He hoped doing that, along with filling the ballast tanks, would ease the rolling effect from the inexorable swells. I prayed we weren't too late in that effort, and that it would make a difference.

Glenn Johnson, our torpedo officer, supervised the cast-off of the torpedoes, having set them to "Safe" and fired over the starboard side. That was the start of our effort to off-load useless weight with the aim of lowering our center of gravity to ease the rolling. I believed the additional antiaircraft guns that were added after the ship was commissioned contributed to our top-heavy condition, so I wanted to dismantle them and toss them overboard, but the seas were too violent to make that possible without the threat of losing men over the side. Instead, I led a small group of seamen to cut adrift the captain's gig. It was swinging wildly at its davits on the starboard side, banging against the deck housing, having broken most of its secured rigging. The driving wind, rain, and swells made it dangerous to be on deck, so we set up a system of rope lines linking each person to the rail to ensure that no one was swept over the side.

Once we got rid of the motor launch, we struggled to jettison all topside ready ammunition bunkers and any other items that could be easily disposed of—including the barrels of our 20 mm and 40 mm guns. It was nearly impossible to detach them, the way the ship was swaying, waves breaking with crushing force across the deck, but we got it done. While we couldn't remove the whole gun, at least the barrels were something.

The process of tossing overboard everything that wasn't bolted down continued in a fevered frenzy through to dawn, the battle for our lives in full swing. Hopes brightened among the crew with the number of items we jettisoned.

We believed it all amounted to quite a bit of weight, but was it enough to make a difference? It was hard to say. Everyone prayed that the top-heavy weight we shed would enable us to ride out the storm.

With all the easily disposable items cast overboard, discussion on the bridge centered on larger items that could be thrown to reduce weight. "The fore topmast, with its radar array, should go," Quarles exhorted. Even though the mast was a hollow steel tube twelve inches in diameter, its great height with the top mounted radar was a lot of weight that we could safely dispose of at this point. "It's useless now," Quarles conceded, "and if rescue is on the way, it will be from a signal Hart sent earlier."

"I agree, sir. It's going down, anyway," I concurred. "We should cut it loose before it bends or snaps on its own accord." Some argued to keep it, but the captain was right, so we sent some seamen to rid us of the mast. As soon as the foremast guy wires were cut, the mast snapped without further help, whipped down by the wind at about the height of the top of the main battery director. The broken beam, however, still clung to life, hanging by unbroken tethers for nearly an hour, swinging back and forth with each roll of the ship, banging against the hull with a dull waterlogged thud, before finally falling over the starboard side and disappearing into the water.

Making sure we didn't overlook anything that would lessen the ship's top-heavy weight, Chief Boatswains Mate Willie Johnson–known to everyone on the ship as "Bull" because of his muscular build and brute strength–along with Lieutenant Pennington and two other seamen, attached themselves to a line tethered to the rail and crawled along the deck through the treacherous, cascading swells to the fo'c'sle where they cast loose the starboard anchor. (The portside anchor, submerged in water because of the list of the ship, was unreachable). Everything counted, every little bit. Besides, even one anchor was heavier than almost all the items that was tossed. Hopefully, it made a difference. Was it enough?

We wallowed dead in the water, without lights or heat, serenaded by the sound of the roaring wind and driving rain, and the breaking seas pounding the hull to keep us company. Everyone prayed for the storm to pass, for the swells to subside, and for the ship to stay afloat until rescue arrived.

The sun emerged behind an overcast, drab, and dreary sky. Mountainous swells, gray as the ship once was, surrounded us on all sides. It was hard to grasp what we had faced in the dark night, but we could see the destruction with the daylight. How had the ship survived?

"Captain, I'm going on the deck to inspect the damage and see if there is anything else we can heave overboard."

"You want help?"

"No, I can handle it." I attached a line to my waist and opened the door. A torrent of water rushed in, as the comber swept over the bridge, knocking me to the floor, landing me in a wet heap in several inches of water. I got to my feet and out the door before the next swell barreled in and tethered my line to the rail. The undulating cliffs of water had to be close to seventy feet. I scrambled sideways down the outside ladder, bent double against the wind, rain, and thick salt spray of the waves lashing over the sea-washed deck, and peered aft. Through the spume I saw a new crack in the deck on the port side by the stack. *Was that always there, a hairline fissure that was overlooked, or did that open during the night? That must be a design flaw in the ship,* I thought. Those cracks let huge amounts of seawater to flow into the engineering spaces which led to the loss of our engines. *Well, there was nothing we could do about it now.*

When I re-entered the bridge, another huge swell washed through the door behind me, flooding the room to our ankles. Quarles hollered, "What did you see?"

"Two cracks on the deck, one on either side of the stack, and I believe that's where all the water was coming from that swamped the engine rooms."

"For shit's sake! I don't know if it would have made a difference if the cracks weren't there. We'll never know."

Communications throughout the ship in our last minutes were disseminated by Quarles through boatswains' mates. Louis Kroll, our assistant gunnery officer, roved about the ship delivering the latest bulletins, endeavoring to raise morale. In good times, he was a walking newspaper belowdecks among the officers, spreading scuttlebutt and making small talk. When he came to the bridge seeking the latest directives from the captain, I saw a man that was resigned to his fate. I think he realized before anyone that our situation was hopeless, and maybe his fanatical movement about the ship was his way of coping. I say that because I saw him take a life jacket on his last visit to the bridge and, as I looked out the window, I watched him slip over the side, and disappear into a large swell. I'm sure he was our first casualty.

I went to assess the situation belowdecks, heading to the crew's living compartment. I stumbled along the companionway, dimly lit with the battery-operated red battle lights, only to find the space flooded by water coming through the ventilation system. Some of the men, with flashlights, were plugging the vents with pillows, blankets, and clothing to stop the inflow, but the items became instantly waterlogged. I saw others holding tight to any structure that was bolted down to avoid being catapulted against the bulkhead. It was a losing battle. I told them, "Don't waste your time trying to plug the leaks. It won't make a difference. Get your life vests on and go topside to prepare to abandon ship."

I worked my way back to the pilothouse, falling several times on the way, as the ship swerved and bounced from the swells pounding her hull. When I entered the room, the water was up to my midcalf. I looked at my watch: it was 1130. The ship was rolling from side to side in a snapping, pendulum motion, sluicing through waves so huge the clinometer reading was threatening to go off the chart.

Quarles saw me. I yelled as loud as I could so he would hear me, "The crew's quarters are flooded! I told the men to don their life vests and get ready to abandon the ship. The clinometer says 61 degrees. Cap, we're on borrowed time. We must abandon now."

Quarles, in a daze of denial, mumbled, "I'll issue the order in a minute."

I looked again at the clinometer; it now read 65 degrees. "Captain, we don't have another minute!" *What the hell is he waiting for?* Looking back to the window, after the last wave washed across the wing bridge, I could see all the starboard side life rafts and floater nets were under water and useless, squandered by inaction to react quickly enough to quit the ship. Water was surging down the stack, through the bowels of the ship, into the dead, cold boilers.

Trying to shake him from his stupor, I screamed in his ear, "Captain, our stack is sucking water! The ship is not going to roll back. We must abandon, *now*!"

Finally, Quarles snapped out of it and gave the Abandon Ship order.

Several of the crew had already taken steps to go over the side, casting off the lashings of the portside rafts and floater nets. Meanwhile, others waited for the signal they had not yet heard, probably fearing the mountainous swells engulfing the ship or hoping for a miracle that she would bounce back and stay afloat.

Believing the ship had only moments left, I made one last sweep to make sure everyone received the order to abandon. I went first to the Radio Room where I discovered the men sitting there unaware, just receiving word from Radioman Paul Klingen who entered the room ahead of me. Dr. Kennedy was attending to Coxswain Clair Raymer, who had a broken leg when a swell jolted the ship, throwing him against a bulkhead. The doc was also administering treatment to Chief Radioman Arthur Tolman, who was injured when a loose bulwark plate flung off and smashed him in the ribs, puncturing a lung. Tolman, in severe pain, groaned loudly, saying he couldn't move and was staying on the ship. Kennedy said he was also staying as it was his duty to tend to his patient.

"Kennedy," I hollered, "abandon the ship now with Tolman! It's going to capsize, and when it does, you'll both go under with her." I was unable to persuade them to leave, so I went to the crew sleeping quarters to double check they had left. It was dark, so I scanned the space from the entry with my flashlight, but it was empty. I left for the bridge.

When I entered the pilothouse, the water was almost up to my knees. Quarles was on the bridge wing giving hand signals to abandon as his stentorian announcement to quit the ship was obliterated by the roar of the wind and crashing swells sweeping across the deck. Chief Boatswain Mate Johnson, seeing the gesture from Quarles, passed the word to the men in his vicinity–clinging like monkeys to the rigging where the mast once stood.

I glanced at the clinometer: 84 degrees. I looked through the window. The captain was gone and in his place was the largest wave I'd ever seen. Beneath its foaming white crown, it was as black as an unlit shaft in a West Virginia coal mine. The windows blew out, the shattered glass flying. The ship was entombed in an avalanche of dark water.

36

THE INEVITABLE

ATLANTIC HURRICANE, MIDDAY 13 SEPTEMBER 1944

Swept off the bridge over the deck railing, I was swallowed in the murky grip of a gigantic eighty-foot swell, crashing into the bulwark. Submerged in an eddy, survival instincts took over. I propelled myself upward with a powerful scissor kick through the briny spume, seeking life-saving air. Although I knew what was coming, I was uncertain of the exact timing and foolishly forgot to wear my Kapok life vest, overlooked in the mayhem of passing word to the crew to abandon the ship. I was only in the water for a few seconds, but it seemed like an eternity with my life on the line.

37

SURVIVED

ATLANTIC HURRICANE, BEFORE NOON 14 SEPTEMBER 1944

We drifted with the Gulf Stream, nourished by the limited food and water stored on the raft. We rationed it to sustain us, if need be, for several days until rescue arrived. The swells were still sizable and the exertion to keep the Carley float from flipping took its toll, creating a tremendous thirst. The sun's intense lemon-colored glare was the new enemy inflaming corneas so that we had to bury our face in the crook of our arms to avoid the intense reflective sea.

A phantom wave on a cross swell shuddered the raft while Melson was dividing the rations, and he went over the side along with two cannisters of water. We searched for him, but somehow, he disappeared. Allphin thought the current took him under the float, where he must have drowned. He wasn't seen again and our supply of fresh water was seriously depleted.

With the loss of the water, I reduced the daily ration to half a cup to ensure it would last for another two days. I hoped that would give enough time for rescue to arrive. I knew that the reduction would lead to tremendous thirst in the sweltering heat and would lead to a temptation to drink sea water. I cautioned everyone again as earnestly as I could, "Don't drink the seawater no matter how strong the desire. It will lead to death. You may not think so, but it will. Take a malted milk tablet. That may ease the urge. We must hang in there until rescue arrives. Hopefully, it will be soon."

The sun beat down relentlessly. Some of the men suffered the effects of sun stroke and became delirious. Arbogast suffered the effects the most, his body unable to cool down. I felt his forehead and could tell he was burning with fever. Without a thermometer, it would be impossible to determine his body temperature, but I guessed it was over 105 degrees. I remembered my father when he died. He slipped into a coma and passed. Arbogast went quickly, burned by heat stroke.

Boyd and Tuttle, afraid they'd suffer from heat stroke after witnessing Arbogast succumb so quickly, hopped into the water next to the raft to cool off and submerge below the beating sun. That was a mistake. Melson's body must have been tangled under the float, and it made a welcome dinner for sharks hungry for an easy meal. The movement of Boyd and Tuttle in the water attracted their attention.

Berman yelled, "I see a fin! Get out of the water."

Before he could react, Boyd was sucked under. I peered down at the water and saw dorsal fins atop ghostly gray shadows. A large white-tip, about twelve feet in length, seized Boyd at waist level, taking him under so fast he made no outcry—the look on his face as he disappeared was one of shocked surprise and horror. Tuttle made it halfway onto the raft when Schultz and Richards grabbed his arms and pulled him up, but a shark chomped on his thigh, severing his femoral vein. The loss of blood was so quick that Tuttle died in a matter of minutes. The blood gushing from his body into the water brought a frenzy of sharks circling the raft so after Schultz said a prayer, we issued a final salute to Tuttle as we pushed his body into the water. He was devoured in seconds, never making it to his final resting place.

Fifteen of us were drifting in the swells. As the day dragged on sunstroke among those on the raft became a problem. Despite our efforts to stop him, Pack gulped several mouthfuls of seawater in a delirious rant. The sodium chloride content and trace elements of potassium, boric acid, magnesium, and sulphate of the water was like drinking a toxic cocktail. He became incoherent, breathing in quickening, irregular heartbeats, telling us, "The girls are coming down from New York in a canoe, and I'm going to meet them." Before we knew it, he dropped into the water and swam away. Another fin was visible and then a mad frenzy erupted.

Our supply of potable water was low, but I authorized an increase to a full cup. I wanted to avoid another person hallucinating like Pack. Unfortunately, Hart suffered the same fate. A search plane passed in the afternoon, so we knew they were searching for us. However, the sun had gotten to him already, and after uttering, "I'm going to the airfield to find out why the plane didn't stop, and while I'm there, I'll bring back sandwiches, for us," he swam off disappearing in a swell. Strong went after him, swimming about a hundred feet, where he was attacked by a white tip. Now there were thirteen of us.

Late that afternoon, the group prayed that the plane that flew over earlier had seen us and would bring our rescue.

Smelsky sat quietly, and Everts, sitting next to him, shook his arm. No response.

"Lieutenant, I think he's dead."

"Sun stroke and dehydration must be the cause."

Schultz said another prayer and we issued a final salute as we pushed Smelksy into the water. There were twelve now.

38

RESCUED

ATLANTIC HURRICANE, LATE AFTERNOON 14 SEPTEMBER 1944

Fighting to block the sun's rays as the treacherous ball of fire faded into the horizon, Greene, cupping his hand over his ear, yelled, "Hear that? It's a ship. Our rescue is coming." Not sure if it was a delirious rant but hoping it was true, we strained to hear the sound he heard, scanning the water seeking visual proof.

It was true. The plane must have seen us and reported our position.

LaTronica screamed, "I see it!"

"It must be *Hyades*," I said. "Who else could it be?"

Snowden, an Edsall-class destroyer escort was our savior. She pulled up slowly with searchlights scanning the water. Once we were spotted, the captain's gig was lowered into the water, making three trips to retrieve us. We had been in the water for over thirty hours–battered, beaten, and inundated. The rescuers were aghast at our appearances as we landed on the deck.

Hyades estimated *Warrington* sank 450 miles east of Vero Beach, Florida, and using that as the starting reference point, and calculating the movement of the prevailing Gulf Stream, rescue vessels *Frost, Nuse, Inch, Snowden, Sawsey, Wooden*, and *Johnnie Hutchins* conducted their search.

Hyades was the first to find survivors around 1650 on 14 September picking up a raft commanded by Lieutenant Davis with several others.

Snowden's sickbay treated us for a variety of maladies: exposure, saline poisoning, saltwater lesions, shock, dehydration, sun poisoning, and shark bites. Some suffered from intense shivering, blurred vision, slurred speech, and lack of coordination. Nearly all of us had swollen, red-and-purple tinged eyes and faces from battling the huge surf.

As we recovered in the sick bay, we learned more than half the crew perished the first day going down with the ship, either too fearful to jump into the mountainous swells or too injured to make it off–like Klingen and Raymer, and Kennedy, who attended to them–while others who made the jump drowned in the swells without a life vest or were victim to an overturned raft. Some drank seawater, went crazy, swam off, and drowned. Sharks ate the rest.

Of the ship's complement of 321, seventy-three survived. Fiddler's Green, the home of the souls of drowned sailors, claimed 248.

EPILOGUE

The day before *Warrington* left Norfolk, I telephoned Ellen to tell her I would be sailing on September 10th on a safe cruise, escorting a supply ship to Trinidad and would call in a couple of weeks upon our return. When she first heard the news about the hurricane in the Bahamas, she became concerned for my safety. She reasoned, however, that the Navy would never dispatch a ship into a hurricane, so her apprehension vanished. She later found out that assumption was wrong.

The storm germinated in the Lesser Antilles and followed a west-northwest path. It grew in strength as it moved northward, reaching peak intensity on September 13th. Unbeknownst to Ellen, *Warrington* became ensnarled in the maelstrom and sank off the coast of Florida. The weather forecasters likened this Cape Verde hurricane to the Long Island Express of '38. Ellen knew about that one because I had told her all about it. This one, when it completed its northward trek into New England, earned its own name: The Great Atlantic Hurricane.

Finally, the news she feared was a reality. *Warrington* was seized in the grip of the hurricane and her crew believed lost at sea. Ellen's parents tried to comfort and console her as she broke into heart-wrenching sobs, to no avail. Although the news was devasting, her parents said surely there were survivors, men who made it on to life rafts before the ship sank and would be rescued. She had to have hope that John would be one of them and would return to her.

Several days passed, and the news reports tabulated the damage, ranking the hurricane as one of the deadliest on record. A total of 390 people died in the storm, of which 340 were lost on ships at sea, most of them crew from *Warrington*. Ellen resolved to stay by the phone until she received news, one way or the other, about my fate. She prayed for good news.

Hyades docked in Norfolk, Virginia, on September 17th, with all seventy-three *Warrington* survivors aboard. As soon as I made it ashore, I raced to the nearest phone booth to call home. Fumbling in my pocket, I realized I had no coins to make a call, so I dialed the operator and asked her to place a collect, person-to-person call. The phone rang once, and Ellen, not knowing if it would be good news or bad news, tentatively answered, "Hello?"

The operator said, "I have a collect call from John Ridgeway. Will you accept the charges?"

A wave of relief flooded over her, and Ellen, gasping said, "Thank God, yes! John, you made it! You're alive!"

"Yes. I made it. I wasn't sure I would, but I did. I guess the Man upstairs knew we were meant to be together, that we deserved our chance at life."

"Oh John! I've been a bundle of nerves waiting by the phone for a call that I dreaded and praying you were safe and that it would be good news. I'm so relieved. I can't imagine what you endured."

"I'll tell you all about it when I get home. We were rescued on the fourteenth by *Snowden*, one of several ships who picked up survivors, and then transferred the next day to *Hyades* for the trip back to Norfolk. That probably led to confusion about who survived and who didn't. Some of the men were in bad shape and unable to talk. Probably in shock. I swear to you, Ellen, I tried to have the cruise postponed until after the storm passed. We knew there was a hurricane in the Bahamas, and we sailed toward it anyway. Sheer madness. We lost 248 men, most of whom went down with the ship. I can't talk about it now. It's too depressing. I should be home real soon. I don't think the Navy will hold us."

"I love you, John."

"I love you too. I'll take the first train to New York as soon as I'm released, but I'm not sure of the schedule, so leave a key under the door mat." With that, we ended the call.

That afternoon—after a brief physical which I passed, except for a date with a dentist soon—the Navy released me. I took the train to New York and arrived home late the next day. It was dark out, and from the street I could see the lights on in the parlor. I stepped onto the porch and quietly took the key from under the mat and opened the door, hoping to surprise Ellen, who was standing by the sink in the kitchen. As I moved closer to her, she heard a squeak from the old wooden floorboard, turned around, and nonchalantly quipped, "Oh, it's only you."

I smiled, breaking into a wide, grimaced grin. Tears welled in her eyes, and she moved to me, leaping into my arms, crying in happiness, "John, you're finally home."

"Yes, I am. Finally."

ACKNOWLEDGEMENTS

Information on *Warrington* was gleaned from "The Dragon's Breath: Hurricane at Sea" by Cdr. Robert A Dawes, Jr., who was captain of *Warrington* until fourteen days before she sank in the Great Atlantic Hurricane of 1944. His book resulted from his own firsthand experience with the ship and her crew, and from his research of the testimony of the seventy-three survivors before the Court of Inquiry. A court of inquiry is not a court in the normal sense of the term but is a formal board of investigation charged with examining and inquiring into an accident and, when directed by the convening authority, making recommendations about the incident. U.S. Naval courts of inquiry were common during World War II, as regulations required a formal investigation whenever a vessel was lost. Their purpose was to examine the circumstances that led to a ship's sinking; to establish responsibility, to determine whether any offense was committed, and to fix blame if necessary. In this case, after all the court of inquiry testimony was heard and evaluated, Commander Wheyland and Commander Quarles, both survivors of the hurricane, were tried by general court-martial, and both were acquitted. John Ridgeway was not aboard *Warrington* and is a fictional character for the story. I purposely added a strain in his relationship with Commander Quarles concerning their differing viewpoints with respect to dealing with the hurricane.

AUTHOR'S NOTE

This narrative incorporates events in my father's memoir, *Letters from the Pacific*, along with his childhood and early adult memories growing up in Glendale, New York, during the Great Depression. His father died when he was eight and he lived in near poverty with his mother and sister. He earned a scholarship to St. John's University and earned a bachelor's degree in accounting in four years while attending school at night and working full-time during the day for a textile company in New York City. He was a graduate of the V-7 naval Midshipman School at Columbia University and was a seamanship instructor at Fort Schuyler. He survived the seventy-foot swells of the Great Atlantic Hurricane of 1944 aboard a 290-ton coastal patrol craft that sailed from Cuba to New York. He served the remainder of the war in the Pacific aboard the USS *Scania*, an attack cargo ship, delivering supplies and military personnel to the islands mentioned in the book. My parents and their friends were members of Tom Brokaw's "The Greatest Generation." They were people who rose above the obstacles thrust upon them. They persevered through the Great Depression and fought in World War II. They shared the traits Brokaw wrote about in his book: a strong work ethic, humility in their dealings with others, a penchant for prudent saving, a deep sense of personal responsibility for their actions, and a strong commitment to religion, family, and friends.

Many of the events and places mentioned in the book are not widely known, but true.

New York City's Grand Central Terminal, the largest train station in the world, with forty-four platforms and sixty-seven tracks, had a secret platform used by President Franklin Roosevelt when he visited New York City because of its direct access into the Waldorf Astoria.

The Guastavino ceramic-tiled arch outside the Grand Central Terminal Restaurant (now the Oyster Bar & Restaurant) is a magical place where expressions of love are whispered.

Paul Cesar Helleu's mural of night sky constellations on the ceiling of the main concourse was indeed designed to depict God's point of view from above looking down on those below.

Barbed wire was installed at Waikiki Beach after the attack on Pearl Harbor to protect against a Japanese invasion, but that didn't stop servicemen and civilians from enjoying this tropical paradise during the war. And Duke Kahanamoku, the Father of Surfing, really did perform a headstand when riding a wave on his surfboard.

Once a year, on Halloween, crowds gather in Machpelah Cemetery in Glendale at the gravesite of Harry Houdini, hoping to see the great illusionist make one last escape.

McDermott Lighting (where Ellen was employed) was founded by my uncle Julian A. McDermott in the early 1940s and continues to this day in Ridgewood, New York, under second-and third-generation family management and ownership. Julian was a prolific inventor of lighting products and had more than twenty patents. I saw his "man overboard" lights on the battleship *USS Wisconsin* in Norfolk, Virginia. He began his career as a chief engineer for Claude Neon, producer of the neon fluorescent lamp invented by Georges Claude in 1915.

The origin of the "Line Crossing" tradition is unknown, but the famous Portuguese explorer Ferdinand Magellan may have been the person to initiate this rite of passage in 1522 when he circumnavigated the earth.

The following events were made to fit the story:

The bikini at Billy Rose's Aquacade at the 1939 New York World's Fair is not historically accurate. While there were two-piece bathing suits worn by women then, the bikini was first introduced in France in July 1946 by Louis Reard. His design was considered too risqué and scandalous that he had difficulty finding a model to exhibit the suit, forcing him to hire a nude dancer at the Casino de Paris for the assignment.

The reference to kamikazes at the Battle of Santa Cruz is not historically accurate. The term "kamikaze" meaning "divine wind," referred to Japanese pilots who volunteered to fly bomb-laden planes into U.S. Navy warships, which was a strategy adopted in late 1944 as Japan's final, futile attempt to reverse the outcome of the war. It was based upon their military tradition of death instead of defeat, capture, and shame. Kamikazes in this narrative were those pilots who knew they were going to crash, so they flew their planes into our ships to inflict as much damage as possible before they perished.

The reference to whiskey and beer at a party during Prohibition was probably true, as there were an estimated one hundred thousand speakeasies in New York City during that period.

Wollman Rink, the public ice rink in New York City's Central Park, opened in 1950 to welcome skaters from late October to early April.

The "Chicken Dance" oom-pah song mentioned at Schuetzen Park is a popular Octoberfest song that was composed by the Swiss accordion player Werner Thomas in the 1950s.